"So," Bobbie said, trying to generate some conversation, "How are things at the library? Is the job going well?"

Suddenly, before I could answer, Margaret looked at me with an almost leering grin. "Yes, Renda. See anything strange in the library lately? Hmm?"

The way she asked the question made my blood run cold because the tone of her voice had changed and deepened. I felt my heart stop as a swirl of darkness seemed to surround her suddenly, and a quick look of pure malevolence flashed in her eyes. Then it disappeared just as quickly as it had come.

When I turned to look at Bobbie and Daniel, I realized that I'd been the only one to witness the eerie transformation as the two of them were waiting for my reaction and had been staring at me. A little voice inside my head started sending out warning signals. Something was terribly wrong.

THE BLOODMANE CHRONICLES

Book 1 — The Awakening

Book 2 — Child of the Dead

by SARA BROOKE

THE AWAKENING

BOOK 1

Dedication

To my little dreamer and superhero.

Chapter 1

I've never minded being alone.

For some people, being alone is the worst thing in the world. They fill their time with countless meetings, dates, texting, and online chatting—anything to stay busy and not face the silence of their thoughts.

For me, it's different. For me, being alone is the only time when I can actually think. It's the only time when my mind is clear and focused. Maybe that's because I've felt alone most of my life, and it is the only time when I am truly comfortable.

My name is Renda Bloodmane. For some reason, my birthmother thought it would be suitable to call me a name that most people almost always mispronounce. I heard it a million times in school...

"Brenda? Brenda, are you present?"

"No, my name is Renda. It's Renda, not Brenda."

"Are you sure your name's not Brenda?"

The conversation was typically followed by a long line of questioning as to why my last name is Bloodmane. And to be honest with you, I'm not exactly sure why I have that particular last name. Many people think that it's a description of my red hair. "Blood" standing for "red" or "in the lineage" and "mane" as another way to describe "hair". But I've never met my birthmother, so I couldn't tell you.

She abandoned me in the hospital, the day I was born.

I was born in a small hospital in Cale, Florida. Literally hours after I was born, the nurses returned to my mother's hospital bed and found it empty. They searched the entire floor for her, but she was gone.

As for my birthfather? Well, she never told anyone who he was, so in the scope of my first several hours of life, I was basically left without any parents or family. My mother's parents had apparently died years ago and since she was an only child, I was put in a foster home almost immediately.

My foster parents, two very kind people named Bernie and Sandra Berkins took care of me, and eventually they filed for adoption. They're great people and I've had a relatively normal upbringing as their only child. But I've always felt—different.

For starters, my parents are very social people and like to spend time with their friends at the country club or enjoy having drinks at their house at dusk. They're always the center of attention, making people laugh with their funny stories and bright smiles. And I do feel very lucky to have them. But the last thing I want to do is draw attention to myself. I wonder if it's because I'm adopted.

My parents told me I was adopted, when I was very young. They're good people, and I know my parents love me, and I love them. But I've always felt an invisible wall between me and everyone else. Sometimes that wall protects me. Other times it shuts me out. Either way, it has always made me aware that I'm a little different.

I'm quite shy and try to fly under the radar. I don't want people taking what I say the wrong way, and so, many times, I don't say anything at all. In college, my friend Bobbie Trillo used to get upset with me quite regularly because instead of going out to keg parties with her and getting into drunken "situations" with fraternity boys, I would stay in my room and read. She'd go out for hours on end, while I'd spend the time in my bed…in flannel pajamas…immersing myself in tales of horror, suspense, or romance.

It's not that I didn't want male attention. I'm a woman after all, with the same needs and desires as all women. But I've just never felt comfortable in social situations, and even though I know I'm not unattractive—I'm just not at ease around outgoing people.

So, needless to say, my life is not exactly the most exciting in the world.

To add to my quiet life, I work in a public library, here in Cale. Now, I know that a small-town library might seem unexciting, but for me, there's nothing better than getting lost in the stacks of books and smelling the old paperbacks resting among the long shelves. It's a place where I feel at ease and can be myself.

My friend Larlene, who also works at the library as the manager, thinks that since I'm a redhead, there's absolutely got to be some fire deep within me that is raging to get out.

I think she may be watching too many soft-porn movies on cable, but who knows. I do love romance novels and movies. Maybe I just need the right guy to draw out my passion.

Anyway, we recently had a small argument about my lack of a social life. I was working on organizing some of our DVD collection, correcting some of the titles that were out of order in the comedy section, when she swooped down on me. That also isn't unusual, since Larlene is close to six feet tall, and I stand at about five feet, four inches.

"So," she said in a breathless gasp. "I've finally found you. What's the plan for this weekend?"

My plans were the same as every other weekend. Rent some movies, and curl up on the bed with my yellow Labrador, Jane (named after my favorite Charlotte Bronte novel, *Jane Eyre*). In fact, I was actually looking forward to watching an old Hollywood epic, *Cleopatra* with Elizabeth Taylor and Richard Burton.

Jane is the perfect movie-watching companion. I've had her since she was a puppy—adopting her from a local animal shelter. In some ways, Jane is my kindred spirit as we were both given a rough start in life, but somehow, we found our way to relatively greener pastures.

Dogs have a way of showing us how to appreciate things in life, and she makes me a better person because of her presence. There is nothing in the world that means more to me than Jane does.

So watching a movie with my best, furry friend in the world seemed like the perfect night.

But divulging this truth would not sit well with Larlene, who enjoyed spending her time online, chatting with any number of lovelorn people on one of the many dating sites she belonged to. Larlene never had any luck finding anyone who was relationship material, but she loved the attention. She also enjoyed hanging out in the local bars in town, something that didn't appeal to me. So I needed to think fast and offer up something that wasn't too dull, but would be a good excuse to keep her pending invitation to spend the evening with a half-dozen martinis, at bay.

"Well, I was thinking about visiting my parents and spending some time with them. I think they're having some friends over."

Larlene cocked her head in my direction and a sly smile appeared on her lips. "Yeah, right. I'll bet you'll be at home with Jane. Don't lie. I see right through you."

Damn. How did she know? "Well, maybe I'll be at the house for a bit, but I'm really going to be busy. I think..."

"Come on, Renda," she interrupted me in a pleading tone. "Let's go out this weekend. We need to relax and have a few drinks. It'll be fun. Please?"

Her face was hopeful, but my mind was made up. There was no way I was hanging out in a bar until the wee hours of the morning. But I needed to let her down easy. She was basically one of my only friends in town. Most of the other locals thought I was too bookish and serious. I'd even heard one of Larlene's friends call me "snobby," which stung, because I don't think I'm a snob at all. I'm just shy. There's a difference. Still, Larlene was well-intentioned and I didn't want to upset her, so I changed my tone.

"I'm actually not feeling all that well. My head hurts, and I think I might be coming down with that flu that's been going around."

To add to the ambience, I coughed and Larlene's eyes softened a bit. "Well, that's not good. I'm sorry you're not feeling well. Maybe next weekend?" she asked and smiled at me, as we finished putting away the DVDs.

The rest of the week passed uneventfully, other than the awful weather. It rained constantly and made the days in the library incredibly dreary. The gray skies cast a depressing mood over everything—as though a heavy blanket was draped over the building.

It was Friday, and a few hours before closing, when something happened that would change my life forever.

I wasn't really expecting anything out of the ordinary to happen. Friday afternoons are usually quiet because most people are getting ready to go out. I have mixed feelings about that. On the one hand, I'm a homebody, and going out to bars isn't my thing, but on the other hand, I can't help but be reminded that even the seniors in my community have busy social lives, while I spend my Friday nights on the couch watching old movies with Jane.

The aisles were empty, making it a perfect time to put away the remaining books that readers had left on tables or chairs. My cart was nearly full as I pushed it along the carpet, hearing the wheels make their telltale squeaking sounds.

My first stop was the horror section. Someone had chosen a great collection of Edgar Allan Poe's most popular stories and the cover was illustrated with a large black raven—in honor of the story with the same name. I do enjoy horror novels and have always wondered about the other dimensions that exist. Surely, we aren't completely alone? I mean, if the world is made up of energy, then where does that energy go when a person dies? Does it completely blink out? Or does it manifest itself in ways that we simply cannot comprehend?

These thoughts were circulating through my mind when I turned the corner and saw a ghost for the very first time.

Chapter 2

I didn't actually see anything strange at first, but the temperature around me felt like it had suddenly dropped several degrees. Goose bumps popped up on my arms as the cooler air surrounded me in a chilly embrace. Taking a deep breath, I briskly rubbed my skin to warm up and continued pushing the cart.

When I turned down the aisle, I was surprised to see a man standing with his back to me. He was looking down, and appeared to be reading something intently. At first, I didn't notice anything strange about him, but as I moved a bit closer, I saw a big red stain on the back of his shirt.

It was blood.

My heart started beating quickly and a list of things to do raced through my mind. I wasn't sure exactly how long it would take for the paramedics to arrive, but clearly the man didn't realize that something was wrong with him as he was simply standing in place, reading a book.

Dropping the novel I was holding into the cart, I started to approach him. "Sir, I think there's something wrong with your..." But I never finished my sentence, because as soon as I started speaking, the man turned around to face me.

He was in his mid-thirties and looked calm, almost disinterested. But that was probably because I couldn't see most of his face. It had been blown away by something brutal... maybe a gunshot blast.

It was unbelievable, but I was looking into the face of a person who couldn't possibly be alive. Blood dripped down from a gaping hole in his forehead and covered most of his face in a red sheen. Part of his mouth was missing, and a smiling, skeletal profile gleamed at me under the library's fluorescent lights.

My mind told me to run. Flee. But then another part of my brain suddenly came alive, filling me with a sense of calm. It was a feeling that I'd never felt before. And in that deep, strange calmness, I heard a gentle, masculine voice speak to me.

I wanted to read for a while.

As soon as the voice entered my brain, it left just as quickly and for some bizarre reason, I didn't want it to go away. Because somehow, I knew that if the voice disappeared—so would this strange, dead corpse.

"Wait, let me help you." And I leaned forward to touch his shoulder. As soon as my fingers connected with the man, he disappeared and I began to fall forward. I had to grab the bookshelf to keep from toppling over.

Not being a very coordinated person, I'm sure I looked like a drunken marionette. And right at that moment, Larlene saw me stumbling around.

"What the hell are you doing?" she asked.

"Uh, I must have tripped on something," I answered quickly, heat rising to my face. "Why are you still here? I thought you were getting ready for a big date."

"Yeah." Larlene sighed. "We'll see how it goes. I'm not holding my breath."

"Is it a guy you met online?" I asked, trying to change the subject so I could gather my wits.

"Yeah, he looks hot in his pictures, but you know how that goes. Guys always post that one good picture from ten years ago, before their beer belly makes its first appearance. So I'm not getting too excited. He's probably really short and has bad teeth."

I burst out laughing. Sometimes Larlene knows exactly what to say to lift my mood. As she waved goodbye and headed out, my smile remained. She was a good friend and someone who really helped me get through the day.

As I turned back to the now-empty aisle, my thoughts returned to the bleeding, destroyed face that had stared at me moments before. Was it a ghost? I'd never seen anything so horrific, but at the same time, so fascinating.

Perhaps I was just hallucinating? Maybe I hadn't eaten enough for lunch? Whatever the case, it was getting late and Jane was waiting for me at home. It was time to pack it up and head out. As I left the library, the memory of the half-faced man continued to haunt me.

Jane is probably one of the smartest dogs in the universe. You might think I'm biased, given that she's my pet, but I seriously think she was born with a special gift. Unlike most Labradors, she doesn't jump all over me and slobber on everything. Nor does she chew the walls, my books, or my shoes.

Instead, Jane is quiet and moves at a slow, steady pace. She listens when called, snorts in agreement when I ask her something, and just inherently knows when I need a little extra love or attention.

The thing I love most about my dear Jane is that every day she waits for me to come home and as soon as I walk through the door of my ground floor, two-bedroom apartment, she meets me with those beautiful doe eyes of hers, while her long tail wags back and forth, signaling true happiness at my return. There's no one on this earth who is more excited to see me than Jane, and so given the strangeness of the day, I was very pleased to see my large, furry daughter at the front door.

"Hi, baby. Are you ready for a cozy, boring night together?"

She sniffed in response, and as I waited for her to run outside and do her business, it occurred to me that maybe it would have been more fun to go out with Larlene instead of sitting at home, watching yet another romantic movie. Plus, I was still unsettled over seeing what I could only assume was a ghost.

Ring!

My thoughts were jarred by the sound of my phone ringing. It was a surprise, as my phone almost never rings. Well, not unless it's my mother calling to check up on me.

Taking a deep breath, I shooed Jane back inside my apartment and picked up the phone on the third ring.

"Hello?"

"Hey! It's Bobbie. How are you?"

"Bobbie! It's great to hear from you. How are things?"

After college, I hadn't spoken to Bobbie nearly enough. To put it plainly, when she became my roommate during freshman year, it was the best thing that could have happened to me. We clicked instantly and she helped me make other friends at school, because she was innately an extremely social person with very few reservations. Despite our differences and the fact that I am socially inept sometimes, we became inseparable and it was terribly depressing to say goodbye after graduation. At least once a year, we'd get together and have lunch or spend the day talking, but she'd been distant the past year or so. And now, with both of us at the ripe old age of twenty-eight, I sometimes wondered if we had anything left in common.

"Well, you know Mom hasn't been doing so well since the divorce," she was saying. "So I moved in with her and I'm working at a local advertising agency here."

Bobbie's parents lived in Macon, Georgia. They were incredibly rich and had gotten divorced a few years back. Bobbie's mother still lived in their mansion and had received full custody of her young son, Daniel. I wondered how he was taking the divorce, and hoped that everything was okay.

"That's too bad. Well, if there's anything I can do, please let me know."

"Actually...I was wondering if maybe you'd like to come visit. It's been so long since we've seen each other and I think it would be fun. Daniel's home for spring break and I can take the week off work to hang out with you. Wait till you see this old house. It's pretty cool."

I hesitated. How much vacation time did I have left? Thinking it over in my head, I realized that I hadn't taken a single day off all year and was owed three weeks of vacation. Maybe a trip to Georgia would be exactly what I needed—after all, there wasn't much waiting for me here besides another night in front of the TV. The last "date" I had been on was nearly three months ago and it had been a disaster (they typically all were). So what did I have to lose?

"You know, I think that sounds like a great idea. I could stay for a week, but then I've got to get back for work. Is that okay?"

Bobbie squealed in happiness on the other end, "Yes! That's perfect! I really miss you and could use some of your wisdom right now."

I had no idea what she meant, but decided it wasn't the right time to push. I didn't have a lot of friends, but I was a good listener and I sensed that Bobbie needed some girl time. "Okay, so let's plan to get together in a week or so. Does that work? Also, can I bring Jane? There's no one here who can take care of her because you know my folks can't handle dogs."

"Yes, that's perfect. We'd love to have her, too. See you in one week! Take care."

As I hung up the phone, it dawned on me that maybe it wasn't such a great idea to impose on her mother if she wasn't in good spirits. Then again, perhaps I could be of help in some way. In any case, I was getting away for a while and that was a welcome change.

One full week in the lap of luxury!

I knew the Trillos were considered high society and that Bobbie's mother was still well-to-do, thanks to very large, monthly alimony and child support payments. Now, I was going to join them for a week of rest and relaxation.

Excitement washed over me and after a double dose of romantic "chick flicks", I had a hard time falling asleep. Perhaps it was also because the memory of my ghostly encounter continued to replay in my mind. So instead of sleeping in the dark, I left a night light on beside my bed.

I also had Jane sleep in the bed with me. Her snores and warm body were welcome reminders that all was safe in my little apartment.

Chapter 3

"Jane! Put your head back in the car!"

She snorted at me, leaving little mucus spots along the window, and then settled back into the seat, putting her head down in submission. I reached out and petted her soft head, feeling badly about yelling at her.

We were finally heading to the Trillos and the weather was very pleasant. The Florida sky was virtually cloudless, its light blue landscape clear and vast. The weather wasn't too hot either, so I was able to leave my windows open as we sped towards the state of Georgia.

The week had been uneventful, with no more strange apparitions at the library. I was almost disappointed, hoping to see something that would confirm the existence of ghosts or poltergeists or whatever I'd seen. But instead, the week dragged on slowly. Even Larlene was lackluster, her date from the prior week a complete dud. The only bit of interest was that Jonny Thomas, a local guy from Cale, had called to ask me out on a date.

I knew Jonny from high school, and for some odd reason, he was still sporting a serious crush on me and had been chasing after me ever since I'd returned to Cale after college. The unfortunate thing for Jonny was that his feelings were most definitely not reciprocated. It wasn't that he was unattractive; he was actually a cute guy, but I didn't feel any connection to him. The few times we'd actually engaged in conversation, it felt awkward and forced. We didn't have anything in common other than we had gone to the same high school. I wasn't looking for Prince Charming, but also didn't want to settle just because I was lonely.

Larlene would tell me to just have sex with him because I'd been celibate for a while…three years in fact. But somehow I couldn't just "open the store" to someone who I wasn't mentally or emotionally attracted to. So perhaps I was fated to be in a platonic relationship with my dog for the rest of my life.

Still—despite my current relationship status—my mood couldn't be dampened on such a beautiful day, and as I neared the Trillos' home, my eyes caught the lush scenery that embraced us.

Macon, Georgia is a sprawling, heavily wooded city, well-known for its Cherry Blossom festival and friendly residents. The air smelled strongly of those famous trees, and I inhaled their fragrance with pleasure as we drove along. The Trillos lived outside the city, in a suburban area where the homes were very grand and stately—relics from a time long gone.

Bobbie had given me directions that were surprisingly easy to follow, and as I entered the long, winding driveway to their home, I was amazed at the beautiful blossoms that surrounded me from every angle. But despite seeing many photos, I was unprepared for the grandiose abode of my closest friend.

The house appeared in the distance, a towering white palace. Easily seven thousand square feet, the front of the house was lined with tall, regal pillars that held up the structure and stood as a powerful reminder of the deep pockets required to obtain such a home. A flight of white stairs led up to a long porch that ran the width of the house. On the first floor, traditional, rectangular windows lined the walls, each framed by neatly set curtains. The second floor was similar to the first, but had odd windows at each end resembling half moons that curved along the edges of the wall. The roof was particularly impressive, jutting up in the center and sharply dropping down along each side.

As my car pulled up on the cobblestone driveway, I sat for a moment while the engine idled. Jane whined to be let out, but I couldn't move. The house was just so—expansive.

Suddenly, my eyes were drawn to one of the curved windows. Despite my distance, I could barely make out what looked like a man staring back at me. It was difficult to clearly see his features, and as I squinted, it seemed as if the man frowned and then backed away from the window.

Maybe it's the butler?

Whoever he is, he's definitely good-looking.

I wasn't sure if people actually had butlers anymore, but given the richness that surrounded me, anything was possible. As I stepped out of my car, the scenery came into view even more distinctly. The house was surrounded by different native trees and the backyard looked like it stretched for miles into a magical, green world.

Despite growing up in nature-leaden Cale, I had never been one to wander around in the woods. Something about the trees and getting lost always kept me close to home and away from places that were undiscovered. In addition, I was not a huge fan of bugs, lack of electricity, or dirt. The one time I'd gone camping, I ended up stepping into a big mass of poison ivy, so my memories of Mother Nature weren't exactly good ones. Still, the Trillos' backyard definitely looked like a place of mystery, but it wasn't a place that I was interested in exploring.

"Renda!"

A familiar voice broke my reverie and caused my heart to skip.

My best friend in the world, Bobbie Trillo, stood on the porch with a big smile on her face. Bobbie was beautiful, her dark hair flowing like a waterfall down her back. Our coloring was polar opposite; she was tanned with dark hair and I was pale-skinned with freckles and wavy red hair. She had eyes the color of dark chocolate. Mine were a light blue. But it wasn't just her beauty or sensuality and confidence that made men flock to her. Bobbie had a warm personality that just welcomed you in, and a smile that could light up an entire stadium. Despite her magnetic appeal compared to my shy demeanor, I'd never been jealous of her. Honestly, how could you compare yourself to an actual living goddess?

Strangely, Bobbie thought the world of me and had made it a point to wrap me up in her comforting friendship. It was an act that made me feel special and cared-for.

"Come here, you crazy woman," she said smiling, holding

out her arms for a hug. As we embraced, I felt relaxed and happy.

"So, how are you?" I asked, as we made our way into the house. I dropped my suitcase by the front door as Jane slowly made her way inside.

"I'm doing fine. Hi, Jane." She knelt down and gave my dog a big hug and kiss.

"Just fine?" I asked. Usually, Bobbie was bursting with excitement to tell me about her latest conquest, and despite her claim to happiness; I could sense an undercurrent of strain.

"Well, it's just that things around here…things aren't great. Mom's not doing so well." Bobbie looked away and cleared her throat, as though she was holding back tears.

"I'm sorry to hear that. If there's anything…" My words were interrupted by the sound of someone slowly coming down the staircase.

"Bobbie," a voice called out. "Is your friend here?"

Bobbie's face immediately looked up with concern. I followed her gaze and watched as an extremely thin and somewhat frail-looking woman slowly approached us. Recognizing Bobbie's mother from photos, I immediately put out my hand to say hello.

"Hello, Ms. Trillo. It's very nice to meet you."

She chuckled quietly and looked away, never grasping my hand. "Just call me Margaret. I feel old enough already. It's nice to meet you…?" She paused and turned back to gaze into my eyes, searching for my name.

"I'm sorry," I stumbled. "My name's Renda. Renda Bloodmane."

"Ah, Renda. Yes, Bobbie's told me so much about you. Has she told you that I'm going mad?"

I didn't know what to say and Bobbie looked mortified. Jane whined and moved her body closer to mine. Margaret didn't seem to notice that Jane was with us and just kept on talking.

"Yes, that's what everyone thinks. But I'm not, you know. It's just that the darkness calls to me. It tells me things."

"Um, Mom?" The voice of a young boy interrupted her, and a child of about nine quickly made his way towards us. "Hi, I'm Daniel, Bobbie's brother. Wow, what a cute dog you have!"

Daniel was adorable, with a mop of brown hair and eyes

that matched Bobbie's. But even though he knelt down and petted Jane enthusiastically, when he looked back at his mother, his expression changed to one of concern and it was clear that he was worried.

I didn't blame him. She looked downright weird. Her hair was plastered to her head as if she hadn't washed it in many days, and her countenance was sallow. She wasn't wearing any makeup and had a flimsy sundress on that probably doubled as her nightgown. It was stained and rumpled. The woman looked thin, on edge, and a little scary.

"Daniel, my baby," she said and wrapped him in a big hug. But I could still see that his face and expression hadn't changed. The entire exchange was awkward, and given what Bobbie had always told me about her vivacious and loving mother, I wondered if the divorce or something more had affected her this way.

Bobbie interrupted my thoughts by immediately grabbing my hand and pulling me up towards the stairwell and away from her mother.

"Renda, let's go upstairs," she said quickly. Without saying anything to her mother, she quickly picked up my suitcase and led me along the winding staircase to the second floor. I turned to say goodbye to the strange woman, but she had already disappeared into the bowels of the house.

Daniel remained and watched Jane as she followed after us.

As Bobbie led Jane and me to the guestroom, I marveled at the size of the second story. Doors lined the hallway, and from my quick count, there seemed to be at least eight separate rooms. The floor plan was U-shaped and wound around the length of the house.

We entered a large room, decorated with a canopy bed and a perfectly matching dresser and armoire. A chaise lounge covered in a beautiful floral fabric that matched the bedspread, sat in the corner, and beside that was a dressing table with an ornate mirror. Everything was constructed from oak, the natural scent of wood filling the air. A connecting door led to a huge bathroom that contained a Jacuzzi bathtub, a separate shower with three rain shower heads, and a double sink.

The bedroom and bathroom combined was bigger than my entire apartment.

It was pure elegance, and I was quite impressed. There was even a large pillow-shaped bed for Jane to sleep on, accompanied by a bowl of water and some dog food set in a silver dish.

"Bobbie, this is amazing."

"Yes, it's home sweet home," she said with a small smile. Then she took a deep breath and her face tensed, "But I can tell from your reaction to my mother that you think she's a nutcase." Bobbie's voice was tinged with sadness. Suddenly, the seriousness of the situation began to seep in.

"Well, I didn't really notice," I started to say, trying to keep things light. But Bobbie had obviously been waiting to tell me what was going on, because she sat down on the bed and immediately started talking.

"Renda, she's been like this for a few months now. We don't know what's wrong with her. She doesn't eat, talks to herself, and says all sorts of crazy things. The doctor thinks she's depressed because of the divorce, but I think it's something else. I think she's having a nervous breakdown."

I didn't know what to say. It didn't take a genius to figure out that there was definitely something wrong with Margaret, but the "what" wasn't exactly clear. Not knowing her well enough, it was hard to make an assertion, so I just sat down next to Bobbie and gave her a hug. When we separated, I spoke softly and tried to be reassuring.

"Look, don't worry. You're here now so you can take care of her. I'm sure that in time she'll start to feel better and let go of... whatever it is that's upsetting her. While I'm here, I'll talk to her, okay? Maybe having someone outside the family to talk to will help."

Bobbie looked up at me with a hopeful smile. "Thank you. You're such a good friend. Look, I'll let you get settled in and then let's grab some dinner downstairs, okay?"

I nodded and she left quickly, giving Jane a pat on the head as she walked out.

Sighing, I sat on the floor next to my furry companion and whispered in her ear, "What was that all about? You sense something's weird here too, don't you?"

Jane didn't make a sound, but just stared at me with her large, soulful eyes. She seemed strangely uneasy in the house and kept looking around as if she was seeing things. I scratched her belly, trying to calm her and she eventually sprawled out on the floor, while I unpacked and got ready.

I felt strange, too. My nerves were on edge and it felt like I was constantly being watched. Feeling foolish, I checked under the bed, the closets, and behind the curtains, just to be sure we were alone. Of course, there was nothing there, but I still felt nervous.

Turning back to my suitcase, I quickly unpacked and got ready for dinner.

When Bobbie and I went down for dinner, the table was set and food was already waiting in steaming dishes. Not surprisingly, the Trillos had a chef who came to the house in the morning, cooked all of their meals throughout the day, and finished it off with a large feast fit for royalty.

The Trillos did not eat at a small kitchen table; rather they sat at a formal, long cedar table that was set with precious china. Everything looked so fancy that I was afraid to touch my silverware. But after taking one look at Margaret, it was clear that she wasn't worried about making a mess.

She was staring off into space, a piece of bread in her hand. In several repetitive motions, she pulled off small pieces of the bread and listlessly shoved them into her mouth. Crumbs were falling everywhere and littered her dress, her plate, and the surrounding tablecloth. When she finished one roll, she would automatically reach for another one. Her plate of food was untouched, but was covered in crumbs.

I tried not to pay attention, and smiled at both Daniel and Bobbie who were embarrassed by their mother's odd behavior.

"So," Bobbie said, trying to generate some conversation, "How are things at the library? Is the job going well?"

Suddenly, before I could answer, Margaret looked at me with an almost leering grin. "Yes, Renda. See anything strange in the library lately? Hmm?"

The way she asked the question made my blood run cold because the tone of her voice had changed and deepened. I felt my heart stop as a swirl of darkness seemed to surround her suddenly, and a quick look of pure malevolence flashed in her eyes. Then it disappeared just as quickly as it had come. When I turned to look at Bobbie and Daniel, I realized that I'd been the only one to witness the eerie transformation as the two of them were waiting for my reaction and had been staring at me.

A little voice inside my head started sending out warning signals. Something was terribly wrong. Trying to compose myself, I took a sip of water and tried to smile.

"Well, um, not really," I said haltingly.

Bobbie jumped in again. "Mom, that's a silly question. Of course she sees strange things. Have you ever been to a library? It's full of freaks!" She laughed and tried to steer the conversation to a lighter place. Daniel and I joined in the laughter, but their mother just looked off into space once more and continued shoving bread into her mouth.

Despite Margaret's weird behavior, Bobbie shared a funny story about a hard-to-please client at work, and we were soon laughing and enjoying our meal. The dinner was delicious—a rich and creamy seafood lasagna and a mixed green salad with granny smith apples and toasted almonds. A member of the housekeeping staff hovered nearby, refilling glasses, and asking us if we needed anything else from the kitchen.

I watched Bobbie's mother closely when she wasn't paying attention. She seemed exhausted, but eventually managed to swallow some of the meal. Her gaze however, made me nervous. Every so often, she would stare at me with eyes that seemed to be evaluating me carefully. It continued on and off throughout the meal and finally, I couldn't help but stare back at her.

Her eyes were dark and piercing, sending off small waves of anger in my direction.

What the hell is wrong with her? Am I wearing the wrong perfume?

The only people who ever glared at me like that were the senior citizens who had just found out that their library books were overdue and they owed a bunch in fees. Otherwise, most people were pretty pleasant.

But Margaret apparently wasn't like most people.

When dinner was complete and dessert was placed on the table, Margaret excused herself. "I'm sorry, but it's time I rested. Nice to see you, Renda."

And with that, she breezed out of the room and left the remaining three of us alone to stare at each other in an awkward silence.

"Are you sure you're going to be okay? Do you need anything?" Bobbie asked for the hundredth time as she stood in the doorway of my room. It was apparent that she felt bad about the way her mother was behaving, so I reassured her that I was all right and she finally left Jane and me alone.

I'd already taken Jane out for her evening walk to do her "business", so we were ready to go to bed. Rushing through my evening ritual, I quickly finished up in the bathroom.

But before I went to bed, I stepped back out into the darkened hallway.

Despite identifying that it was irrational, I was afraid of being alone. I looked in the direction of Margaret's bedroom at the end of the hall, and realized that it was the one with the crescent-shaped window. The one where I'd seen the man earlier.

What would a man be doing in her room? Was he a servant? I hadn't seen him at any other time or place around the house. It was very strange.

Her door was shut, and all was dark. But I knew she was in there, and my blood chilled a bit. The woman was clearly disturbed and it was strange to be sleeping so close to her. Trying to push the thought out of my mind, I quickly stepped back into my room, shut the door, and locked it for good measure.

Jane snorted in approval and settled into her doggie bed for the night.

I leaned down and gave her a quick kiss, and then pulled the covers over my body letting sleep take over.

Chapter 4

Sometime in the middle the night, the sound of Jane's whimpering woke me up.

At first I struggled to remain asleep, because I'd been dreaming about attending a large party, dressed in a beautiful gown. My lover was waiting for me at the foot of the stairs, but I was taking my time descending as the other patrons watched me in awe.

In my fantasy, I caught a glimpse of myself in one of the mirrors that lined the slanted walls that followed my descent down to the first floor.

I looked stunning—my red hair was swept up in a bun and a simple strand of white pearls adorned my neck. At the foot of the stairs there was someone waiting, but I couldn't make out his face, only that he was dressed in a sharp tuxedo. He had thick, dark hair that fell rakishly over his brow.

And of course, he was tall and fit. My perfect dream-man who would only last for a few amazing seconds.

As my feet reached the bottom of the stairs, I heard whimpering and the dream faded away.

When I opened my eyes, Jane was staring right at me. She had her head resting on the mattress and was whining for me to wake up, her eyes wide and alert.

"What is it girl?" I whispered, rubbing my eyes in exhaustion. A quick look at the cheap, light-up watch on my wrist indicated that it was three o'clock in the morning.

Jane went to the door, looked back at me, and then started scratching at it. It was what she did when she wanted out. I was worried that she was going to mar the wood, so I quickly got up.

"Stop, Jane," I whispered, making my way to the door. Hesitating, I wondered how dark the hallway would be, but there was no choice. If my dog had to go out, I'd need to find my way through the house and lead her outside.

Unlocking the door, I opened it slowly and peeked out. At first, I didn't see anything because my eyes were trying to adjust to the deep blackness of the hallway. But within a few seconds, I began to make out shapes in the distance, and I noticed an impossible set of orbs glowing and bobbing in mid-air.

The orbs looked perfectly round and hazy, but as I squinted to get a better look through my glasses, they began to take shape and started to look like people. Only, I couldn't distinguish any faces or color. They just looked like people-shaped floating white things. And the "things" floated back and forth along the hallway.

As I stood in shock, one of the white things stopped and started to float towards me. Unsure as to what to do, and frozen in fear, I backed up, but Jane growled and stood her ground. The white thing continued to float towards me until suddenly, a door opened in another part of the hallway and banged against the wall.

The sound of the banging door seemed to frighten the white, floating objects, and they all scurried in different directions, vanishing in unison. The only strange object that didn't vanish as quickly was the one that had started floating towards me. It hung in the air, several feet away from us and then finally disappeared.

My attention was drawn to the door that had opened, and the person who was now moving out of her room into the hallway.

It was Margaret.

Even in the darkness, I could make out her madness. Her flimsy bedclothes stuck to her body in flattened, sweaty clumps. She walked slowly down the hallway, and as she neared the stairwell, I could see that her eyes were open but gazing out into the distance without focusing on anything. Her hair stuck out in different directions, and her breathing was loud and harsh.

I was worried she might fall down the stairs, but couldn't

bring myself to say anything. To make matters worse, my feet were frozen in place.

Jane growled and backed up, standing close behind me.

Watching, I waited for something awful to happen, but instead, Margaret descended the long staircase without tripping or falling. It was as if she was being guided by an unseen force… as if she was a marionette.

Suddenly, my strength came back, and I was able to speak once again.

"Margaret," I whispered loudly.

She ignored me, so I stepped to the edge of the landing, looked down, and this time said out loud, "Margaret."

She stopped and turned to look at me. Her eyes were dead— this I could see, even in the darkness, and she held a finger to her lips as if to indicate "Shhh…"

What the hell?

Jane suddenly barked and left my side, bounding down the staircase and following Margaret who had now disappeared around the corner.

I rushed down the stairs to follow them both and found myself on the first floor. Not being completely familiar with the house, I was disoriented for a moment, unsure as to where to go. There were several hallways surrounding me, and it was possible that I was going to get lost.

The sound of Jane's bark guided me down the hallway straight ahead. It took me past the dining area to the rear of the house, where the vast kitchen was. I stood for a moment and looked around nervously. The silver pots and pans hung from their large hooks and glinted in the moonlight. A block of knives rested atop the counter, and for a split second, I considered grabbing one of them to use as a weapon. But an unfamiliar male voice interrupted my thoughts and entered my mind…

You're not going to kill your host, are you?

Spinning around wildly, I searched for the voice that had just questioned me. But there was no one in the kitchen.

A door to the rear of the kitchen was swinging silently back and forth, and inky darkness seeped into the opening. It was the door to the backyard.

Once again, I hesitated. The backyard was terribly creepy, even in the daylight. I didn't like the woods, or forests. Heck, even shrubbery rubbed me the wrong way. It was too dense. I had seen enough horror movies in my time where people got lost in the woods, only to be chopped up by some maniac with a chainsaw. But Jane was out there and even from my vantage point, I could hear her barking in the distance.

I had to follow.

Still in my bare feet, I gingerly stepped outside and planted my toes in the wet, mushy grass.

Ugh. Gross.

Crickets chirped loudly around me, and the air was extremely still and warm.

To my left, a line of Adirondack and lounge chairs surrounded a huge s-shaped swimming pool. Several bistro-style tables, protected by big white umbrellas were located at the far end. An outdoor kitchen sat in the corner, complete with an oversized grill, stone oven, a long prep counter, a fridge, and a large rectangular freezer.

Well, the rich certainly know how to do backyard barbecues the right way.

To my right was a separate garage that housed the Trillos' cars, which were no doubt all luxurious and sporty. And in front of me lay a vast, open expanse of tall trees and thick shrubbery, merging together into one big fortress of darkness.

I took a deep breath and tried to calm my racing mind. During moments of panic, I typically talk to myself, because it usually helps me remain calm. So as I walked slowly towards the dark woods, I began chattering away...

It's going to be fine. She's probably just going for a walk. In the middle of the night. Lots of people go for walks in the middle of the night, right? I'll just get Jane and return to the house and in the morning, I'll have a serious talk with Bobbie. She can tell me the whole story, because clearly, her mother needs help. But what the hell were those floating white things and that male voice...and okay, this self-talk really isn't working.

As I entered the woods, I could barely see Margaret in the

distance, her white negligee glowing eerily. Jane was nowhere to be found, but I could hear her panting and little "woofs" every once in a while. It was unlike her to take off without me, but I figured she had a good reason and tried to keep my frustration at bay. Besides, I was too scared to be annoyed and just wanted to get us safely back to the house.

Maneuvering through the woods was difficult. Despite the dewy-softness of the grass, I kept stepping on little twigs and stones that were scattered about, which made me utter an endless string of "ouches".

Note to self: next time wear shoes when chasing a madwoman through the dark woods after midnight.

The thought made me giggle, until a smattering of wicked tree branches hung down and scratched at my face, almost as if they were trying to pull me back. I fought against them and tried to keep up.

Finally, I came upon a small clearing up ahead. As I got closer, I could see Jane planted on all fours, growling menacingly. I'd never seen her act like that as she was normally the meekest, kindest dog in the world.

"Jane," I called out, trying to get her attention. But she wouldn't look towards me and focused her attention straight ahead.

I finally reached the clearing and saw why my most beloved companion was growling.

Margaret stood several feet away. Her legs were spread and she had both arms reaching up to the sky as if she was praying. Her eyes were rolled back into the sockets, revealing nothing but eerie white orbs. Her mouth was open and she was moving her lips, but no sound was coming out. As she waved her hands, I was shocked to see that the sky above her had started to grow ugly, with storm clouds circulating in a rhythmic fashion above her head. The wind had suddenly whipped up and was swirling around us, sending the surrounding trees in a frantic, frenzied dance.

Then Margaret laughed—a horrible, scary sound.

At the awful noise, Jane whimpered and ran in my direction. I was terrified that the woman might attack me, so I ran back into the woods toward the house. Jane raced ahead as if to help guide me back. Pain shot through my feet and arms as I stumbled along over tree roots and through hanging branches.

My chest was beginning to hurt from the exertion, but I didn't stop until we reached the backyard where the lawn chairs and open space welcomed us back. I stopped to take a breath and looked down at Jane who was panting heavily and staring at me with frightened eyes.

But there was no time to waste.

I quickly went inside and flew up the stairwell towards Bobbie's room. As I pulled open the door, she immediately woke up, a terrified look on her face as she sat up.

"Whaaa?" she asked, unable to form words, still hazy from sleep.

The words tumbled from my lips so quickly that it was hard to compose a coherent sentence. "Bobbie, something's wrong with your mom. She's outside in the woods, and she's completely lost it. You've got to come with me."

Bobbie didn't try to calm me down. Instead, she jumped out of the bed, flicking on the light. When she saw my face, she immediately started freaking out.

"Renda! Your face is all scratched and bleeding. What happened to your feet? Your arms? Did you go outside without a flashlight or shoes?"

I hadn't even realized how much damage had been done during my race through the woods. But given the situation, I decided it was best to ignore the cuts and pain.

"Look, let's not worry about me right now. You're mother's out there. We need to get her back inside."

Bobbie agreed and we both grabbed our shoes and flashlights. The commotion woke up Daniel who stood in his bedroom doorway, his eyes wide with fright.

"What's wrong?" he asked in a small, scared voice. "Is everything okay?"

"Yes, everything's fine," answered Bobbie, who knelt in front of him and whispered words of comfort into his ear.

I backed away, not wanting to frighten him with my scratched and bleeding face. Jane stayed by my side and waited with me until Bobbie was able to get him back into bed.

When she returned, she looked frightened but serious. "Look, we've got to get Mom back inside and then we'll take it from there."

I agreed and we quickly left the house, followed by Jane. With flashlights and shoes on, the woods seemed less frightening. We moved around the trees and arrived at the clearing, which seemed a lot closer this time. I also noticed that the weather had once again settled and the swirling wind was gone.

And so was Margaret.

Where is she? She was just here!

Sighing with frustration, I looked at Bobbie who seemed both relieved and concerned that her mother was no longer standing there. I was worried that she might not believe my fantastical story. After all, it sounded crazy—even to me.

"Bobbie, she was here. Seriously."

"Renda, I believe you," she answered, looking back in the direction of the house.

But there was something in her voice that didn't quite resonate. Like, maybe she believed me—to a point. I had a feeling that this might cause problems, because if she wasn't willing to face what was going on with her mother, it would be impossible to help her.

"Let's go back to the house," she directed, heading back towards the woods.

I remained in place for a moment, and looked around. Even though Margaret was gone, I still sensed that something was wrong. There was a heaviness in the air that felt as if something was watching us and lying in wait. The darkness of the night was suddenly electric, and I felt that if I stayed in the spot for several more minutes, the evil would reveal itself.

"Renda, let's go!" Bobbie shouted.

Jane barked in agreement.

Turning, I exhaled slowly and followed them out.

We found Margaret lying in bed, sleeping peacefully. Her arms were casually thrown over a mass of white blankets and her snores traveled gently through the air. To the casual observer, she appeared to be completely relaxed.

Daniel, who was still awake, had joined us, and we all stood watching her for a moment. Even Jane came to the side of the bed and sat beside Daniel, almost as if to protect him. It felt strange to stare at the woman while she slept, but the fact that she'd somehow made it back to the house without any of us seeing her, including Daniel, was even stranger. She hadn't passed us on the way out, and I knew for certain that she hadn't initially followed me back to the house. So her return was a mystery.

It also made my story about seeing her outside seem ridiculous.

Bobbie led Daniel back to his room and said goodnight to me quickly. She barely looked in my direction and mumbled something about her mother probably going to get something to drink in the kitchen. The comment annoyed me because we hadn't seen Margaret on the way out, so she'd obviously been missing.

Bobbie didn't believe me. I knew that as clear as day.

As Jane and I turned back down the hallway to my room, I nearly screamed when I noticed that there was a white glow emanating from the doorway. Turning back towards Bobbie's room, I thought about getting her but something held me back. I didn't want to appear hysterical if we came back to my room and nothing was there.

She might think I've lost my mind.

But I also didn't want to move in fear that the light would go away.

Taking a deep breath, I walked towards the doorway. I was nearly at the point where I could turn the corner and see what was glowing, when a voice from behind me spoke.

"You're not crazy."

I nearly peed in my pants. It was the same male voice I'd heard in my head earlier in the evening when I'd been in the kitchen. The one who'd questioned whether or not I needed a knife.

Flipping my head around, I saw a man standing before me. He was tall, with wavy, black hair. His stature was strong and fit, and his face was all hard angles. Sharp cheekbones framed a straight nose, well-shaped lips, and a square chin. But his eyes—his eyes were dark brown and piercing—and staring at me with a powerful intensity.

His clothes were strange. They were black and looked old fashioned, and he had some kind of gun in a holster on his hip. Somehow, the outfit suited him perfectly. In some odd way, he looked like a man from the cover of a steamy romance novel. But, given the circumstances, I was not feeling particularly romantic.

I was terrified.

"Who-who are you?"

As I spoke, the expression on the man's face turned to one of shock. He took a step closer to me and tilted his head in confusion. Up closer, I could see how handsome he was.

"What are you doing here?" I asked again.

This time, the man backed away and straightened himself. "My name is Cole. Cole Drake." He spoke with a strange British accent, and his deep voice resonated through my ears.

"Nice to meet you," I said quivering. "I'm Renda. What are you doing here?"

Cole stared at me for a moment and then pointed to my room. "Don't ask any questions. I'll return later." Then he turned and walked in the other direction, his body literally disappearing into thin air.

My brain was screaming at me to do something, but I had no idea what to say or where to go. In the span of twenty-four hours, I'd experienced things that had never happened to me before and were just too extreme to comprehend. Jane whimpered beside me, and I realized that she hadn't growled at Cole. Perhaps she knew that he wasn't going to hurt me?

What the hell was going on? Who was Cole? A ghost?

Why was I seeing things that weren't real?

My doorway no longer glowed, so I finally went back into my room and shut the door. Jane sighed and settled into her bed for the night. Looking at my watch, I estimated that it was nearly sunrise, but my body didn't care, and I fell into a deep, dreamless sleep.

Chapter 5

Iawoke to the aromatic smell of freshly brewed coffee. Opening my eyes slowly, I could see bright rays of light streaming through the blinds and bathing the room in a warm glow.

Surprisingly, Jane had slept in and was now looking at me from her bed with drowsy eyes. I smiled at her and swung my legs over the side of the bed, preparing to get up—when the craziness of the night before hit me like a sack of bricks.

Leaning back against the pillow, I thought about Margaret's strange behavior and the white floating orbs.

Then my thoughts moved on to Cole. I hoped I would see him again.

If I'm going to be haunted by a dead guy, at least he's a handsome dead guy.

Questions continued to plague my mind as I finally got up and took a shower. Despite my cuts and bruises from the night before, the hot water soothed my aches and pains. Once I was ready to face another day, I headed downstairs for breakfast.

As I descended the stairwell, it dawned on me how normal everything appeared. Almost as if the prior night's events had been washed away by the sun's sterile glow.

Bobbie and Daniel were already eating breakfast at the kitchen table. And surprisingly, Margaret was down there with them. The trio was chatting amicably and didn't falter when I entered the room.

I stood there for a moment, unsure of where to sit, when a member of the help staff ushered me to one of the seats and placed a plate before me. It took only moments before my cup was filled with aromatic coffee, and a steaming plate of eggs and bacon stared up at me.

"So, Renda, how did you sleep?" Margaret asked, looking at me with a smile on her face. She appeared rested and healthy.

"Fine, thank you."

"Well, that's good. I got a good night's sleep, as well," she said cheerfully, taking a sip of coffee.

Both Bobbie and Daniel stared at me, waiting to see what I would say next. They both looked a bit tired and neither greeted me directly. Instead, they just continued eating their breakfast and talking about shallow things like the weather and current TV shows.

I ate my breakfast in silence, annoyed that they weren't addressing the obvious. Their mother had been roaming the woods like a crazy banshee, and I was the only one who was willing to admit it. Summoning up a bit of courage, I decided to tread on dangerous ground. Things needed to get resolved and the worst they could do was throw me out.

But what about Cole?

Ignoring the small bit of concern in my mind, I put down my fork and stared at Margaret with purpose. "Ms. Trillo, last night I saw you leave the house and walk into the woods. Do you remember that?"

For a second, her eyes flashed, like she was about to snarl at me. But instead, she gave me a big smile. "No, I don't recall that happening. Are you sure you saw me?"

"Yes, it was definitely you. You went outside into the woods. Do you have trouble sleepwalking?"

She cleared her throat and chuckled. "No, I don't think so. Maybe you were having a dream."

"It wasn't a dream. I saw you..."

Suddenly, Bobbie interrupted me. "Renda, I think I'm going to have to leave you alone this morning for a few hours. I've got to pick up a few things from the office. Will you be okay if I leave you here?"

Irritated at the interruption, I looked down at my plate. "Yeah, I'll be fine."

"Bobbie, do you want me to drive you into the city?" Margaret asked.

"Sure, Mom. That would be great!"

The two began a new conversation about going shopping for some clothes, and I chose to tune them out. Once breakfast was over, they both left, promising to return in a few hours. I decided to grab a book and sit outside and read while Daniel went upstairs to play videogames in his room.

The climate outside was typical Georgia weather—hot. But there was an occasional light breeze that made it less muggy. I found it strangely comforting and settled into my chair, hoping to get some color on my pale skin.

After reading for a few minutes, I put the book down in my lap and looked out at the woods. Then I turned and looked up at the house.

I couldn't sit still. There was something out there—in the distance—and I needed to find out what it was.

Conjuring up every bit of courage in my bones, I put my book down on the chair and slowly walked towards the woods. In the light of day, the greenery didn't seem that scary.

It's just grass and a bunch of trees, right? Nothing to be afraid of.

I slowly walked into the forest, careful this time to push the branches out of the way. Although no one had talked about it during breakfast, I knew that I had a small network of tiny scratches on my face and arms and didn't want to mutilate myself further.

I was finally able to make it through the woods and once again arrived at the meadow. The air still felt heavier here, but my surroundings were less ominous than the night before.

Exploring the meadow turned up nothing other than grass, rocks, and bugs. There were no strange markings anywhere, no notes, no infamous "stone left unturned". I was about to leave when suddenly I heard a voice in the wind. It formed a single word.

Mine.

I stood frozen in place. Had I imagined it? No, because I heard it again...

Mine.

The wind suddenly stopped, and a putrid odor filled my nostrils. The stench reminded me of rotting garbage. But I had no idea where it was coming from.

I looked around and didn't see anything, but the smell remained. Feeling helpless, I called out, "Who's there?"

Silence.

Then—I heard a name whispered several times in my ear.

Elial.

Elial.

Elial.

The wind suddenly blasted through the meadow, making me jump. It occurred to me that perhaps I should have brought Jane, but she was in the house napping. So I was alone.

Impossibly, a dark form began to appear in the center of the meadow. I rubbed my eyes, but the form remained and a voice emerged from its depths.

"I am Elial!" it shouted. "And you take heed. The woman is mine!"

The horrible voice reverberated through the air and shot through my head, making me extremely dizzy. I tripped and fell to the ground, banging the side of my face on a large stone.

"I am Elial. Demon of the woods. And you take heed!"

My head now hurt so badly that it was nearly impossible to lift it up. Blood dripped onto the grass and I felt my nose burn with a nosebleed.

"Please," I whispered.

It was too much to take. My eyes glazed over and everything went dark as I fell into unconsciousness.

I emerged from the darkness, thanks to the sensation of Jane's long tongue. She was licking my face, trying to wake me up. It was actually quite ticklish and despite my precarious situation, I started giggling.

"Stop it, Jane!"

She barked and hopped around, pleased to have been successful in her mission to get me off the ground, but it took me a few moments to stand. My nose had stopped bleeding, but my head hurt like someone was hitting it with a mallet.

Checking my watch, I was surprised to see that I'd been out for nearly forty-five minutes and immediately knew that I needed to get back to the house as quickly as possible. I didn't want to worry Bobbie any more than necessary.

At the same time, it was important for me to process what had just happened.

Suddenly, I heard a voice in the distance call my name.

"Renda! Are you out there?"

It was Bobbie. Quickly, I wiped my face to erase any bloodstains, and taking a deep breath, calmly walked towards the woods. Bobbie stood amidst the trees looking at me with a concerned frown.

"Are you okay?"

"Sure," I lied. "I was just taking a walk and was actually heading back to your house."

"Okay, well, you've gotta see the new clothes I bought."

As she led me back to the house, I didn't turn around once, but the name of my new enemy continued to burn in my mind.

I am Elial.

The rest of the day passed uneventfully, which was good considering I had nearly suffered a concussion out in the woods.

I didn't see Margaret, and Bobbie kept us busy. We spent time talking about her job and her latest exploits, clothes, my life—the only topic that was off limits was her mother. We did talk a little bit about the divorce and how hard it had been on everyone, but Bobbie kept switching the subject every time the topic of her mother came up.

Normally, I would have been frustrated at the obvious avoidance, but I was nursing a headache from my earlier fall and was seeking some normalcy, so I welcomed the casual conversation about other things.

Bobbie chided me about being single and working at the library. She felt that I should branch out and use my college degree in English Literature to do something more, like teach high school. But I gave her the same excuse I gave everyone—I worked in the library because I simply hadn't figured out yet what I really wanted to do with my life. There was nothing I was inherently good at, other than reading books and keeping my life as mellow as possible. Of course, that hadn't been the case throughout the past forty-eight hours, but I kept those thoughts to myself.

Bobbie then switched the topic to what our plans were for the week. She hadn't organized anything special, but wanted to go shopping, hit the clubs, and find ways to get into trouble.

Typical Bobbie.

She knew that I wasn't into the socializing and that her club-hopping notions were probably not going to turn out the way she wanted, but I indulged her—smiling and listening.

We talked for what seemed like hours, until the rays of light through the windows started to fade and then disappeared altogether. We caught up on so many things that I basically forgot about the strangeness of my afternoon, and immersed myself in the closeness of a friendship that always seemed to regenerate itself when we were together.

In the meantime, Jane spent her time exploring the house and alternated her afternoon between Daniel's room and ours. She seemed to be having a great time.

After a while, my stomach grumbled loudly and we both laughed. It was nearly dinnertime, and the only break we'd taken was to let Jane outside. Bobbie looked out of her window, shaking her head slowly.

"It's crazy. We've been talking forever. I think dinner's ready. Mmm, something smells good."

I sniffed the air and caught the aroma of what smelled like roast beef. My mouth watered at the thought of another delicious meal, but at the same time a small voice of worry chided me that now was not the time to let my guard down.

As we rose and left the bedroom, I looked down the hallway warily. With the onset of nightfall, the house seemed a little more mysterious as darkness began to crawl into the corners. I began to experience a strange, ominous feeling and was happy to be heading downstairs, which was brightly lit and bustling with activity.

Don't want to hang out here and wait for ghosts.

Downstairs, the formal dining room was set with a feast

fit for a king. Tender slices of medium-rare roast beef were laid out on a beautiful silver platter, along with a matching gravy boat filled with a dark, rich sauce. Next to the platter, a fluffy mountain of mashed sweet potatoes beckoned. Plates of various roasted vegetables dressed with a balsamic reduction and seasoned with aromatic herbs, along with crusty French bread and a bowl of creamy butter, rounded out the delectable meal.

It was an insane feast for a handful of people, but I reminded myself that the house staff also ate from the pickings and probably took some food home for their families.

Margaret greeted us warmly as we arrived at the table.

"Hi, girls!" she chirped happily.

Despite her smiling face and warm welcome, I was suspicious. I hadn't forgotten about my little run-in with Elial, and even though I wasn't sure what I had encountered, it couldn't be good. And the woman it had been screeching about had to be Margaret.

It wanted her.

And it didn't want me getting in the way.

Suddenly, Daniel's sweet voice interrupted my thoughts. "Renda, we're going to watch a movie tonight with Mom. Do you want to join us?"

Normally, I would've been thrilled to settle in and watch a good flick, but the idea of spending more time with Margaret than necessary wasn't appealing. So I politely declined, citing exhaustion. Bobbie rolled her eyes at my statement, but I didn't care. My body was tired after the strange experience in the field and I was looking forward to getting some rest. I needed time to process everything I'd seen and heard.

So once dinner was over, I said goodnight to the group and went upstairs to my room, Jane following close behind me. The trio remained downstairs and curled up on the couch in their family room. They planned to watch a comedy and the telltale smell of popcorn soon wafted towards me as I made my way to the bedroom.

I didn't like being upstairs by myself. The floating orbs, the strange man who no one seemed to know—when I'd asked the house staff if there was someone working with them named Cole, I was greeted with blank stares—and my new acquaintance, Elial, all had me on serious edge.

In order to avoid any chance encounters, I went directly to my bedroom. Jane followed behind me and whined as we entered. I quickly shut the door...locking it once more.

"I know. We're not having much fun tonight," I murmured. "But we'll be rested up for tomorrow. You've already gone out, so go to bed."

She looked at me with her large eyes, snorted, and then turned her back on me, settling down into her pillow.

I got into my own bed and stared at the ceiling. The lights in my room were still on, and I decided it would be best to keep them that way until morning.

Chapter 6

I'm not sure if it was the chatter or the banging that woke me up first. But what I do know is that there was such a terrible racket going on outside my bedroom that it was peculiar that no one else had woken up yet.

As I slowly opened my eyes, I could hear various noises outside my door. There seemed to be several people talking—some with strange British accents that sounded clipped and distinct. Looking over at Jane, I could see that she was awake as well and was literally sitting at the door with her back to me. She looked over her shoulder at me as if to say, "Come on. We've got to see what's out there!"

So I decided to be brave and find out.

Sitting up, I slid my feet into my favorite green slippers and slowly shuffled to the door. Jane hadn't moved and remained in her upright position. She didn't greet me as I walked up, nor did she turn her head for a gentle petting.

When I opened the door, she raced out and disappeared into the darkness. I whispered her name, trying to get her to come back, but it was impossible to see where she'd gone.

I was immediately distracted in my effort to find her, because the hallway was now filled with a strange yellow glow and it helped my eyes adjust to a very unusual sight.

There, in the middle of the hallway, was a large group of people, but there was something wrong with them.

One woman was leaning over the railing, rocking back and forth and singing songs to herself, while a trail of vomit leaked out of the side of her pale mouth and traveled down her neck, staining her old fashioned white blouse.

Sara Brooke

A man was slowly walking down the hallway, dragging an ax behind him, but he was missing one of his arms.

Two children played together in the center of the hallway, but they were both badly burned.

And there were many more people, but they all looked injured or...dead.

My mind raced and threatened to shut down altogether. In the midst of the chaos, small white orbs traveled up and down the hallway. Once in a while, an orb would stop and then grow until it became one of the ghosts. Other times, an orb would simply flit around back and forth until it connected with a wall and disappeared.

"It's a strange sight, isn't it?"

The voice came from behind me and nearly caused my heart to stop.

It was Cole.

Turning around, I answered as calmly as I could, "Um, yes. What is all this?"

Cole stood there amidst all of the strange people, yet despite his handsome profile, seemed to fit in perfectly. Perhaps it was the fact that he was pale like the others or that he was wearing clothing not of this era. But unlike the others, he made my heart race from fear and something else—was it attraction? I couldn't be sure. It didn't matter. He was as weird as the rest of them, and I needed to be on my guard.

"You can see us," he said quietly. "It seems you're able to bridge the gap between our worlds."

"Are all of you...dead? Are you ghosts or something?"

Cole sighed as if I was asking an obvious question and motioned towards my bedroom door. "Why don't we go inside and I'll explain."

I hesitated, and he seemed even more annoyed. "Look, if you want to understand what's going on here, you must listen to me, young lady. Otherwise, I'll leave you be."

Not wanting him to leave, I turned back towards the doorway and gasped when I nearly bumped into one of the children. It was the little girl, her badly burnt face shining in the strange glow that cleared the darkness. She was missing most of her hair and a few burnt patches stuck up in different directions. Her eyes were milky and lost, but she seemed to know exactly where I stood, because she took my hand in her small, charred fingers and asked, "Want to play?"

I immediately felt strange pinpricks of heat seep into my skin and nearly passed out in shock, when Cole spoke up from behind me.

"Not right now, Claire. Go play with your brother, and we'll join you in a bit."

Even though her features were marred by smoke and fire, I could see her disappointment.

"Okay," she said and dropped my hand. She started to walk back to the hallway, but turned around again and smiled at me, her white teeth in stark contrast to her black skin.

"It's nice to meet you."

"It's nice to meet you, too," I whispered.

"Make sure you turn your bedroom light off first," Cole instructed, "I haven't manifested enough energy to project against the light. And don't worry about your animal. Here she comes."

Almost as if on cue, Jane appeared in the hallway and happily trotted over to us. Whatever these "things" were, she wasn't afraid and seemed to enjoy the attention. As she passed the ghosts, some of them stopped to pet her and then returned to whatever it was they were doing. By my count, there were at least thirty men, women, and children loitering in the hallway.

I wasn't all that keen on turning off the light, but something inside my mind urged me to be brave and trust that this strange man wasn't going to hurt me. I flipped off the light switch and was surprised and relieved to see that as Cole made his way into the room, the yellow glow from the hallway seemed to follow him.

It dawned on me that the yellow light was actually emanating off these beings, like a halo of energy radiating outward.

Walking over to the bed, I sat down and watched Cole. His body gently glowed, but his dark eyes stared piercingly in my direction. Despite myself, I felt a slight shiver of sexual excitement. Dead or alive, he was hot. But I shrugged it off quickly and addressed him as calmly as I could.

"Okay, so we're in my room. Now, tell me who you are."

Cole leaned up against the wall and folded his arms in front of him. He looked hesitant suddenly, as if afraid to say the wrong thing.

So I relaxed my gaze and tried again.

"I'm glad you're here. Please tell me what's going on."

Cole's lips turned up in a small, almost undetectable smile and I could tell that he was pleased at my interest.

"As I've told you, my name is Cole Drake. I was born a long time ago in London, England."

"How long ago?" I asked, interrupting him. Cole gave me an irritated look, so I shook my head and allowed him to continue.

"Long after the American Revolution, my family traveled over from England, settling in Macon. We had a good life here in Georgia, but then things changed. A feud with a neighboring family spiraled out of control and led to trouble—and ultimately, my death."

My face paled at the mention of the obvious, but it wasn't until Cole pointed to his midsection, when I noticed that there was a dark spot lining the black garb he was wearing. I hadn't seen it there before, and as I watched, the spot darkened and then suddenly disappeared.

"Yes, I was shot to death. It was a rogue move by a member of a neighboring family sworn to destroy the Drakes. But as you can see, I didn't disappear into some theoretical place they call heaven or hell. My soul remains here—on this land. I forever remain restless between two worlds." He then paused and looked at me for a response.

I had nothing to say. The whole thing was crazy. A shooting? Dead people chatting in the hallway? It was all too fantastical for my brain to understand, and yet—I was slowly, amazingly, coming to terms with what was happening around me.

Cole was waiting for an answer; so instead, I asked the only question possible. "Why can I see all of this? Those people out there…they're making a ton of noise. Why can't anyone else hear them?"

"Because you're special, Renda Bloodmane. There are only a

few people who can see through their world into ours. You're one of them. Maybe you've always been able to and never realized this ability."

I thought about the man in the library. He'd obviously been dead too, but I'd seen him standing there as clear as day, reading his book. Is that when everything had started?

And now, would I see dead people all the time? How would I ever be able to sleep?

"Don't worry, Renda," Cole said softly, as if he could hear my thoughts. "You won't always see us. It takes energy for us to manifest. And that is a slow process."

I looked up and noticed that he looked tired suddenly, and his shape wasn't as clear. The dresser that he was leaning against was now becoming slightly visible behind his body. In a panic, I realized that he was starting to disappear.

"Yes, I am starting to fade. It happens to us. We can manifest our shape and form into actual solid beings, but it takes stored energy for that to happen. We need time to regenerate so that we can once again project ourselves. So depending on how 'real' we want to appear, it may take hours or even days."

"But you can't leave. I have so many questions," I sputtered, not wanting him to disappear.

"I must," he said quietly. "But I'll be back as soon as I can. And, Renda, you must be careful. You've made contact with someone who's not like us. It's a demon. A terrible force of energy that doesn't need to regenerate because it was never human. You must stay away from Elial until you're able to better handle the dark force. Do you understand?"

Cole's body was now fading fast and had become almost entirely translucent. But he struggled to finish his thoughts.

"Stay away from Elial. I'll help you, but you must listen to me. Stay away from the woman he inhabits. Trust your thoughts. And I'll do my best to help you. We all will."

His words chilled me and I stood up, reaching out as if I could stop him from disappearing. But as the last words left his lips, he vanished, and a warm breeze swept through the room in one final exhale.

Jane whimpered in unhappiness, and it was exactly how I felt.

I didn't want him to leave. There was something about the way he looked at me—the way he talked to me—that had awakened a fire deep within my core. I could feel a surge of energy coursing through me that I'd never felt before. It was an amazing sensation. But there were other emotions churning through my blood, as well.

Fear.

Awe.

An uneasiness of the future.

Why was this happening to me?

In an effort to hold on to some of the magic and mystery of the evening, I quickly went to the door and opened it, hoping that some of the restless spirits were still haunting the hallway. It would be proof enough that I wasn't going completely insane.

As the door swung open, I peered into the hallway.

All was dark.

Disappointed, I turned back to my bedroom, when a soft voice whispered in my ear. It was Claire's voice—the little girl who'd lost her life in an apparent fire.

"We're glad you're here."

Chapter 7

Morning came to greet me like an old friend. The warm rays of sunlight brightened up the room, and Jane added to the ambience with her characteristic snorting. My eyes opened slowly, and the colors came into focus.

It was hard to believe that anything but wonderful things could happen in such a cheerful, comfortable place. But the prior night's events quickly crept into my mind, darkening the world with a gothic shroud. Things were not wonderful. And I wasn't sure if I'd ever be able to trust my own sanity again.

Lying against the soft pillow, I felt the heaviness of my situation.

Was I losing my freaking mind?

Dead people roaming the hallways…handsome ghosts from the past…it was too much.

Sighing, I turned my back so that I was facing the wall and pulled the covers over my head. Getting the day started wasn't very appealing. It was much nicer to keep my head under the blanket and away from anything—undead.

But Jane wasn't having any of it. She poked her nose under the blanket, snorting loudly as if to say, "Come on, Mom!"

I groaned and kept my head under the covers. "Leave me alone, Jane. I'm not getting up. There are too many ghosts in this house, and I don't want to deal with that crazy woman who lives here."

"Oh, really?"

Bobbie's voice cut like glass through the air.

Shit.

I sat up quickly and tried to apologize. "Bobbie, hey, I'm really sorry. I was just…"

"Don't worry about it. You can leave if you like. I'm going to take a trip to town for a while. Hope you can stand hanging out here." She turned and left the room before I could say anything else.

Jane whined again and looked towards the door. Aggravated, I slid out of bed and led her out of the room and down the hallway. In the daylight, everything looked normal. The door to Margaret's room was still closed, so I assumed she was sleeping and I quickly rushed downstairs to the front door. As Jane and I exited, I saw Bobbie's car take off down the driveway and disappear into the distance.

I had no idea how long she'd be gone, so after Jane did her business, we both went back upstairs, and I got ready for the day. A long, hot shower felt wonderful, but I continued to look around—fearful that I might find some ghastly dead person starting at me while I bathed.

Luckily though, the dead stayed away and gave me a chance to blow dry my hair and get my clothes on. The aroma of a hot breakfast wafted up through the rafters, and I could smell eggs and other delicious treats. My stomach rumbled in annoyance, and I headed downstairs to face the rest of the family.

Daniel was sitting at the breakfast table by himself, munching on a piece of toast and reading a comic book. He looked up as I approached and gave me a close-mouthed grin, motioning for me to join him. The table was laden with jumbo blueberry muffins, thickly sliced toast, fresh fruit and preserves, and creamy butter. The sideboard contained various hot dishes including fluffy scrambled eggs, sausages, and hearty oatmeal sprinkled with cinnamon and raisins. I poured myself a cup of rich, dark-roasted coffee and reached for a muffin.

Jane trotted over and sat on the floor between us, her eyes hopeful that we'd drop some food on the floor by accident.

Daniel reached out and patted her on the head. Jane wagged her tail in reply.

It amazed me how wonderful Jane was around children. I knew that she'd already brought a certain amount of comfort to Bobbie's adorable little brother. It made me feel good about our visit, even though I wasn't getting the full story from my friend. She was clearly uninterested in delving too deeply into her mother's psyche and that was causing a rift between us.

We ate breakfast quietly as Daniel read his comics and I thought about how to apologize to Bobbie. Her earlier entrance into my bedroom had been so quiet that it had been impossible to detect her presence. Still, what I'd said was rude, and I wasn't one to fight with my friends (the few friends that I had). In addition, I desperately needed someone to talk to about my "visions", so a speedy apology was appropriate and necessary.

I noticed that Margaret was still upstairs in bed and mentioned her absence to Daniel. He looked at me sadly, his large eyes filled with a despair uncommon for a child his age.

"Mom's been in bed a lot lately. She has good days and bad days, but the bad ones are starting to win."

I was about to say something, when the sound of maniacal laughter traveled down the stairwell and into the dining area, interrupting us with its chilling trespass. Daniel was now terrified and he stopped eating, looking in the direction of the stairs.

The laughter stopped and then started again. It continued for several seconds and would then peter out, like a CD that was being played, pausing every few moments. The noise carried on for a bit and we just sat there, listening to the strangeness of the laughter, frozen in our chairs.

Finally, I could take it no longer and stood up abruptly. My chair nearly toppled over, but I caught it, while motioning for Daniel to stay put. "I'm going upstairs to see what's going on."

"No," he started to beg. "Don't leave me alone. Stay."

"Daniel," I replied more calmly than I felt, for his sake, "don't worry. I'll just check upstairs to make sure everything is fine and then I'll be right back. Jane will stay here with you."

Jane snorted in agreement.

"That's okay. I'm going to go to my friend's house down the street, all right?"

I nodded and figured it would be better to let him go than stay in the house with his crazed mother.

Daniel turned and left the kitchen, followed by Jane who seemed to have made a new best friend.

I was now alone and it was time to face Margaret.

Elial.

As I slowly climbed the stairwell, the noise began again, but this time it sounded more like chuckling and less like laughter. And when I reached the top of the stairwell, the sound stopped altogether. I stood in place for a few minutes, almost daring the maniac to start laughing again, but nothing happened.

And then, something did happen.

The door to Margaret's bedroom opened by itself.

It swung open slowly, and then stopped moving—as though mocking me in its frightening simplicity. My feet wouldn't work and remained glued to the floor, as the realization that my life had become a series of strange and terrifying events suddenly washed over me. I felt nauseous, and for a moment, I wished and prayed that things could go back to the way they were.

I closed my eyes and envisioned my apartment in Cale. In my mind, I could see myself sitting on the bed with Jane, watching yet another Jane Austen flick on the BBC. But this memory that was usually so comforting now seemed colorless and vague.

You were meant to do this.

The sound of Cole's calm voice cut through the silence and swirled around my head. I could now sense that he was somehow with me and this feeling gave me enough comfort to lift one foot and then another.

I was finally standing outside Margaret's bedroom, staring at the doorway. She wasn't making any sounds, but the laughter and cackling had definitely been coming from within.

I took a deep breath and stepped inside.

The bedroom was vast and elegantly decorated, like one of those perfect rooms you see in decorating magazines. In the center, sat a huge bed with four golden bedposts carved in the shape of angels. Margaret was in bed, asleep.

Or so I thought.

As I neared her silent form, I could see that her eyes were closed and her chest rose and fell gently. She wasn't thrashing or sweaty, and looked almost peaceful. Leaning down to get a closer look, I whispered, "Ms. Trillo, are you awake?"

Suddenly, her eyes flew open and to my horror were completely white and empty. She flashed an evil grin and grabbed my neck with both arms, pulling me down on top of her. I struggled and tried to free myself as she began cackling louder and louder, the sound filling the room with its evil.

"Try to get free now, my little librarian!" she screeched and cackled.

I could barely breathe because my face was being smashed against her bony chest, and despite Margaret's frail appearance, she had an iron grip. I panicked, trying to get away, when suddenly a loud voice boomed and resonated throughout the room.

"Let her go!"

It was Cole's voice, and it had an immediate effect. My attacker quickly loosened her grip and fell back on the bed. As soon as I was free, I fearfully backed away.

Margaret was no longer moving, but I wasn't taking any chances.

Not knowing what else to do, I ran back to my bedroom and quickly snatched my laptop and purse. After that, I went back into the hallway, which was thankfully empty and took one more look at Margaret's bedroom before fleeing down the stairs. As I tore through the living room on the way to the door, I woke up Jane who'd been taking a nap in the downstairs living room. She followed me outside and I let her jump into the passenger seat. Then we sped away.

Chapter 8

It took me several minutes to stop shaking. My hands were trembling as they gripped the wheel. It was surreal to drive by such elegant homes on a warm, sunny day when I had just experienced one of the most terrifying moments of my life.

I needed to get away from that cursed place.

I needed to think.

Jane whimpered as she watched me drive in an unknown direction. She could sense my panic and wasn't comfortable with my countenance. Leaning over, she placed her head on my lap and snorted—her eyes fixated on my face.

"I know, baby. I know. Things are crazy. I just have to figure this out."

We were starting to get close to the city, so instead of merging onto the highway, I pulled over onto a residential street and drove around aimlessly until we approached a park. It was nearly empty, with the exception of a woman reading a book under a tree. It was the perfect place for me to stop and reflect on what had happened, and more importantly, what I was going to do.

I parked the car and led Jane over to a secluded spot, instructing her to "sit and stay" while I opened my laptop and grabbed my cell phone from my purse. Not knowing whether dogs were allowed in the park, I figured that being as hidden as possible would be a good thing. I chose to ignore the disdainful look we received from the lone reader who seemed annoyed at our intrusion. The woman then got up and moved to a bench that was far away, which was perfectly fine with me.

I never could understand people who didn't like dogs. In

my opinion, Jane was the sweetest soul on the planet and had the purity of love that I'd only ever experienced from animals. People on the other hand, could be horrid and mean. Or in Margaret's case—possessed by a demon.

Flipping open my phone, I dialed Larlene's number.

She answered on the second ring.

"Why, hello there, Ms. pain-in-the-ass," she said in typical Larlene fashion.

"Hi," I answered, trying to keep my voice as calm as possible.

"Where the hell are you?" she asked, forcing me to engage in several minutes of small talk about my recent impromptu vacation. After a few moments of discussion, I realized that it wasn't the right moment to share everything that had happened over the past several days. There was too much to tell, and not enough time. I needed some immediate answers.

"Larlene, I've got a question for you."

"Sure, shoot."

"I can't tell you why right now, but I need a little info on some demonic stuff. Can you help me?"

Larlene giggled and responded gleefully, "Cool! Are you doing a séance or something? You know, those people in Georgia are into all sorts of black magic. In fact, I just saw a movie that—"

"Larlene," I interrupted. "Please."

"Okay, okay. What do you need info about?"

I didn't even want to say its name.

"Can you give me a little information about a demon called Elial? It's for a short story I'm writing. I'm feeling very creative lately."

Larlene snorted. "Sure, hang on. I've got all sorts of research sites I can pull from. Did you try Googling it?"

"Yes," I answered as I typed the name into a Google search. All sorts of strange items came up, but nothing that led me to the answers I needed. "But I couldn't find anything. Can you check into some of our demon books?"

She sighed and started typing into the reference PC that was loaded with our catalog of books. Then she put me on hold for several frustrating minutes and finally came back on the line.

"Found it!" she exclaimed.

"Great, so what can you tell me?"

"Well, hold your horses there, missy. I still have to get the book from the shelf. Hold on a few more minutes, and I'll be right back."

So I sat and waited some more, fruitlessly trying to find something on the Internet that would lead me to the answers I needed.

"I'm back." Larlene breathed into the phone. "Um, let's see. I've got this book called *Demons of the Medieval*. It looks like this Elial you're talking about isn't one of the mainstream demons that you hear about in all those crazy horror movies and..."

"Larlene. I really need that info."

"Sorry. Here goes..."

As she shared the story of Elial, it became quite clear to me that I was in serious trouble.

Elial has been described in several different ways, the most popular as the Tree Demon or Demon of the Woods. It is unique in its maleness. Many demons possess the ability to manifest in female or male form, but Elial is always described as a male.

Legend has it that the demon Elial is a manifestation of the sorrow encountered by the suffering of the trees. Every time a tree is cut or burnt; every time an insect burrows itself into the bark and cuts through the meat of the trunk; all pain that is inflicted—every moment of destruction—that is Elial.

He therefore feeds on pain and suffering and seeks it out— primarily from women. He is known to hide in the darkness of the shadows and await his victims. When a woman stumbles into his presence, he initially fills her with peace and sexual fulfillment. She knows not what is happening and is powerless to stop it. And in many ways, she does not want to stop it because it feels so good to her.

But the intense, wonderful feelings are masking Elial's true deception, for he is feeding, starving her of her life source. With each moment of his bonding with his victim, he is injecting the blackness of night into her cells and polluting her essence with his evil.

She will become weak, both in mind and spirit, and she will not be able to fight him.

The only thing that can save his victim is the strength of those who love her. The commitment to protect and honor her will save her soul. But the battle will be difficult, for Elial does not like to lose. He will remain embedded deep within the soul for as long as possible, feeding off his victim until there is nothing left of her. His victims sometimes do not survive.

Larlene continued to read from the book, but my thoughts were already racing in other directions. A battle? I would be forced to fight a battle against some crazed demon that didn't like to lose?

I was just a simple librarian from Cale, Florida! It was absolutely absurd to think I could defeat such a creature, wasn't it?

You are different.

Damn that Cole. Why was I hearing his voice in my head at the most inopportune times? I didn't want this fight. I just wanted to go home and put my head under the covers.

"Renda, are you listening to me? Do I need to keep reading?"

I'd forgotten about Larlene, who'd been droning on and on and had begun reading about another demon.

"No, no. Thanks for the information. I really appreciate it."

Larlene paused for a moment and then hesitantly asked, "Renda, what's really going on? I know you. This is one helluva strange request."

I wanted so badly to tell her what was happening. To have someone understand what I was going through. To confess.

But somehow, I just knew that it wasn't the right time. I would eventually tell her what was going on; but first, I had to figure out how to save Bobbie and her brother from the evil force that was trying to steal their mother away.

"I'll explain later. Thanks so much for the info. I'll call you in a few days."

"Okay...Renda?"

"Yes?"

"Be careful, okay?"

A tear escaped my eye as I said goodbye and hung up. Jane whimpered and snuggled up next to me. But this time her warm, furry body didn't comfort me. It was time to go back to the Trillos.

The drive back to the mansion was difficult. Part of me just wanted to turn the car around and head south to Cale. A few times I actually pulled the car over and sat with the engine idling, debating whether or not it would be best to just walk away from the situation.

But I couldn't do that to Bobbie. She was my dearest friend and she needed me.

And part of me wondered if I left, would it mean the end of my contact with Cole? I was drawn to him—even if he was dead.

And then there was Daniel. The poor child was stuck in the midst of a nightmare. What kind of life would he have with a possessed mother?

I realized there was no choice but to return to the house. As the large white mansion came into view, the anxiety in my body increased. I pulled the car around and stopped in the driveway, looking up at the window that I now knew was Margaret's bedroom. This time, there was no one standing there to greet me.

The air outside felt tense and still. There was no immediate movement around the house, and to the casual onlooker, it might have appeared perfectly normal.

But I knew better.

Erring on the side of caution, I quickly opened the front door and walked through the house, Jane trotting beside me. I then went back outside to the backyard. Since Bobbie wasn't home, my strategy was to stay outside until she returned and then try to talk to her about what was happening.

Plus, Elial was now a part of Margaret, so I wasn't all that excited about returning upstairs.

What if she attacked me again?

The idea of an attack happening once more filled me with dread, but instead of dwelling on it, I started to think about how to react the next time it happened. Cole's apparent intervention had helped me escape (though he'd remained invisible to me after it happened), but I couldn't count on him every time I was in trouble.

I needed to figure out how to combat the demon.

All the horror movies I'd seen regarding demonic possession usually involved someone from the Church dressed in special garb, as an exorcist. They usually carried a cross, and a Bible, and chanted passages while sprinkling holy water on the possessed person.

Was that what I was supposed to do?

The thought of having to behave in that manner was beyond me because for starters, despite being raised a Christian, I didn't wear a cross and rarely ever went to church. Holy water wasn't something I readily had available, and a Bible? I wouldn't even know what passages to read.

I opened my laptop and began searching on the Internet; first by typing in "exorcism" and then "demon". At first, the typical websites came up that involved the Vatican, or priests, or other people "of the cloth". Other websites with horror movies appeared, and many of the sites didn't contain factual information and were for "entertainment purposes only".

The different websites became a blur as I searched through the links, only taking breaks to use the bathroom. After a while, I couldn't stop ignoring my rumbling stomach, so I decided to go inside and grab a sandwich. As I stood up, Jane snorted and proceeded to follow me inside.

When I entered the kitchen, I could see that the chef had already started preparing for the evening meal. Bobbie had told me his name was Roy Garvey, but everyone called him Chef Roy. He was an older African American gentleman who had worked as a cook in the Army. Bobbie's uncle had been a commander on the base and had been friends with Roy for many years. Margaret had hired him when he'd retired.

Chef Roy was an amazing cook (as I had experienced from all of his meals), but we hadn't had any time to talk because he was always bustling about in the kitchen. This time, however, it seemed rude to just barge into the kitchen and not say anything, so I tried to strike up a conversation.

"That looks delicious."

Jane snorted as if in agreement and plopped herself on the floor close to Chef Roy.

The chef looked over at me, winked, and then gave Jane a biscuit from a container on the counter. I shook my head at Jane. She was now Chef Roy's friend for life. We both laughed as Jane devoured the treat.

"Yes, I like to get started early so the Trillos can eat dinner at around the same time every day...Ms. Trillo likes it that way."

I noticed his tone change when he mentioned Bobbie's mother.

"She's not doing so well, is she?" I asked.

The chef sighed and kept his focus on the food. "No, she's not, but we just try to mind our business and not get involved in family matters. It's better that way. I've known Ms. Trillo for a long time, when things were better." Chef Roy looked up and smiled, his eyes warm in thought. "She used to laugh and tease me about my meals, telling me that I was trying to fatten her up like the evil witch in Hansel & Gretel. Those were good days."

He looked back down and continued to chop greens for the salad. "But I'm afraid those days are long gone now. Ms. Trillo's not been doing well for some time. I've even called her uncle for help, but he isn't sure what to do, either."

I pressed him, again. "Don't you think she needs some serious help?"

This time, the chef put down his knife and gave me a sad smile. "Ms. Renda, I've known Ms. Trillo for years. She's like a sister to me. She always treated me like family. When I cook for her kids, it's like I'm cooking for my own. But we hear things in this big old house. There's noises when there shouldn't be and things don't always end up where you put them." He noticed my expression and laughed. "There's ghosts and there's people who act like they're ghosts—all quiet and in the shadows. But Ms. Trillo, she's always been so alive. I hope she gets back to that place. I hope someone can help her..." His voice trailed off, and I could see tears dripping down his cheeks.

Reaching out, I took Chef Roy's hand, and gave it a gentle squeeze.

"I'll do whatever I can."

He smiled at me and quickly wiped the tears away. "Well, I'd best be getting back to supper. We're having roast duck tonight. It's gonna take some time to prepare. Don't you worry, it'll be all right."

I stood and watched him for a while, and then went back outside. Jane stayed in the kitchen, content to watch Chef Roy and beg for scraps.

After eating my sandwich, I returned to my Internet search. I cruised around for a bit when finally, I clicked on a link for a website that was entitled *The Chosen*. It was about people who have the ability to communicate with the dead. It wasn't about psychics or astrologers, but rather about regular people who find themselves bumping into ghosts and ghouls.

The site was dark, illustrated by different images of strange, scary beings. But in the center, it contained a candle with a caption that read: The Chosen are beacons of light not only for the living but also for the dead. They are the directive force that can change circumstances occurring in the space between reality and the world of the spirits. This powerful inclination can create change in both the realm of the living and the realm of the dead.

I continued reading about how *the Chosen* were able to defeat evil, but at a price…

The curse of the Chosen is the ability to interact with and defeat evil. Therefore, they are always in the midst of uninvited beings and specters. Keeping 'real' life intact and not losing oneself to the seduction of darkness is the key. Evil will always try to seduce with its promises of power and immortality. Many of the Chosen have become ill or psychotic due to a constant battle with the darkness.

At this point, I pushed my laptop away and took a deep breath, staring out at the gently swaying trees in the distance. If the website was telling the truth, whatever "gift" I had or possessed could inevitably drive me crazy if I wasn't careful. And there was the possibility of defeating evil without having to delve into all of the religious mumbo jumbo that was typically required.

No special black robes for me.

Looking back down at my computer screen, I was stunned to see that the screen had gone blank. Frustrated, I hit the "back" key on my computer, but it took me back to the search engine. Fruitlessly, I attempted to find the website of *The Chosen* once more, but it had seemed to disappear altogether.

I was about to begin searching again, when I heard Bobbie's car pull into the driveway. I gently placed my laptop on the chair and walked around the house to greet her.

Bobbie had already turned off the engine and was starting to get out of the vehicle as I approached. She eyed me warily and had obviously not forgiven me for my callous remark earlier in the day.

"Hey," she said calmly as she emerged from the car and swung her purse strap over her shoulder. "I'm surprised to see you're still here. I mean, you are staying with a crazy woman and her kids after all."

Pain shot through my heart at the sound of her words. The last thing I wanted to do was upset my friend. If anything, I needed to try to help her before it was too late.

Walking over, I put my arms around her shoulders and gave her a hug, whispering, "I'm sorry. That was a horrible thing to say. Please forgive me."

Bobbie relaxed her stiffened stance and pulled away, still eyeing me carefully. "So, do you really think my mom's crazy?"

"No, but we need to talk. There are some things I need to tell you that might help you understand what's happening. Can we sit outside and chat for a few minutes?"

She agreed to hear me out and I followed her into the house. To my surprise, Margaret was now awake and was sitting at a table near the living room, a coffee cup in hand. She barely acknowledged us as we walked through and remained still, staring out into the distance.

A physical chill shot through me as we passed the woman. I almost expected her to reach out and grab me, but thankfully, she ignored us both. Bobbie didn't seem to notice her mother's reaction, but it was very obvious that something had a hold on the poor woman.

At the same time, Daniel walked through the front door and

greeted his sister with a big hug, as though he was hanging on to her for dear life. She looked a little surprised, but then knelt down next to him and asked, "Hey, buddy, why don't we go out for ice cream tonight after dinner?"

"Sure! Renda let me play at Jack's house for the day and it was totally fun."

Bobbie gave me a "look" and I felt a little guilty that I'd let him play at a friend's house all day, instead of hanging out with him myself. I'd been so focused on my research that it had just seemed easier to let him go have some fun. In hindsight, I wondered if it would've been better to keep him at the house with me.

I made a mental note to spend a little more time with Daniel and to show more interest in what he was up to. I ruffled his hair and he smiled at me, then went off to his room to play video games. Jane emerged from the kitchen and trotted after him.

Bobbie and I grabbed a few cookies that Chef Roy had baked for us and a couple of glasses of milk and headed outside. The sky was beginning to turn a dark blue, and the moon would soon make her appearance. The weather had cooled down somewhat and a gentle breeze blew through the trees, rustling the leaves. It was such a beautiful landscape that it was hard to believe that evil existed within this domain of serenity.

The Chosen are cursed to live with the knowledge of darkness...

We sat down on opposite lounge chairs and smiled at one another. But a sliver of tension was beginning to snake its way into my veins and through my blood. I knew that within the next several minutes, my dearest friend in the world would either think I was a complete lunatic and never look at me the same way again—or perhaps, even worse—would hate me and send me back to Cale.

It was a chance I had to take. There was no other way.

"So," she started, opening up the conversation, "what's going on with you?"

I took a deep breath and told her everything, beginning with the library encounter, the ghosts in the hallway, Cole, her mother, Elial...everything.

Surprisingly, Bobbie didn't interrupt me. She just listened, her eyes growing larger and her lips tightening, as I spoke. I talked for what seemed like an hour and when I was done, the sky was purple and the evening was fast approaching. Chef Roy had already called for us to come in several times and had even joked that he'd feed our dinner to Jane. But the seriousness of the situation was all encompassing as we kept talking. Fleetingly, I wondered if my dog was getting a few bites of my delicious supper.

"So," I asked hesitantly, "What do you think? Do you believe me?"

Bobbie didn't say anything. She looked out at the landscape and I could see that she was quietly crying. We remained silent for minutes that dragged on and on, until she finally looked at me with shiny, wet eyes.

"Renda, what do you expect me to say? What you're telling me is crazy. My mother is possessed by a demon? You're seeing dead people? What is this, a horror movie?" She made a weak attempt at laughter.

"Bobbie, I know what I'm telling you sounds crazy, but you've known me a long time and have I ever lied to you? Have I?" I pushed her, struggling to break through.

She sighed and shook her head. "I don't know, Renda. No, you've never lied to me, but since you've been here…you've not exactly been yourself. So what do I know?" She stood up and walked away, leaving me alone under the darkening sky.

My mind whirled in frustration. I knew it was hard to believe what I'd said, but Bobbie had told me from day one that her mother was behaving strangely, so she obviously knew that something was wrong.

Perhaps she didn't want to believe that it had anything to do with the paranormal, but it was imperative that she open up her mind to the possibility.

Otherwise, her mother could be in mortal danger.

Chapter 9

Dinner was awful. The food itself was good, though I wasn't a big fan of roast duck. But the conversation was non-existent and Margaret was taking her dinner upstairs in her room. Daniel, Bobbie, and I ate in silence and didn't even try to engage in small talk.

I felt terrible. It was clear that Bobbie didn't believe a word I'd said and was just content to watch her mother spiral down into madness.

Even sharing her mother's attack on me earlier in the day hadn't made an impression. The idea of giving up was beginning to sound better and better, when the phone suddenly rang.

It was the first time I'd heard the phone ring and it was loud, because there were landline receivers in every room. Daniel jumped up and grabbed the nearest portable, placing it to his ear and chatting excitedly into the mouthpiece. While he talked on the phone, the silence between Bobbie and I remained.

"Guess who that was?" Daniel asked happily, returning to the table.

"Who?" asked Bobbie, barely paying attention.

"Jack. Since we had so much fun today, he wants me to sleep over his house tonight. Can I? Please?"

It struck me as odd that he was asking for Bobbie's permission and not his mother's. But given the circumstances, he probably wanted to avoid his mother until she "got better".

"Sure. Do you need me to drive you there?"

"Nah. He lives just around the block. I can take my bike."

"Are you sure?"

"Yeah," Daniel said happily. But then, his countenance

darkened slightly, "Can you tell Mom that I'm going over there? She didn't have a good day today."

Bobbie nodded and excused him from the table. We could hear Daniel bound happily up the stairs and it was only a few moments before he raced back down again, yelled out a goodbye, and left the house. Jane barked as if annoyed at his departure and then settled back for a nap at the foot of the stairwell.

The uncomfortable silence was too much to bear.

"Look," I said, "You don't have to completely believe me. Just give me some time, and I'll prove to you that what I'm saying is true. What I really need is for you to trust me and let me try to help."

Bobbie kept her head down and didn't meet my gaze. "You know, I'm aware that there's something wrong with Mom. That's one of the reasons I wanted you here. You've always been so sensible and level-headed. I'd hoped that you would help me convince her to go to a therapist or maybe you could talk to her yourself. But now, you're expecting me to believe something that's totally out there." She stopped and looked me straight in the eye. "And that's not helping at all."

Standing up, she turned away and stormed out of the dining room.

I sat there staring at my uneaten duck and truffle risotto. It looked like a feast fit for a queen. But I felt like the court jester.

After finishing whatever portion of my meal I could, I slowly walked up the stairs. This time, I could see flashes of light dancing across the walls of the hallway, but the ghosts had not yet made their appearance. Perhaps they were preparing for their evening festivities, but I wanted no part of it.

I was depressed and feeling low because Bobbie didn't believe me. Even Jane decided to remain downstairs napping. Not wanting to bother her, I didn't call for her to join me. If and when she needed to be taken outside, she would undoubtedly let me know by whining outside my bedroom door. So I took my isolation and carried the heavy weight as I entered my bedroom.

The light was off in the room, so as soon as I flicked it on,

I was shocked to see that Cole was sitting on my bed. He was hunched forward, deep in thought and looked up as I entered.

"What are you doing here?" was all I could ask in confusion. But a part of me was secretly excited to see him.

He looked the same. Darkly handsome and absolutely as mysterious and brooding as ever. His dark hair glistened in the light and his eyes fixated on me in concentration. It had been a while since a man had been able to generate such a powerful effect on me. Despite the fact that I knew he was dead, I was reacting the same way I would to a living man.

I found myself gazing at his broad shoulders, tight chest, and the bulge that was undeniable between his strong, powerful legs.

What am I thinking? He's dead! And here I am, staring at his crotch!

Heat rose to my cheeks and I quickly looked away. It was insane to be sexually excited by a dead guy. But my life was taking all sorts of crazy turns, so why not?

If Cole noticed my gaze, he gave no indication. Instead, he motioned for me to sit down next to him. I could feel warmth radiating from his body, which surprised me because he was dead.

Well, technically this was not his dead corpse, but his spirit. *Perhaps spirits could be warm?*

I decided to ask him.

But just as I opened my mouth, Cole chuckled. "You're surprised at how much heat my body generates. Well, allow me to explain. We're ghosts, but we must generate energy in order to project ourselves into your world. So what you're feeling is the energy that's allowing me to appear real to you. And I have mass also. Touch me."

I looked at Cole uncertainly.

"Okay."

Reaching out, I placed my hand on his wrist. I felt an intense sensation the moment my skin connected with his. Warmth passed through his wrist and traveled through my hand and up my arm like a hot stream of water, gently washing through my body. The heat also traveled between my thighs and in that moment, staring into Cole's eyes, I didn't care that he was dead.

I wanted him.

After a moment, he pulled his wrist away, and coldness returned to my blood. It wasn't painful, but it filled me with emptiness and my whole psyche felt shallow without his radiance pulsing through it.

Cole chuckled apologetically, "I'm sorry, but I only have enough energy to remain in your world for a short while. When you touched me, the energy I stored was seeking regeneration, so it flowed out of me and into you. It's nothing personal." He looked away, almost embarrassed.

"That's fine," I responded, not sure what to say either. But the awkwardness passed quickly, because Cole stood up and began to pace the room.

"Renda, your encounter today with Elial was dangerous. You've got to be more careful. From now on, you should only approach the woman he's possessed if you're with me. I can help you defeat him, but you're too vulnerable on your own. Because I am on the same spiritual plane as a demon, I can see them easier than you and can also detect their weaknesses. In addition, you are a strong conduit of inner spiritual strength. I can help you find a way to attack him. Every demon has a weakness, but it is through another spirit that you have the best chance of finding it. Plus, our energies combined will make for a stronger attack as well as a shield."

I nodded. He was right. My earlier encounter was recent enough to still make me shudder and there was no way I was going to attempt to contact the demon, let alone fight him, on my own.

"We need to see how strong he is. All of the others want to be rid of him, as well. He's a dark and evil force and wants the spirits here under his control," Cole stopped and looked at me, his eyes heavy with concern. "Demons are devourers. They eat everything in their path; corrode it with a dark energy. He's already beginning to destroy some of the spirits in this home, and he won't stop until he's taken over everyone."

"So, what do we do?"

"First, we need to contact him. Together. This will show him that you are not alone, and there are others who will do battle with you, if needed."

My brain started screaming at me in protest. Face Elial, again? So soon after my recent run-in with him? I wasn't sure I could do this.

"Wait, wait. I'm not sure this is the best idea. You saw what I had to deal with today! Why should I put myself through this again? I don't think I can handle all of this. And you need to be straight with me and give me the whole story. Don't keep secrets when I'm putting my life on the line this way." I started to step back and felt perspiration pop up on my forehead.

Cole walked over and placed his hand on my shoulder. Heat cascaded through my body once more, but this time I felt a calming sensation despite the excitement that was coursing through me. "You'll be okay," he said gazing at me. His eyes flashed, and for a split second I thought I saw something deep and caring in them, but it was gone as soon as he stepped away.

"We don't have much time. Let's go, Renda."

My knees felt wobbly and the world was hazy as I stood up carefully. But surprisingly, I wasn't afraid. Cole's sturdy presence was giving me courage that I'd never felt before. In all of my years, I'd never felt this way in the presence of another man, and a little voice inside my head warned me that I was swimming in a deep pool with no shallow end.

Surprisingly, Cole was able to push the door open by himself (as opposed to walking through it), though I wasn't sure if he did this for his benefit or for mine. As we entered the hallway, it was lit with flashing orbs and ghosts. Some of them still appeared ghastly in their deathlike state, but I was no longer afraid and as we walked down the hallway, they didn't pay much attention to us.

The children were there too and as we passed, Claire grabbed my hand in hers. Again, warmth radiated through me, but it was a smaller amount of energy and made me feel giddy with happiness. She smiled up at me through her burnt, destroyed face and I smiled back. I no longer saw her ravaged skin, but rather the beauty that generated from a deeper place within her spirit. And despite my inability to connect with children who were alive and in my world, I felt a deep connection to the ghost who had taken an immediate liking to me.

Cole saw what was happening and knelt down beside the little girl, gently removing her hand from mine. Despite his tough countenance, he visibly softened and whispered something into her ear. She smiled at him and once again began to play with the little boy who I assumed was her brother.

Standing up again, Cole gave me a stern look and motioned towards Margaret's bedroom. I noticed that none of the spirits loitered near her room or doorway. In fact, they all steered clear as if they knew that something bad awaited them if they ventured too close.

To my horror, the door to Margaret's bedroom once again opened by itself. Part of me wanted to run and get Bobbie and prove to her that this was all real. But another look from Cole convinced me that we had to venture forward and not falter.

We passed through the doorway into the bedroom. It was so dark that it was hard to see anything, but as my eyes adjusted (thanks to the moonlight streaming in through the window), I could see Margaret lying asleep in bed.

Her face was white against the darkness, and it was apparent that she was getting sicker. Dark circles painted her eyelids, a network of deep wrinkles dug into her forehead, and there was a new cluster of sores that looked like acne along the sides of her face. I could smell her breath as she exhaled, and it was sour.

Cole motioned for me to join him at her bedside and I obeyed, despite the fear now welling up in my body. As we both stood over her sleeping frame, Cole spoke carefully, "Beast, we see you. The darkness of night cannot hide your evil face. We know your name, Elial. And now, we are ordering you to leave. It is time to leave this house in peace."

Margaret's eyes suddenly opened as if she'd been shocked by a live wire. Her head turned mechanically towards us, and she began to cackle in a deep, unnatural voice.

I instinctively backed away terrified that she might grab me again. Cole reached for my hand and held it tightly. Immediately, the warmth and comfort returned, as well as the inherent reminder that we were standing very close to each other. But I knew that Cole's energy wouldn't last forever, so I quickly dropped his hand to conserve whatever energy was keeping him with me.

Margaret looked at us and spat out, "Ha! You think a corpse and a librarian can stop me? I am Elial. I am as old as time and infinite worlds deep. My power is more than you will ever know, and I will continue to feed. Yes, feed. This woman is nothing but my vessel."

Suddenly, the voice stopped and now Margaret began to thrash in her bed.

"Noooo," she moaned as her head twisted back and forth. She closed her eyes and then opened them again. This time, I could sense that she was back with us—maybe for only a brief moment.

"Help me," she whispered and then fell back against the pillows. Cole pulled me away from the bed, and I could tell that he sensed something bad was about to happen.

As soon as we were standing a few feet from the bed, Margaret's eyes opened once again. This time, she cackled and leapt up, so that she was standing on the bed. Her back was hunched over, her arms were outstretched, and her fingers were curled like claws.

I nearly wet my pants in fear, but everything happened so quickly that it was hard to comprehend. The woman leapt out of her bed and landed cleanly on the floor. She then kicked the door fully open and raced out of the bedroom, nearly knocking Bobbie out of the way as she turned the corner and descended the stairs at an incredibly fast pace.

"Bobbie," I shouted, running out of the room. My friend stood, frozen in place, a terrified look on her face. I could tell she was in shock, so I shook her until she began to respond.

"Bobbie! Snap out of it. We've got to get your mother!" I shouted, trying to get her to speak to me.

Her eyes finally focused on mine, and she began to babble, "Did you see her? She looked crazy! What are we going to do? What are we going to do?"

"Bobbie," I instructed, holding her shoulders tightly. "We've got to follow your mother. Will you come with us?" She looked at me slightly confused, and I realized that she could not see Cole.

I looked back at the ghost to see what he thought we should do, and he simply motioned for me to hurry up, so I decided now wasn't the time to begin introductions.

"Look, let's go. We can figure out the rest later."

She nodded dumbly, and we quickly grabbed our shoes, put them on, and then raced down the stairs, out of the house. Cole was much faster than us and ran ahead, a glowing flash of light. But as fast as he could move, he kept his pace manageable so that I was able to follow the glow of his energy in order to stay on track and in the right direction.

We ran through the kitchen and out the back door, into the darkness of night. The air was warm and humid, the trees ahead of us standing straight. They almost looked like an army to me, guarding their natural realm of mystery. But there was no time to admire or fear the unknown, and we ran straight ahead into the darkened woods.

Cole's glow helped me keep on track, but Bobbie was having a difficult time in the dark. She kept stumbling and alternatively cursing and sobbing. A few times, I had to stop and help her keep going. But Cole's light never dimmed or disappeared. He was always waiting for us to catch up.

We finally made it through the mess of trees and shrubbery and arrived at the now infamous clearing that seemed to be the spot for everything—bad. But to our surprise, Margaret was nowhere to be found. I looked around for Cole and saw him standing at the northern corner of the field, looking up.

He saw me staring at him in confusion and motioned for me to come over to where he was standing. His face never lost that serious, slightly irritated look, and I had a feeling that things weren't good.

As Bobbie and I approached him, she gasped. She saw it first—or rather—she saw her mother first.

My eyesight has always been a source of weakness, and I wear contacts basically all the time. Sometimes I wear glasses. But regardless of the hardware, I've never had great night vision. So it took me a moment longer to focus on what Cole and Bobbie were looking at. And once I did, I almost wished for blindness because the vision was one of the most horrifying I've ever seen.

Margaret Trillo, or what she had become, was hanging on to a tree like a monkey. Her arms and legs were wrapped around a tree trunk that was about fifteen feet high, and her head was tilted back as she cackled and laughed loudly at the night sky.

But the laughter sounded amplified, like a multitude of voices screeching at the same time in different decibels and tones. It was the same sound that had frightened Daniel and me earlier in the day.

Cole had a tight look on his face and he immediately turned to me.

"Renda, there's nothing we can do right now. The situation is worse than I thought, but I can assure you that she will return to the house by daybreak. Elial will need her rested in order to continue to drain her life energy. In the meantime, we need to get some advice on how to handle this, and I've got a person in mind who can guide us. We've got to move quickly though, my energy levels are depleting faster in the presence of such pure evil."

I could tell from Cole's pained look that Elial was indeed starting to siphon off some of his energy and the urgency to not lose him took over my thoughts, sharpening my resolve. Walking over to Bobbie, I grasped her hand and pulled her away from the horrific scene.

"We've got to go," I instructed her.

"What?" she yelled. "You want to leave my mother up in a fucking tree? We can't leave her here!"

Taking my friend's terrified face in my hands, I focused my energy on calming her as quickly as possible. "Look, I don't know if you trust me, but you have to find a way. We have to leave your mother here. She'll be fine. I know it sounds crazy, but if we stay out here, we're actually making things worse. Trust me."

I could feel the inner turmoil churning in my best friend's heart, and for the first time, I could see that she wanted to trust me. It had become such an unbelievable situation that she undoubtedly needed something to hang on to.

"Can we leave her here? Are you sure?"

I nodded yes and managed to lead her out of the clearing. She held my fingers tightly in her hand and walked behind me, like a child following her mother. We walked slowly, and Cole once again remained ahead of us so that his light could lead us out of the woods.

When we got to the house, I took Bobbie upstairs and into her bedroom. She was in shock, and thankfully, it was making her sleepy.

Gently tucking her into bed, I whispered in her ear, "Don't worry. Everything will be all right, I promise."

Her eyes were already closing as I left the room.

Outside, Cole was leaning against the wall, looking more tired and dimmer than ever. His hands were trembling as he looked at me. "Is she asleep? I was able to reach inside and calm her mind enough to slow her metabolism and get her to nod off."

Was there anything he couldn't do? I nodded yes, and followed him down the hallway to a small alcove that contained a table with a potted plant on it. During the day, the alcove was simply a nice touch to the house and didn't serve any main purpose. But now, in the dead of night, it was occupied by a small, wrinkled man who sat cross-legged on the floor and rocked back and forth. As we got closer to the ghost, I realized that he was a Native American, and while he rocked, he slowly chanted in a low, deep voice.

Cole brought us as close as we could get, and I sat down on the floor, not far from the strange elderly man. It was amazing how real the ghosts were, especially since I was now unafraid to view them in closer proximity. At my present vantage point, I could see the man's weathered skin and deep wrinkles lining an obviously wise face. He had long grayish white hair that fell to his shoulders and a feathered headdress resting atop his head. The man was wearing the type of garb I always imagined a Native American from the past would wear. His eyes were cast to the ground as he continued to murmur and chant.

"He is a sage. One of the wisest I've ever come across," Cole explained in a fading voice. "He was there when we arrived in the New Land and guided me through many trials and tribulations. His name is Adahy, which is Cherokee for 'Lives in the Woods'. Adahy is familiar with the darkness that can descend on nature and should be able to tell you about Elial."

Despite the understanding that I might be the only living person amongst numerous members of the spirit world, I had to ask, "Is Adahy...is he dead?"

Cole sighed as if I was the most ignorant person on the planet. "Yes, Renda. We lost Adahy to illness. The settlers...we brought many diseases with us to the New World. Unfortunately, Adahy succumbed to a terrible sickness and died in our midst. But like me, he couldn't pass over. On his deathbed, he told me that there was something very important he'd have to do and only then, could he pass over."

As Cole spoke to me, his skin grew paler. To my dismay, he was becoming translucent. I knew the evening's events had been too draining, and he was fading fast. Standing up, I reached out to grasp his arm, but my fingers slipped through into nothingness.

"Don't leave. I'm scared," I admitted, feeling ridiculous in my blatant weakness. But even as he began to disappear, Cole smiled.

"You'll be fine," he whispered. "I'm always here. You just can't see me." And with that, he disappeared, leaving me with the strange man, who I now knew as Adahy.

I sat back down opposite the chanting ghost, and spoke carefully, "Adahy, can you help me? Do you know who I am?"

The man stopped his chanting and looked up at me. When our eyes met, I was relieved to see that he had a kind expression.

He smiled at me with familiarity.

"Of course I know who you are," said Adahy. His voice was clear and loud, without a slight trace of an accent. His English was perfect, which surprised me.

"You hear me, the way I can be heard. In order for us to communicate, I must speak your language, my dear. But like our friend Cole, my time in your world is limited. So please listen to me carefully."

As he spoke, it seemed as if all the ghosts in the hallway had drawn closer, because I could feel heat all around me now. My back was warm and hot air coursed along my arms. It was not an unpleasant feeling.

"The demon you are facing is a strong one," said Adahy. "He is a culmination of all the evil we've seen on our precious planet for all the years it has been cultivated. Elial is from the very beginnings, when good and bad were first born. His evil tendencies caused him to fall from grace, forcing him to live amongst the humans and the forest they needed for survival. He is not something you can destroy, but you can banish him as he was banished centuries ago."

"But how can I banish him?" I asked. "I'm just a regular person. I'm nothing special. I think this is all a mistake!"

Adahy chuckled, but looked deeply into my eyes with the wisdom of a sage, "Renda Bloodmane, you know better than that. We've been waiting for you for a very long time. It is now that you are blossoming and becoming one of the chosen few who can bridge the worlds and bring peace. There is an extremely delicate balance between our realms and without anyone to protect that balance, there will be immense suffering."

He suddenly took a deep breath, and I realized that this long speech had drained him of the energy he required to remain in place. Trying to not fatigue him anymore than necessary, I urged Adahy to tell me what to do.

"You must be strong. You must use the love around you to protect this woman who is possessed by the darkness. She is losing her battle, and you will have to fight for her. Reach deep inside, and fight from your essence...your core. You will not defeat Elial through weapons. You will defeat him through your words and your beliefs."

Adahy was beginning to disappear, but he fought to finish his thoughts.

"I have remained here for this battle. Cole does not realize it, but I have remained for you. And I will try to help you, but I have very little time left. My fate calls for me to accept this. As does yours."

With those words, Adahy completely disappeared, as did all of the ghosts in the hallway. Without looking, I could feel the heat temper off and a coolness spread throughout the space. The sound of footsteps echoed in my trembling ears.

Margaret had returned from the woods. She climbed the stairs unsteadily, gripping the banister. I turned to face her; unsure as to what I was dealing with.

Had Elial taken complete control?

"Renda, I know you're trying to help me," she whispered. Her voice sounded dry and raspy. "I don't know what's happening to me, but everything's getting so hazy. It all started after I began painting in the woods. It seemed like such a good idea at first, but then I started losing track of time and I started imagining things. My heart was broken from the divorce and there was a man. I could never see him closely, but he whispered things to me. He made me feel better. But now, the voices are constant. I can't get them to stop."

She was standing right in front of me now and trembled as she fought to communicate. I could see how thin she'd become and realized that in a better place, she was probably a very kind, intelligent person. But she'd given in to weakness and to deception, and now was clearly paying the price.

I knew that her moments of clarity were slim, so I reached out and gently touched her arm. "Margaret, don't worry. I'm going to help you. I promise."

She smiled thinly and looked away. "Thank you, child. I hope you're right."

As Margaret shuffled away and left me alone in the hallway, I exhaled deeply. It felt as if I'd been holding my breath for hours. And it was amazing that Bobbie hadn't woken up when her mother had come up the stairs. Somehow, Cole had been able to deeply sedate her.

Walking over to the balcony, I placed my hands on the railing and looked out at the darkened house. Jane stood at the bottom of the stairs and stared back at me. She turned her head to the front door, beckoning for me to take her out for her last "bathroom break" of the evening, so I went downstairs.

When I opened the front door, the warm air once again greeted me, and I decided to take a short walk around the entrance to give my dog the chance to get a little bit of exercise before we went to bed. Despite the late hour, I wasn't tired. My entire body was jittery and my mind was filled with thoughts that needed to be sorted out.

It had been an intense day.

As we walked together under the tall trees, the crickets chirped loudly, and periodically a frog would sing its throaty ballad. The calmness that had descended on the Trillo property was in stark contrast to the show Elial had put on earlier. It was a shame that evil had found its way to such a beautiful place.

I thought about Cole—his strange moodiness, intense stare, and the mystery surrounding his persona. How tedious it must be for him to haunt the mansion year after year, invisible to the living world. And what a waste of a life! In just the few exchanges we'd shared, I could tell that he'd been a strong, ambitious man when he'd been alive. Now, that was all gone and he was forced to face a ghostly existence—day after day—year after year.

Was he lonely like I was? Did he feel like no one quite understood him? Did he yearn for a connection with someone? Or would that delay his passing over to the other side? It seemed like trying to hold him here was a selfish act that would prevent him from the ability to rest in peace.

And why do I desire him?

My head hurt from all of the questions and thoughts and I just wanted to go back inside and try to sleep, but Jane was slowly searching for a spot to mark her territory and hence, delaying our return to the house. Normally, I would have been irritated by her deliberate manner, but the walk was helping to dissolve my nervous energy, so I tried to be patient.

We walked to the end of the driveway and turned around to head back to the house, when I heard someone behind me. It wasn't the crackling of leaves or the sound of someone breathing heavily that alerted me to the presence; it was the feel of a familiar heat that could only mean one thing.

Something was exuding energy.

I turned around and was surprised to see a woman standing in the middle of the driveway. She appeared to be in her mid-fifties and wore clothing similar to Cole's but fashioned for a woman.

She smiled at me, and I could see that she too was dead, though it wasn't immediately apparent how she'd lost her life.

"Please, don't be frightened," she said softly.

"Who are you?" I asked.

"My name is Lillian. I'm Cole's mother."

Chapter 10

Lillian wasn't as strong as Cole and remained somewhat translucent while we stood and talked. To my surprise, Jane wasn't the least bit concerned and after she did a perfunctory sniff of the woman's shoes, found a spot to plop herself down.

There was definitely a strong resemblance between Cole and his mother, though I wasn't immediately sure why she wasn't in the house with her son.

"Renda, I'm so glad you're here. There's evil in that house, and I'm so worried about Cole."

"Why aren't you in the house with him?" I asked, confused.

The ghost smiled at me. "Because, my dear, I've already transitioned to the other side. But I've come back to speak with you. It's that important. You have many trials ahead, but they will prepare you for the reason you've been chosen."

"I'm not sure I understand. What do you mean?"

"You must listen to me, Renda. This is a very important time, and you will be tested each step of the way. Demons are strong, but they can be beaten. The more important thing here is that you continue onward. My son will help you, but he is very proud and vulnerable. Take care of him if you can and show him that he can let go of his pride and pain."

Part of me wished I had something to write with so that I could take notes. Lillian was speaking so quickly that it was hard to remember everything she'd said. And to make matters worse, her form was beginning to fade away.

"Renda, I must go now. But please be strong. And remember, you are chosen. We will help you from afar, but to truly succeed, you must pull from within and remember your core. Your birthright."

As I stood and watched, she completely vanished and I was once again surrounded by the darkness.

When Jane and I returned to the house, I looked around quickly, wondering if anyone else would visit me. But to my disappointment, the hallways were dark and quiet. It seemed as if even the ghosts had gone to sleep.

I left my bedroom door unlocked and prepared for bed. It didn't matter, anyway. Ghosts could pass through objects and would find me if they wanted to.

As I lay under the covers, I thought about Cole. Was he watching me as I lay in the darkness? Would he come to me at night? The thought both thrilled and frightened me at the same time. What would it be like to make love to a man who was already dead, but could manifest himself through the energy of the world?

If it felt anything like when he'd briefly touched me, I might not survive the experience. But oh, the fantasy of it all! Much too intense for a small town librarian.

Smiling to myself, I finally allowed sleep to come and sweep me into its protective arms.

Chapter 11

"Renda. Renda, wake up, we need to talk."

My tired eyes opened slowly and took in the colorful flowers on my comforter. But the calming view was immediately interrupted by Bobbie's hands pushing away the blankets and trying to turn me over to face her. I was instantly annoyed.

"Bobbie, what time is it? It feels really early."

"Yeah, it's about six in the morning."

"Six? I only went to bed around two. I'm exhausted. Can we talk in a few hours, after I've gotten some sleep?"

But she wasn't having it and kept begging me to wake up until a loud snort from Jane cleared my foggy head.

"Okay," I said, sitting up and leaning my back against the bed frame. "What is it?"

Bobbie looked disheveled and tired. For once, I didn't see her glorious natural beauty shining through. She appeared concerned, stressed out, and pale. "What do you mean 'What is it?' How can you ask me that question! What are we going to do about my mom?"

Sighing, I closed my eyes. Bobbie finally believed me and was willing to cooperate, but I didn't have the immediate answers she needed. Still, there were some thoughts churning in my brain and I knew that it was best to share them. I needed all the help I could get.

Taking a deep breath, I explained to her what Larlene had shared about Elial and how the demon could be banished from the person he was possessing. Numerous websites describing Elial's weaknesses had all pointed out that those closest to the possessed would need to somehow show their loyalty and commitment at the time of reckoning.

I still wasn't sure when that "time" would be, but given that my vacation would be ending soon, it would need to arrive within the next few days. In addition, Margaret's condition appeared to be worsening, so we didn't have much time to lose.

Bobbie confirmed that her mother was getting much worse. She described to me the early onset of her mother's symptoms, which had begun manifesting themselves several months back.

"Renda, she was fine at first. I mean, she was struggling with the aftermath of the divorce, but that's not surprising, or unusual. As you may know, my father basically packed up and moved to Europe for the year to open up a business in Barcelona, Spain. In the meantime, he left us all here to pick up the pieces. Mom took it very badly. She would leave the house with her painting supplies and an easel and disappear into the woods for hours. She said that the alone time helped her paint, but after a while we didn't see any progress in the artwork she was creating and began questioning what she was doing out there. And then, she started acting weird. She would talk to an invisible person sometimes, other times she would just zone out altogether and then she started sleeping a lot."

Bobbie described her mother's worsening physical appearance, as well. Before the divorce, her mother had been heavier, always carrying twenty pounds of extra weight. But after the divorce and during the time of the "painting in the woods" excursions, her weight began to drop off until she diminished into the thin, fragile creature she now resembled.

Both Bobbie and Daniel were concerned, but visits to the doctor were futile. Diagnosed as "slightly depressed" and "fatigued", their family doctor recommended a psychiatrist, but by then, Margaret was too weak to take the advice. So instead, she stayed home where her condition grew worse and worse.

Desperate to help her mother, Bobbie had called me in the hopes that maybe I could convince Margaret to see someone or seek immediate medical attention. My initial diagnosis had been frustrating, because Bobbie wanted her mother to get help the logical way. But now, there was no doubt that something bad was happening, and there was no "normal" cure for the ailment she possessed.

As she spoke, my best friend's eyes filled with tears that poured down her cheeks, but she continued on. It was as if a river of truth was flowing out and she needed to saturate me in her frustration and pain. I listened as quietly as possible and allowed her to tell me everything.

When Bobbie was done, she let out a deep sigh and dropped her head into her hands. I could hear quiet sobs as her body heaved.

I leaned over and hugged her tight, while keeping my mouth closed.

What pure hell she and her brother had been through! Dealing with all of this, and with no one who would believe them that the situation was getting worse.

Bobbie had no one. I was her only hope. And this realization struck me deep within my heart.

A strength I'd never felt before began to surge in my veins.

There was no backing down.

I would stay with the Trillos until Elial was destroyed.

Or until he destroyed me.

I wasn't sure what to do for the rest of the day. After all of the advice I had been given the night before, it seemed like the best course of action was to wait for nightfall when I could once again speak with Cole and the others, and to continue preparing for what was certain to be a battle with the demon.

Daniel was still at his friend's house, and Bobbie had to run to the office for a few things, so she asked me if I wanted to come with her. At first, I wasn't sure it was such a good idea, but it occurred to me that a bit of normalcy might do me some good. So we got ready and hopped into her BMW for a quick ride to town.

The weather outside was overcast and for the first time that week, it appeared that rain was on the way. Scattered dark gray clouds hung low in the sky and the humidity was unbearable, causing my normally wavy hair to get kinky and frizzy.

Bobbie had applied some makeup and once again, looked

stunning. Staring at her, I wondered if Cole would be more attracted to her if he saw us standing next to each other. The answer was pretty clear, but I tried to push the thoughts away because it was all so absurd.

This isn't a beauty contest. I have no reason to get jealous. What's wrong with me?

We didn't try to engage in small talk and just listened to the pop music playing from her satellite radio. Staring out the window, I watched as buildings whizzed by and the landscape changed from green, to the gray of the concrete buildings lining the streets.

As we pulled into a city lot, Bobbie asked me if I wanted to go up into the office with her or if I preferred to wait in the car.

"I'll just wait," I said, and gave her a phony bright smile to confirm my happiness with the decision.

As she left, I watched her small frame disappear within the large building. Sighing, I was prepared to rest my head on the window again when I found myself staring face-to-face with a homeless woman.

She was peering into the window, while foam and spittle dripped out of the side of her mouth. Her eyes were rheumy and wet. And her face was heavily lined with the wrinkles that etched themselves into her skin as reminders of the rough life she'd experienced.

I wasn't sure if she was alive or dead, because no one had explained to me whether or not ghosts were visible in the daytime. So instead of remaining in the car, I decided to get out, even though I knew she might be dangerous. But I figured that at this point, there was no use in being scared when restless spirits were lurking around every corner.

As I pushed the door open, the woman backed away and then stood, staring at me. I noticed that her clothes were ratty and torn and appeared wet in the sunlight.

"Can I help you with something?" I asked.

At the sound of my voice, she looked terrified and ran off. But I didn't miss the fact that as she attempted to cross the street, her body disappeared into thin air—amidst the cars and buses.

"She's just scared, that's all," said another voice from behind me. Whipping my head around, I found myself standing inches away from a construction worker whose face was horribly disfigured. In fact, his head looked like an oversized egg—with the top lopped off.

Trying not to gag, I took a deep breath and attempted a smile. "Well, she's got nothing to be frightened of. I wasn't going to hurt her."

"Oh, we know that, miss. But living people never notice us. There aren't many that can do what you do. We're around all the time, but most people never know we're here. Take a look around."

I'm not exactly sure what happened at that moment, but it felt like something clicked in my brain, and once my vision cleared, the world changed right before my eyes. The cobwebs or haze or whatever had been obscuring my view before was suddenly cleared completely away.

The road was filled with ghosts.

They were everywhere.

And I wasn't sure exactly how I knew they were ghosts, but I just knew. Some of them were horribly disfigured or missing a limb. Others were crawling along the ground and some were acting normally. In fact, some of the spirits were walking along, talking amongst themselves.

"So," I asked the man, "how is it that these spirits can manifest in the daylight? Do they have to store up energy?"

He laughed, which was a gruesome sight as most of his mouth was squished together, so I tried not to pay attention and kept my gaze on the circus around me.

"I'm impressed that you know so much about us. Most people think ghosts make you feel cold. It's the biggest crock of shit out there. We may take some energy from a room, dropping the temperature slightly, but if you're really close by, you'll feel heat. Some people who're near ghosts think they're sweating because they're nervous, but their body temperature is simply going up because we're setting off energy. It's really the world's biggest myth. Look for hot spots…not the cold ones. Remember, cold doesn't really exist. It is just the absence of heat—but heat, well that's our energy all bundled together. It's pretty easy to understand, even for a regular guy like me."

I nodded and waited for him to continue.

"Those of us who haven't passed over for whatever reason learn that first. If you want to move around like you did when you were alive, or at least try to, you've got to store up energy to do that. But those of us who're stuck outside like this have figured out how to store it and keep it regenerating." He pointed to the sun, which was barely visible through the low hanging clouds. "It's a big ball of freaking energy. And it keeps us 'outside spirits' moving at a regular pace. The guys stuck inside or who keep themselves in those haunted houses...they're missing the boat. You gotta stay outside. It's safer and a helluva lot more fun."

His words were intriguing. So if Cole would allow himself, he could regenerate and stay with me for hours? Days? The idea was attractive, but I was worried about how my new vision would affect my ability to move around. Would I constantly be bumping into dead people everywhere I went?

The construction worker seemed to notice my concern. "I know we're all over the place, but don't worry. The few of you who can actually see us have to turn on your special sight to see our two realms at once. I'm not sure how you do it, but you can turn it off, too. You've just got to focus on the dimension you're in and tell yourself to shut it off. Why don't you try it?"

I stood still and closed my eyes tightly, willing myself to close off the area of my brain that was new and pulsing with energy. Trying to dull my thoughts, I shut out the sounds of the spirits and clenched my fists in concentration.

"Renda, what are you doing?" Bobbie asked.

My eyes flew open and Bobbie stood in front of me with a concerned look on her face. But I wasn't worried about what she thought because...

The world was normal again.

I'd done it! Somehow, I'd shut off the visions of the spirits. Now, if I could only control it more easily.

"Renda, are you okay?"

"Yes, yes. Sorry, I just needed some air."

"So you left my car on and just stepped out onto the curb?"

Realizing how ridiculous I looked, I stepped away from the road and got back into Bobbie's car, ignoring the strange looks she was giving me.

"Do you want to grab some lunch?" she asked.

"Sure, that sounds good."

She drove us to the center of the small downtown area and parked alongside the road.

We stepped into a restaurant that featured loud rock music, colorful pictorials on the wall, and a bustling setting. In other words, Bobbie's favorite kind of place.

My preference was a quieter bistro or café, but I figured now was not the time to be anti-social. As we slid into the booth, the waitress asked us for our drink orders and quickly shuffled away.

The menu was full of fried, fattening foods, so I tried to find something that wouldn't kill my stomach. I've always been a little delicate when it comes to food. When I was a kid, the family doctor diagnosed me with a "Hiatal Hernia", and hence, prone to gastric problems.

The cuisine at the restaurant wasn't going to be kind to me—I could tell that already—so the hunt for a healthy option was on.

"While you spend an hour on the menu, I'm gonna run to the ladies' room," Bobbie said jokingly.

As she left the table, I continued to scour the menu for something remotely healthy to eat. Suddenly, I noticed something out of the corner of my eye. It was a man standing by the entrance with his back to me, but the hair and the body type looked like Cole's.

My heart started beating quickly at the thought of him coming to the restaurant to meet me. How had he known that I would be here? Not wanting to stare, I dropped my head behind the menu and peered around again.

The man was gone.

Disappointment flooded my heart. It hadn't been Cole. Just some guy who looked like him. It seemed unfair that I was fated to see hundreds of restless souls crowd the streets, but the one man I wanted in my presence had such a hard time manifesting himself to me.

Fighting down frustration, I greeted Bobbie as she returned to the table and soon after we ordered our cholesterol-laden lunches.

After lunch, we returned to Bobbie's car and headed back to the house.

The drive back was as silent as the drive out, but this time, my stomach was queasy and it wasn't from the meal. The sun's undeniable daily descent was an indication that nightfall would soon come and then I would be surrounded once more by a dark and mysterious world that was now my life.

"How do you think the rest of the day will go?" Bobbie asked, staring straight ahead. I wasn't sure if she was asking me or herself, so I remained quiet. She didn't seem to notice and continued, "I hope Mom is doing better. Especially since Daniel is coming home today. He really shouldn't have to deal with this."

The circumstance with Daniel was a tough one. Part of me agreed with Bobbie that it was better for her brother to be as far away from the house as possible, but the other part of me recognized that the only way to beat Elial was to have loved ones close by. So despite the danger, it was better for Margaret if Daniel was home and within reach.

Instinctively, I looked at the upstairs windows as the car pulled up the driveway, hoping to catch a glimpse of Cole or any of the other spirits. But there was no one there and even though I focused on "seeing something", no one manifested.

As we entered the house, it was cold and quiet. Bobbie called out for Daniel, but he hadn't returned home yet (who could really blame him?) and Margaret was nowhere to be found. We walked through the downstairs wing and read a quick note from the kitchen staff saying that they'd gone home and everything for dinner was warming in the oven.

As we passed the stairwell, I stopped for a moment and looked up at Margaret's bedroom. Her door was closed, which indicated she was still in bed. Bobbie came over and stood beside me, her eyes also focusing on Margaret's bedroom.

"I'm going to go upstairs and check on her," she said.

"Are you sure that's such a good idea? Maybe I should go with you."

Bobbie shook her head. "No. I've got to see this for myself. Maybe she'll talk to me."

She didn't wait for my response and quickly turned around, going upstairs and disappearing from my view. Not sure what to do, I decided it would be better to head towards the kitchen as opposed to standing at the foot of the stairs.

Jane was napping by one of the tables, no doubt hoping to find a morsel of food on the floor. She rarely begged at mealtimes, but she did tend to stay close by in hopes of snatching some "people" food.

"Hi, Jane," I said, petting her gently on the head. "Has anyone let you out since I've been gone?"

The baleful look on her face was a clear indication that the answer was no. So I pushed open the back door and let her run out onto the warm grass. She barked happily and ran around, quickly sniffing and looking for the perfect place to mark her territory.

I turned my face up to the sky that had cleared since the earlier hours and closed my eyes against the brilliant warmth. It was the first time all day that I'd had a quiet moment to myself without any strange spirits invading my privacy. The heat felt good, but it started to get almost too warm.

Something was near me. I could feel it.

Not wanting to panic, I slowly lowered my head and opened my eyes. Brightness struck me from every angle and spots swam in front of my eyes as I struggled to adjust to the natural lighting.

When my eyes finally regained their focus, I looked around quickly, trying to detect the source of the unnatural warmth. But the backyard appeared empty. Concentrating on the invisible "lever" in my mind that could help me see the unseen, I squeezed my eyes together and focused on trying to reach the spirit realm.

But for some reason it wasn't working.

Frustrated, I opened my eyes again and decided to rest on one of the lounge chairs. The efforts of the afternoon had positively drained me, and all I wanted to do was take a nap. So I flopped down on the lounger and closed my eyes. The twinkling sound of Jane's tag comforted me as she made a spot for herself right next to the chair.

Sleep didn't take long to visit me, but once it did, my dream unraveled itself quickly and mercilessly.

I knew it was a dream because when I opened my eyes, the sky was dark and stormy. My body was still resting in the lounge chair, but the colors around me were different. Almost too rich and vibrant, like paintings still fresh on a canvas.

Rising from the chair took extreme effort and everything felt soupy and slow. The air was hard to inhale, filled with so much moisture that the humidity was stifling. Searching for relief, I decided to walk into the relative coolness of the darkened woods.

Walking through the woods was not a pleasant experience. Despite the fact that I knew I was in a dream, the shrubbery and branches still managed to attack me as I made my way through the rough darkness. My shoes had somehow disappeared as well, and my feet were raw and pained from the constant chafing of rocks and sticks.

I emerged into the clearing, but things looked very different now. The sky was a dark shade of purple, with black clouds angrily colliding upon one another. The wind had started to pick up and now I could see that Bobbie and Daniel had appeared. They were standing off to the side, holding hands and looking absolutely terrified.

In the center of the clearing, a small, dark cyclone had begun to twist and turn. At first, it was a miniature twister, bending back and forth as it spun on its apex against the flat terrain. But then, it began to grow in size until it was close to seven feet tall. I watched the phenomenon twist and bend until it took on the shape of a person.

Margaret emerged from the blackness and stepped out onto the grass. She was grinning, but her mouth was too wide and stretched unnaturally across her face. Even in the darkness, I could see that her eyes had turned completely black and were glaring at me with intense hatred.

"You can't stop me!" she screamed as the wind continued to pick up, howling in disdain all around us. Bobbie and Daniel pulled closer together and looked away from what had once been their mother.

In the dream, I somehow knew that their behavior was the wrong way to react. My brain silently chided me that the offspring of the woman still trapped in a battle with the demon needed to show their support and be strong, not cower away in the shadows. But my voice wasn't working and all I could do was watch in frozen terror as the events unfolded.

The Margaret-creature began to rise off the ground until she was floating in the air, her feet dangling like talons against the vicious wind. She laughed in large bellowing overtures, spittle flying from her face and shooting out everywhere.

Suddenly, I felt a hand on my shoulder. When I turned around, there was no one there, but a voice whispered to me, "Bring them together. They must hold on to her and say the words *Recéde Daemon* over and over while you put your hands on her face. You and you alone, will be able to extract the demon from her. But you will have to do it with your bare hands."

It came to me in a flash.

The mental lever that the construction worker had helped me identify.

I would need to use it while I was holding on to Margaret and then I would have to pull Elial out of her, and then as quickly as possible shut him down.

Dear Lord. How was I going to do that?

Margaret laughed and shrieked at me, "You won't be able to, you little bitch. I'll kill you first. I'll kill you!"

With those words, her body flew through the sky and straight at me. Trying to deflect her assault, I put my arms up as our bodies tumbled to the ground.

And then I woke up.

Screaming.

Bobbie was standing over the chair, trying to wake me up by gently shaking my shoulders. She looked as terrified in real life as she had been in the dream.

"Oh my God, Renda! Are you okay? You were screaming in your sleep."

I rubbed my aching temples.

"Is your mom okay?"

Bobbie frowned. "She was asleep. Again. What are we going to do?"

I knew the answer to that.

We would have to take action.

And there was barely any time left.

Chapter 12

"What do you mean—we have to exorcise my mother?" Bobbie shrieked.

Since I'd woken up from the nightmare, it had been difficult trying to communicate. I knew that Margaret's condition was worsening but was relieved that she hadn't tried to attack Bobbie or Daniel and was basically in a sleep-coma. That was actually safer than her floating around the house, screaming and spitting insults at everyone. Plus, I was certain that if the situation got to that level, the ghosts in the hallway weren't going to simply cower in the corners of the darkness.

Simply put, everyone was going to need to fight. And the sooner Bobbie faced the facts, the better.

But she wasn't taking the news well, despite the fact that it was calmly relayed, by a groggy, disheveled, redheaded librarian. The more I tried to explain to her that a battle was going to be necessary, the more upset she became.

"My mother isn't freaking Linda Blair from *The Exorcist*!" she exclaimed, looking at me with anger and confusion. "And what makes you think that you're qualified to do this? I mean, in all the years I've known you, you've never gone to church once. So what do you think you're going to do, huh? Chant some phrases and sprinkle water on her?"

At this point, I'd had enough. My head was still pounding from the nightmare, my entire body felt sleep deprived, and everything that was once normal had turned abnormal. In other words, my patience had run out.

Standing up quickly, I grabbed Bobbie by the shoulders and looked her dead in the eye. "I'm her only hope and if you want your mother back, you'll listen to me. Do you understand?"

She didn't answer, which gave me the encouragement to continue.

"I know what we need to do and you'll need to be a part of this. Daniel too. And I'll probably be getting help from some others who you either don't see or realize are there. Whatever happens, you have to believe in me and in your mother."

She looked at me fearfully, but I could see the realization starting to form in her eyes.

"You have to believe me that I'm doing my best, and I want to save your mother. You have to believe that for some crazy reason, I've been chosen to do this. And lastly, you have to believe that others will be helping us. We're not alone."

By the end of my speech, my voice had taken on a pleading tone. I understood now that if Bobbie refused to stand beside me and help that it wouldn't work. She had to be there. And she had to believe.

We stood in silence for what seemed like hours. I stared at Bobbie as intently as possible, almost willing her to believe me. The concentration shifted the lever in my brain and all around my peripheral vision, I could vaguely make out shapes that had appeared out of nothingness and were encircling us. They too were waiting to see if she would help, and I hoped that their warmth and support would somehow seep through her skin and thaw her conventional thoughts and beliefs. I knew that I was asking her to believe in something that wasn't normal, and that she would have to stretch the boundaries of all that she deemed as part of reality, to join me in saving her mother.

"I believe you," said a small voice from the doorway of the house.

Daniel was standing still, watching us with large eyes and pursed lips. I wasn't sure how long he'd been standing there.

"Daniel, did you hear...?" Bobbie couldn't finish the question.

He nodded slowly and never took his eyes off mine. It was in that moment when I realized how smart the child was and his ability to shift his sensibilities, despite everything he believed.

"Yeah, I heard. I think Renda is right. We need to help Mom.

She's getting really bad and if we don't do something, we'll lose her." His voice cracked and tears began forming in his eyes, spilling down his cheeks.

Bobbie quickly went over to him and kneeled down, wrapping her arms around his body and pulling his thin frame to hers. They cried and hugged while I watched. After a few moments, Bobbie looked up at me with tears in her eyes.

"Okay. We'll do it your way. Help us, Renda. Please."

Shortly after our talk outside, the three of us went into the house for dinner. Earlier in the day, Chef Roy had cooked a hearty Italian meal, and it didn't take us long to pull it from the oven and set the table.

Sitting down, we each silently served ourselves and ate with nervous energy. Given the quiet, I had time to think about the fact that I had one more night to meet with the spirits and try to garner as much knowledge and work up as much courage as possible in order to do the right thing. No one had specifically told me that the battle would take place in little more than twenty-four hours, but it was something innately emblazoned in my mind.

Waiting a few more days would most certainly mean failure.

After dinner, Bobbie announced that she was going to bed early and Daniel mirrored her comments. They both looked at me, hoping that I could give them some sort of guidance, but the time wasn't right. So instead, I assured them that everything would be fine and advised them to go to their rooms and try to fall asleep as quickly as possible. My hope was that once the house settled down, I would be able to roam freely and that Cole would reappear.

Cole.

I'd not forgotten him for even a minute. The thought of having him near me made my heart do a quick dance within my chest. I knew that any infatuation was a dangerous thing but couldn't help hoping that he'd reappear. The idea of being alone with him in my room was a delicious yet nerve-wracking possibility.

After taking Jane out for her evening business, the four of

us went upstairs together. There was a strange unity that had begun to form between us, and we now moved together almost needing to be close and understanding that our friendship was a necessary weapon. Once we got to the landing, each of us moved to our separate rooms, steering clear of Margaret's bedroom.

Her door was closed and there was no sound coming from inside, but we didn't want to test fate, and frankly, everyone was exhausted and unable to handle another night of commotion.

My heartbeat sped up and I once again walked down the darkened hallway towards my bedroom. To my disappointment, it was empty and I wasn't sure whether the ghosts were taking a break or still regenerating for their evening visit. Cole was nowhere to be found, either, so after loitering for a moment, I finally decided to go to bed.

Shutting the door, I gave Jane a soft pat on the head and slipped into my bed. Not wanting to fall asleep yet, I sat up against the pillows and once again tried to shift the lever in my brain that allowed me to see ghosts. I squeezed my eyes shut and concentrated as hard as I could.

"You know, you really shouldn't try so hard," a male voice teased.

My eyes flew open and to my delight, Cole was standing a few feet away from me, leaning up against the wall. He looked devastatingly handsome as usual, and my breath caught in my throat at the vision of such masculine beauty. His hair was tousled and hanging over one eye and despite his casual stance, his gaze was piercing.

Not sure what to do, I gathered my blankets about me like a protective fort and motioned for him to sit down. Cole suddenly looked a bit hesitant, but then smiled and sat beside me.

"How are you?" he asked.

"I'm okay, just a little nervous. I'm pretty sure tomorrow's the day I have to deal with Elial."

He nodded in agreement and leaned forward. "Yes. That's why I'm here. We need to visit Adahy again. I'm not sure you're ready for all this."

"Neither am I. I'm still trying to figure out how I'm going

to be able to pull this off. My ability…it doesn't always come so easily. I'm afraid that once we're in the heat of it, Elial's going to be too strong for me."

Cole put a finger to my lips to silence me. I could feel warmth radiating off him and I just wanted to kiss the tip of his finger. Feeling embarrassed, I looked away.

"Renda…I'm sorry. It's just…" Cole stuttered, and I looked back at him. His face had softened and he seemed confused. But there was something else there. For a split second, I saw—desire.

The world disappeared around me and I could no longer hide what I was feeling. The aching and hunger to be connected to this man overtook me, and I allowed it to guide my actions. Pushing the blanket aside and ignoring the burst of energy that seeped into my skin, I grabbed his shoulders and kissed him deeply.

The sensation was unlike anything I'd ever felt before. Instead of feeling bursts of energy, I felt a warm sweetness travel through my veins like a drug. Cole's mouth tasted wonderful and when his tongue touched mine, I was overcome by the strongest sexual feelings I'd ever experienced in my twenty-eight years.

Pulling him to me, I felt his electric body on top of my own. He groaned in passion, and I could feel his maleness growing and straining against the tight fabric of his pants. More than anything in the world, I wanted him naked and inside me.

"Renda," he whispered in my ear, "We must stop. I need my energy for tomorrow. But I'm aching for you…"

I ignored his pleas and pushed his body tighter against me, wrapping my legs around him. My actions were bolder than I'd ever allowed myself in the past, but an overwhelming sexual hunger was tying me up and wouldn't let me go. My insides felt like melted chocolate, and yet—I needed more of him. Wanted more of him…

"Now isn't the time, my children."

At the sound of Adahy's voice, we both pulled away and sat up quickly. Looking at Cole, I could see that his face was red and his breathing was labored. It was amazing to me that I'd had such an effect on him. But I could also tell that I'd drained him of some important energy.

"Adahy," he said as calmly as possible, "We were just coming to see you."

The ghost smiled at us and waved his hands. "Yes, I know that. But time is running short and we must talk. I will sit here, okay?" He pointed to the ground and gracefully lowered himself into a comfortable sitting position.

Cole and I got up from the bed and sat on the floor with Adahy, making a small circle. We watched as the Shaman sang and chanted, waving his hands about. While he was chanting, I snatched quick glimpses at Cole who seemed to be entirely focused on the ceremony before us.

Incredibly, a small cloud of smoke appeared in mid-air as Adahy continued to chant. It hung in place for a moment and then flew towards me and flowed over my face. It was odorless and seemed to evaporate against my skin.

Adahy opened his eyes and smiled. "Now, you have the spirit of strength within you. There are many forces standing with you, Renda. You have to trust that you are not alone. This is the first of many battles, but it's necessary for you to transform. Remember the words *Recéde Daemon*. No matter what Elial says or shows you, you must continue to recite that phrase until you feel the force lifted out."

"How will I know he's gone?"

Adahy grew serious, his dark eyes boring into my own. "There will be a moment when his evil will threaten your own spirit. You'll feel it like a poison trying to enter your veins—all the vile and filth that can be mustered in a single breath. But you must fight it, Renda. We will all be beside you."

The sage then instructed me to ensure that Bobbie and Daniel were close by—but not too close. They would need to recite the same phrase over and over while they held each other. And then Adahy finished his instructions with a very frightening reality.

"Renda, I feel it's important that you know. You could lose your life in this battle. Elial is very strong and will try to drain you of life energy in order to remain within his vessel. Margaret is providing him with the sweetness of human life... it is like nectar to the demons who have been cast down. They're without hope, without sanctuary. And that is very difficult for those former angels who felt the light of God's love on a regular basis. They will do whatever it takes to regain even a drop of that light."

After speaking those words, Adahy took my trembling hands into his. I immediately felt the energy transference and his age-old strength. It was strange, but I could also tell that he was able to connect with humans longer than most ghosts without losing his ability to manifest.

"Renda Bloodmane, granddaughter of the Bloodmane heirs of the spirit realm, I give you the protection of the mighty and the mysterious." He leaned over and kissed my forehead. A burst of light filled the room and he disappeared.

Cole took a deep breath and stood up quickly. He began pacing the room and appeared worried.

The air was heavy around us and Adahy's words were burned in my mind.

I could die?

How had it gotten to this point? Or had it always been this serious and I'd just chosen to ignore it?

And if I survived this, would there be a way for me to find others from my family? The other heirs? Were there even any other heirs?

"We can't let this happen," Cole mumbled angrily. "I won't lose you to this evil creature."

He continued pacing and then sat on the edge of my bed, putting his head into his hands. I could see the outline of bright energy lining his body and once again marveled at how magnificent he was.

And how vulnerable, as well.

Standing up, I walked over to the bed and then knelt down in front of him. As gently as possible, I touched his soft hair, and he lifted his face to meet mine. His eyes glistened in the darkness, and without saying a word, he leaned forward and gently kissed my lips.

When we parted, I felt like tumbling to the ground, but instead I spoke the words we both needed to hear.

"Cole, I've got to get to sleep. Tomorrow's coming and we

both need to be prepared. I want to ask you something."

"What?"

"I need you to try to leave the house and spend some time outside. It will help keep you strong for the battle."

Cole jumped from the bed and angrily lashed out, "What are you talking about? I can't leave this house! Why would you suggest something so absurd? Do you not realize that I'm dead? I'm dead, Renda! I can't leave."

It dawned on me that Cole had been sedentary for so long that he didn't realize that the sun would help him regenerate for a longer period of time. And he wasn't taking my suggestion very well.

"Look, I've spoken to others...others like you. And they've told me that being outside is the best way to regenerate and stay in your lifelike form for the longest period of time. Can't you just try it?"

Cole now stood with his back to me and when he responded, I could hear the anger and frustration in his voice. "Renda, you know nothing. For me to venture outside could mean that I never return to you. It's a big step for someone to take. Apparently, you don't really care if I return or not." And with that, he swept out of the room.

I ran out into the hallway, looking for him, but was greeted only by the other house ghosts who continued in their activities. Orbs flew back and forth, dancing around my head while others who were manifesting themselves only casually looked my way.

Suddenly, I felt a small, warm hand gently brush mine and when I looked down, Claire was standing next to me with a sad look on her face. I knelt down so that we were eye level and realized that her once-frightening appearance no longer impacted me. Instead, I saw her as the girl she'd once been... beautiful and vibrant.

"Hi, there," I said gently. "What's wrong, Claire?"

"He never leaves the house," she said quietly. "He's been angry and lost here for so long that he doesn't realize there's other ways to exist. But since you, he's been happier. He thinks of you and wants to be real for you."

I realized that she was describing Cole and nodded in agreement.

"So," I asked, "how can I convince him to leave?"

The little girl shook her head and looked down the hallway. "I'm not sure you can. With those of us who live in the spirit realm, it's very hard to change our patterns. We've been here for so long that we don't even consider that there may be other ways to leave. Mommy used to tell me about heaven and hell. But I don't remember any of it."

It was strange to me how her vocabulary vacillated from that of a young child, to a wise adult, and then back again. But it didn't matter. She was sharing insight into Cole and that's all I wanted.

"Well, I don't know if heaven or hell exist, but I've been told that there are other ways to inhabit the living world and for longer periods of time."

I explained to her what I'd been told about the sun and the ability to better regenerate when outside in the presence of the world's most natural energy. But by the time the little girl began speaking again, I'd realized my mistake.

"It hurts for me to be outside," she said quietly. "The only place where it feels good is in this house. So that's where me and my brother stay."

"Do you remember what happened to you?" I asked.

"Yes," she said so softly that I could barely hear her. "Mommy was getting supper ready, and I was helping her. She needed to get something from the cupboard, so she left me alone to watch the food cook. I don't know why, but the fires found me. Everything started to catch fire and my brother tried to help me, but he got caught in the fires, too."

She was crying now, and I could see the tears dripping down her tiny cheeks.

"When the fires stopped, we tried to find Mommy. We looked everywhere and something was telling us to leave her alone and go towards the new place. But we didn't want to. We stayed here...together. And one day, we hope our Mommy will find us."

My heart wept for the little child and without even thinking about it, I gathered her body into my arms and hugged her. The energy from her spirit enveloped me in a sweet, gentle aura and then—she was gone.

The hallway darkened suddenly and all of the ghosts disappeared. In the distance, I could hear an evil cackling coming from Margaret's room. It started out low and then rose in pitch and volume until it seemed to be coming from everywhere. I watched as Daniel ran out of his room and into his sister's.

I backed away and went into my own room, locking the door behind me. Jane was on all fours, pacing and very nervous.

"It's okay. Let's just go to sleep."

But despite my self-assured words, I sat on the floor and gathered her into my arms. Her comforting dog-smell helped to calm my racing heart and eventually, I was able to get back into bed.

It was a long time before either of us was able to succumb to dreams and darkness.

Chapter 13

The new day welcomed me with gray skies and a light drizzle that saturated the world with a gentle sheen. My ears awoke to the sound of water dripping on the leaves outside my bedroom window. The Trillos' home was in a small neighborhood and nowhere near any main roads, so it was easy to lose oneself in the sounds of nature that were amplified by the lack of traffic noise that generally polluted the atmosphere.

I slowly opened my eyes and was immediately overcome by a myriad of emotions, each one fighting to take over my mood. But it was difficult, because half of me was overcome by a growing fear of the battle that was to come and the other half of me couldn't stop thinking about Cole.

Eventually, thoughts of Cole overtook my mind.

I need to touch him again.

Our sexual chemistry was undeniable and exciting, but we hadn't parted on such good terms. If anything, he'd stormed out of the room in anger. I was unaccustomed to the ferocity of such emotions and certainly had never felt this way about another man in my life.

Even the memory of Cole caused me to ache with desire and a sense of urgency. There was something so powerful and yet so vulnerable about him that I was conflicted as to which was the more prevalent. The fact that he was also a ghost was a challenge.

Who am I kidding? It's the Mount Everest of romantic challenges! I could see it now.

"Mom and Dad, this is Cole. You can't see him because he's a ghost, but he's a terrific guy."

What kind of future could I have with a ghost?

And speaking of the future, if Cole was unable to leave the Trillos' home, how would I ever see him again after I left? I wasn't sure if I could even get through the ordeal, but if I was able to defeat Elial, how would we ever meet again? Would I have to visit Bobbie in order to see him?

Sighing, I sat up and leaned against the wall. It had not escaped me that this could be my last morning alive, but for some reason I wasn't terrified or worried. After all, I could just get in my car and never come back. But the thought of my life in Cale returning to its sedate normalcy was almost unbearable to consider.

How could I go back to working at the library, listening to Larlene talk about her dates? Would the ghosts still haunt me and create havoc in my life? And what about Cole? Would I ever meet someone who made me feel the way he did?

Questions continued to tumble through my mind, and all I wanted to do was hide. Feeling ridiculous, I threw the covers over my head and snuggled underneath the warmth, trying to will myself to fall back asleep.

"Are you going to sleep all day? Something tells me that's not going to help you."

At the sound of Margaret's voice, my head immediately popped up. I felt vulnerable and caught off guard, but I tried not to let her see my fear. I wasn't immediately certain who I was talking to either, as Elial always seemed to be more forceful, and Margaret, somewhat meek.

She smiled and when I saw the tired look in her eyes, I could tell that Margaret still had a weak hold on herself. But I didn't want to get too close in case Elial was bent on attacking me prematurely. And I wasn't sure how much control the woman had left. There were black circles under her eyes and her face had taken on a grayish pallor. She was skeletal and her teeth looked dark under chapped lips.

"How're you feeling, Ms. Trillo?" I asked carefully.

She sighed and looked away. "Please, call me Margaret. I'm feeling really strange today. It's like my head's not connected to my body or something. I'm going to spend the day in bed."

"That's probably a good idea," I offered, trying to expedite her departure.

She turned to go and then looked back at me. "Thank you, Renda."

"For what?"

"I know you're trying to help me. And I appreciate it. Something tells me that I'm not going to—"

And she fell to the floor in a dead faint.

I jumped out of bed and called out for Bobbie. It only took a moment for my friend to emerge in the doorway, still wearing her pajamas and looking very scared.

"Oh, my God," she whispered and together we lifted her mother and carried her back to her room.

It took an enormous amount of effort to carry the woman, even though she was as thin as a rail. But I hadn't eaten breakfast yet and librarians aren't exactly known for their feats of strength.

Finally, we managed to get her back into bed without any mishaps.

Margaret was still breathing, but it was coming in jagged breaths. As we stared at her, the enormity of what was coming began to fully settle on my shoulders.

"Renda, we've got to help her. She's fading fast."

I nodded and turned away, leaving Margaret's bedroom. As I walked back to my room to prepare for the day, my steps felt heavy. Thoughts of Cole threatened to turn spiteful.

He should be here helping me right now.

As quickly as the thought entered my mind, I erased it.

Perhaps Elial was already trying to get inside my head and turn me against the things I held closest. And like it or not, I'd become linked to a ghost who now haunted, not only my physical spirit, but my mind, as well.

After my shower, I quickly got dressed and headed downstairs. On my way down, I noticed that several ghosts were mingling about. They weren't ghosts I recognized and were all dressed similar to Cole.

Figuring that my mental lever had somehow become

disengaged and was allowing me to see both realms, I instinctively wondered whether to close it down and focus on the present. After all, I needed the practice.

But I also needed my strength and figured that if I began trying to mess around with my "gift" so early in the morning, it would drain me for what was to come.

So I just ignored the different ghosts and headed to breakfast. Strangely, it was empty except for Bobbie and her brother. There were a couple of boxes of cereal on the table and a pitcher of milk.

Seeing my confusion, Bobbie gave me a small smile.

"I decided to give the house staff the day off. Given all the stress around here lately and our upcoming night's festivities, I figured it would be better if we weren't disturbed." She chuckled quietly, but it came across strained and phony.

She's terrified. Because there's a good chance that I won't be able to help her mother tonight. And then we're all screwed.

I decided to smile and hide the anxiety that was bubbling up inside my chest. Picking up the box of cereal, I poured myself a bowl and tried to focus on the little brown flakes.

My appetite was virtually non-existent, but I tried to eat something. A little voice inside my head reminded me that eating would be crucial. The worst thing I could do was to fight evil on an empty stomach.

The comedy of the situation tickled me, and I let out a little giggle. Bobbie and Daniel both stared at me as if I was crazy, shook their heads, and continued eating their breakfast.

After a few moments, I decided to speak up.

"We need to let your mother get some rest, and I think the best thing to do is to leave her alone just for a little bit so that she's not distracted by noise in the house. And then tonight, we'll need to get her out of bed and bring her out to the field. Once she's there, you'll have to listen to my instructions, and maybe, we'll be able to help her so that tomorrow…everything will be back to normal."

Both siblings continued to stare at me, but instead of asking questions, they just nodded and continued eating. I could tell that they were mentally drained and open to any assistance possible, despite how strange that help may seem.

As we continued eating, I watched as an old man passed by the open window. His eyes were open and sightless, but somehow he was managing to take a stroll in the backyard.

Another ghost. Another new member of my strange neighborhood for the dearly departed.

After breakfast, I went upstairs and grabbed Jane's food and water bowls, bringing them downstairs to the kitchen. As I walked in, I noticed several plump female ghosts dressed as cooks moving around the kitchen. They seemed friendly, so I felt better about leaving Jane with them.

My furry sweetheart gave me a small "woof" and settled down on the tiled floors.

After that we all piled into Bobbie's car and headed to town. No one went upstairs to say goodbye to Margaret, who was lying in bed, presumably asleep.

As Bobbie's car pulled out of the driveway, I looked up toward the house, hoping to catch a glimpse of Cole in the window. But there was nothing but the reflection of the grayish skies staring gloomily back at me. I also looked around the grounds as we sped past, hoping that he had taken my advice and ventured outside, but once again I was disappointed. There were definitely ghosts milling about but none of them were my beloved, mysterious Cole.

We pulled out onto the main stretch of road and the skies opened up once more, raining down on us. The roads were slick, so I cautioned Bobbie to slow down. She didn't pay attention to me and kept moving forward as if she couldn't wait to put as much distance as possible between us and her mother.

The wet trees bent and turned in the wind as the storm grew heavier. Finally, Bobbie addressed me.

"Okay, so where do you want to go, Renda? Please, pick a place."

I just wanted her to slow down, so I mentioned the first place that came to mind.

"The library. Let's go there. I need to find something."

Sighing, Bobbie agreed and despite Daniel's groans in the

backseat (I'm sure he was hoping for something a little more exciting), she drove to the local library, which was a few blocks away, and slid into a parking spot near the entrance. Running together in the rain, we made it to the front door without getting drenched. As soon as we were inside, I felt more comfortable.

For some reason, libraries have always been able to soothe me with their familiar smell and calm energy. And this time was no exception. As we entered, I noticed some tables lining the walls and motioned for Bobbie and Daniel to meet me there. I needed to find these books alone.

They agreed and we split up in different directions. It didn't take me long to navigate the medium-sized library and within minutes, I was able to find the section on the Occult. The titles were varied and strange, but after perusing some of the options, I was finally able to pull a volume that comprehensively covered my enemy.

It was entitled *Demons of the Ages* and had a photo on the cover of a man standing in fear while a horned creature threatened him with an angry gaze and hooves as fists. The coloring was dark red with heavy, black lines outlining the figures. The author was a man I'd never heard of and the copyright date on the inside was 1947.

I thought for a moment about bringing the book back to the table, but decided that it might frighten my companions. So instead, I sat on the floor with the book in my lap, and started to flip through it.

I had chosen well. The book described the different demons that had been cast down from the heavens and had the different creatures alphabetized by name. Each one was described in several pages of illustrations and textual descriptions.

It didn't take me long to find Elial's evil face glaring back at me from the yellowed sheets. And beads of sweat immediately popped up on my forehead when his name came into view.

The name *Elial* was written in a dark scroll. And the illustration adorning the section was horrific. It was an image of a creature hanging from a tree, like a monkey. The demon had a misshapen head with pointy ears and bulging eyes. Sharp teeth hung from its mouth and claws gripped the tree tightly.

The demon had its head back and was laughing at the sky.

The book slipped from my hands and tumbled to the floor. Shaking, I put my head in my hands. How was I going to battle this age-old evil? I wasn't strong—I wasn't anything.

"You are a Bloodmane. You're stronger than you realize," whispered Adahy in my ear.

What did that mean?

Who was I?

I yearned to learn more about my biological mother and father. It was so hard sometimes to just operate on good faith.

Adahy wasn't manifesting behind me, but his voice was enough to give me the strength I needed to continue reading. Picking up the book, I rubbed my eyes and focused on the text before me.

The pages described Elial in very specific terms as one of the oldest fallen angels. When in God's service, he'd been responsible for the health and beauty of nature, watching over the creatures that lived off the land. But Elial had angered God because he was lazy and only paid attention to the largest and noblest of creatures, while the tinier animals suffered under his neglect. According to the book, Elial was responsible for some of the most ruinous disasters such as fires and famine because of his ardent neglect and favoritism of the boldest.

To punish Elial, God cast him down to earth and forced him underneath the ground he was supposed to protect. Now, he was less than the creatures he'd neglected—a bottom dweller forced to live amongst the worms and the tiniest of creatures.

According to the tale, Elial was furious with his fate and chose to hide amongst the trees, waiting to attack the weakest of victims. He seemed to like broken-hearted women because he could manipulate them, calm them with his ability to control nature, and then—when they least expected it—he would possess them and drain them of their life force.

The illustration that accompanied this text was of a woman who was clearly in crisis and was leaning back, barely holding herself up on a set of stairs. She was using the railing as support, while Elial hung in the air, his tongue exposed and flicking towards her.

It made me think of Margaret, all alone and vulnerable after the divorce. How she must have suffered. Enough so that Elial was able to make his move and attack her while using natural seduction and the most evil of tactics to stun his prey.

The last few paragraphs of text caught my attention. It explained things I already knew—that Elial could be defeated through unity and positive strength. But the interesting thing I uncovered was that he could never be satisfied with just one host. He would hop from host to host when tempted by something or someone more vibrant and attractive.

According to the book, Elial was so arrogant that he always felt that he could do better (sounded like some of the men I knew). Therefore, his Achilles heel was that he was always seeking something more powerful. This tendency kept him from fully draining his victims and left him constantly "on the prowl". The illustration beside the text showed the demon standing on the shoulder of one woman, while hungrily eying a much younger girl standing off to the side.

It was at that moment when my mind clicked, and I fully understood what I needed to do to defeat the demon. The thought made me dizzy for a moment, but I quickly regained my footing and decided that no matter what, I was going through with it.

No matter what.

Placing the book back on the shelf, I returned to my companions who were sitting at the table, talking softly about what was going on. They both looked so worried that it saddened my heart. Bobbie's face was drawn and tired while Daniel's eyes seemed resigned and older than his years.

I had to help them. The consequences didn't matter.

Settling into one of the chairs, I gave them both my most encouraging smile and tried to be as noble as I could. This new role wasn't easy for me, but I was fast realizing that shyness wasn't going to get me anywhere anymore.

"Listen, I don't want you guys to worry. We just need to stick together tonight and no matter what, don't try to stop what I'm doing."

"Renda, are you sure you know what you're doing?" Bobbie asked uncertainly.

I wasn't.

"Sure. Don't worry. It will be okay. Just follow my lead and we'll be fine. Why don't we grab some lunch and go to a movie? I think it'll be a good distraction."

Bobbie agreed and we took a quick look outside before leaving. The rain had stopped just in time for us to head to the car and grab a quick bite.

After lunch, we decided to see a movie. Given the circumstances, watching something humorous was a good distraction, and Bobbie picked an entertaining film about a couple on a crazy vacation at sea. All sorts of mayhem unraveled, and kept us giggling and laughing.

Despite my nervousness, I was able to lose myself in the film and relax. Given the past several days, there was a simple joy in doing something so normal and typical. I glanced over at Daniel who was chomping on his popcorn and happily watching the movie. It made me feel good and for some odd reason, gave me hope.

Suddenly, I felt a hand reach out and squeeze mine.

Bobbie looked at me in the darkness with a smile on her face.

I squeezed back and tried not to cry.

But it wasn't easy.

I loved them as if they were a part of my own family. And I knew that Jane felt the same way—particularly about Daniel.

Sipping some of my soda, I rested my head back on the seat and tried to focus on the rest of the movie.

After the movie, we got up and slowly returned to the parking lot. No one wanted to go back to the house, and as Bobbie's car came into view, Daniel suddenly stopped. I noticed that he wasn't walking with us and I turned back to see where he'd gone.

He was standing in place and crying, tears running down his face in thin rivers. Shaking, he looked at us and said miserably, "I don't want to go back there."

While my heart broke for him, it was clear that Daniel was expressing the emotions that both Bobbie and I were feeling. He was just honest enough to admit it. So not waiting for Bobbie to handle the situation, I walked over to him and knelt down so that we were eye level.

"Daniel, don't worry. You trust me, right?"

He sniffled. "Yeah, I guess. But you're just a girl."

His comment made me pause for a moment and then both Bobbie and I burst out laughing. Eventually, Daniel joined us and gave me a hug. As I embraced the little guy, my thoughts raced with his words.

I was just a girl. An inexperienced, awkward, and socially inept girl. A girl who was about to step way out of her league to help cure an illness that didn't exist in any medical journal or scientific article. Because in situations like this, dabbling with demons wasn't something you could learn how to do.

Sink or swim, basically.

Grabbing Daniel's hand, I led him to the car and let him sit in the front, while I sat in the back.

Bobbie started the car, and we were off.

We rode in silence, only interrupted by the sound of the DJ on the radio chirping away about some nonsensical contest for free tickets to see a boy band in concert.

The skies were still gray, but the rain had momentarily stopped.

As we drove along the streets of Macon, I watched the beautiful greenery of the trees and shrubs race by my window. Sights like these were taking on a different meaning now that I might not live to see them again. So I tried to take in everything that passed before my eyes, allowing the visions to burn into my mind as if branded by an iron.

I saw small birds drinking from pools of water along the street, watched a teenager ride happily on his bike, and children gleefully play on a colorful playground set against the green woods. In a sudden, impulsive gesture, I unrolled my window and took a deep breath. The smells of rain and earth filled my nostrils with calming aromas that helped to slightly ease my nervous energy.

Bobbie looked at me in the rearview mirror. Her eyes were large and thoughtful and I wondered how much of my instructions she actually believed. Did she realize how dangerous the next few hours were going to be?

It was scary.

Just a few weeks ago, life had been simple—maybe even boring. Now I was fighting some terrible demon who wanted nothing more than to destroy my friend's mother and quite possibly me, as well. It was just such a freaky feeling to be teetering on the verge of a mortal battle.

As I thought about it, drops of perspiration began to appear on my forehead, and I quickly wiped them away.

The car entered the woods that enveloped the Trillos' house and almost immediately, the sky seemed darker. Heavier clouds appeared to be moving in, swollen with rain.

Rolling my window back up, I inhaled sharply and tried to calm myself, but my nerves were on high alert. No form of meditation could help me now.

As the colonial mansion came into view, I watched it grow larger and larger until it loomed over us like a silent sentinel. A flash in one of the windows upstairs caught my attention, but I didn't even try to get a better look. The ghosts were all around me now, and I was beginning to get used to seeing things that no one else did.

As we got out of the car and entered the house, Jane met us at the front door. She was happy to see me and then ran outside to mark her territory. I motioned for Bobbie and Daniel to go inside without me (though they seemed reticent) and told them to stay downstairs until I returned.

"Jane!" I called out, feeling a familiar annoyance.

She'd already raced toward the trees and was now bounding back and forth with the energy of a dog that slept approximately twelve hours a day. Back in Cale, it seemed as if she stored up all her energy for the exact moment when I came home, so that she could achieve her goal of tiring me out within fifteen minutes of walking in the door.

Right now, she was sniffing around one lucky tree and finally found her spot. While she did her thing, I looked around anxiously. Everything seemed so overcast and—gray. It was depressing and I felt a heaviness build up within me.

I wondered about Cole. How angry was he?

Part of me couldn't imagine that he would leave me to face Elial alone, but given his moody temperament, I wasn't so sure. He hadn't manifested at all during the day, which wasn't unusual normally, but I'd hoped that he would take my advice and try to regenerate with help from the natural light.

The sun wasn't cooperating either and was stubbornly remaining behind a mass of heavy clouds. So perhaps it didn't really matter.

"Renda!"

I looked in the direction of the doorway and saw Bobbie standing there, a look of terror on her face.

Chapter 14

"I mean, she's just sitting there! Is there anything we can do?" Bobbie's voice was a bundle of jittery nerves. And with good reason.

As she explained it to me, she'd returned to the house with Daniel. Given that the cleaning staff was out of the house, everything had been very quiet and still.

They'd walked past the stairwell and noticed that the door to their mother's room was ajar. But instead of going upstairs to check it out, Bobbie had kept them downstairs and led her brother into the dining room, hoping to distract him with some milk and cookies.

Once they'd entered the dining room, they found their mother facedown, with her face resting in a pile of macaroni and cheese. It was a ghastly sight. At first, Bobbie thought her mother was dead. She pulled Margaret's face out of the mushy mess and checked to make sure she was still breathing.

Miraculously, the woman still had a pulse and was breathing (albeit wheezing a bit from the obstruction she'd been lying in) and was now sitting straight up in her chair with pieces of macaroni still stuck to her face. Parts of her skin were bright orange from the cheese, which Bobbie was trying to wipe away.

Margaret's eyes were open, but they were lifeless, without a flicker of any recognition. I'd heard about possessed people being in a catatonic state, but to actually see it firsthand was much more frightening than I'd imagined. She was like a statue—her entire body upright and unmoving.

"We need to get her to bed," I said quickly.

This wasn't part of the plan!

The timing wasn't right. It was still daylight outside, and I wasn't sure how things would go if the ghosts I needed help from weren't able to manifest. This was a situation that we hadn't predicted, and I wasn't ready.

At the sound of my voice, Margaret's head turned in a robotic fashion until she was facing me. Her eyes narrowed as an evil smile transformed her mouth into jutted, ragged lines. Her lips were chapped and bleeding, and a network of veins had appeared along her pale skin. She looked as if an outline of a map had been drawn on her face.

The sudden motion and change in her mother's appearance caused Bobbie to jump back in fear, pulling Daniel behind her as if to shield him from the horrific transformation.

Margaret stared at me for a moment, hate pouring from her eyes. I could almost feel the temperature in the room drop suddenly, as if the demon was pulling all the available life energy from everything it could possibly reach. This was a different feeling than what the ghosts released.

It was cold.

Dead.

Evil.

"Ms. Bloodmane," the demon cackled, "how nice of you to join us. How is my favorite librarian?"

My heart raced within my chest. This all felt wrong and I wasn't sure what to say. Backing away from the table, my mind was a flurry of useless thoughts.

"My, my, my...you're at a loss for words. How unfortunate. Because there's a lot I want to say to you. For starters, why are you still here? You need to go home. There's nothing you can do to me and if you try," Elial paused and chuckled, "Well, let's just say...you're not going to have a home to go back to."

Suddenly, the bowl of macaroni flew off the table and crashed into the wall. Cheese and pasta flew everywhere, and Daniel let out a terrified scream. Bobbie pulled him back and held him tightly in her arms.

Now Margaret began to rise from the chair. But not like a normal person would. Her body actually appeared to be floating off the seat as her body straightened. And once she was fully upright, she floated a few inches off the ground.

I'd never been so frightened and unprepared in my life. Everything was happening too fast and I didn't feel any help coming from the ghosts in the house. We were alone in the dining room with a demon that was ready to attack.

Margaret opened her mouth and let out a huge scream. The sound was so loud that I toppled over, gripping my ears to block out the painful, razor-sharp shriek. Then there was a loud crash and all went silent.

Bobbie, Daniel, and I slowly rose to our feet and stared in amazement at the room. Every piece of furniture was upside down. The table, the chairs, even the china closet was topsy-turvy.

And Margaret was gone.

"You're supposed to stop this," Daniel said suddenly, accusingly.

He was angry, but he was also terrified—tears welling up in his eyes.

At the sight of the child's youthful rage, something suddenly snapped in my mind and the fear disappeared.

He was right. I couldn't just cower in the corner, no matter how terrified I was.

I needed to pull myself together and remember all I'd learned over the past several days. It didn't matter that it was in the middle of the day and a thunderstorm was threatening outside.

It didn't matter that I was only a librarian.

None of it mattered anymore.

I walked over to Daniel and put my hands on his shoulders. "You're right. I'm going to stop this. Now you've got to promise me that you'll listen to what I say...no matter what. We've discussed this already, but I'm going to say it again...no matter what...you must listen and not try to stop me. Okay?"

Even though I was speaking to Daniel, Bobbie answered as well and came up to me, putting her hand in mine. She squeezed it tightly and the three of us looked at each other with the unspoken understanding that the time had come.

Chapter 15

The sky had darkened considerably within the hour, and was now crowded with swollen clouds. As the dangerous weather moved in, the temperature dropped dramatically and a cool wind began blowing through the trees. Like sentries, the trees seemed to be watching us, waiting for something to happen.

I stood at the back door with Bobbie and Daniel at my side as we stared out into the woods ahead. Margaret had raced into the depths of the darkened forest and could be lost to the world if we didn't follow. But it seemed like a lifetime away—the grass separating us from the trees—the last safe terrain we would tread.

We would venture in—but would we all venture out?

The question hung unasked and unanswered. I felt a small hand grip mine and as I looked down, Daniel was gazing up at me—his brown eyes calm and trusting. Smiling, I kissed the top of his head and smelled the clean scent of his hair. In the space of one week, I'd become much more comfortable around children and was feeling protective over the little souls who trusted me.

"Okay, guys," I said with much more confidence than I felt. "Are you ready?"

They both nodded silently, and I suddenly thought about Cole.

Where the hell was he?

Here we were, ready to go into the unknown; and the one ghost I fully trusted and needed was nowhere to be found. A pang of anger rushed through my mind and served to strengthen my resolve.

As we walked away from the house, something made me turn back. Looking at the upstairs window, I could see a small worried face staring back at me.

Claire.

Her milky eyes gazed at me and I understood that this battle wasn't just for the living, but for the dead, as well.

I waved at her and she stared at me for another moment, and then disappeared.

Bobbie turned and looked in the same direction, then turned to face me with confusion written on her face. But she didn't ask anything—just kept moving forward.

As we neared the trees, thunder grumbled in the distance and I could see a flash of lightning in the sky. We were going into the heart of the storm and would be surrounded by trees, which wasn't a smart move. Any flash of lightning could ignite the woods and put us in a very precarious situation. But we had no choice—the woods were the only barrier between us and the clearing. And despite not seeing Margaret anywhere, I was pretty confident that we would find the sick woman hiding where we'd seen her the other night.

So we pushed forward. The storm began whipping up even more voraciously, and the trees swayed back and forth, creating a sea of branches and twigs that appeared everywhere and reached out to grasp us in their sharp claws.

Daniel whimpered, so I allowed him to walk directly ahead of me as I tried to cradle both of us from the onslaught of rough terrain. My arms were attacked over and over again as the branches flew against us. As we fought our way through Mother Nature's assault, I could hear Bobbie grunting behind me.

It was a tough trek and more than a few times, one of us cried out in pain. My arms were now covered in red scratches and blood dripped down tiny slits caused by the angry branches. My hair was also flying everywhere, and I was constantly stuck in a sea of red strands that were sticking to my face, flying into my mouth.

But we pushed forward.

The clearing was up ahead, and we finally managed to

disentangle ourselves from the branches that continued to scratch and pull on our clothing and skin.

"Look!" shrieked Bobbie.

It was nothing any of us had ever seen before. The sky above the clearing was black, with white clouds rolling quickly by as the wind howled and screamed. It felt as if a hurricane was bearing down, but strangely, the rain hadn't started yet. As we all entered the clearing together, we scanned the field but couldn't find Margaret anywhere.

A sharp pang of fear stabbed my heart. What if she wasn't where we expected and was hiding somewhere else?

Daniel began to cry and clutched his sister's arm in terror.

Combined with the constant gusts and onslaught of moaning wind, it was hard to concentrate.

But I had to try.

Standing by myself, I clenched my eyes closed and concentrated ferociously. I knew the ghosts were near us, but couldn't see them.

Sweat beaded my forehead as my mind repeated the same words over and over again...

I need to see you.

I need to see you.

I need to see you.

Suddenly, a scream broke my concentration. I opened my eyes and didn't see anything at first, but something dripped on my head, and my eyes shot up to the sky.

Margaret was hanging mid-air, her hair whipping about like snakes on Medusa's head. Her eyes were black orbs and she laughed maniacally while heavy ropes of spittle dripped from her mouth and landed on my head.

My stomach lurched in disgust.

"You can defeat him," Adahy's voice whispered. "Stop trying so hard. You know what needs to be done."

His words calmed my frayed nerves and I took a deep breath. Staring up at the shrieking woman, I called out, "Elial. Come down here and face me directly. Stop hiding in the clouds!"

I could hear Bobbie gasp behind me in terror, but I didn't turn around. Pulling together all of my courage, I maintained my stare and didn't look away even when the demon hissed at me.

As Margaret began to descend, the horrible transformation of her face became even clearer. I'd seen many horror movies about demons, but this was worse.

Margaret no longer resembled the woman I'd met several days prior. Now, her eyes were completely black and dark circles deepened under her lids, sunken down to the bone. Black veins lined her face and covered every inch of skin in snakelike, winding spirals. Margaret's mouth looked larger too and impossibly wide. Even her teeth were different. These teeth were pointed and gray, barely concealed by chapped purple lips that were bleeding in many places.

She was the scariest thing I'd ever seen and my mind kept screaming at me to run far, far away. But I stood my ground, even when the creature's feet finally touched the ground, and she was inches away from my face.

"Bobbie and Daniel," I instructed, "don't move. I don't care what you see or what she says. Don't move. Now, hold hands and start repeating 'Recéde Daemon'. Do it, now!"

Bobbie and Daniel began to repeat the words over and over again. The demon inside Margaret looked at them disdainfully and then laughed in my face.

I smelled the horrible stench of demon-breath and tried not to gag or close my eyes. Being so close to the creature was sickening, but I did my best to steady my nerves and remember all that Adahy had taught me.

"Recéde Daemon," I said, but my voice was barely a whisper. With shaking hands, I attempted to put my arms around the woman.

Margaret/Elial looked at me and spat out, "You're a nobody. A librarian. A nerd. A nothing, with no boyfriend, no life, and barely any friends. Your own parents abandoned you because you're such a loser."

The words stung deep within my heart. Because deep down, a part of me believed what Margaret was saying. My parents had both deserted me—left me in a hospital with no one to care for me. I didn't know where I came from, or where I was going.

Tears formed in the corners of my eyes and dripped down my cheeks. I wanted so badly to fight back—to say something. But the pain was unbearable.

Suddenly, Margaret pulled back and punched me in the chest—hard. Dots swam in front of my eyes as pain erupted along my upper body. My knees buckled, and I crumpled to the ground. Barely able to breathe, I tried to lift my head and saw that the possessed woman was now approaching Bobbie and Daniel.

"Why, hello there, my little kiddies." She sneered. "Are you here to watch Mommy kill our guest?"

Bobbie was crying, but was continuing to repeat the verse, Recéde Daemon, over and over again. She tried to ignore her crazed mother who was now walking in circles around her and Daniel as if trying to decide where to strike next.

"Leave them alone," I whispered and tried to rise. My chest was on fire and everything was hazy now—coming in slow motion. Out of the corner of my watery eyes, I could see Adahy standing by the trees. His eyes were closed and he seemed to be chanting, but I couldn't hear anything over the screaming winds and the constant cackling coming from Margaret's throat.

The demon looked at me trying to get up and spat on the ground.

"You stupid bitch. Get back down," she roared.

Suddenly, an invisible force hit me across the back and I tumbled forward. Blood flew out of my nostrils and the ground shook beneath me. I fell face forward and smelled the rich scent of dirt as I tumbled into a mass of grass and rocks.

A heavy feeling overtook me then, and I considered giving up. I could barely breathe, blood was now pouring out of my nose, my chest was on fire, and a deep exhaustion was creeping into my brain. As I closed my eyes and rested my head against the solidity of the ground, a familiar voice called out to me.

"Renda, don't give up. Please, I can't lose you."

It was Cole. I couldn't see him, but I knew somehow that he was there. With tears streaming down my face, I raised my battered head and looked out at the field. I could see Margaret continuing to threaten her children, and I was still able to see

Adahy chanting in the distance. But where was Cole?

"I'm behind you. Turn around."

He was standing behind me, with a concerned look on his face and his hands clenched in nervous fists.

He'd come outside! He'd ventured past the threshold to help me!

I tried to smile, but my face hurt and I could barely breathe. It was impossible to speak.

"I know you're hurt, but you can't give up. You've got to try to get up. Come on, Renda." And then he put out his hand.

When I grasped Cole's strong fingers in mine, the haziness in my eyes cleared up almost immediately and a powerful sense of strength flowed through me. It was an amazingly rejuvenating sensation, but I knew that I was draining him and needed to let go.

But Cole wouldn't let me.

"Cole, we need to stop."

But his beautiful face just stared at me with a mixture of caring and sadness. "No, Renda. This is what you need. Take my energy. Take all of it. I want you to have it."

Tears coursed down my cheeks as he held me tight, and his energy flowed into me. I could sense so many things now as I connected to him. It was a strange, but incredibly touching sensation.

His loneliness, sadness, desire, need, memories—all of it was pouring out of him and flowing into me. In turn, he was intermingling with my own thoughts and hopes. He was finding his way into my deepest secrets and fantasies that I'd locked away within the innermost private areas of my mind.

But I wasn't embarrassed—just incredibly sad to watch him fade. At first, he simply looked tired. Then I could see the struggle as he tried to hold himself whole for me. And then his form became softer until I could see right through him.

Before he disappeared, Cole leaned over and placed his lips on mine. He was already so translucent that all I felt was a warm wind as our mouths connected and then—he was gone.

"Isn't that sweet. A love affair between a loser and a dead guy." Margaret cackled.

I turned to face her now, feeling much stronger. For a split second, I could sense a flicker of fear in her dead eyes, but then it disappeared and was replaced by a sense of amusement.

The demon moved closer to me and smiled again as it began to speak.

"Renda, Renda, Renda. You've always been alone and now you're alone again."

I stared at the creature, unsure as to where the speech was going and continued to recite the verse that Adahy had taught me. But Margaret didn't seem to care and continued speaking.

"Just like Mommy and Daddy, just like anyone you've ever cared for, he's gone now. Yes, you've drained that pathetic ghost from all of its energy and now...he's never coming back." It giggled. "Aren't you tired of being alone?"

Margaret was now standing inches away from my face and peered at me almost inquisitively. "Wouldn't you like to feel whole? Don't you want someone to love you?"

Incredibly, the woman morphed from a horrific beast and now resembled Cole. His dark eyes stared at me, and his gorgeous lips parted in a gentle smile.

"Come here, Renda," he said. "You don't have to be alone. Let's be together before it's too late. Elial is helping me regenerate. Let's make love. You want that, don't you?"

Despite the weather, my friend, and her brother chanting behind me and everything I knew to be real—my body started to react. I began to tingle at the thought of feeling Cole's hard sex against me, in me, moving deep inside me.

It was crazy, but I started to move closer to him.

Be careful, Renda—it's a trap.

I could hear Adahy's voice warn me, but there was no need. I knew what needed to be done.

"Stop, Renda!" shouted Bobbie.

But it was too late. I'd already embraced what looked like my beloved Cole and as soon as my body connected to his—it was clear that it wasn't Cole. There was no warmth or energy flowing between us. Instead, the thing wrapped its arms tightly around my back as evil flowed into me.

It felt like tar was entering my veins, because they stung

as an icy chill spread through my body. Somewhere inside my mind, I wondered if the sensation was what death felt like.

As Elial entered me, my body grew heavy and hazy. I could no longer stand fully upright, because it felt like sand was filling every empty space, every cell. Staggering away, I groaned and searched for something to hold me up.

Bobbie tried to approach me, but I waved her away. I was infected now and fearful that the demon would try to jump to someone else. Somehow, despite his intention of completely possessing me—no doubt to suck up all the remaining energy that Cole had given me—I was still hanging on to myself...barely.

Margaret was lying on the ground and suddenly spoke. "Where...where am I?"

Her children ran to her, and as they hugged and cried, I knew that at least part of the job had been done.

Don't try to fight me, Elial whispered inside my head. We're one now and you'll never be alone again. I'll help make you powerful and loved.

"Shut up," I muttered, staggering toward the trees. I had to get away from people and be alone. And as I stumbled into the forest, I could now see various ghosts looking at me sadly. They weren't ghosts I recognized, but they all backed away as I approached, fearful of what was now rooted inside of me.

I stumbled through the trees for what seemed like hours. In the distance, my name was shouted out once in a while, but I ignored it and pressed forward into the deepening woods.

If I die here, then Elial has lost.

The thought perpetuated through my mind numerous times throughout the afternoon as the day settled into dusk and then into night. It was dark now and nearly impossible to see where I was going.

Finally, I sat down on the ground, and dropped my head between my knees. Elial's voice was intermittent, but every time he spoke to me, it created immense pain within my skull.

How had I failed so miserably? Adahy had said that to defeat the demon, I had to protect the victim with love and verse—and with my own abilities.

But instead of expunging the creature into the sky, I had taken it within myself.

An empty victory indeed.

I was tired, cold, thirsty, and scared. Curling up on the ground, I attempted to sleep.

The dream came upon me quickly. It was extraordinarily vivid and clear, as if it was actually happening.

There was a woman with long, red hair. She was beautiful, despite the fact that her clothes were worn and she wore little makeup. I could see that the woman was seeking counsel from an elderly man who was sitting behind a mahogany desk. They were both in an office with dark, stone walls. A distant wind howled outside.

The two people were in the midst of a conversation that I was intruding upon. Neither of them seemed to notice me, and they continued in hushed voices.

"But what am I supposed to do?" the woman asked in a nervous voice.

The man stroked his long gray beard and pondered the question for a few moments before he responded, "You need to be careful, Evelyn. The gift is a special one, but it's not the world's best-kept secret. There are those who know and they'll do whatever it takes to find you. As you know, it's something that many have used to their advantage. And some will not stop until they have it—and you. My advice is to leave her. Leave her where no one knows, where no one can harm her. And then, when the time is right, you can reunite."

"No!" the woman cried out. "How can I do that? How can I abandon her? She's my only child. She'll never know."

The man smiled. "Yes, she will. When the time is right, she will. But there's no time. Here's what we'll do…"

The voices faded and now I was just watching the two discuss matters as the image of the room began to grow smaller, like a camera zooming out to project a larger image.

The beautiful woman was pregnant. Was she pregnant with me? Who was the old man?

Where were they?

I could feel pain as the dream faded away and when I opened my eyes, darkness flooded my view. The harsh woods cradled my sleeping body, and everything felt cold and horrible.

Suddenly, a voice in the distance called out my name.

Renda.

Renda.

It was the woman's voice from my dream. Standing up shakily, I slowly navigated through the woods. The voice continued to call out my name and was now getting louder.

Renda.

Renda, over here!

A small glowing orb appeared in the distance. It was partially blocked by the mass of dark branches and leaves, but I followed it until I was standing a few feet away.

The orb started to bounce up and down like a ball and then elongated as it drifted toward the ground. I was now aware that ghosts tended to inhabit these little round spheres until they fully materialized, so I figured that I was in the presence of another one.

As the light began to take the shape of a woman, the sound of crackling leaves behind me caused my entire body to jump. Turning around, I searched the darkness but couldn't see anything.

When my head turned back to face the glowing shape, I wasn't surprised to see that the woman from my dream was now standing in front of me. She looked older and had different clothes on, but I clearly recognized her.

"Who are you?" I whispered.

"My name is Evelyn. Renda, I'll explain everything to you at a later time, but right now we've got to work quickly. The demon inside you isn't strong yet, but in a few days he'll be able to completely take over your mind and soul. We've got to stop that from happening."

"So what do I do?"

"Listen to me carefully. You need to embrace me, the way you embraced the creature. Don't worry about draining me— just hang on as long as you can. It's going to hurt, and you may feel like letting go, but don't. And we'll have the help of one more friend."

I was about to ask her who the other person was, when the sound of twigs crackling once again caused me to turn around.

My heart stopped for a moment and then Jane raced out of the woods. She ran up to me and gave me huge dog kisses as a welcome.

In the midst of all that had been going on, I'd completely forgotten about my most loyal friend in the world. When Bobbie had called me into the house, I'd left Jane outside while we encountered Elial and the rest was a blur.

Had she been in the clearing with us? I couldn't remember now, but it didn't seem to matter. All that mattered was that she was with me now, and I knew that her love and loyalty would be strong allies in the battle against Elial.

The woman seemed more anxious now and waved me over. "Come on, Renda. I'm keeping the demon neutralized, but I won't be able to maintain this level of control for long."

Indeed, I was already starting to feel the evil awaken within me and begin to try to pull me away from the light. Every step toward the woman was increasingly difficult.

Once I was standing within her glow, I could see how beautiful she was. Her red hair danced in the moonlight and flowed around her. Jane whimpered and got closer to us as well, her furry body rubbing against my bare legs.

As we connected, my brain suddenly erupted in pain.

Stop! No! No! No!

Elial was shrieking inside me now, and each time he did it felt like a sword stabbing me right through the skull.

"No," I moaned, but despite the pain, I wouldn't let go of the woman's body. I held her tightly and felt pure energy flowing into me.

I was being attacked by pleasure and pain at the same time. Part of me was searing, as Elial tried to hold on while vivid memories from the woman flooded my brain.

A childhood, running through the fields…

A man she loved…and lost…

The joy of finding out she was pregnant…

The sadness of losing the child…

Was this woman my mother? I wanted so badly to ask her, but the damned demon was hanging on so tight. It was unfair, it was wrong, it was...

Anger and rage flooded me like I'd never felt before. It consumed me with such a vengeance that I couldn't think or do anything else except bellow out the phrase that I'd been taught was the weapon against this evil, age-old creature that was intent on destroying me.

"RECÉDE DAEMON!"

My voice bellowed so loudly that it seemed to reverberate throughout the woods. It erupted from deep within my throat and propelled forward with such aggression that I was pulled from the glowing woman who was trying to save me, and flew several feet, hitting a tree and landing on the ground.

There was a loud shriek in the air and then all went silent.

And dark.

Chapter 16

The first thing I felt was heat. But it wasn't an uncomfortable, scorching heat, rather a gentle warming on my skin that seemed like a gradient spreading out until it vanished entirely at the furthermost points of my body.

I wanted to remain in the darkness because it felt safe and secure. But something was pushing me to wake up. It was a tiny nagging sensation in the back of my mind that became more and more insistent as time went on.

Finally, I allowed myself to rise from the coma-like slumber I'd been immersed in and my eyes opened to a room filled with light. The blinds covering the windows were open and the sun was happily beaming through the glass, casting bright spots along my blankets and exposed skin.

"She's awake!" shrieked Bobbie who had apparently been sitting beside my bed, waiting for me to wake up.

But how had I gotten there? My mind raced, trying to remember my last moments of consciousness. It took a moment, but then it all came back to me.

The woods.

The woman who'd appeared out of nowhere in a shroud of glowing light.

Jane.

The anger that had surged through me and wiped out any last restraint.

Elial.

Suddenly, I sat straight up in the bed. The world tilted a bit and my head roared with an intense headache, but it was a welcome sensation because pain was the only thing in my head.

The voice was gone.

Elial was gone.

"Renda," Bobbie cautioned, "I think you'd better lie back down. You're not one hundred percent right now. Let me get you a glass of water."

I drank some of the cool liquid and then looked closely at my friend. There were a million questions running through my mind.

"How did you find me? Where did you find me?"

Bobbie explained that after she and Daniel had reunited with their mother, they had turned to talk to me, but I had already disappeared into the woods. It surprised me that I'd moved so quickly because at the time it felt as if I could barely walk.

Bobbie ended up leaving Daniel with her mother and had raced after me, calling out my name as she tried to navigate through the brush. But I was too far away, and she eventually went back to the clearing to check on her family.

Once she got her mother home, she'd quickly called some friends and a group of twenty people set out looking for me. There had been a lot of ground to cover, because the Trillos' house backed up against a natural preserve that extended out for miles until it finally ended at the state border.

The group had divided up the woods, so that they could cover more ground. Unbeknownst to them, Jane had already run ahead and was searching for me, as well.

"How did Jane find me?" I asked.

As I spoke her name, Jane (who had been sitting anxiously by the bed) leapt up and rested her head on my chest.

I could tell she was very relieved that I was okay, and I was extremely happy to see her—giving her a big kiss on her cold, wet nose.

According to Bobbie, when we had initially found her mother sitting comatose at the dining room table, I'd left the front door open. So Jane had taken her time outside and eventually come in. But by then, we'd already entered the woods and had our encounter with Margaret/Elial. Once Bobbie had returned to the house, as soon as she opened the back door, Jane went outside looking for me.

The group had spent several hours searching and was about to contact the authorities when they'd heard Jane barking in the distance. One of the groups (which included Bobbie) was nearby and had followed the sounds when they found me, lying on the ground—unconscious and bleeding.

According to Bobbie, despite being in the middle of the woods in the dark of night, I appeared to be peaceful in my slumber and didn't stir when one of the men in the group picked me up and carried me back to the house.

Once inside, they'd checked to make sure I was still alive and doing okay—putting me in my bed and watching over me while I slept. Bobbie and Daniel had taken turns watching Margaret and me while we both rested from our ordeals.

"I can't tell you how thankful we are that you saved our mother. Why did you run into the woods like that?" Bobbie asked.

I quickly made the decision to keep my intermittent possession quiet. It wouldn't do any good to worry them all over again. The bottom line was that Elial was gone and Margaret was safe.

"Can I see your mother? Is she feeling all right?"

"Yes, Renda. I'm right here," said a gentle voice from the doorway.

As I turned to look at Margaret, my breath caught in my throat. Now that Elial was no longer feeding off her body, she looked reborn. Her cheeks were pink and alive, and her eyes were normal and vibrant.

"You're okay," I managed, feeling a tidal wave of emotion come over me. The tears started to pour down my cheeks without any reservation, and I felt as if all the bones in my body were turning to Jell-O.

"Yes, my dear. I'm fine. Thanks to you." And then she came over, and gave me a tremendous hug. We clung to each other for several minutes, forever bonded by what we'd shared and more importantly, by our mutual survival.

When Margaret emerged from our hug, she had tears in her eyes, as well. But she smiled a thankful grin, and I was happy to see that her teeth were normal and perfect.

"Now," she said, "I'm going to have Chef Roy fix you some breakfast so that you can get your strength back. Does that sound good?"

"But you need to get your strength back, too," I said in a wobbly voice.

"I'm feeling fit as a fiddle, don't you worry about me. Chef Roy's already been stuffing me full of his homemade chicken soup and dumplings," she replied, giving me a wink. We all laughed at her restored sense of humor.

I nodded happily. After she left the room, Bobbie and I stared at each other for a moment.

"You saved my mom. How'd you do it?"

I leaned back against the pillows and tried to answer as best as I could, carefully keeping out any parts that would seem farfetched and fantastical.

The rest of the day was strange. When I finally had enough energy to get out of bed, I went to take a shower. Removing my clothes, I gasped at the condition of my body. My arms were covered in scratches and bruises, I had a dark spot along my chest (where Margaret/Elial had punched me), and when I turned to look at my back, it was scratched and bruised, as well.

Everything hurt. When the hot water sprayed over my body, I moaned in pain.

After spending only a short time under the spray, I gingerly dressed and was thankful that I'd packed a long pair of pants and a long-sleeved blouse. It would help cover up just how damaged I was.

Jane whined outside the bathroom door and stayed close by my side.

As I descended the stairwell for a late breakfast, I didn't notice any ghosts milling about and wondered about Cole. I'd drained him of all his energy, so obviously he would need time to manifest. But I missed him and wanted to be close to him.

Would he be proud of me? I'd succeeded in my mission, but for some reason didn't feel an enormous sense of satisfaction. Perhaps it was because I was also still wondering about the woman who'd appeared in the woods and helped me defeat Elial.

Who was she? My mother? Another ghost? If she was my mother, did that mean my mother was dead?

A lump formed in my throat as I approached the table and tears threatened again. The exhaustion of the past week was finally fully descending upon me and I had so many questions. Despite being around people who cared about my well being, I felt more alone than ever.

Bobbie was already sitting at the table waiting for me and noticed my sad face. She rose and came to give me a hug. As we embraced, it helped ease some of the pain in my heart. I hadn't told her about the woman who'd appeared in the woods. Instead, I simply explained that I was so tired and confused after the ordeal that I'd stumbled around the woods in a haze and then simply passed out.

"Let's eat something, okay?" she offered.

The brunch was delicious and despite my inner turmoil, I ate two helpings of the feast. Margaret and Daniel joined us, and I was amazed at how quickly the Trillos had returned to normal. Now, they joked and laughed together. The familial bond that was becoming apparent in their presence was both comforting and saddening. It demonstrated what I'd helped them achieve and also what I felt was missing in my life, despite having my own family.

Or maybe I was just missing Cole and feeling sorry for myself.

The rest of the day passed along quickly. We spent a lot of time together in the earlier hours, talking, reminiscing, and looking at photographs of when Bobbie and Daniel were younger. It seemed to help Margaret heal as she bonded with her children.

Later in the day, Bobbie went to the gym for a quick workout and Daniel went to play videogames with a friend, which left Margaret and me alone in the house together. She made some coffee, and the two of us sat at the kitchen table.

"Renda, I wanted to spend some time alone with you. I'm sure you know why."

She wanted to understand what had happened to her, so I explained as much as I could about Elial. But when it came to how I'd exorcised him, the words were difficult because I wasn't sure how much she would believe.

"Margaret, I know you'd like details about how I helped get rid of Elial. But I'm not sure you'll think I'm telling the truth."

"Renda," she coaxed, "please go ahead. After what I've been through, I'd probably believe anything. You can trust me."

So, I did.

I told her about everything. The ghosts, Adahy, Elial, being chosen—and finally—about Cole. It took nearly an hour to recap the entire ordeal, but once I was finished, tears were pouring down my cheeks and exhaustion set in. Despite having experienced the entire set of events myself, it was an effort to recount everything because of the enormity of it all.

In essence, my life had been utterly and completely changed forever in the span of a week. And now that I'd served my purpose, what was next? Was I supposed to return to the library in Cale and my life there? How would things ever go back to normal?

Margaret seemed to sense my turmoil and took my shaking hands into hers.

"I believe you," she said. "I saw things too when that... that thing was in my head. I saw all these shapes and things floating around me and could never identify what they were. But you always came across so clearly. Whenever you were in my presence, I always felt a sense of peace. That's how I knew that I could trust you."

She hesitated for a minute and then continued gently, "The ghost you call Cole, you really care for him, don't you?"

I nodded.

"Well, if you want to stay here for another week and try to reconnect with him, you're more than welcome. Bobbie has to get back to work and Daniel will return to school, but you can stay here alone with me if you'd like. Would that help?"

It was an attractive offer, but also unrealistic. I had to return to Cale, because my vacation was over and my boss at the library probably wouldn't appreciate me disappearing for another week. So as much as I wanted to take her up on it, I declined.

"Thanks so much, but I have to go home tomorrow. I have to

get back to work. Thank you for believing me. I'm so happy that I could help you. You deserve the best in life and now, you can live in peace—away from the darkness."

Margaret smiled and we talked for the next hour about moving forward and finding happiness in our lives.

As the sun began to set, I sat outside and watched the trees sway in the distance. I had no desire to ever venture into the woods again. But somehow, I had the feeling that it wouldn't be the last time.

"There you are!" exclaimed Bobbie who was freshly showered after her workout. She was beautiful as always and seemed rejuvenated from the physical activity.

"Did you have a good workout?"

"Yes, I did. Why don't you hit the gym?" she teased. "I mean, you're skinny and all that, but given your new vocation as a demon-slayer, you probably could use the muscles!"

I giggled at her joke, and she sat next to me on the lounge chair.

"I'm really gonna miss you, Renda. Are you sure you have to leave tomorrow?"

I nodded and gave her a knowing grin, "Yes, I do. The library awaits. But don't worry. I'll be back soon."

She looked away and sighed. "Yeah, I know. But I just want you to be happy."

The conversation was heading in a heavy direction, so I changed the subject. "You know what would make me happy?"

"What?" Bobbie asked.

"A big dinner. Let's go eat!"

She laughed and we headed back inside.

Since it was our last dinner together, Margaret had asked Chef Roy to whip up something spectacular. And he'd outdone himself.

The table was full of colorful, delightful food and many of my favorite dishes had been prepared, including spaghetti carbonara, schnitzel cutlets, and a fluffy broccoli soufflé.

As Chef Roy prepared to leave for the day, I gave him a big

hug and thanked him for his wisdom. He winked at me and whispered, "I knew you'd help this family."

It was a delicious dinner. We dug in and devoured the food quickly, eating way too much. We topped it all off with rich chocolate cake and washed it down with aromatic coffee.

After the meal, we sat and talked for a while longer and then, it was time for bed. As I ascended the stairwell, some familiar ghosts greeted me with their pale faces and then resumed their activities.

But Cole was nowhere to be seen.

I took my time getting ready for bed, hoping that he would appear in the hallway. After brushing my teeth and using the bathroom, I stepped back into the hallway, hoping to see him one more time. It was filled with ghosts...but he did not appear.

Jane and I went outside for her final bathroom break, but no one greeted me there, either.

And then, back to the house, where the ghosts continued in their nightly rituals. All of them, except for Cole.

As I headed back to my bedroom, Claire and her brother were playing right outside my doorway. I knelt down and watched them for a while. Neither paid me much attention, but the little girl would occasionally look in my direction and smile as I watched them play with imaginary dolls and blocks.

Suddenly, I felt a warm hand on my shoulder. I turned around quickly, expecting to see Cole, but instead it was Adahy. Trying to hide my disappointment, I smiled. But Adahy was too smart and could sense that I wasn't happy.

"Ahh," he mused. "Come with me, Renda Bloodmane."

I patted the little girl on the shoulder and followed the shaman into my bedroom. Once inside, I shut the door, and we both sat on the floor opposite each other.

"You did well, little cricket. But there are many battles ahead. I sense you are sad. Why?"

"I was hoping to say goodbye to Cole before I left here. But he isn't manifesting himself. So I guess I'll see him when I see him."

Adahy seemed to darken at my words. His smile disappeared, and he stared at me with serious eyes.

"You cannot fall in love with one of us. We are a part of another realm—whispers of this one. Your friend Cole helped you in your battle. But he may not reappear, as you took all of his energy. Sometimes, when a spirit loses strength, the transition to the final place is easier. I cannot see if he has moved on or not. But you cannot hope to see him again."

Adahy's words cut me like a knife.

Never see Cole again?

How would I survive?

"You must go on, Renda. There is much for you to do. If Cole is still part of the realm of the spirits, he will find you. If not, you must understand that forming a connection to the dead is a dangerous one."

Suddenly, Adahy smiled.

"But now is not the time to talk of danger or of sad things. You have succeeded in your first quest. There will be many more and you must be prepared."

"But who was the woman who helped me? I wouldn't have succeeded without her."

Adahy seemed surprised at my question. "Woman? I don't know what you mean. There was no woman on the field. Did you receive help from another source?"

I wasn't sure how to answer, so for the second time that day, I decided to keep quiet about the mysterious visitor who had helped me defeat Elial. If Adahy thought that I'd done it on my own, then it was probably better to leave it that way.

"I'm not sure. I thought I saw someone, but perhaps I'm wrong."

The ghost frowned at me. "Renda, be careful. You are newly awakened and there is much for you to learn."

"Will you continue to teach me?"

He smiled again. "No. For now, I must remain here. I'm not bound here. None of us are. But this is the land I choose to be connected to. And there is a responsibility to the other spirits who reside within these walls. The children you encountered for example. They rely on the elders for guidance as they float between your realm and ours."

The look on my face must have been one of pure concern,

because Adahy shifted closer to me and spoke more gently. "Don't worry, Renda Bloodmane. There will be others who will protect you. By now you should know that Elial's words were purely falsehoods. You aren't alone and never will be. You are *the Chosen*."

Adahy's form began to fade and I panicked.

"No, don't leave me here. How will I know what I'm supposed to do? What if I never see any spirits again?" My babbling was humiliating, but I didn't want him to leave. It felt too final.

"Don't worry," Adahy repeated as his form faded. "You'll know when you're needed. There's no need to concern yourself with that. Just keep yourself safe. Be well, my sweet cricket. Be well."

And with those words, he disappeared into the air, a warm wind signaling his departure.

I found our parting strange. In the living world, you would hug each other or shake hands to say goodbye. But I was discovering that with ghosts, goodbyes were quick and always connected with a sense of unfinished loss. The same rang true for Adahy's parting. There was still so much I wanted to ask him, so much he'd said that was unclear.

A knock on the door interrupted my train of thought. The knock was soft and uncertain, almost as if the person on the other side wasn't sure whether or not to come inside.

"Come in," I called out.

The door opened slowly, and little, beautiful Claire with the burnt face and blind eyes came into my room. She was very shy and slowly moved toward me.

"Come here, you little troublemaker," I said smiling, patting the floor next to me.

"Why are you sitting on the floor?" she asked.

"Well, I was just talking to Adahy, but he had to go. So I was just sitting here...waiting for you."

A large grin spread on her tiny face, and she seemed happy with my answer. She sat down next to me and sighed. "You're the only one who can see us. Why is that?" she asked.

"I guess other people in my realm don't look very closely, because if they did, they'd definitely want to play with you and your brother. You're both adorable."

"No, we're not," she said quietly. "I know we're all burned up. But we don't feel sick or anything. We're just kids and we just want to find our mommy."

Despite knowing that I would end our chat more quickly than normal, I took the child's hand in mine and felt her energy pour into my veins. Looking into her sweet, destroyed face, I whispered, "You're never alone. I'll be with you always. Just call for me and I'll find you. Goodbye, my sweet angel."

She embraced me fully and our bodies fused as her innocent energy wrapped us in a pink haze. Then she was gone but not before I heard her cheerful giggle as she departed.

I returned to the hallway to say goodbye to the rest of the ghosts and then got into bed. But it was difficult to sleep. My body was full of unrequited passions and I ached for Cole.

Turning away from Jane's gaze, I reached under the blanket and touched myself as I thought about Cole's naked body against mine. As my body shivered with self-induced pleasure, I thought about his eyes, his lips, and his strong muscles straining against me. But my orgasm was half-empty because Adahy's words continued to repeat themselves in my head.

What if Cole was truly gone? I was leaving in the morning and many miles would be put between my soul and his.

Tears found my cheeks, and I cried myself to sleep.

Chapter 17

Iwoke up the next morning and was immediately filled with apprehension and disappointment. Despite my hopes that Cole would return to at least say goodbye, he'd been a no-show. And now, I was leaving and not returning for many months—if ever.

Bobbie was immediately at my door, asking if she could help me pack and continued to ask me to reconsider staying at the house for at least a few more days. Once again, her words tempted me because I thought it might give me a better chance to see Cole, but the other side of me knew that the quicker I put distance between myself and the Trillos' home, the sooner I could begin healing from the whole ordeal.

It didn't worry me that I might continue to see spirits. I actually welcomed the idea as I'd become quite comfortable with the ghosts around me. In truth, they made me feel needed and a part of something. But I didn't want to keep pining for a man—a dead man—who apparently didn't feel the need to even say goodbye.

Or might be gone forever to heaven or wherever spirits went when they were finally at rest.

So, as difficult as it was, I finally said goodbye to the Trillos and promised I'd keep in touch regularly. Bobbie gave me a hug and Margaret did the same while whispering in my ear, "Thank you. I'll be in touch very soon. And I promise not to go wandering in the woods from now on."

It was a funny and touching thing for her to say, and we both laughed.

Jane said her goodbyes as well and enjoyed plenty of petting from our gracious hosts who'd grown quite attached to my long-legged, furry daughter. Many treats were gobbled down until I finally had to stop the indulgences or I'd be dealing with dog vomit in my car on the way home.

As we pulled away from the house, I couldn't help but look at the same window that I'd seen when we'd arrived, one week prior. Cole had stared out of that window, discovering me before we'd even exchanged a word. Now, there was no one there, but I knew that all of the familiar ghosts would still float through the hallways night after night, seeking a salvation they would never find, yet finding a strange form of comfort in their infinite routines.

The thought made me sad.

My car pulled out of the driveway and as we sped past the trees, I looked toward the spot where I'd seen Cole's mother. It looked different in the daylight—normal and empty. It struck me that I rather preferred the way it looked at night.

As we drove out of Macon and back onto the highway, I noticed that ghosts also roamed the side of the road. Many of them were victims of car crashes, their bodies mangled and destroyed. Not wanting to be distracted the whole way home, I decided to shut off my second sight and the visions disappeared into the air.

Jane looked at me when I made the mental shift, her eyes reflecting a sense of understanding as if she was aware that I didn't want to be bothered by the dead.

"I know, I know. Maybe it's a gift, but I'd like to feel normal for a while and I don't want to think about him. Okay?"

Jane snorted and looked in the other direction, leaving me to my thoughts.

We drove for a few hours in silence and when the Cale sign came into view, my heart dropped in my chest.

I was home.

Chapter 18

Nothing had changed and everything had changed.

Coming home was uneventful. Despite having been away for a week, no one had called, except for my mother to say she'd watered my plants and left my mail on the kitchen table.

No one had missed me, and I decided to keep my second sight turned off for a while.

Life at the library was the same, too. Several days after I returned, Larlene and I went to lunch and even though I felt strange being so honest about my ordeal, she had a million questions, so I told the truth. As I spoke, she sat upright in her seat, leaning forward with large eyes.

"Oh, my God. That is absolutely insane," she sputtered. "You're like...gifted!"

I laughed at her reaction and immediately remembered why we were friends. With Larlene, you could tell her almost anything, and she'd take the news in stride without question. However, she wasn't so quick to let me off the hook as it related to Cole.

"So, are you never going to see him again? He sounds totally hot."

Sipping my iced tea, I looked down into the glass. I missed Cole every day, but was trying to rebuild my heart and it was taking longer than I'd expected. "No, I don't think I'm going to see him again. It's been several days and I think it's time to move on."

"No!" she shrieked. People turned to look at us, and I felt heat rise to my cheeks.

"Shhh, don't be so loud. There's nothing I can do. It's over."

Larlene leaned forward in her seat and whispered conspiratorially, "How do you know that? Maybe he's just...I don't know...maybe he's just resting or something. You can't give up if you've found true love!"

"True love?" I shot back. "How can I find true love with a ghost? He's not real, Larlene. And apparently, he's not missing me at all. It's over. Let it go."

My tone surprised her, but she backed off, and we continued talking about the spirits that I could now see. Larlene was interested in ghost hunting with me, but I turned her down flat. She was making me feel like a carnival sideshow freak, and I wasn't interested.

Our lunch ended in a somewhat bleak mood, and we both parted ways once arriving back at the library. I couldn't help but feel more alone than ever. So I figured maybe it was time to turn my sight back on.

The rear of the library was lined with comfortable couches for people who just wanted to read and not be disturbed by the constant opening and closing of the front doors, or the people who found it necessary to speak to their friends while browsing the aisles. It was a perfect spot for me to focus on lifting the lever in my mind.

Sitting down on the soft couch, I leaned back against the cushions and closed my eyes. It didn't take long before I felt a familiar shift in the innermost reaches of my mind. Opening up my senses to the other realm was quite relieving, like a dam releasing water in a rush of easing pressure. It wasn't quite like the release from an orgasm, but it definitely felt good.

Suddenly, I became aware of a person sitting next to me. My blood froze because it couldn't be anyone who was living as I would have heard the person approach and felt the cushions compress under the weight of another human being.

I was sitting next to a ghost.

Lowering my head slowly, I took a deep breath. It had been several days since I'd seen my last ghost, so I wasn't sure how it would affect me. I carefully opened my eyes and shifted my body, so that I was able to inch away slightly.

Nice and easy. No need to rush this. Just relax, Renda.

As I turned my head, my nerves began firing on all cylinders, because I was sitting next to the man I'd seen before the visit to the Trillos.

The man who I'd seen reading a book.

The man with the destroyed face.

Only now, his face was normal, as he sat and read the book clutched in his hands.

I stared at him in surprise with my mouth half-open. He didn't pay attention to me at first, but then turned and noticed my look of surprise.

"Hi," he said in a strong voice. "I was wondering when you'd come back, so that I could say goodbye."

"Say goodbye?" I managed. "What do you mean?"

The man stood up from the couch and turned to face me. "You know me, Renda. Don't you remember? Think..."

I couldn't recall his face or his voice, but there was something about the man that looked familiar. Now that he was uninjured, I was able to see the features on his face, the eyes, and the chin— the countenance that looked...like mine.

"Daddy?"

The man smiled gently and knelt in front of me, so that I could look closely at his face.

"Yes, my dear. I've waited so long for you to recognize me, so that I could move on to the next stage of my existence. This library was the last place I visited before my life ended. But I couldn't bear moving on until we were able to say goodbye. I've manifested here every day for the last twenty-eight years."

Tears were streaming down my face and I couldn't think of anything to say.

My father reached out and wiped a tear from my cheek, his strong energy gently warming my skin.

"Don't be sad. You're loved so much. And I've watched you grow up from the time you were a child browsing the stacks, to the beautiful woman you've become. My sweet Renda, I'm so proud of you."

My heart filled with happiness at his words.

"What happened to you?" I asked.

His eyes turned away from mine as a sign that he didn't

want to discuss it, but I knew time was running out, so I pressed him for information.

"Daddy, what happened to you?" I repeated.

"It was a misunderstanding, that's all," he said. "A stupid misunderstanding."

"But you were killed, Daddy! That doesn't sound like a misunderstanding to me. What happened?"

My father grew serious and stared at me with the same eyes I'd seen in the mirror so many times. "Listen to me, Renda. You need to be careful. Your gift is a wonderful thing, but it can also be something very sought after. Keep your eyes open and if you need help, be sure to call on the spirits for support. You're a part of their realm now too and most of them will help you in the event of an emergency."

"And what about my mother?" I asked urgently. "Where is she? Is she still alive?"

My father took my hands in his. Energy flowed through him and I felt his essence and his love. As we connected on the most basic level possible, he leaned over and kissed my cheek. When he pulled back, his body was already beginning to fade, but he had a smile on his face.

"I'm going now, my child. Don't worry. It will all make sense to you soon. Be safe and know that I will always love you."

"Bye, Daddy," I whispered as he disappeared into the distance.

The book he'd been reading was still lying on the couch, and to my surprise—it was real. When I turned it over, I looked at the title on the cover.

Sleeping Beauty.

I laughed and cried at the irony of my father's last gift to me.

I was asleep no more.

Chapter 19

The rest of the week passed quickly.

The visit from my father had calmed my nerves. In fact, my whole outlook was different, and I decided that if I was to live my life anew amongst the spirits, then I would have to try to make some changes.

It was Friday, and my cell phone rang in the early afternoon hours. When I looked at the phone number on the screen, I recognized Jonny Thomas's number. Sighing, I quickly debated whether or not to answer.

I still missed Cole and really didn't want to talk to Jonny. But I realized that if I was going to turn over a new leaf, it needed to be on all fronts. And what better way to start than trying to give people a chance?

"Hello?"

Jonny seemed nervous and excited at the same time. He stumbled at first and then finally got the words out. "Hey, Renda. Was wondering where you've been. Went to the library, but your friend said you were out of town for the week."

"Yes," I replied carefully, not wanting to talk about my experience. "I'm back. What's up?"

"Well, I was wondering if you wanted to go out tonight and see that new comedy about the sorority girls who decide to start a major league baseball team. You interested?"

Truth be told, the movie looked ridiculous, and all I really wanted to do was go home and hang out with Jane, but I was trying to do things differently. So Jonny was in luck.

"Sure. That sounds like fun. Why don't we meet at the theater?"

Jonny was silent for a minute—no doubt in complete shock that I'd agreed to go out with him (he'd been asking me for many years to no avail). But he finally got it together and told me that the movie started at seven-thirty. I agreed to meet him outside the theater.

As I hung up the phone, the skies grumbled in aggravation. It was going to be a stormy night, so perhaps it was good that I'd be inside a movie theater. Picking up the books that were scattered on a nearby table, I hurried to get things cleaned up.

It had been a very long time since I'd been on a date. In fact, it was nearly impossible to find anything to wear because I hadn't been shopping in nearly six months. My mother was always chiding me about the fact that I still looked like I was living in the '80s, but honestly—who had time to update a wardrobe? I also had no interest in hunting through the racks for something that looked good on me.

After nearly twenty minutes of sorting through blouses, I finally found something that looked semi-decent—a black blouse with a plunging neckline. It was probably the only piece of clothing I owned that was the least bit sexy, and I felt uncomfortable revealing so much of my chest, especially since I wasn't really interested in Jonny.

I didn't want to give him the wrong impression.

But I needed to get out more. So making myself look presentable was part of the plan.

To augment the outfit, I applied some dark red lipstick and blush. Then I added mascara and a spritz of perfume, and I was all set.

Jane watched me disinterestedly. She was undoubtedly annoyed that I was going out and not sitting at home watching a movie with her.

"Aww, don't be jealous, Ms. Jane," I said jokingly. "I'd rather be home with you, but I've got to rejoin the land of the living." I laughed at my own joke, but Jane just snorted and went to lie on her doggie bed.

I took one last look in the mirror and was startled by my transformation. Not one to usually be impressed by what I typically saw staring back at me, I was amazed at how a little bit of makeup changed my image. My red hair was shiny and full, my eyes deep and pensive, and my lips plump and glossy.

I actually looked sort of—sexy.

Shrugging my shoulders, I headed outside into the dark night.

The theater was packed with people, because in Cale, there wasn't much to do on a Friday night. The weather was awful as well, with a slight drizzle already beginning and dark clouds rolling against the night sky. The air was still warm, but an intermittent wind plowed through, messing up carefully sprayed hairstyles and washing away eye makeup.

I closed my umbrella and stepped under the awning outside the theater. Staring out into the distance, I squinted and searched for Jonny. The sea of people made it hard to identify anyone. There were many locals who I knew, but I wasn't interested in being social.

There were other people, too. I'd left my second sight active and could see the ghosts milling about. It wasn't difficult to distinguish one from the other. The ghosts were pale, some translucent. Others hadn't manifested yet and were floating orbs in the air. They swirled around people and flitted in and out, completely invisible to the throngs of the living.

All except for me.

I'd become accustomed to searching for Cole, always hoping he'd appear amongst the orbs and restless spirits. But he never manifested and I was growing tired of searching. The focus it took was exhausting and depressing. And now I was on a pseudo-date with a man I wasn't even remotely attracted to. It was enough to make me turn around and consider heading back to my car...

"Renda!"

Jonny's voice carried over the throngs of moviegoers and I could see his tall frame ambling through the masses, trying to reach me. A burst of anxiety hit me and all I wanted to do was run far away and hide.

Why am I like this? I'm acting like an idiot.

Trying to give him my brightest smile, I greeted Jonny with as much gusto as I could muster.

"Hey there! How're you? I thought you might be standing me up."

He grinned and rubbed my shoulder. At the touch of his hand, I instinctively shrugged it off and backed away. Jonny noticed immediately and his grin wavered, but he quickly resumed his composure and looked toward the theater.

"I think the movie's about to start, so let's go in. I already bought the tickets online."

I was impressed. Not having to stand in the rain and wait for tickets was a plus. Perhaps the night would turn out better than I thought.

We headed inside.

As expected, the movie wasn't a masterpiece, but it did make me laugh several times. And Jonny was a perfect gentleman, never making any sudden moves.

As the movie played on, I looked over at him. He wasn't unattractive, but I felt absolutely nothing inside. No butterflies, no skip of the heartbeat—nothing. It was as if my heart had gone to sleep and it would take electroshock therapy for it to do anything more than simply function.

Jonny noticed me staring at him and smiled back at me.

Worried that he might be getting the wrong impression, I whispered, "I'm going to the ladies' room."

He nodded and returned his attention to the movie.

Making my way out of the theater, I slowly walked to the restrooms. Most of the movies playing were in full swing, leaving the hallways empty and dark. It felt strange walking alone down the empty hallway, but it was better than trying to pretend that I was interested in Jonny.

When I was halfway to the ladies' room, I felt a warm breeze against my arm. It had come from behind me, so I turned around and was greeted by another warm gust—this one hitting me in the face. I blinked and rubbed my eyes.

What the hell was that?

I searched the perimeter, but there were no ghosts around. Just me, standing there looking ridiculous. Still, something about the wind seemed familiar.

Several minutes ticked by, and nothing happened. The air around me cooled and then settled once more. I quickly went into the women's bathroom and when I emerged several minutes later, Jonny was outside waiting for me. People were also milling about and leaving.

The movie was over.

"That movie sucked, didn't it?" Jonny asked. Before I had a chance to respond, he continued, "I've got an idea. You look too beautiful to end the night. Why don't we grab some ice cream at The Diner?"

The Diner was a popular hangout that looked exactly the way it sounded. It perfectly mimicked an old-style diner from the '50s, fully equipped with a jukebox and waitresses who were dressed in large poodle skirts with matching sweaters and bobby socks. But what made The Diner so good was its food. It had the best desserts in town and a mint chocolate chip shake sounded really good to me.

"Sure. Why don't I meet you there since I have my car?"

Jonny looked a bit disappointed but agreed to meet me at the restaurant.

Once I pulled up to The Diner's parking lot, I was pleased to see that it wasn't too crowded.

Yet.

The crowd always came back to the eatery later in the evening when they had the "munchies" from too much drinking in the bars.

As I entered the restaurant, I noticed that Jonny had not yet arrived, so I grabbed a booth and waited for a waitress to take my drink order. As I looked around, I noticed a man standing in the distance with his back to me, facing the jukebox. From the back, he was tall with dark hair and resembled…Cole.

My heart started beating fast and I could feel my body temperature immediately rise in excitement. I wasn't sure what to do because if I got up, I'd lose the booth, but if I didn't and it was Cole, then I'd never forgive myself for missing him.

Taking a deep breath, I looked down and said a little private prayer. It was now or never.

"Hiya," a happy voice greeted me. The sound was such a surprise that I jumped and banged my knees against the table.

"Ouch!"

"Sorry, Renda. It took me forever to get here. I hit every traffic light on the way over. Did you order yet?"

I tried to move around Jonny to see if the man was still standing at the jukebox, but he was gone. Disappointment washed over me. Now I was stuck.

"No, I haven't," I mumbled and sat back down.

Jonny didn't seem to notice that I was completely deflated and began to talk immediately. He rambled on and on about the movie until the waitress arrived.

Her presence was a relief, and I tried to smile at her as she took our order. She looked harried, a loose strand of hair hanging in her face. She was an attractive woman, but hours on her feet every day were obviously taking their toll.

"Thanks, I'll get your order," she said once we were done. She turned to me and winked. "You know what. I must be going into menopause or something. I just got my first hot flash on my way to your table."

"Really?" I asked. A thought was beginning to form in my mind, but I didn't want to succumb to it. Not unless I was completely sure.

"Yeah," she said, mopping her forehead with a handkerchief. "I just started feeling these hot blasts of air that ain't coming from anywhere in particular. Must be my clock winding down or something. No worries, I'll be right back." And she took off in the other direction.

It was at that moment when I realized that I needed to get home. Every nerve in my body was on edge, and there was a little voice in the back of my mind giving me a constant nudge.

"Oh," I murmured and grabbed my stomach.

Jonny looked at me with concern in his eyes. "What's wrong? Are you okay?"

"I don't know. All of a sudden, I'm not feeling so well. I think I need to go home."

The look on Jonny's face broke my heart. He was absolutely crushed. But it was time to go, and I couldn't wait a minute longer. Standing up from the table, I went over and kissed him gently on the top of his head.

"I'm so sorry, but I've got to go home. I have this stomach problem and when I feel this way, it usually means that I'm going to spend the rest of the night running back and forth to the bathroom."

As soon as the words tumbled out of my mouth, I felt heat rise to my face.

Did I really have to use the dreaded bathroom excuse?

I felt guilty for a moment, but silently told myself that I needed something good enough that would help get me out of the situation I was in without offending my date who was well-intentioned, but just not for me.

My words worked, and Jonny backed away a little. "No problem, I totally understand. Do you need me to drive you home?"

"No, that's okay. I'll be able to make it back. Go ahead and enjoy your ice cream and I'll call you tomorrow. Thank you for a lovely evening."

Jonny nodded miserably.

I quickly exited and got into my car. On the drive home, I looked in the rearview mirror and could see my eyes shining almost feverishly. I wasn't sure why I was so excited, but there was hope racing through my veins.

Parking the car outside of my apartment, I slowly stepped outside and looked around. The night was darker than ever and the rain had stopped, allowing for a humid shroud to soak up all the air.

Unlocking my front door, I immediately welcomed the cool blast of air conditioning that hit me as I entered. As if on cue, Jane raced outside, looking for a place to do her business—leaving me standing in the doorway.

I peeked inside and looked around, straining my eyes to identify anything in the dark. But to my disappointment, the apartment was empty. Not even waiting for my dog to come back in, I sank to the floor and began to cry.

My despair was so quick and powerful that I was helpless within its strong grasp. Tears poured down my face as I wailed in despair. All of my pain and loneliness emerged. I wanted Cole. Because with him, I could handle the spirits. I could find a way to discover the true purpose of my life and not wander aimlessly through the hours. Without him, I was unsure where to turn, who to help, and who to love.

I loved him. This I finally realized. Despite our brief encounters, he'd saved my life and the energy of his spirit still ran within my veins. He was a part of me now and to have him ripped away so quickly was something I couldn't face.

Jane whined from the doorway, but I ignored her. My sadness was threatening to completely overtake me.

Looking up at the darkened ceiling of my living room, I spoke to the universe in a strong, angry voice.

"Why can't Cole come back to me? Come back to me, Cole! I need you!"

Jane whined again.

I still didn't acknowledge her.

It didn't matter. She couldn't help me.

"It's not fair," I cried. "I can't go through this alone. It doesn't matter to me that he's dead. He's not dead to me. He's warm and loving and smart and…"

"And what?" a voice asked teasingly from behind me.

I tuned to the doorway where Jane stood panting happily. Standing next to her in the darkness, outlined by the glow of the moonlight, wearing regular clothes, and sporting a small smile…was Cole.

My heart leapt in my chest, and my breath felt as if it had been pulled out by force. I couldn't speak and just sat there with my mouth open and my eyes wide.

He was dressed in tight blue jeans and a dark buttoned-down shirt that clung to his strong arms. He looked wonderful. His body glowed with the familiar energy of his source, but strangely the glow was less intense. Instead, it was a thin, muted shimmer along his skin.

Cole didn't say a word, but instead led Jane back inside the house and shut the door behind him. We were now surrounded by darkness, with the exception of the gentle glow he emitted. He then moved closer to me and put out his hand for me to grasp in order to rise.

I resisted at first, afraid and unwilling to drain him when

I'd just gotten him back. But Cole shook his head and motioned with his fingers for me to grasp his palm. Trusting his request, I grabbed his hand tightly. Instead of feeling a jolt of energy flow through me, I only felt a slight shock, which then subsided quickly.

I was perplexed at this change in him, but didn't care. All that mattered was that I could touch my love and not worry that he would disappear.

Standing in front of the man and ghost who I loved and wanted more than anything, I felt the heat rise to my face and delicious pangs of desire race through my veins to every point of my body. My hands shook, my breath came in gasps, and I felt overwhelmed by all of the feelings bursting inside me.

Cole laid his hands on my face. Again, I felt a slight shock and then—nothing. He put his face inches from mine and then kissed my lips gently.

As his lips touched mine, I felt a slight tingle and then softness. It wasn't enough, and I pulled him closer to me, kissing him deeply, my tongue searching for his and finding it easily. We tasted each other and kissed more fervently, our moans escaping into the darkness.

We both sank to the ground, kissing and pulling our bodies closer and closer together until we were literally almost glued to one another. I could feel all of his muscles straining against his clothes, and I felt an unyielding passion like never before. I wanted to feel his skin against mine, feel his energy flow through me—feel his maleness fill me.

I forgot time and space—everything disappeared as we kissed.

Slowly, Cole began removing my clothes and as my garments floated to the ground, the cool air kissed my skin and was immediately replaced by his hands and mouth. He kissed along my shoulders, making me shiver with desire before moving down to my breasts. I gasped at the feel of his warm, moist mouth. I had never felt such pleasure in my life.

I didn't want him to stop. But then he slowly made his way downward to where I had begun to burn with a fiery yearning. When Cole's tongue touched my shivering femininity, I thought I would explode. The feelings were so intense that tears sprang from my eyes and traveled down my cheeks. He lifted his head and looked questioningly up at me.

"Are you okay?" he asked, his voice shaking with passion.

"Yes." I breathed back and began to remove his clothing.

Cole's chest was muscled and lightly sprinkled with fine, black hairs. There was a deep scar on his left torso. But it was not bleeding and despite its severity, was not fresh. As I removed his pants, my breath caught in my chest.

He wasn't wearing underwear.

My love had a sizable erection that shook and quivered with passion.

I ran my fingers down the length of his strong shaft and traveled farther down his thighs. It was impossible that any man could be made so perfectly, but my dear ghost, my dear love... was perfect. And he was waiting for me to quench his desire.

How long had he waited to make love to a woman? How long had it been since he'd felt the stirrings of passion?

I didn't want to sit and wonder, because my own needs were calling and there was no time to think. My soul was vibrating with a hunger that I'd never known, and it could only be satisfied by the merging of our bodies.

Naked, we both lay on the ground, side-by-side staring at each other. I wasn't sure how this was happening and how Cole was able to maintain his presence without losing all of his energy, but somehow he was manifesting without transferring his energy to me, which allowed us to touch and kiss.

But would it allow us to make love?

I was nervous suddenly. It had been a long time since a man had been inside me. And I wasn't sure if I was the best lover. Certainly, I didn't have much practice.

Cole propped himself up and looked into my face with his strong, intense eyes. "Are you ready?" he asked.

I nodded.

Leaning down, he kissed me gently at first and then his kisses became more fervent. I began to feel like the fire in my body might completely consume me if he didn't press his body against me, so I pulled his strong frame on top of me and moaned as the initial shock of his energy was replaced by the warmth of our bodies rubbing against each other.

We moved in unison—like two sticks rubbing together to generate a flame—and soon, the flame engulfed us both as we touched and kissed and finally, melded together.

I gasped as Cole slipped inside me. He was larger than most men I'd been with, and yet his size helped to ease the ache and fill my yearning with a delicious satisfaction that only fanned the flames of my passion further and further.

Thrusting inside of me, Cole pushed his sex deeper and deeper, but I wanted more—pulling on his body—wanting him as close as possible.

We began to move together and his thrusts became more fervent. I could hear his breathing begin to get more shallow and desperate. It occurred to me that even though he was a ghost, I could hear his breathing, and I made a quick mental note to ask him about that once we'd settled down.

But we weren't settling anything just yet, and we both began to moan louder and louder as our passions grew and intensified. Then I felt Cole get even harder inside of me and the sensation sent me over the edge. Feeling my insides explode in complete and utter sweetness, I moaned in ecstasy and allowed the waves of passion to flow over me.

Moments later, Cole stiffened and bellowed as an orgasm overtook his body. It was the most majestic of experiences, feeling my lover's body stiffen and succumb to the purest of pleasures while mine slowly ebbed away into a feeling of relaxation and utter completeness.

Cole rested his face against my chest for a moment and then he rolled off me onto the floor. I turned away from him and felt my emotions explode within my chest as the tears dripped down my cheeks.

My heart felt like it was swollen double its normal size, and I couldn't grasp what had just happened.

"Renda, my darling. Please look at me."

Slowly, I turned my body to face his and looked into the strong eyes of the man I now loved. The man who was a ghost. Who'd been dead for years.

Who had somehow just made love to me.

"Please," I whispered. "Please, tell me what just happened?"

Cole smiled and propped his head up on one hand. "Well, let's just say—I've been practicing."

I listened eagerly as he shared his own journey with me.

When my battle with Elial began, Cole could sense the danger and decided that he had no choice but to venture outside. How else would he be able to help me? In order to do so, he consulted with Claire, who had been outside a few times at night and helped him take that first step. But as soon as he passed over the threshold, he began to feel his energy quickly disappear. Giving his final reserves to me drained him of nearly everything.

After the battle with Elial, Cole found himself a shadow of a spirit. But he had also become eligible for the spirit world's "mercy clause," which was the ability to pass along to the final realm because he had made peace with the living and gotten closer to the core of true energy. ·

Despite this opportunity, Cole chose to remain—not wanting to leave me behind.

It took him several days to regain enough energy to communicate with other spirits, and he eventually sought out Adahy for guidance. The sage was surprised to see him, but quickly agreed to help Cole find his way back to me.

For days, the two practiced different techniques. Cole emerged from the house, and once outside, learned how to harness the strength of the sun to regenerate himself. Over and over again, Adahy drained energy from Cole's center and forced him to regenerate almost as quickly as he lost his strength. They practiced for hours and once the sun went down, Adahy taught Cole other things.

He taught Cole how to contain his energy—a trick that was difficult for even the sage to accomplish. To harness the life source and keep it contained and circulating through the body like blood required incredible concentration and focus. Cole described the hours he spent doing nothing but training himself to restrain the flow of energy even when he felt as if he would disappear from exhaustion.

But the real test came from a chance encounter with Margaret. Cole decided to manifest himself to the woman one evening after Bobbie and Daniel had gone to bed.

She'd been sitting on the couch watching a movie when he came into the room. At first, she didn't notice him, but Cole sent a warm blast through the air that immediately caught her attention. When Margaret looked in the direction of the heat, he turned on as much energy as possible without completely burning himself out.

Margaret had been possessed by evil, so even though she was free of the demon, she was more inclined to see creatures who passed between the realms and to Cole's luck, she did see something.

"Who's there?" she'd called out, frightened by the strange shadow she saw floating in front of her.

Cole spoke quietly, "Don't be afraid. I'm not going to hurt you. Please. I'm a friend of Renda's. I need your help."

To Cole's luck, Margaret did hear him—barely.

"I think I heard you. Yes, I'll help. What do I need to do?"

Cole didn't answer and simply approached the woman. She flinched as his shadow grew near but did not move away. Somehow, she knew that whoever the spirit was, it wasn't going to hurt her.

Cole put out his hand and gently touched her arm. Margaret felt the movement but didn't pull away, despite feeling a surge of heat.

As he continued touching her arm, Cole immediately felt his energy begin to enter the woman's veins. Straining, he struggled to keep his energy inside and focused carefully on what Adahy had taught him. The energy leak began to thin out until it progressed to a drip and then subsided entirely.

Margaret looked at Cole and smiled. She could now tell that he was safe as some of his energy had traveled through her body and given her insight into his life, dreams, and desires. She remained still as he held her arm and controlled his energy flow.

"Thank you," he said softly when it was over.

"You're welcome," Margaret replied. "If you want to try

again tomorrow night, I'll be sitting here at nine. Come find me, dear spirit."

And so he had. Cole returned to practice with Margaret every night for several days. On the final night, when he pulled his hand away, he was surprised to see Margaret staring into his face with tears in her eyes.

"You're so handsome," she'd whispered and Cole immediately knew that it was time to find me.

"Thank you, Ms. Trillo. You've given me a gift of immense value. I will never forget your kindness."

Margaret smiled and said with a wink, "And I'll never forget yours. Now go find Renda."

Cole had then set out to search for me, but on the way decided to change his clothes to surprise me—another trick he'd learned from Adahy.

Finding me at the movie theater, he'd decided to send me some warm blasts of energy for fun. He then watched me at The Diner, while sending more blasts my way that got interrupted by the motion of the waitress walking past. Finally, he could wait no longer and decided to ride with me on the way home.

"How come I didn't see you?" I asked incredulously.

"That's another trick I learned," Cole joked. "How to remain hidden from the eyes of '*The Chosen One*'. And that one I'm going to keep to myself for now."

"Okay, smart ass, don't answer that," I threw back at him. "What about your injury? The one that ended your mortal life?"

"Oh, you mean this?" Cole asked and turned over on his back, showing me his scar. He ran his finger over the deep cut that remained dry. "This was an added benefit. Adahy and I realized that by circulating energy throughout my body, we were able to heal wounds. Or at least, the appearance of wounds."

His eyes darkened suddenly, and I realized that Cole was thinking about his own state of being. He was still dead—despite the new rejuvenating abilities he'd discovered. But I didn't want to think about it during such a special time. And I didn't want him to think about it, either.

"Let's not worry about wounds and the past. Let's live in the moment."

And with that, I pulled his naked body to mine once again and began kissing him in a way that generated a passionate flame. Within seconds, we were both on fire again.

Sometime in the wee hours of the night, Cole lifted me up off the floor and placed me into my bed. I was very tired, and my eyes were threatening to close. He looked tired too and to my dismay, I could begin to see the paleness return to his face.

"Don't leave me, Cole. Please," I mumbled, struggling in a battle with my Circadian rhythm.

Even between my tired eyelids, I could see his face sadden and grow paler.

"My sweet girl," he whispered in my ear. "It's time for me to go. But please don't worry. I'll be back in the morning. Just give me a little time to rest."

Then he kissed me and I fell fast asleep in the embrace of his warmth.

Chapter 20

When I awoke the next morning, I didn't immediately remember all that had happened. My body felt drained of all energy, and I was surprised to find myself naked in bed. Sometime overnight, Jane had decided to hop up on the bed with me and was now sleeping on my mattress, her furry head resting on my legs as she snored loudly.

Cole.

The memory of the last twenty-four hours suddenly hit me like a lightning bolt. Sitting up quickly, I looked around my room for any sign of him. But I was alone with Jane (who was quite annoyed at my sudden movement).

I slowly sat back against the pillows and rubbed my forehead. Had it all been a dream?

No, that couldn't be it. Why would I be naked?

And I felt sore in a place that couldn't be reached unless there was a man nearby—a man with a sizeable...

"Good morning," said a familiar voice, breaking my train of thought.

Cole was by the window, leaning against the wall in a casual manner as if it was absolutely normal to appear out of the clear blue. But I didn't mind the intrusion one bit.

Leaping out of bed, I ran over to him and gave him a hug, not even minding the little jolt of energy as our bodies connected.

If anything, I welcomed it.

"Wow," he said as we parted. "That was certainly a wonderful greeting. Good morning, m'lady. How are you feeling?"

I loved his accent and the way he addressed me in such a polite, respectful manner. No doubt in his day, men were much more proper and appropriate. He was still intense and serious, but in the past hours, I'd discovered that Cole could also be affectionate and loving.

"I'm feeling great. Can you stay for a while?" I asked. It felt weird to see him in the daytime. But surprisingly, he looked normal. His skin was a bit pale, but the rest of him was alive and alert.

"Yes," he replied with a mischievous grin. "I was actually thinking that perhaps we'd take a shower together to get you all cleaned up."

There was no need to debate further, so the two of us went into the bathroom.

Cole undressed first, and I watched as his clothes dropped in a pile on the floor. I couldn't take my eyes off his gorgeous body. He was perfect in so many ways, even his scar was beautiful as it stood out in defiance against his skin. I knew that the scar was a result of the deadly bullet that had ended his short life, but I chose not to think about it. How could I, when we were standing naked together in the shower under the warm spray?

The droplets of water beaded our eyes and hair, and through the rainbows of moisture, I could see Cole watching me intently. But we didn't speak. Instead, he pulled me against him, and we kissed underneath the warm spray.

Our kisses became more fervent, and we slowly sank down into the tub, slippery and aroused. Within minutes, my breasts were in his mouth, and I started moaning.

Despite our passion, there was a calm voice in my mind warning me to be rational. It spoke to me in a gentle, but stern tone.

Be careful, Renda. Remember, he's dead. He's a spirit. You need to make sure you don't lose yourself in a situation that can never be real.

But I was falling. And there was no other option. I couldn't face the future without him. There were too many uncertainties and dangers ahead. Adahy and others had warned me that the battle with Elial was just the beginning. All of my dreams were pointing towards a future filled with potential pitfalls. Who else could I trust?

Cole could sense my hesitancy and stopped kissing me. He

turned the water off and grabbed our towels, but instead of drying off, he stood and watched me carefully.

"You're worried I might disappear again, aren't you," he said quietly.

"No, it's not that exactly. But I'm not sure how to react to all of this. I mean you're still a ghost, and there's still so much I don't understand. How do I move forward with my life? How is anything ever going to be normal again?" I was starting to babble and panic.

Cole took my hand and sat me down on the edge of the tub. "It's understandable that you're confused. Perhaps I'm not as emotional because I've had time to experience my anger, grief, and confusion. But I've also been feeling more clarity than ever before. And I've waited a long time for you. So I'm willing to continue to follow this journey until we know where it leads. Can you trust me?"

I looked at his serious, handsome face and reached out, tracing circles on his pale cheeks with my fingertip. "Yes, I do trust you. But please, be patient with me. It's going to take time for me to understand what my purpose is."

He nodded and we sat in silence, feeling the heaviness of my words permeate the air.

Cole sat and watched as I ate breakfast, while periodically staring out the window. He never ate anything and sustained himself on energy alone.

"Your town, Cale, seems to be filled with many mysteries. It feels strange for me to have ventured outside of Macon, but now that I'm here, I wonder if this is a safe place for you."

It was a strange thing for him to say, and I wasn't sure if I fully agreed. In fact, I felt a bit defensive at his remark.

"Cole, I can't just leave my hometown. My parents are here, my friends are here, and my job is here. This is where I grew up."

At the mention of my parents, he looked at me with an interested gleam in his eye, "I would like to see your parents. Do they possess the same traits as you? Like your red hair?"

"No, they're my adoptive parents. My father died shortly

before I was born, and my mother abandoned me in the hospital on the night of my birth." Saying the words made me feel ashamed, and I looked in the other direction.

"I'm sorry. That must be very difficult to talk about."

I diverted my eyes to the colorful tablecloth covering my breakfast nook. "Yes, it is. I saw my father's spirit when I returned to Cale. We at least got a chance to say goodbye."

"How did he die?" Cole asked.

"He was…murdered," I answered quietly. "And I think he was killed because of me. Cole, I'm not sure why I was picked to have these abilities, but someone wanted to hurt me. That's the only reason I can imagine my mother abandoning me. She couldn't have just dropped me like that. There had to be a reason."

Cole came around to my chair and knelt on one knee beside me. "I'm certain she loved you. And I'll help you find out what happened to her. If she's a spirit like me who hasn't passed on to the other side, there are ways to find her."

I nodded, but was desperate to change the subject. Despite my closeness to Cole, I didn't feel comfortable talking to him about my past. Not yet. So I changed the subject to something a bit more casual.

"Would you like me to give you a tour of Cale? It's not very big, but I think you'll find it quaint."

He nodded, and after I washed and dried the dishes, we got into my car for a quick spin around town.

The sun was shining brightly and the clouds seemed to have dissipated after the prior night's rainfall. It was humid, but a light breeze passed through every now and then. I left the windows down so we could enjoy it. Privately, I wondered how long Cole could remain with me as he was starting to look tired, but I was afraid to ask. I just wanted us to be together as long as possible.

We passed the downtown area and the movie theater. I showed him where I'd gone to school, the library where I worked, and the small shops that lined the streets. We talked casually and he seemed happy and relaxed.

As we neared one of the largest cemeteries in town, I noticed that Cole's gaze became more focused and concerned. At first, I thought it might be because we were passing the Mecca of the dead—the physical resting place for the dead outside of the spirit realm.

But as we drove by, I too started to stare more intently.

There was a young child in the cemetery. But she was alone.

And she was dancing amidst the graves in a strange dance that reminded me of the "Mayfair" dances I'd seen in several movies. She skipped back and forth and twirled her skirt as she danced in small circles.

A car horn honked behind us in irritation at my slowing speed.

Pressing my foot more firmly on the gas, I turned to look at Cole. He was still staring out of the window at the cemetery with a concerned look on his face.

"What was that?" I asked. "Was it a spirit? I couldn't tell."

"No, it was a child. A living child. Is that normal behavior, Renda?"

I shook my head no and stared straight ahead as we drove back to my house. It felt wrong to just drive away, but I was in traffic and for some reason, I didn't feel like investigating the situation further. I just wanted to be alone with Cole and in his arms.

Still, the strange scene left us both serious and pensive and somehow, the light happiness of the day had been tainted by the eerily dancing child.

When I parked my car in front of my apartment, I turned to say something to Cole and immediately gasped.

He was fading fast, his body becoming translucent. But there was a smile on his face.

"Don't worry," he promised, "I'll be back later this evening. Have a good day, my sweet Renda."

He disappeared quickly in a blast of warm wind that ruffled my hair and tickled my cheeks. And once again, I was alone.

But this time, I wasn't concerned. Cole had come back to me and that was all that mattered. With that thought in mind, I exited the car and went into my apartment. Jane was sitting by the front door and greeted me with her usual exuberance.

As I knelt down to pet her, I was overcome by exhaustion. Despite getting some sleep the night before, I needed a few more hours.

It was time for a nap.

As I lay down on my pillow, thoughts of Cole flitted through my mind. The memories of his body against mine were comforting and helped me drift to sleep.

I'd been asleep nearly an hour when the ringing of the phone woke me up. At first, I tried to ignore it, because I desperately wanted to stay hidden within the comfortable clouds of my dream. But the phone continued to whine incessantly and I finally reached out to grab the receiver, knocking half the books off my bedside table in the process.

"Hello?" I asked in a raspy voice.

"Renda. Is that you?" Larlene asked on the other line. Her voice was shrill and full of tension.

"Yes, it's me. What's up?"

"Well, I've got a favor to ask you. Actually, it's a favor for a friend of mine, but I feel really weird asking you about it."

Larlene's cryptic words were enough to jolt me out of my dreamlike state. Sitting up, I leaned my back against the pillows and tried to concentrate, though my head was still a bit fuzzy.

"What's going on?"

"Well," she said hesitantly. "My friend's daughter's been acting weird lately. She's been talking to 'invisible friends' and things like that."

"That doesn't sound unusual," I said. "A lot of children have imaginary friends. Not sure how I can help here."

"Well, that's not all of it. She's also playing in the cemetery."

Memories of the strange child dancing amongst the gravestones appeared in my mind in vivid detail. The little girl we'd seen on our drive through town was no doubt the same child that Larlene was describing. Now I was concerned.

"Yeah, that is kinda weird. Anything else I should know?"

Larlene made a strange cough and then cleared her throat, "Her mother was checking in on her last night after hearing some strange sounds. She came into the room and didn't see anything at first, but when she was about to close the door, something caught her attention."

"What did she see? Stop being so dramatic!"

"I'm not being dramatic," Larlene snapped. "You're so impatient. Anyway, my friend was about to close the door when she saw a dark shadow hanging over her daughter. She thinks something is haunting her family."

There was a pause and I waited, fully aware of what Larlene was going to ask.

"Can you help her, Renda? I mean, you did say you solved that possession in Macon and that you've got some kind of gift. They've really got nowhere to turn—nowhere to go. Will you at least talk to her?"

I thought for a moment and decided it might be better to give this one some thought before simply agreeing to an unknown, potentially dangerous situation.

"I'll call you back."

Hanging up the phone, I walked over to the window and looked out at the darkening sky. I wasn't sure when Cole would return, but knew that when he did, we'd have some things to talk about.

The situation with Bobbie was one thing, but was I really prepared to handle another spiritual nightmare?

The answer came to me as I stood and watched the wind play through the trees. It wasn't in the form of a simple "yes" or "no". It came to me in a series of visions.

The field where Elial and I battled...

The woman in white...

Margaret thanking me for saving her life...

Daniel clutching my hand in desperation...

And Claire, the little girl with the burnt face and purest of hearts, with her innocent smile and blind eyes.

I would help Larlene's friend because I no longer had a choice in the matter. I'd been chosen to keep the realms peaceful and interconnected. My life had been interrupted by the love of a ghost and the guidance of a sage, and coupled with these gifts was my responsibility to those who suffered.

As I thought about my upcoming challenges, someone

knocked on my door. It was strange, because I rarely had any
visitors.

Jane barked and paced restlessly in front of the doorway.

I didn't see anyone when I looked through the keyhole, so I
opened the door slowly.

"Hi," a little voice said.

Looking down, I saw the little girl from the cemetery. I
wasn't quite sure how she'd gotten to my house because I lived
nearly two miles away from where she'd been playing. But there
she was—standing in my doorway. She had stringy blond hair,
and close up I could see that her face looked smudged as if she'd
been playing in the dirt. Her little fingernails were also dark
and looked filthy. Her shoes were worn and muddy.

"Hi there," I said. "Do you want to come in, honey?"

The little girl shook her head and simply looked up at me
with big, suspicious eyes. "No, my mommy says I shouldn't talk
to strangers."

The comment baffled me. "So why are you here? How did
you get here?"

"They told me to come here. They told me you're a good
lady. I hope we get to play together sometime. You seem nice."

Jane whined and nudged the girl's leg with her head. In
return, the little girl smiled and petted her gently.

*Opening the door wider, I tried to determine what to do next. I've
got to keep her here long enough so that I can call Larlene. What can
I give her?*

"Wait here. I'll be right back." I held up one finger indicating
that she should wait a minute and rushed quickly to the kitchen.

It took a few moments, but I was finally able to find a box of
semi-stale chocolate chip cookies that I hadn't polished off yet. I
quickly returned to the door with my box of cookies, but the girl
had disappeared, leaving Jane alone in the doorway.

I went outside and looked around, but she was gone. Almost
as if she'd evaporated into thin air.

After a few more minutes of searching, I finally turned
around and walked back to my apartment. But I didn't shut the
door just yet. Instead, I stood and stared out into the distance
and watched the sun begin to set behind the clouds while the

warm winds continued to tousle my hair. My eyes were wet with tears, but my resolve was solid.

I thought about my father and our last moments together.

It was the beginning and the end.

Sleeping Beauty had indeed awakened and was ready to face the evils that lay ahead.

CHILD OF THE DEAD

Chapter 1

The wind talks to me.

Ever since I was a child, I have always loved to listen to the gusts moan in anticipation of an oncoming thunderstorm. As the trees sway and bend in rhythm to the wind's song, I listen to their music.

The wind is a perfect example of something that is normally ignored by most people.

I am not like most people.

The world has become a strange and mysterious place ever since I first saw my father's ghost in the library where I work. Before that, I was a small-town librarian who did my job, went home to my best friend Jane, who just happens to be a dog, and immersed myself in the land of imagination on TV, or in the pages of a good book.

But then I started seeing dead people. Everything changed after that.

It's a gift or so I've been told by some of the spirits who've befriended me. One of the wisest spirits—Adahy, a Native American shaman who lived way back in colonial times—told me that my gift is something to be revered as well as feared. He also foretold that there were more trials ahead, and that my ability to exorcise a demon out of my friend's mother was just the beginning of my journey.

My ability to see the dead also led me to the love of my life. Cole.

Cole had been killed during colonial times in a duel gone wrong and was never able to pass along to the Great Beyond. Instead, my handsome lover roamed the halls of my friend

Bobbie Trillo's home in Macon, Georgia until we crossed paths during my visit. His black hair, intense dark eyes, and lean, muscular build made me weak with desire, but it was his powerful, yet gentle soul that I connected with.

After I'd exorcised the demon Elial from Bobbie's mother, the horrific creature entered my body and it was only through the help of a mystical ghostly woman that I was able to banish him for good. The woman remains a mystery to me, though I am determined to find her again, one day.

But Cole had disappeared from sight, and I'd returned home to Cale in a state of despair. Despite trying to forget him and immersing myself in work—even going on a date with another man—nothing helped. I was near the end of my sanity, when Cole finally appeared to me and professed his love.

It was the first time I'd ever made love to someone who touched the innermost depths of my heart and soul. And, of course there was the small matter of Cole being a ghost.

Since Cole's return a few weeks ago, my life has been hazy and out of focus. Unlike most spirits, Cole is able to regenerate his inner energy so that his manifestations last longer. And he is able to touch me without losing his essence.

In some ways, this is an incredible advantage because we can interact for hours. Sometimes Cole is able to maintain a bodily form for nearly half a day before vanishing. But it also creates a conundrum, because he follows me around at work. I know I sound ungrateful to have a sexy man following me around all day. But I'm the only one who can see him, so I have to work twice as hard to not get caught talking to him, otherwise the library patrons and staff would think I was off my rocker.

To make matters even trickier, my close friend Larlene also knows about Cole. We work together and we're passionate about books and literacy. But other than that, the only thing Larlene and I have in common is that we both have brown eyes. As for the rest, Larlene is about six-feet tall, with big brown hair and a personality to match. I'm five-feet-four and a redhead, and while my temper can certainly get the best of me sometimes, I'm usually pretty low key and quiet. Larlene, on the other hand is extremely social and outgoing. She's also very blunt and can make me blush in an instant with all her questions about Cole's "manliness." So, I try to keep our discussions about him to a minimum.

This is my life. And I wouldn't have it any other way.

"So, is he here?" she asked me for the hundredth time that day.

Thankfully, Cole had run out of energy and had disappeared to regenerate so I didn't have to worry about lying to her.

"No, he's not. He's…resting."

Larlene snorted and looked me straight in the eye. "Renda, I know you're tired of hearing the same questions all the time, but I think it's totally cool that you have this majorly hot guy who is available whenever you need him."

I laughed at her blunt observation. It truly was wonderful having Cole with me, and he'd changed my life for the better. We watched movies together, took long walks through town, and just spent time getting to know each other. It wasn't always easy when we were in public, because to the common eye it appeared as if I were alone—but it didn't matter.

I never felt alone.

Cole made me feel like I was finally a part of something. Being adopted into a family of two very loquacious parents was something I appreciated, but never quite felt comfortable with. I was an introvert, who spent more time thinking than talking while my adoptive parents were very gregarious people. At parties, they could fill the room with their stories, and bask in the spotlight. Not that I wanted attention. I was always quite happy just blending in.

But with Cole, it was never uncomfortable or strange. He listened better than anyone I'd ever met, and never judged me when I was tired and didn't feel like talking. Our personalities flowed together like the gentle currents of a stream.

There were times when we didn't even have to speak at all. We would just lie on my bed and gaze at each other. Those moments, while very intense and romantic, also frightened me because I could feel my heart growing larger and larger as if it would nearly explode. In all of my almost-29-years of life, I'd never felt that way about another person. So vulnerable.

"Hey, are you listening? I was telling you about the Marcks. They have a daughter, Katie, who's been acting strange lately."

Larlene's question pulled my thoughts away from Cole, and I remembered the little girl we'd seen roaming the cemetery. We were driving by at the time, and saw her dancing among the gravestones. A strange sight indeed.

Even more strange—hours later she showed up on my doorstep. And when I turned away to get her some cookies, she'd disappeared. I had no idea how she'd made it to my house on her own.

A week had gone by, and I could only assume that this little girl was indeed Katie Marck.

"Larlene, I think I've seen this little girl. Last week she came to visit me."

"She did? Why didn't you say anything?"

I wasn't sure why I hadn't mentioned it. Perhaps I'd been so wrapped up in Cole that the rest of the world had taken a back seat. Or, maybe, I just didn't want to deal with it. Part of my so-called gift opened me up to things that were dark and dangerous, and I'd been so happy with Cole that everything else seemed like an unnecessary risk.

But now, I felt guilty. Clearly there was something strange going on with Katie and instead of trying to help her, I was hiding away in the arms of my lover.

"I'm sorry. You're right, I should have told you. It just slipped my mind. So, what's going on with her?"

Larlene sat in a nearby chair and motioned for me to join her. The library was quiet, so we had a rare chance for privacy.

"Well, you know a little bit about what's going on, but things are getting worse. Katie is disappearing from her bedroom at night and her parents are finding her outside in her pajamas. The weird thing is that she's often just standing in place—like she's a statue or something, you know?"

Given my new circumstances, I'd been reading a bit about possessions and hauntings, and a passage from one of the books suddenly came back to me.

The haunted subject is sometimes overcome by spirits or demons in its realm. This can lead to momentary paralysis or even put the subject into a catatonic state. The subject will often appear to sleepwalk and find himself/herself in an unknown location, having walked for several hours, unaware. In such situations, it is best to lead the subject back to safety and allow for sleep to take hold. After the subject has rested, it is unwise to ask questions about the event, as there will be no recollection of it ever having taken place. Paranormal experts however, do recommend keeping a close eye on the affected person as they can be a danger to themselves if they wander into a body of water or a busy street, as has been reported in many instances of fatalities associated with such occurrences.

The book had gone on to describe what kinds of behaviors were associated with a possession and what were specific to a haunting. The differences were pretty easy to identify, if you knew what you were looking for. What Larlene was describing to me didn't sound like a possession, but more like a haunting. I wasn't sure how I felt about this, because I'd never handled a haunting before—other than my own.

But either way, there was no time to waste.

"I'd like to meet her."

Chapter 2

Despite my best efforts, Larlene insisted that she drive and accompany me to the Marcks' place. So after work, I went home to walk Jane, and then Larlene picked me up.

Larlene had called the Marcks while we were still at work, and I could see the conversation had been tense. Her normally cheerful face was scrunched up in concern as her eyes darted back and forth from me to the floor. It didn't seem like the Marcks were all that happy about me visiting them, but she insisted, and they finally conceded to talk about what was happening to their little girl.

On the ride over, I looked over at Larlene who was gripping the steering wheel tightly and staring straight ahead.

"Are you okay?" I asked. She seemed stressed out.

"Yeah, I'm fine. It's just that Katie's mother, Anne, isn't the easiest person to get along with. I know her from some volunteer work I used to do at the animal shelter. She's kind of quiet, but she's got a pretty sharp tongue sometimes. I think she's going through a rough patch because her husband was out of work for a long time. Money was tight, and they had to move to a different part of town. Lots of people around here judge. It's been hard on her family. So, just be aware that while she wants your help, she's not going to be very friendly."

I didn't respond and just stared out my window. Why was I even willing to help these people if they weren't sure whether or not they wanted my help? It just made things more difficult. It reminded me of when I told my friend Bobbie that her mother was possessed. Her initial resistance to believing me made things much more difficult. If I was facing the same challenges with Katie's parents, it could make things tough from the very beginning.

Larlene pulled down a street that I wasn't familiar with. The houses weren't the nicest, and it was in an area that was inhabited by mostly blue-collar laborers. The area wasn't in the slums per se, but it was definitely a step below middle class.

Children stared at us as our car drove past. Many of the homes were in some state of disrepair and the front yards were littered with broken-down vehicles, rusting bicycles, and a few had cars resting on cinder blocks.

The Marcks' house was small like the other homes on the block with bars over the windows, and a fragile roof in need of repair. But it was freshly painted in a muted gray, as though they didn't want to attract attention to themselves.

A few stuffed animals sat on a plastic lawn chair on the neatly trimmed grass, smiling a perpetual greeting.

We approached the screen door and rang the doorbell.

No one answered, and we stood awkwardly waiting for someone to let us in. After a few moments of silence, Larlene reached over to ring the bell again when the door opened.

The little girl who I'd met the week before, the one dancing amongst the gravestones, stared at us from the doorway. She was barefoot and wearing faded pink leggings with a long purple T-shirt that had a picture of a princess on the front. Her pretty blonde hair was tied in a high ponytail with a little pink elastic band. Even in her worn-out garb, she was a beautiful little girl. Her big, round eyes were a deep blue, her smile of greeting bright and welcoming.

I was taken by how happy she was to see us. The last time I saw her she'd known about me somehow, but hadn't seemed all that comfortable in my presence. She'd disappeared shortly after arriving at my apartment. But now, Katie was all smiles.

"Hi, I'm Katie. Do you want to come in? Mommy's in the kitchen."

Larlene nodded and I followed her inside.

The muggy interior was a clear indication that the Marcks were trying to save money on electricity. I wondered how they managed to get through each day coping with the Florida heat.

Inside, the sliding windows were open, letting in the occasional feeble cross-breeze. In the living room, a loveseat that had seen better days was made more cheery by a colorful quilt. Two wooden chairs with worn upholstered cushions stood on either side of the loveseat. On the walls were framed drawings of trees, puppies, and kittens—no doubt Katie's creations.

Sweat beaded my forehead and I wiped it away as we entered the small kitchen. The aroma of stew from a crockpot hung heavily in the humid air.

Interestingly, Anne Marck was already seated at the compact wooden table. The slim, dark-haired woman clutched a glass of iced tea, the condensation leaving a small ring of water on the tabletop.

Oddly, she didn't offer us something to drink or even get up to greet us. Instead, she simply glanced in our direction and motioned for us to sit down. She also told Katie to go "play in her room" with a limp wave of her hand.

"I'm sorry," she said softly, tucking a strand of hair behind her ear. "We're just exhausted. Katie's been a real handful lately."

Her greeting gave me a quick chance to introduce myself. "Hi," I said. "I'm Renda Bloodmane. Nice to meet you."

"My name's Anne," she replied. "And I know who you are. I'm just not sure if you can help us."

Larlene cleared her throat and attempted to intervene. "Hey, let's not make any assumptions right away. Renda's done some amazing things and she may be able to help Katie. Just give her a chance."

Anne turned her gaze to me, her blue eyes, so like her daughter's, were fixed intently on mine. It made me uncomfortable, and I instinctively wanted to look away. But I steadied my gaze and forced a smile to my lips.

"Why don't you tell me what's going on with your daughter?"

Anne blew out a breath, but said nothing. I patiently waited, gazing back at her, until she looked away and began speaking. And what she told us was chilling...

It began six months ago, when the Marcks went to the cemetery to visit the resting place of Gertrude Dexler, Anne's mother.

The woman had passed away the year before, and the Marcks made it a point to visit her grave regularly. During their visits, they would place a bouquet of flowers on her headstone and take some time for contemplation.

On this one particular visit, Katie was bored and kicking rocks along the ground. She was singing songs out of tune, irritating her parents who were trying to focus on the moment.

Not even thinking about it, Anne motioned to a nearby tree. "Why don't you go play by that tree, Katie? Give Mommy and Daddy a few moments alone."

Katie smiled, exposing her missing front teeth, and ran off in the direction of a large oak tree that shaded a wrought iron bench, painted white.

About fifteen minutes later, Anne went to look for her daughter and couldn't find the little girl.

"Katie!" she called out, a worried frown marring her brow.

"Brent," she said to her husband. "I think Katie's run off somewhere. Can you help me find her?"

They searched the nearby graves, but Katie was nowhere to be found. Anne's heart pounded in her chest and perspiration began to drip down her back. The fear of losing her child to some perverted, horrible predator flashed through her mind, and she forced it away.

Suddenly, she could feel eyes watching her. Turning her head, Anne saw Katie behind a large, ornately carved headstone. Two angels reached out to each other from opposite ends of the stone, their fingertips touching.

"Katie? Katie, what are you doing?"

No reply.

Katie was crouched up in a ball. Her arms were wrapped around her legs and her head was down as she rocked back and forth.

Anne reached out to touch her daughter's shoulder when Katie suddenly looked up at her.

Her eyes were entirely black.

Stunned, Anne stumbled back and nearly tripped over a random pile of rocks that lay nearby. As she reached out to steady herself, she could see that Katie was now standing and looking a bit frightened.

Her eyes were normal once more.

"What happened? Why are you hiding over here?" Anne asked, trying to calm her trembling voice.

"I saw the people," Katie said. "They were really sad, but when they saw me, they started to smile. They wanted me to play with them, so I went over to where they were. But they are really hard to see. So, I had to sit and concentrate. Is that okay?"

Anne wasn't sure how to react. Katie seemed all right and no worse for wear so she decided to simply lead the child back to her husband. And, for some reason, she didn't share with him what had just happened. The whole situation felt so surreal that she couldn't bring herself to repeat it.

But things started to escalate after that. At first, Anne would hear Katie talking in her room. She'd check on her and Katie would be staring at the wall as if there was someone there. But the room was always empty.

Several times Brent saw strange shadows move along Katie's bedroom walls and then disappear as he approached. At first, he thought it was the nightlight, or a car driving by, but then he witnessed something that chilled him to the bone...

One night he'd gone into Katie's room to check on her and a dark cloud was floating above Katie's bed, with a claw protruding from its center. It seemed to be reaching for the little girl, as if to pull her into its blackness.

Brent swept Katie up in his arms, ran to his own bedroom, and placed her in bed with Anne. He then ran back to Katie's room but the cloud had vanished.

Since that night they had allowed Katie to sleep with them, and everything seemed peaceful for a few days until their daughter began asking if she could play at the cemetery. Concerned once more, they said no. "The cemetery is not a place for a child to play," they told her.

But Katie didn't listen. Given that it was only a ten-minute walk from their home, she was able to sneak away on three separate occasions. And each time, Anne would find her daughter sitting in front of the *angel headstone or on the white, wrought iron bench under the oak tree chatting animatedly to herself...*

At this point, Anne stopped talking. With a shaky hand, she picked up a spoon, plunging it into the glass. She stirred the liquid, watching as the red-brown surface twisted and turned in a miniature whirlpool.

I felt like this was the point where I was supposed to say something, but Larlene jumped in first.

"Soooo...that's really crazy. But like I told you, Renda has experience with this stuff and she might be able to help you. Right, Renda?"

Clearing my throat, I tried to think of something to say. I hadn't really experienced anything strange since we'd been in the house, because I'd forgotten to turn on my special sight that allows me to see the dead.

While in Macon, a friendly spirit had explained to me that this ability wasn't always active, which was a good thing because otherwise, I would have a hard time functioning. The dead are all around us and if I had my sight on all the time, I'd be too busy gaping at the spirits floating around me to get anything done. So I had it "turned off" most of the time. In order to turn the ability back on, I had to mentally lift an invisible lever in my mind, which in turn, switched on my inner sight.

To be honest, part of me was afraid to turn it on. I wasn't sure exactly what was happening to Katie, but it sounded like she was being haunted by numerous spirits, and I wasn't really all that eager to meet them. Still, both Anne and Larlene were staring at me expectantly and I knew I needed to do something.

"Okay, let me see if I can figure out what's happening," I said, and stood up.

Very carefully, I closed my eyes and lifted the lever in my mind. I could feel the telltale shift of the world around me as the middle realm came closer to my energy and revealed itself. Sometimes, when I lifted the lever, I felt as if the world was slightly hazy, and I was walking through air that was heavier than normal—almost like a fog.

When I opened my eyes, I was staring straight at the living

room, away from Larlene and Anne. Everything looked the same, just a bit darker than before, which was normal in my altered state.

Suddenly, I heard low ominous murmurings coming from what I could only assume was the child's room, down the hall. The house was small enough for me to easily identify where the bedrooms were located.

The door to Katie's bedroom was shut, but it was obviously her room because of the cheerfully painted sign that bore her name.

The sounds were much louder now, but they sounded strange to me in that they weren't the voices of young spirits, which I initially assumed were contacting her. They sounded low and rough and spoke in a strange dialect.

I touched the knob unsteadily, and as soon as my hand connected with the metal, the murmuring stopped. Silence enveloped me and the only thing I could hear was my own shallow breathing.

Slowly opening the door, I looked inside and was greeted by an explosion of pink.

It had all the makings of a childhood fantasy. Princesses danced in a painted mural spanning the entire room. A collection of dolls of various sizes, sat smiling on a small shelf in the corner. Katie's bed was covered in a beautiful pink and purple hand-made quilt that rivaled the one on the loveseat.

Despite their financial situation, Katie's parents had clearly put a great deal of effort into the whimsical space. It looked like the bedroom of a very perky little girl, but where was Katie?

A low shuffling sound came from inside the closet. A painted purple vine with little pink flowers adorned the door with a jaunty flair.

"Katie?" I called out, approaching the closet.

A little giggle greeted my question, and I smiled. The little rascal was playing hide-and-seek.

I reached out and turned the doorknob. As expected, Katie was sitting on the floor of her closet. Surrounded by toys, she looked up at me with a smile.

"Hi! Did you come to play with me? They told me you'd come."

I knelt down so that we were eye level. There was no hint of guile in her eyes, just a shining purity bestowed upon the young and innocent. It touched me for some reason, and I gently lifted a strand of golden hair that had fallen over her eyes, and tucked it behind her ear. "Yes, I've come to play with you. Can I sit here beside you?"

"Sure. What's your name again?"

"Renda."

Katie moved over and we sat together in the cramped closet. I looked around, hoping to see some of the spirits who'd been talking to her, but there was nothing there.

Settling back against the wall in the closet, I took a deep breath and chose my words carefully. Despite not knowing much about Katie or the spirits that haunted her, I didn't want to appear too inquisitive so I chose to be more matter-of-fact in my tone. "It's fun talking to spirits, isn't it?"

The little girl gave me a small smile and looked around furtively. "Yes, they keep me company. And I like them. But sometimes, they're very loud and don't let me concentrate."

"Really?" I asked, trying to keep the concern out of my voice. "What do you mean? Do they bother you? Do they ever scare you?"

Katie shook her head, her expressive eyes wide, "No, they don't scare me. But they do bother me sometimes. Some of them are...they're old and weird. And they speak in weird voices."

My heart started beating quickly. "Weird? Do they act weird?"

"No, they just look weird...Kind of wrinkled and strange. Almost like little old people...There's one!"

I turned my head and there he was.

A small man was standing just outside the open closet door. He was wrinkled, with white hair standing up in all directions. He wore brown trousers, a dingy shirt that most likely used to be white, a skinny blue tie, and a gray overcoat. He carried a walking stick in one hand. His clothes didn't look modern, but were certainly from the late 20th century. There was no indication as to how he'd died, which was commonly recognizable in many of the spirits I encountered. But one thing was for certain. He didn't appreciate my intrusion.

His eyes glared at me and he *growled* as I gaped at him in shock. Then he vanished into thin air, leaving us both sitting in stunned silence. For a moment, I couldn't think of anything to say. But, Katie launched a bunch of confused questions at me.

"Why was he so mad? They've never been mad before. They're always so nice to me. Why was he mad, Miss Renda?"

I wasn't sure. But whatever the reason, it couldn't be good.

"Thanks so much for having us over, Anne," Larlene said as we headed for the front door.

I'd sat with Katie in her closet for a while longer, but nothing else had manifested. It was extremely odd, because normally, spirits weren't afraid to approach me and openly came into my space. Sometimes they were aware I could see them, and other times, they simply didn't care. But this time, the room had remained empty as if the spirits knew I could see them and weren't happy about it.

It was an unusual experience, and the first time something like that had occurred since my second sight had manifested. I made a mental note to visit Katie again and figure out how to make the creatures show themselves.

They won't be able to hide from me.

Anne didn't seem all that thrilled about allowing me to spend more time with Katie but eventually, she conceded and agreed to make plans for me to visit one afternoon after work.

It wasn't going to be easy to dedicate this much time to the little girl because I had a life after all, and I didn't want to miss out on my limited time with Cole. But I figured he could accompany me and provide some much-needed guidance if things got too complicated. He might also be able to communicate directly with unfriendly spirits should we encounter any.

As I adjusted my seatbelt on the passenger side of Larlene's car, I noticed Katie watching me from the window. I swallowed a sudden lump that formed in my throat.

Her mouth was turned down and her eyes gazed at me forlornly.

I silently vowed to do whatever it took to help her.

Chapter 3

As Larlene pulled up to my place, anticipation bubbled in my chest. I hadn't seen Cole all day and knew that he would be arriving soon. It typically took him half a day to regenerate so that he'd be able to spend ample time with me, and once he returned, he was full of energy.

Oftentimes, full of sexual energy.

Anxious to see him, I gave Larlene a hug goodbye and hurried into my cozy apartment. As soon as I opened the door, Jane came bounding out and nearly knocked me over.

A hearty, yellow Labrador, Jane was named after my favorite author Jane Austen. She was typically ready to race around the neighborhood several times when I got home from work. But after doing her business in the front yard, she had enough sense to realize that her owner and best human friend was too tired to go for a jog. It was part of the strange but beautiful bond we shared, and one that I was thankful for.

"Okay, let's finish up and head back inside," I said as she raced around looking for the perfect spot to pee.

As I watched her, a gentle breeze kissed my forehead, and I relaxed for the first time all day. It was good to be home.

Without warning, male arms crushed me against a firm chest.

I gasped down to my core, a delicious shiver running through me.

Turning around, I beamed at the handsome, strong face of Cole Drake. He was my lover, my confidant, and my best friend in the world. Despite the fact that he was dead, I was falling hopelessly in love with him.

My inner voice niggled me about getting too involved.

I ignored it.

At least, for now.

As Cole and I kissed, Jane grew irritated at being ignored and nudged the back of my legs with her wet nose, pushing me toward the door.

Laughing, I petted her soft head and we headed inside.

Sharing a meal with Cole had initially been a strange experience. After all, he was dead and therefore didn't need food or drink, so it was always slightly awkward eating in front of him.

As I scarfed down my turkey sandwich, a typical Renda-hates-to-cook-meal, Cole shook his head as he watched me eat.

"What?" I asked around a mouthful of turkey.

"That can't be healthy," he said arching a thick, black brow, and pointing to the bag of potato chips beside my plate. Cole had told me about the food he'd eaten when he was alive. Yes, in colonial times they didn't have processed food or junk food. Everything they ate, they either hunted or grew themselves.

I arched my eyebrow back at him and popped a few chips into my mouth, crunching loudly.

"How about you let me cook for you?" he asked. "I'm not a professional chef by your modern-day standards, but if you bought some proper groceries, I could make something healthier for you."

Shaking my head, I took one more bite of my sandwich and left the rest on my plate. Cole was caring and I loved him but sometimes he was a know-it-all. I sighed and stared out the window. I had more important things to worry about than eating a gourmet meal.

"Look, something happened today that you should know about. I've been asked to help with a haunting. Or at least, I think it's a haunting."

Cole reached out and squeezed my hand. His energy gently seeped into my skin, immediately filling me with warmth. Concern glimmered in his eyes. He was right to be worried. I'd barely survived my last attempt at trying to "save" someone.

Settling back in my chair, I recapped what happened at the

Marcks' home. I described Katie and reminded him of the day we'd seen her dancing at the cemetery.

Cole listened carefully until I was done and then stood up and paced the room.

"The man you saw in her room. It sounds as if he was like me, a person who walks between the realms. But I am concerned at his reaction. There are those of us who have averted the gateway to Hell through the ability to haunt and consume souls. Those spirits are quite dangerous, Renda. You don't want to spar with them."

"I may not have a choice," I said, my voice rising in indignation. "There's a little girl whose life may be at stake here. Something is really wrong, and she's being targeted by these spirits. I need to find out why."

Cole walked up to me and put his hands on my shoulders. "Well, at least let me help you. You don't have to handle this by yourself. Not anymore."

I smiled and kissed his cheek. But inside, anxiety was wrapping itself around my heart.

Trying to get our minds off the stress of the day, we took a bath together. As the warm water enveloped us in a gentle cocoon, I used the bath sponge to gently massage Cole's muscular chest and arms. It still amazed me that when he manifested, his body was so solid. So present. And yet as the hours passed, I knew that this strong, virile man would eventually vanish into ghostly energy once more.

He smiled and leaned his head back as I rubbed the sponge up and down his chest.

It was so strange to touch a man in such an openly sensual manner. In all my life, I'd never been so free, so wanton. But with Cole, everything seemed easy and when he took the sponge out of my hand and began to kiss me, I allowed him to pull my slippery body on top of his.

His hardening erection pressed against my sex in an urgency that revealed his passion. Together we rubbed and touched, until his cock was resting against my opening and then I gasped as he entered me with one strong thrust.

Moaning, he rocked against me as our passions ignited hotter and hotter. Cole never climaxed the way living men did—that is, he never ejaculated within me. But he did spasm violently when he reached orgasm, his penis throbbing inside me.

And as we exploded together, in our unique way, I soared up and up as every cell in my body, every fiber of my being, cried out in pleasure and love. For this man—this ghostly, handsome creature—had completely and utterly captivated me.

After the bath, we dried off and snuggled in bed together. I cherished these moments of complete intimacy and peace, fully aware that soon Cole would vanish, and I would wake up alone. When we made love, he disappeared sooner than usual, because of the energy he expended.

As he described it to me, it was harder to recycle his life force when he was focused on achieving sexual release. The very nature of the act caused him to lose valuable reserves of power.

So I knew time was short and could already see his skin becoming pale and translucent.

It was one of those ever-constant reminders that despite our deepening relationship, we had embarked on a strange journey that was unknown to both of us. In the past, I never felt the need to confide in others about my life, because I was content being on my own. But since getting involved with Cole, I wished I had someone else to share my feelings with about what was happening.

I thought about Adahy, the Native American spirit who'd helped me at the Trillos' and had served as my spiritual guide. I hadn't seen him since I'd left Georgia, and oftentimes I wondered if he'd ever come back. He was incredibly wise, and I knew he could help me figure everything out.

But he remained elusive, and when I asked Cole about him, I couldn't get a straight answer. Instead, my beautiful spirit lover would gaze off into the distance and make some remark about Adahy being "anchored" to the house in Macon and reluctant to leave the other spirits who relied on his wisdom.

It seemed strange that Adahy remained out of sight because, after all, he'd been the one to help Cole figure out how to regenerate his energy and travel the distance to find me. But, he wasn't able or willing to take his own advice. And now, Katie Marck presented a new challenge that I wasn't sure I could handle without him.

As Cole disappeared back to his strange limbo state where he was able to regenerate and conduct a form of "spirit sleep" as he called it, I lay in bed thinking about Katie.

She was so small and vulnerable. Even though I sensed that she was blessed—or cursed—with a similar type of gift as me, given her tender age, she seemed unable to handle the changes that were occurring. It also didn't appear that she could decipher which spirits were good and which ones were dangerous.

The curse of the innocent.

I remembered reading in one of my books that children were often victims of evil spirits, because they were entirely too trusting and were so excited that someone from the "ghostly" world was communicating with them that they often became conduits—pulling in the energy around them and not discriminating against the darkness.

The strange and scary man in her room wasn't a friendly spirit, but why hadn't Katie deflected his advances? When I'd asked her about him, she'd been vague and just giggled. I wasn't sure whether it was nerves or simply childish behavior that led to her actions.

And how was I to help her? Where was I going to start?

The cemetery.

Cale's cemetery was the main location for most of the burials in town and was also home to a large mausoleum that offered a final resting place for the town's elite who had gone to the Great Beyond.

I'd never visited the Cale Cemetery. My parents had never allowed me to go when I was growing up. If they ever had to attend a funeral they preferred that I stayed home, telling me that a cemetery was no place for a child. Even after my grandmother died, my parents insisted that I not accompany them to the graveside service.

At the time, I hadn't really minded. The idea of spending time amongst the dead wasn't appealing. But now, I wondered why they'd been so adamant that I stay away. Had there been a reason? It was difficult for me to recall, but somewhere in the back of my mind there was a memory starting to emerge.

I can't do this right now. Too tired. Need sleep.

Outside, the crickets cheerfully congregated to produce some of nature's most beautiful music. I listened to them chirp and sing and my eyelids grew heavy.

But before I fell asleep, I couldn't help thinking of little Katie in her pink room, in the little house on the other side of town.

Chapter 4

Iwas lying in bed, when inexplicably, my body lifted and I was sitting upright, but floating in mid-air. Ghostly white-robed figures walked by me, on either side of my bed, in an eerie, silent procession. Stunned, I tried to scream for them to go away but no sound would come from my throat.

I woke up screaming.

Jane barked at me as I sat up in bed, a sweaty, terrified mess.

Though my nightmare had been brief, my heart pounded like a wild bird in my chest.

The darkness seemed less ominous now, and I wondered why I'd been so frightened. It wasn't like I'd never seen ghosts before.

But these ghosts seemed...different. Bone-chilling cold shook me to the core as they'd shuffled by me, almost as if they were devoid of any essence or energy. Not spirits of the dead, but different entities altogether.

It was impossible to fall back asleep. I stared at the ceiling and tried to think of calming thoughts but my brain raced over the events that had unfolded in the past twenty-four hours.

I got out of bed and paced the apartment. Walking through the darkened living room, I passed the windows and paused to pull back one of the blinds. Jane got up from her dog bed and came pattering after me. She sat up, her head tilted to one side, a curious look on her face.

Outside, the night was clear and calm. The trees were still, indicating a high level of humidity. The roads were empty as if the world were "on hold" until the sun came up.

But I knew better.

Before my mind could kick into full gear, I pulled on a pair of sweatpants and sneakers, then grabbed a T-shirt from the dresser.

Jane whined and looked at me as if I were crazy.

I wondered if she was right, but knew that I had to go. It was time to see it for myself and now was as good a time as any.

The cemetery.

Maybe I was crazy, and I knew that Cole would be furious with me, but there was something driving my actions. I wasn't sure if it was Katie's innocent face, or the odd creature I'd seen in her bedroom, or maybe the dream I'd just had. But nothing was going to stop me.

As I opened the front door, Jane bounded out ahead into the night. She didn't even look back, and simply went straight to my car as if to say, "Don't even think about going to that place without me."

Sighing, I opened the door to the backseat and let her in.

Once my dog was safely inside, I got into the driver's seat and backed out of the driveway, turning onto the main road and heading straight toward Cale's main cemetery.

As I drove, my gaze fixed on the inky ribbon of pavement, the night's darkness welcoming me into its solitude.

The roads were deserted, making the drive an easy one. At night, the streetlights in Cale were left in the "hazard" position and simply blinked yellow or red, so I was able to easily maneuver through the town until I arrived at the wrought iron gates that greeted visitors to the final resting place of their loved ones.

I pulled into the empty parking lot of the cemetery. Eerie shadows slithered along the ground, illuminated by the blue-white glow of the moonlight slicing through the heavy branches.

In the back seat, Jane whined, clearly not wanting to be in a cemetery in the middle of the night. She seemed to be arguing with me in her canine-manner to turn the car around and go back home.

Well, it certainly wasn't my favorite place to be either, but I'd come this far, and I was determined to investigate.

Stepping out of the car, I mentally turned my "spirit sight" back on and waited a moment to get my bearings. I'd learned over the past few weeks that sometimes spirits could be very close by, so it's best not to rush into any situation.

Thankfully, the spirits hadn't ventured into the parking lot. It was strange to be alone here, surrounded by burial plots and yet so much natural life—trees, birds, insects, squirrels.

Jane exited the car and nervously paced around the vehicle. Instead of marking her spot as she normally did, she stayed close to me and whined every now and then.

Taking a deep breath, I mustered up all the courage I had.

"Okay, girl. Let's go. "

Together we walked from the parking lot to the cemetery gate. To my relief it wasn't locked and we were able to get in. A paved path began at the gate and wound its way through the cemetery, taking visitors past rows of headstones, and ending at a dome-shaped mausoleum with white arches.

My blood chilled as spirits began to appear around me, first as orbs of light then as human specters. They were of different ages and races, all showing me how they died, and despite the fact that I had grown used to seeing ghostly figures it was always a shock at first.

The spirits I came in contact with hadn't moved on. Instead, they were stuck in between the realm of the living and the road to their final passage.

They floated through this world, unable to let go or cross over, anchored here by thwarted loves, lives caught short, and sometimes...with vendettas that they could never carry out.

Cole had been one of those spirits, until he'd met me. He could have crossed over to the Other Side, but he'd chosen to stay with me and haunt my world instead.

And I was thankful for that—despite knowing in my heart that it was a selfish desire.

But right now, Cole was in a different realm altogether, and I was walking through a cemetery in the dead of night with my loyal dog to protect me.

It was pure insanity.

The spirits were everywhere now—orbs floating past my

head and swirling around us as we walked along the path.

Jane snorted and shook her snout as if to ward them off. She seemed to tolerate them, like pesky flies. The only spirit she reacted positively to was Cole. She adored Cole.

I wasn't sure what we would find. Yes, there were dead people all around us, but they were harmless, pathetic creatures scurrying and shuffling about.

One woman sat atop a headstone, talking to herself, a gaping wound in her chest—her cause of death. A man sat on the ground near her, reading a book with sightless eyes.

Despite it all, we kept moving.

We'd walked halfway through the cemetery, when I saw the mausoleum. Its huge dome glowed in the moonlight, the columns on either side stood as silent sentinels. I was about to take a step forward, when a voice from behind me called out.

"Renda."

I turned around to face a spirit I hadn't seen in many weeks.

Adahy hovered in the shadows, gazing at me with solemn eyes, his lips set in a firm line. Dressed in traditional Native American garb from the early days of the Americas colonization, his body was lean and well-toned, even though he'd been very old when he'd died. A headdress of feathers rested atop his long, wavy gray hair.

Even though I was happy to see him, I was surprised that Adahy had ventured miles away from Macon. A complex and wise sage, Adahy hadn't been comfortable traveling away from the Trillos' home and had remained there for years with the spirits that roamed the mansion. He was often a comfort to the younger creatures who hadn't passed over to the afterlife and who needed guidance.

Adahy had also been the one to guide Cole towards me, teaching him how to regenerate energy in a manner that would allow him to be touched without the telltale draining of the source that kept manifestations present. But Adahy himself was never interested or perhaps even capable of traveling long distances, and I'd often thought about him and wondered how he was doing. The sage knew quite a bit about me somehow, and had warned me about a challenging future ahead.

Instinctively, I stepped closer and reached out to give the spirit a warm welcome, but he moved back.

"No, Renda. My energy is weak. As you know, I'm unaccustomed to traveling away from my central source and it's taken quite some effort for me to visit you. But now that I'm here, we must talk. Quickly."

"Okay, I'm sorry. It's just very good to see you."

The sage smiled at me, but the sound of Jane whining caught his attention. "Your companion is nervous for you. And she's right to be worried. Renda, you shouldn't be here. You're not ready yet."

His words both frightened and irritated me.

"What do you mean? I'm not doing anything wrong. I'm just—"

"You're stepping into darkness that is beyond your knowledge," he interrupted. "I have foreseen the journey you've begun and it's not safe for you. The spirits haunting the child aren't strangers to you or your family. You must be careful."

The world seemed to have grown darker around me. I shivered and stepped closer to Adahy. "Are these spirits demons? Like Elial?"

I often thought of Elial, the demon who'd possessed my friend Bobbie's mother. The creature had been known as the "Demon of the Woods" and had one objective—to attach to his female victims and slowly suck the life out of them. Thankfully, I'd intervened but I knew that Elial wasn't dead. He was just weakened and would soon move on to his next victim. That was the way demons operated.

Adahy shook his head. "No, they're not demons who are fallen angels, seeking revenge on the human race to spite their former father, God. These are true evil spirits...people who died, but were so entirely blackened in spirit that they scorned the light and were shunned from Hell because of their desire to outrank Lucifer himself.

"These are terrible entities that have no interest in anything but capturing the life spirit of a human and destroying anything or anyone that comes between them and their objective. They are responsible for terrible tragedies including insanity, suicides, murder, even wars. They are able to cloud thought, possess, and destroy. We call them the "Rashas," which means the "evil ones" in the language of the Judaic ancients."

I was having a hard time processing this.

Worse than demons? How could that be possible?

Memories of the battle against Elial flashed in my memory...

The feeling of possession as the demon penetrated my skin and wrapped himself like a serpent around my soul...The evil eating into my veins like a spiritual cancer...The final expulsion of the creature as his vile energy flew out of me like putrid phlegm.

How could anything be worse than that?

"Rashas do not commonly venture to places of heavy spiritual gatherings," Adahy continued, taking my silence as a cue to keep going. "Before today, you've never seen any. They don't like to congregate with the more peaceful spirits and only travel in packs of their own. But now that they've encountered you, you are in great danger. They feel your energy and are trying to lure you into their dark grasp. They want you and all that you represent. Do you understand?"

Nodding slowly, I looked toward the mausoleum. It was very dark, but I could now see shapes curling around the corners like tendrils of smoke reaching out to the oxygenated sky. Adrenaline started to pump through my veins and I realized that Jane and I needed to get out of the cemetery.

Quickly.

When I turned back to Adahy, he was gone but I could hear his voice in the air, "Run, Renda. Run!"

Jane barked and began to race back toward the car.

I followed Jane as fast as I could, my shoes slapping against the concrete. Behind me, I could hear wailing. It started out as a low hum, and then began to pick up speed and intensity. Soon, other voices joined in the wailing, like an eerie chorus. I could hear it echo all around me.

Impossibly, the air began to shift and pull me back, as though a giant vacuum cleaner was trying to suck me into a dark void. As I ran, I could feel my clothes lift and stretch as the force of the wind pulled on them, but even though there were horrible sounds behind me and the world had turned into one big lopsided tornado, I didn't turn around to see what was going on. Memories of movies where one of the characters turned to stone at the sight of Medusa's face kept flashing through my mind.

There was no telling what would happen if I got sucked in.

I could finally see my car ahead.

Jane had reached the vehicle already and was pacing back and forth nervously, barking at me to hurry up.

My hand touched the pad on my key ring and the telltale beep of the locks clicking open gave me hope that I might get out in one piece.

Willing myself not to look back, I opened the back door for Jane who quickly bounded inside. I reached to open my door, when a terrible screeching broke the silence like a million pieces of glass shattering around me.

Unable to help it, I looked toward the sound and instantly wished that I hadn't.

A thunderous cloud of gray smoke had emerged, filled with hundreds of ghostly faces all floating together. The entity undulated and rippled as it flew toward me, gathering speed and looming larger the closer it got. And then it opened its mouth, and I froze as a dark, swirling, twisting smoky snake slithered out, seeking its prey.

It was one of the strangest, most terrifying things I'd ever seen, but there was no way in Hell I was hanging around to be that snake's midnight snack.

As quickly as I could, I slammed the car door and roared out of the parking lot. Running over the curb, I maneuvered the car out of the cemetery and onto the main road.

As we sped away, I focused my eyes ahead.

Don't look back. Don't look back.

My hands shook as they clenched the steering wheel, and beads of sweat poured down my forehead in great rivulets.

Jane whined in the backseat but didn't try to comfort me. She seemed traumatized as well and laid her head on her paws as we drove along the deserted streets of Cale.

When I pulled up to my place, I quickly shut off the engine, let Jane out of the car, and we ran inside, locking the door behind us. I rushed from room to room and turned on all the lights. With the apartment now shining as bright as the morning sky, I got in bed, still shaking with fright.

Jane didn't even wait for an invitation and hurled herself onto the mattress, curling up beside me with her eyes open and alert.

Together, we remained in this position until the sun came up...the horrible mass of ghostly faces flashing through my mind.

Chapter 5

"Renda. Renda, my darling, please wake up. You're going to be late for work."

The sound of Cole's voice roused me out of a light sleep that had mercifully taken over at around five o'clock in the morning. My head pounded with a migraine, my stomach hurt, and the memories of my night in the cemetery washed over me in a sickening deluge.

Suddenly, Cole's voice grew panicked. "Honey, you need to look in the mirror. Something's wrong."

My heart stopped at his words and my eyes flew open in a flash. Had I turned to stone? Had the Rashas somehow stolen my eyes, my mind—my soul?

Without saying a word, I rushed out of bed and ran to the mirror.

From behind me, Jane whined.

I now knew why Cole was worried. My face looked fine—nothing strange had happened there. But my hair was another matter.

There was now a white streak in my hair. It wasn't large, but it definitely stood out against my bright, red mane.

I couldn't move. I stared at my metamorphosis like a stunned deer in headlights. To anyone just glancing my way, it looked like a fashion statement, or a quirk of nature, or just some premature white hair. But to me it looked awful.

I was marked.

My legs grew weak and I sank to the floor in a crying heap.

Cole wouldn't want me now.

No one would.

Letting out a sob, I rested my head in my hands and let the tears soak through the gaps in my fingers and onto the clothes I had slept in from the night before.

Jane jumped from the bed and nudged my arm with her wet nose, trying to comfort me.

But Cole, strangely, remained seated.

After a few moments, I raised my tear-stained face to look at him.

His shrewd eyes were narrowed, staring at the white streak.

That instantly pissed me off. I'd just been through hell and back and all he cared about was my hair? The nerve!

"Thanks a lot," I said in a huff, rising from the floor in anger and feeling bipolar as I'd only just been sobbing moments before, "I know that I look a bit strange right now, but you have no idea what I've been through. Jane and I saw some pretty messed up things last night in the cemetery, and—"

"And you came in contact with a group of Rashas," Cole said, finishing my sentence.

"How did you know that?" I asked indignantly, now standing with my hands on my hips.

"Only an encounter with a horde of Rashas could have done that to you," he answered. "And I suggest you calm down. My reaction has nothing to do with your hair and everything to do with the fact that I can't believe how stupid you were."

My eyes widened. I opened my mouth to reply but I was too shocked to form any words.

Cole stood and paced the room. When he started to speak, he wouldn't even look at me directly. His voice was calm and controlled, but he was holding himself so tensely that he was clearly furious.

"I only know about the Rashas from Adahy. Before I left to find you, he explained to me about the different beings that roam in our realm, because he was fearful I might come in contact with them and wanted to ensure I was safe. But never in a million years did I think that you'd encounter them first." He pinned me with his gaze. "And you must promise me to never do something that reckless again."

"Well, I'm sorry," I said in a snarky tone. "But I needed to see the cemetery for myself and find out what was haunting Katie. Something just seemed to be pulling me there. I don't know. It was awful though. Oh my God, it was just horrible."

I began crying again in frustration, relieved that Cole wasn't appalled by my appearance. He was just upset that I'd ventured out on my own. A wave of emotions flooded me, and I felt ridiculous for behaving in such a crazy manner, but hell, I'd just received a supernatural dye job from some scary ass monster ghost, while at the same time, being chastised by the man I loved most in the world.

Not a great start to my day.

Cole walked over and wrapped his arms around me. He held me tight for a moment, and then pulled away slightly to kiss my lips.

His tongue flicked against mine and despite my despair, my body responded. This time, the wetness that had begun to build between my legs wasn't just pleasure—it fueled my need for release…to let go of the horror that had plagued me.

Without reservation, I grabbed Cole's hand and led him to the bed. I lifted my lips for his kiss, as we fell onto the mattress. Boldly, I stroked him through his pants, feeling him harden against my fingertips.

He groaned as our bodies, seeking fulfillment from the ache that was now overtaking us both, joined together in a sensual union.

I rested my head against the pillow and gazed into Cole's eyes. His face was already beginning to look a little pale and drained from his exertion of sexual energy.

While I always basked in the wonder of our lovemaking, I also felt sadness afterwards because it used up Cole's precious energy so quickly. I knew he would have to leave for at least the rest of the day so he could regenerate. That meant I had to get through the day without him. My shift at the library began within the hour and that left me little time to contemplate the events of the past night. Not to mention, my new hairdo would no doubt attract attention from Larlene and others.

As if able to read my thoughts, Cole reached out and gently

moved the white streak of hair away from my face where it had fallen.

"Don't worry, darling. No one will say anything to you. But you really need to be more careful. No more venturing into the cemetery without me, okay?"

I nodded without saying a word but a new idea was already forming in my mind. I had to visit with Katie again. There was so much I needed to know. Without more information, how was I going to help her?

Cole sighed, his body becoming lighter under the sheets. He was fading quickly, and I knew that our time was short.

"Renda, I'm tired and need time to regenerate. Be careful. I'll be back later." He leaned over, kissed my forehead, and then vanished.

Chapter 6

"What the hell happened to your hair?" Larlene shrieked. A few patrons turned around, shooting frowns at us.

Damn. I'd been trying to hide behind the stacks at work all morning. After Cole had disappeared, I only had about twenty minutes to get ready for work, so I grabbed a quick shower, threw on some clothes, dragged a comb through my frizzy hair, and raced out the door with a cookie in my mouth and a muffled goodbye to Jane, who woofed in reply, and no doubt promptly fell back asleep. Needless to say, I wasn't looking very spiffy, and I wasn't able to cover my new "winning" streak.

Larlene, never one for subtlety, got straight to the point. "You look like a total mess," she whispered loudly. "I mean, your hair looks kinda cool, but I'm not a big fan of white. And white streaks with red hair aren't really a good combination. Are you going to fix it or what?"

Normally, I would have been incredibly annoyed with this line of conversation but given the past twenty-four hours, there were other things on my mind.

"I know it looks weird. I'll fix it later this week when I have a chance to pick up some red hair dye. In the meantime, can you call Katie's mom and let her know that I'll be stopping by to visit this afternoon?"

Larlene screwed up her face and eyed me suspiciously.

"So what are you going to do when you're over there?" she asked.

"It's not a big deal. I just want to see how she's doing."

I continued shelving the pile of fiction books I had in my cart, ensuring that the titles were properly alphabetized.

Larlene regarded me for a moment as though wanting to ask me more, but a question from a young mother with a toddler interrupted her so she left to help the woman.

I let out the breath I'd been holding and relief washed over me that the Spanish Inquisition was over for now. It left me with time to concentrate on what I might be able to accomplish later.

My plan was to visit with the Marcks and try to get Katie to talk about her new "friends". If the Rashas were the ones contacting her, she clearly didn't see them as dangerous. I also had a feeling that they might be working hard to garner her trust, so I'd need to venture carefully. Plus, Katie's mother wasn't all that welcoming, so I wasn't expecting a warm greeting.

Oh, boy. This should be fun.

When I pulled up to Katie's house after work, I didn't notice anything out of the ordinary. I'd wanted to remind Larlene to call Katie's mother before I left, but the day had been busy with book returns, a charity fundraiser meeting, student term papers, and chatty elderly patrons taking some respite from the sweltering heat. When I finally had a chance to talk to Larlene, she'd already left for the day. It didn't matter, though, as I was determined to see Katie.

The house looked quiet and oddly lonely. There were a few children playing down the street, but it seemed as if the pervasive Florida sun was keeping everyone indoors where the fans were whirring behind protective walls.

I remembered that Jane was home and would need to go out, so this visit would have to be quick. Not that I was intending on a long, drawn-out conversation.

Just need to get more information and then I'm outta here.

As I walked up to the front door, the gravel of the driveway crackled underneath my feet. I noticed a different trio of stuffed animals perched on the lawn chair, as though Katie was letting them all get a turn outside. I smiled at that.

"Hello? Is anyone home?"

I knocked on the door several times, but no one answered. Feeling like a total trespasser, I turned the knob just to see if the door was unlocked, and the metal twisted easily in my hand.

Pushing the door open, I stepped into the darkened interior, which felt as hot and humid as the swamps of the Everglades. The morning-old smells of coffee and bacon hung in the stale air.

My stomach turned. My sense of smell had always been strong and sensitive. In fact, during my childhood, I had a hard time with breakfast smells like eggs, making me nauseous. Over the years, the tendency to get sick from strong aromas had waned but now, standing in the doorway of the Marcks' home, I was feeling queasy.

The sound of laughter floating in from the backyard caught my attention. I knew I had a few minutes at least to look around, but I left the door open behind me just in case a quick getaway was necessary. As my eyes grew accustomed to the dark, I was thankful that nothing seemed out of the ordinary. My second sight was turned off and hence the world seemed normal and quiet.

Giggling sounds from the backyard drew me to the window. Katie and Anne were sitting on the grass, a variety of dolls of different shapes and sizes arranged in a circle for a tea party. Most of the dolls looked old, as though they'd been purchased at a thrift store. Their hyperactive terrier was chasing his tail, causing fits of laughter from Katie and her mom.

I smiled at the sweet display and felt a bit guilty for spying. But, this moment also gave me an opportunity to do some snooping.

Heart racing, I rushed down the hall. Katie's bedroom, which faced west, was aglow from the afternoon sunlight filtering in through the blinds.

I wondered where I should search first. There were shelves with picture books and coloring books, trinkets such as beaded bracelets and colorful headbands. But nothing out of the ordinary.

Then, I spied something interesting.

A kid's sketchbook of construction paper and a box of crayons lay beside Katie's pillow. Curious, I picked up the book and began flipping through it.

The first few drawings were simple depictions of her house,

showing her parents standing on the lawn holding hands and her dog smiling beside them. Katie had written Mommy, Daddy, and Pixie, next to her illustrations, in bright pink, purple, and yellow. I wondered why Katie hadn't included herself in the pictures of her family. Was I reading too much into the doodles of a little girl or was there more to it?

But then, as I flipped through the pages, the drawings began to change...

On one page, a stick-figured man with a dark red circle for his head and a black, open mouth was holding his arms up to the sky. Another picture showed a mass of tiny stick-figured people floating in the sky above a row of headstones.

And finally, Katie had drawn herself lying in bed, with a mass of black loops above her head. Her mouth was turned down in a sad frown.

The images became darker and more ominous as I kept turning the pages.

I was wrong. The Rashas weren't always nice to Katie. Otherwise, how could a child have drawn such disturbing pictures? Were they terrorizing her as they had terrorized me in the cemetery the night before? I couldn't tear my eyes away from the drawings.

"Hi, Miss Renda. Do you like my pictures?"

I dropped the book with a startled gasp.

Turning, I saw Katie in the doorway smiling at me. Her mother, standing next to her, was definitely *not* smiling.

Crap. I'm in big trouble.

"Yes, I d-d-do," I stuttered, as I clumsily laid the sketchbook back on the bed.

"I like your new hair! Want to draw with me? Mommy, can she draw with me?"

Anne stared at me hard and then turned back to Katie with a softened look on her face. "Sure, honey. But first, let me speak to Renda for a moment." And with that, she gave me a look and stepped out of the room.

I followed her out to the hallway.

Anne crossed her arms over chest. Her eyes narrowed and it was clear she didn't appreciate me snooping about.

"Look, Renda. I told you that it was okay to spend time with Katie. But from now on, please make yourself known when you come to our house. I know you're trying to help. Just please be respectful.'

"I'm so sorry, Anne. Please accept my apology."

She glared at me for a moment, then with a reluctant nod, turned and walked away.

I felt terrible, but there was nothing I could do now. I'd already trespassed and been caught red-handed. Plus, Katie had just come out of the room and was staring at me with an expectant, happy face.

So, I went back into her room and sat on the floor with her while she chatted away about her tea party with the dolls in the backyard.

The little girl was awash in excitement as she showed me several beaded bracelets that she'd made with her mother. I didn't want to interrupt her chatter as I wanted her to feel comfortable with me.

Katie didn't seem to notice that I hadn't spoken a word in nearly ten minutes and when she tired of talking, she grabbed some fluorescent crayons and began to color on one of the pages in a princess coloring book. She focused on carefully coloring within the lines, her little forehead scrunched up in concentration.

It seemed like a good time to ask some questions, so I approached her carefully.

"I heard that you like to spend time in the cemetery. It's a very peaceful place with lots of trees and birds chirping. I bet there are lots of bunnies there too."

Katie didn't answer and continued coloring.

I decided to try again. "Do you have any special friends you talk to at the cemetery?"

Still...nothing.

It was as if I wasn't even speaking to her. Frustrated now, I remembered one of our earlier conversations and tried something else.

"Katie, do you remember when you came to my house?"

She smiled and nodded while continuing to color.

"When you came to my house, you mentioned that 'they' told you I was nice and that's why you came over. Who are 'they', Katie?"

She stopped coloring for a minute as if deep in thought. Not looking up at me, she responded slowly, "They are the little people in the sky. And they talk to me about things."

The little people in the sky?

"What kinds of things do they talk about?"

Katie now looked up at me with an expression of uncertainty on her face. "I'm not sure if I can tell you. They made me promise to keep it a secret."

"I promise not to tell anyone what they say. They told you I was nice, remember? So, they probably wouldn't mind if you shared their secret with me."

"Well, if you promise not to tell…" She looked around as if fearful that someone might hear her. Then she turned back to face me.

"They tell me that I'm special, and they want me to fly with them. But, I'm scared to go up into the sky. Are they going to get mad at me, Miss Renda?"

I wasn't sure if the Rashas were getting impatient with Katie's reluctance to drop her guard and give in to their suggestions. Thankfully, she was too frightened to take them up on their offer to "fly." But how long could she deny them what they wanted?

After catching a glimpse of the monster of death that had floated toward me in the cemetery, there was no doubt in my mind that Katie wouldn't be able to keep the darkness at bay for long. Eventually, the Rashas would break her down and then, there was no telling what could happen.

Katie was waiting for a response, so I tried to downplay her question, while still giving her good advice. "I don't think they're going to get mad at you, but you should trust your instincts. If you don't want to fly, you don't have to. Only do what you're comfortable with."

"My *stinks*? Is that something smelly?" she asked.

We both laughed and I reached out and tapped her nose.

"An in-*stinct* is a very strong feeling that we have inside us.

It helps us decide what is right and wrong for us. It's important to always pay attention to that feeling."

She smiled at me and nodded, apparently satisfied with my answer, and then leaned over to give me a big hug.

Katie smelled of baby powder and summer flowers, reminding me of the little ghost girl I'd met in my friend Bobbie's home in Macon. She was a friendly spirit who'd touched my heart while I was staying there, helping Bobbie's mother free herself from a demon.

The ghost child, a little girl named Claire, had been killed in a fire, her face horribly disfigured. But she had a smile that could brighten a room and the purity of innocence reserved especially for children.

Before discovering my gift, I'd never really been drawn to kids. I couldn't even picture myself married, let alone a mother. My parents had adopted me when I was a newborn, and I was an only child. I'd spent my childhood pretty much in my own little world, much in the same way Katie was spending hers. But my experiences with these little girls were helping me focus on my purpose. I could use my gift to protect the good in this world and beyond. And as I held Katie in my arms, I realized that there was no way I was going to let anything bad happen to her.

Not on my watch.

During my drive home, Cole returned—materializing in the front passenger seat. In the early days, he was able to surprise me with his manifestations and would seemingly pop up out of nowhere. But now, I was able to detect his return. It usually began with a gust of warm wind, followed by a sensation of being "watched." Within minutes, Cole's body would slowly appear until it had solidified into the man who was fast becoming the most important person in my life.

Now, he sat comfortably in the car with a self-assured grin on his face. But his smile faded when he saw my pensive expression.

"What's wrong? I thought you'd be happy to see me."

"I am happy to see you," I said, keeping my eyes on the road.

"So, why do you look so serious? And where are you returning from?"

This line of questioning surprised me because I simply assumed that Cole kept track of my every move, even when he wasn't fully manifested. But it was clear that he didn't know about my visit to Katie's house. Cole hadn't shown up at the cemetery either and that worried me.

If Cole couldn't "see" where I was at all times, he wouldn't be able to help me if I was in danger.

Trying to keep my voice calm and steady, I glanced at him and smiled before returning my gaze to the road ahead. "I was visiting Katie. It was enlightening to say the least. I think—"

"You shouldn't be going there alone!" Cole shouted, obviously furious.

I didn't answer and kept on driving. It was the second time in less than twenty-four hours that he'd chastised me like a child. Not exactly winning points with me.

"Did you hear me?" he pressed. "I thought we talked about this. This situation is dangerous and the Rashas could seriously harm you. You need to be more careful and wait for me before taking that kind of risk."

At this point in time, something inside my brain just *snapped*. Perhaps it was the lack of sleep from the night before, or the fact that I was dealing with some frightening realities that no one— including Cole—could protect me from. Or maybe I was just feeling overwhelmed in trying to be some sort of superhero, when in reality, I was just a nerdy librarian from small-town Cale. Whatever the case, I'd had enough and my brain switched into adrenaline mode. My hands acted on their own, and I pulled the car off the main road, into a semi-empty parking lot. The quick movement caused the car to screech and lurch forward as I shifted the gear into *park*.

A red haze swam before my eyes and I turned to Cole angrily. "I've had enough! Stop telling me what I can or can't do. You don't have any right."

Cole looked incredulous. "What do you mean, I don't have any right?"

"Well, for starters…you're dead. And secondly, you haven't

been here to protect me over the past few days when some pretty bad stuff happened, so don't try to protect me now *after the fact*. I can't sit around and wait for you to return to me, every time I have to do something. It isn't fair, and you shouldn't expect that from me!"

As soon as the words left my mouth, I felt awful. Even though what I was saying was true, Cole didn't deserve the poison that had just spewed from my lips. I opened my mouth to apologize, when he silenced me with a dark look. Turning away, he stared out the window before he began to speak again.

"You're right. I can't protect you all the time. I can't be with you day and night. You deserve someone better. A living man."

"Wait..." I sputtered, realizing that I'd just made a huge mistake.

"No. Don't say anymore." He turned back and I could see the pain in his dark eyes. He managed a half-smile and reached out to caress my face.

I leaned into his touch, tears falling from my eyes.

Then he pulled away and to my horror, he vanished before I could say another word, leaving me alone in my car.

"No!" I shouted. "Don't leave me. Oh, God, I'm sorry Cole! Please, come back!"

I drove home in a blur of tears. The sun was setting, and everything around me seemed darker. Lonelier.

I prayed that Cole would forgive me for being such a total bitch and hoped that perhaps he might be waiting for me when I got home. As I pulled into the driveway outside my apartment, my heart bounced within my chest in hopeful anticipation.

After I opened the door, Jane came bounding out of the apartment as usual, a little more desperate to relieve herself, because I'd left her home for far too long. But no one else was there to greet me.

After we went inside, I checked each room, calling out to Cole—begging him to come back, apologizing for my stupidity. But he didn't respond or return to me.

After an hour of calling out to him, I managed to swallow a few bites of a peanut butter and jelly sandwich and then curled up on the couch, tears coursing down my cheeks. I felt so incredibly alone that I didn't know how I'd managed to exist before Cole. My mind continued to replay the last few moments together in my car and how he had gently caressed me.

Come back. Please. I need to feel your touch again.

Jane, sensing my despair, hopped up on the couch, usually a no-no, and laid her furry head on my leg.

I rested my head atop hers, smelling her familiar scent and then curled up beside her. When my eyes could no longer stay open, I whispered Cole's name before falling asleep.

Chapter 7

Sunlight streamed through the window and warmed my legs as morning greeted me, but I still didn't want to move. My entire body ached from the awkward position in which Jane and I had slept, but that was nothing compared to the ache in my heart.

As I slowly unfolded myself from the couch, I called out to Cole again but he didn't respond. My second sight was no help either. Jane and I were alone.

Getting ready for work was a painful, arduous task. After taking Jane outside to do her business, I stood in the shower as the hot spray hit my body. Numbly, I lathered my hair, thinking of Cole and what he must be feeling after our fight.

After downing a cup of coffee and a few bites of toast, I let Jane out once more, then like a zombie, I trudged to my car barely noticing the clear blue sky and sunshine.

The library, usually a welcome sight, loomed ahead of me. The last thing I wanted to do was bump into Larlene who would ask me a million questions about Katie and Cole. So instead of making my usual morning rounds, I headed straight for the conference room and began working on a budgeting project.

The hours rolled along, and thankfully, I was left alone for most of the morning. But as lunchtime approached, Larlene finally found me.

"Hey, I looked everywhere for you this morning. Sorry that I ran out so quickly yesterday. Had a date, but it sucked." She shrugged and opened her mouth to speak again but stopped, her eyes widening.

My pain must have been stamped on my face for all to see.

I was heartbroken and certain that I'd chased away the only man I'd ever loved. I dashed away my tears with the back of my hand.

"Renda, what's wrong?" she asked.

"I think I've lost Cole," I managed to choke out, before completely breaking down in tears.

Reaching out, Larlene held me in her arms as I sobbed onto her shoulder.

I blurted out the entirety of the past few days—the cemetery, the Rashas, Cole's inability to protect me, Katie's confession...

When I was done, she sighed loudly and reached for my hand.

"Renda, I know you're a mess about Cole, but you've got to help Katie. You can't let this go. It sounds like she's in serious danger."

I knew Larlene was right. Whatever I'd seen in the cemetery wasn't going to disappear anytime soon and it had its sights set on the little girl.

"Larlene, I totally agree with you, but how am I going to do this without Cole? I'm such a novice at all this."

She squeezed my hand again, and flashed me an encouraging smile.

"Don't worry. You're stronger than you think, and I'll help you in any way I can. But there's something important you need to know. It's the main reason I came looking for you."

"What is it?"

"It's Katie. Her mom found her this morning, unresponsive in her bed. It's like this weird coma. She's in the hospital."

Cale's hospital was surprisingly calm and holistic. The fact that it was located amidst a forested area of heavy oaks and dense foliage added to the natural ambience. The chief of staff had been interviewed on the local news recently, claiming that the oxygen released by the greenery helped patients "heal faster" and created a healthy environment around the medical facility.

But we didn't notice any of this as we found a parking spot and entered the building in a rush of anxiety. My mind was racing with questions.

What if my trying to help Katie ended up putting her in even more peril? Have the Rashas finally penetrated her soul? Were they "punishing" her for saying no to the flying, or had they finally convinced her to say yes, and this was the result?

We were allowed admittance into the patient ward and suddenly, I found myself surrounded by spirits. After turning it on in the morning, I'd kept my "sight" on all day in the hopes of encountering Cole, but now, I wished I'd remembered to turn it off. I'd forgotten what Adahy had told me about certain places attracting more spirits than others, especially hospitals.

Most of the ghosts looked as though they had been patients when they died. Some of the poor souls wore expressions of bewilderment on their faces—as though they were in shock from either an unexpected death on the operating table, or heart failure after a procedure.

One man, who was dragging himself along the walkway with an IV attached to his arm, looked up, and our eyes met. Realizing that I could see him, he reached out and touched my shoulder. The contact immediately sent a shock through my body and his despair flooded my senses so completely that I fell back against Larlene in agony.

"Renda, are you okay?" she asked.

I gasped, trying to regain my footing, and when I looked up, the spirit was gone.

Sometimes contact with living people drains weaker spirits immediately, and they can no longer manifest. But this was one of the few times that a spirit had actually touched me, unprovoked. Typically, they kept their distance. But he was likely desperate to communicate with someone.

When I began seeing spirits, I realized that most of them just wanted to tell their stories—they wanted someone to listen to them. To hear them. To acknowledge their existence. Since they no longer had a human body, they were invisible to the average person.

Their energy was on a different plane. The spirits who realized this and made peace with it could move on but the ones who didn't, forever haunted the world they left behind.

"Yeah, I'm fine. Let's keep going."

But something wasn't right. More spirits began manifesting along the path as we walked. Flanking us on either side, they gaped at me with hollow eyes. My senses kicked into overload as dozens of ghosts passed by me. It was like trying to get through a gauntlet of the dead.

They began crowding around me so close that the air escaped my lungs. Terror consumed me. I was drowning in their desperate energy, overwhelmed with one thought.

Escape.

Letting out a shriek of fear, I ran...

Larlene, who was totally confused, chased after me and called out, "Renda, wait! What's wrong?"

The spirits swarmed me in a terrifying crush of ghostly fervor. Everywhere I turned, I saw dead eyes and clawing hands. Falling to the ground, I curled up in a ball and forced myself to turn off the sight, despite feeling shocks from every angle now as the creatures clawed at me.

Turn off! Turn off!

I silently focused on shutting off the vision and scrunched my eyes closed as decrepit hands continued to grab at me. It was maddening, but finally...mercifully, it stopped.

Until another hand touched my shoulder...

"Get the fuck away from me!" I shouted, and then realized it was only Larlene.

She jumped back, her eyes widened in shock. Several orderlies had joined her and circled me carefully.

"I'm...I'm so sorry. I just had a panic attack."

"Are you sure?" my friend asked, still keeping a safe distance and obviously unsure as to how to react.

Standing up, I smiled at the orderlies and forced myself to pull it together. People were staring at me and giving me the "she's a nutcase" kind of look.

"Yes, I'm sure. So sorry about that. I'm okay. It won't happen again."

One of the orderlies raised an eyebrow as if trying to decide whether or not I needed sedation. I gave him my sincerest smile and tried to assure him that I wasn't an insane person. Plus, we were now in the children's ward, so the hospital staff was even more insistent that we not frighten the young patients.

It took several minutes of convincing, but they let us go—much to my surprised relief—and we finally made it to Katie's room. We knocked and a muffled voice told us to come inside.

Larlene pushed the door open and we walked in.

Nervously twisting a tissue around her trembling fingers, Anne sat in a chair opposite the bed. The cartoon characters painted on the walls seemed a sharp contrast to her worn expression.

I glanced at the mural of a cobblestone walkway that looped around the room and ended at a spectacular palace. Pretty flags flapped in an imaginary breeze and a beautiful, smiling princess gazed out of a window. It made me wish for an escape to my own imaginary world, where I could let go of the burden of death and spirits. Except Cole. He was the only spirit I would gladly have with me for the rest of my life. My wonderful prince from a bygone era.

But my prince had deserted me.

Swallowing my heartache, I made my way to Katie's bedside. Thankfully, Anne didn't keep me from approaching her daughter, and frankly, I had no intention of letting anyone get in my way. I had a feeling that the recent procession in the hospital ward was a warning from the Rashas to keep me away from Katie. I'd need to keep my sight turned off for a while until I could figure out exactly what was happening.

Katie was lying on the bed, her lovely blonde hair fanned out across the pristine white pillows, and her face was pale. But what disturbed me the most was that her eyes were wide open—staring out into nothingness.

I took a deep breath, saddened for the sweet child who, just yesterday, had been so full of light.

I watched her for a moment, and while she did appear to blink regularly, there was no sense of recognition in her eyes. She looked like a wax figure.

"She's been like that since this morning," Anne commented from behind me. "Went into her room to get her up for school, and she was just lying there. Like a fucking doll." She choked back tears and looked down in her lap.

I continued to stare at Katie and then leaned down and whispered in her ear, "Katie, it's Renda. Can you hear me? Are you flying with them?"

The child didn't respond but remained frozen in place.

I was about to try again, when the doctor came into the room. Tall and dark-skinned, with glasses perched on the end of his nose, his brow furrowed at the sight of us.

"Well, that was quite a scene you put on outside, young lady," he said, addressing me directly. "I'm not sure it's best for you to be here. Katie's still unresponsive and we need to keep her as calm as possible until we can figure out why she's catatonic."

I waited for Anne to agree with him, but she surprised me.

"It's okay, Dr. Franklin. These girls are friends of the family. I'm not sure what happened outside earlier, but I'm fine with them being here."

The doctor seemed unconvinced and gave me another *look*. He then turned back around to face Anne and ignored Larlene and me entirely.

"Mrs. Marck, Katie's test results have come back, and frankly, we're a bit surprised. The good news is that everything seems to be working fine. Her organs are all functioning properly and we couldn't find any evidence of an epileptic seizure or any other impairment in her brain. So far we have found nothing of a physical nature that could tell us why she's in this catatonic state. We would like to keep her here under observation until we can figure out what's going on. Is there anything she might have experienced? Any sort of trauma?"

I looked over at Anne and waited to hear what she would say. Instead, she shook her head and wiped a tear away from her cheek.

I felt terrible for the woman. She may not have approved of my visiting Katie, but it was clear that she loved her daughter. Without thinking, I went over to her and put a comforting hand on her shoulder for reassurance.

Anne looked surprised by my actions but then gave me a slight smile.

"Until Katie regains full consciousness, I'd advise that you limit the number of visitors, Mrs. Marck. We've got to ensure that Katie remains as peaceful as possible and is surrounded by people she trusts—family and close friends. It might also be good to bring some toys from home or other objects that are familiar and comforting. We've found that sometimes patients like this will respond to familiar things like toys and the gentle voices of loved ones."

The doctor gave me another disapproving look before he made his exit.

Once we were alone again, Larlene broke the silence.

"Well, at least we know she's not seriously sick. That's good news, right?"

Anne ignored her and turned to look at me. "You know what's wrong with her, don't you Renda?"

I was surprised at her directness, but my instincts urged me to be open and honest.

"Yes, I think I do. But, you may not believe me."

Anne shook her head. "Don't worry about what I think or don't think. We're past that now. What's going on?"

Very carefully and calmly, I explained my theory and the reasoning behind it. It felt strange telling the woman about the Rashas and how Katie had confided that she wasn't entirely comfortable with the requests they were making of her, but Anne listened attentively and didn't interrupt.

Instead, when I was done, she lowered her face to her hands and rocked back and forth. A low moan came from her throat, as though she was experiencing a deep pain.

When she raised her head, there were tears in her eyes but there was also a softness reflected back at me that I hadn't seen before. She motioned for me to sit beside her, so I pulled up a chair while Larlene leaned against the wall and waited patiently.

"Renda, there's something I need to tell you," she said quietly.

Fear rose in my heart.

Oh shit. She's going to tell me that she's like me— *another Chosen One…*

Anne could see that I was nervous and put a hand on my knee. "Don't worry, this isn't anything bad, but it may help you understand why some of this is happening. We've never told anyone about this, because we've been frightened of the consequences—but you need to know."

"What is it? Tell me. Please."

Anne took a deep breath and then spoke quietly, her sad eyes staring deeply into my own. "Renda, I have to tell you something. About your background. Something you don't know."

I looked at Anne in surprise. I'd only recently met her through Larlene .

How does she know anything about me, or my past?

My heart started beating faster.

"Renda," Anne continued, "Your father's brother...is my husband. Katie is your cousin."

I couldn't believe it. I actually had an uncle! The knowledge made me dizzy.

Why didn't my uncle reach out to me years ago?

Why had no one told me?

Anne had known who I was, so why had she acted like she could barely tolerate me?

In all of my life, I'd never known any of my biological relatives. My adoptive parents had told me that after my birth mother disappeared, there was no one left to take me in. Her parents had died and my father as well as his parents had also passed away.

"Tell me the whole story. I want to know."

Anne took a deep breath and spoke slowly. "My husband was adopted. He never knew he had a biological brother until your father contacted him. Your dad was already married to your mother at the time. My husband was a teen when they met all those years ago. They spent some time together, getting to know each other, and then a few months later, your father died and your mother disappeared."

My mind raced crazily, and threatened to shut down altogether.

Weeks ago, my father had appeared to me at the library to say goodbye before crossing over. He'd been waiting for years for me to finally sense his presence. But he'd never mentioned anything about a living brother. Spirits did tend to be rather mysterious about what they could or couldn't reveal. Was my father unable to tell me the truth because of some "ghost code"?

Before I had a chance to ask Anne more questions, we heard a sound from the bed.

Katie!

We rushed to her beside and watched as her head shook in tiny tremors, and her lips struggled to form words. Her eyes were still open, but seemed even wider now—almost as if in panic.

Anne stood in shock, seemingly unable to move.

Larlene reached for the "call" button and pressed it.

In the meantime, I leaned closer to Katie's face and urged her to speak. "Come on sweetheart, tell us. What is it?"

"Help me," she whispered and then her body went rigid. She fell back on the pillow and closed her eyes.

The next hour was a mess of nurses, tubes, and activity.

After Katie's momentary bout of consciousness, the room filled up quickly with people trying to figure out what had happened. She was connected to different wires and machinery as the medical staff went into emergency mode. Her vitals weren't dropping per se, but had slowed considerably, indicating trauma had taken place.

Tension wrapped itself around me like a vise. The severity of the situation had only been heightened by Katie's words.

Help me.

While I observed the team working on her, my inner voice was repeating the same words over and over again.

They can't help her...No one can help her...No one—but you.

The realization was only heightened by the insanity of the past twenty-four hours.

The Rashas, Katie's coma, and now this new revelation that I had living blood relatives. There were so many things I wanted to ask Anne, but it wasn't the right time. She was standing a few feet away from us, as close as she could get to Katie without getting in the way of the doctor and nurses. Her arms were wrapped protectively around herself and her eyes were red and teary. It was obvious she was barely hanging on by a thread.

Larlene interrupted my thoughts by lightly tugging on my arm and whispering, "Let's go outside for a minute. I need to talk to you."

I cast a quick glance back in Anne's direction but she didn't appear to notice, her eyes locked on her baby girl. So I followed Larlene into the hallway.

The orderlies from earlier in the afternoon were chatting by the nurse's station. They both looked at me with disdain as we stepped outside.

I tried to ignore them and focused on Larlene.

"Renda, are you okay? That was some crazy shit in there. Can't believe you guys are related?"

"Yeah. I'm pretty shocked too. Did you suspect anything like that?"

Larlene looked at me as if I was off my rocker. "Are you kidding? I had no freaking clue! I've been friends with Anne for a while, but she never said anything to me. And what did she mean about being scared of the consequences or something like that?"

I had a feeling that Anne knew more about my ability than she'd let on and the responsibilities that came with it. Perhaps she was worried Katie would develop the same "gift" that I had? I had a sinking suspicion that my connection to Katie had something to do with the Rashas haunting her and I needed to know the entire story, or I wouldn't be able to save her.

"Maybe we should go on home," I conceded. "I need to take Jane out anyway. But I'll be back tomorrow.

Larlene agreed and left me in the hallway, briefly stepping back into the hospital room to let Anne know what our plans were. She returned within minutes. "They're still working on Katie, but she seems stable for now. Let's go."

As we walked out of the children's ward, I couldn't help but feel nervous as we moved through the hallways. I kept my second sight turned off and never looked back even when it felt like the creatures of the night were nipping at my heels.

When I finally pulled up to my apartment nearly thirty minutes later, I was exhausted. The day's activities had drained me of my ability to think clearly. I just wanted to curl up on the couch with Cole and watch a movie.

My heart shuddered at the reminder that I couldn't do that, because Cole wasn't around, and I wasn't sure if he would ever come back. It's not like I could text him and tell him I was sorry. Or call him and leave a message. He existed in another realm. His amazing ability to regenerate and be with me had been a precious gift.

A gift I'd foolishly rejected.

Sighing, I opened the front door and stood to one side, expecting Jane to come bounding out. But instead, she exited slowly and kept looking back at the doorway as if to indicate that there was someone there.

My heart leapt in my chest.

Cole had come back!

But instead of my beloved, I was surprised to see Adahy sitting on the floor of my apartment. He looked up as I entered and motioned for me to join him.

Used to visiting with Adahy in this way, I sat down on the floor next to him and waited for him to speak.

In his lifetime, Adahy had been a Cherokee shaman. He'd died in colonial times and always appeared to me dressed in his traditional garb, made of soft buckskin. On his head, sat a headdress of feathers sticking straight up in proud tradition. Wrinkles outlined his leathery skin, a testament to his many years on this earth. His hair was gray and wavy, falling past his shoulders.

But it was Adahy's eyes that always drew me in. They shone with kindness, patience, and an infinite wisdom.

He regarded me closely, and I felt the walls that were holding up my inner strength—come crashing down.

Tears spilled from my eyes and I sat and stared at him in despair. I'd been hoping that Cole would have returned by now. He'd been away for twenty-four hours. He never disappeared for that long. The realization that he might truly be gone for good, began to sink in.

Adahy moved closer to me, and a musky scent filled my

nostrils. When he began to speak, I was impressed, once again, by his fluid English and modern manner. Spirits were able to communicate with the living in many different ways and Adahy spoke English because it was what I understood.

"Don't cry, Renda. I know things are difficult for you, but you have to be strong. There's so much to learn and time is running out for me."

I looked at the sage and could see that he wasn't smiling or as self-assured as I'd seen in his previous visitations.

"But I have so many questions. Did you know that I have an uncle?"

Adahy nodded. "Yes. Please don't be angry and allow me to explain."

He took a deep breath...

"Your mother and father met under the strangest of circumstances, and the reason I know this—is because I was there. It was years before you were born and they were young and just getting started in the world...

"Part of a hiking group, they met each month and traveled the Southeast, looking for new terrain to explore. The group spent hours trekking through this land's massive brush and undeveloped natural treasures.

"The group decided to hike through the woods in Macon, Georgia. They set off, not far from the Trillos' home and moved through the same wilderness my ancestors had occupied. The hikers were all protectors of nature and treated the woods like a special sanctuary.

"It was on this particular trip that your parents met for the first time. Your mother was new to the group, but your father was a seasoned hiker and noticed her immediately. Perhaps it was because she had an inclination to stumble over rocks and twigs. Or perhaps it was because she was strikingly beautiful and captured his heart with her innocence.

"Whatever the case, I was the first to witness it.

"At the time, I was passing through the woods and noticed the two of them walking together. This was not unusual, as the woods they were trespassing through had been recently visited by another group of hikers.

I didn't fear being noticed because only people with your gift can see me, so I was able to move about freely.

"Renda, I'm not sure why I was so bold at the time, but I decided that I wanted to get a closer look at the young couple. I could sense their auras were different than the other souls that occupied the land of the living. They had a glow to their spirits that was unusual.

"It was surprising, but it also called to me.

"As I moved closer to them, I was shocked when their eyes turned to gaze upon my own. They had actually seen me and started to walk toward me.

"At first, I wasn't sure how to react. It was the first time in more than two hundred years that I had made contact with a living person. For years, I'd simply floated through the pathways between our realms and found solace in comforting the dead who needed to understand why they had died and what they needed to do if they wanted to move into the light. But these people...they were alive and could see through the wall dividing our two planes. It frightened me."

At this point, Adahy paused, and I stared at him wide eyed. It was nearly impossible for me to imagine this wise man being frightened of anything, let alone my parents. But his words were bringing some peace to my continual longing that ached for more knowledge about my true heritage, so I urged him to continue.

"Your mother spoke to me first. She was very gentle and said hello. Your father smiled as well, but was more reserved and unsure how to approach a Native American in the middle of the woods dressed in traditional clothing...I remember our exchange like it was yesterday..."

At this point, Adahy did something strange.

He took my hand and all of a sudden the air shifted around me, twisting and twirling like a cyclone. My breath felt as if it was being sucked out of my lungs, and I struggled to find a sense of equilibrium. It was a bizarre sensation, because I was still sitting down, and yet at the same time was caught in a whirlwind of colors and sounds.

Adahy was transporting me to another time and place.

Within a minute, the swirling sensations stopped and all was still.

But I was no longer in my apartment. Instead, I was sitting on the ground in the middle of the woods.

Birds chirped around me, and I could actually smell the aroma of grass after a recent rain. The air was humid and shrouded me in the warm cloak of summer.

I was sitting alone now, because Adahy was standing a few feet ahead of me, talking to two people. I could see that they were male and female, but their faces were blurry—like the view from a camera lens that was out of focus.

Frustrated, I tried to stand up but was unable to move. Panic set in until I heard Adahy's voice floating in my mind.

Shhh...relax, Renda. You are here to observe as a visitor in a time past. Just watch and learn.

Then, the people standing with Adahy began to speak.

"Hello," said the woman. It was my mother. My birth mother and father! And I was getting the chance to see them as a young couple.

Hot tears welled and coursed down my cheeks.

Adahy didn't answer and instead, just stared at the couple in amazement.

"Um, are you lost?" asked the man.

My mother laughed at her companion's clumsy attempt to greet this strange Native American man.

"I'm sorry. Don't pay any attention to him. It's very nice to meet you. Do you speak English?"

It was only then that Adahy spoke. "Yes, I do. My name is Adahy. Do you see me?"

My mother laughed again. "Of course we do. Why wouldn't we?"

There was a moment of silence, and I watched as Adahy reached out and touched my mother's arm.

It was hard to tell, because everything was out of focus, but it seemed as if her eyes glazed over at his touch. My father's lips parted, but before he could intervene, Adahy withdrew his hand.

The whole scene reminded me of the first time I'd met the

wise sage. I could almost imagine the awe and fear that my mother was experiencing because it was never easy to discover that you'd just made contact with the dead.

But she seemed to be handling it well. She was now speaking to Adahy in a low voice while my father stood nearby and watched carefully.

It was hard to hear what they were saying, but I could tell that Adahy was explaining his circumstances and how he'd died.

My mother listened intently and when he was finished, she grasped his hand and they walked away together, but for some reason, my father remained where he was.

"No. Don't leave…" My father cried out as they walked away. He watched as they disappeared from view, and then glanced up at the sky as if to say a prayer. "No. Please, no. Not her, too."

His voice was filled with desperation and fear and even though the woods began disappearing around me, I could feel his sadness. I tried reaching out to him but it was too late…

The vortex dragged me in once more and this time, I didn't fight it. I tried to steady my breathing as I let the cyclone sweep my mind into its twisting centrifuge and bring me back to the present day. Seeing my mother and feeling my father's pain had left a terrible ache in my chest. I wanted to be back in my apartment with Adahy and Jane.

And Cole…

My breath returned to normal as the familiar surroundings of my apartment came back into view. The carpet in my living room replaced the wet grass in the forest, and the muggy summer air transformed into the cool air conditioning that flowed steadily from the vents in my living room.

When my vision cleared, I was still sitting on the floor, but Adahy was gone. No doubt, the transfer of energy to allow for such a vivid memory had drained him of his essence.

Why is it that when anyone shares information with me about my past and my existence, it leaves me with even more questions about myself?

I wanted to know why Adahy took my mother's hand and led her away. I wanted to know why my father hadn't gone after them and why he'd prayed to the skies. He'd obviously found her again because I was born sometime later. But how and why did they both have this gift? And why hadn't my father told me this when he saw me that day in the library to say goodbye?

So many questions plagued me, and I knew the answers would not be forthcoming any time soon.

Jane nudged my arm with her snout and whined for some attention.

I pulled her large, furry body against mine and gave her a hug. It felt good to hold her close, when everything in the world seemed so alien and remote.

After eating a simple supper of cheese toast—I didn't have much of an appetite—I curled up on the couch with Jane and put on the BBC. A film adaptation of *Pride and Prejudice* came on, and I sincerely tried to focus on the romance between Elizabeth Bennet and Mr. Darcy. But it was impossible to concentrate.

I kept thinking about Cole.

Why was the situation so tenuous with him? And why did he have to disappear when things got difficult? He'd done it in Macon as well, while I was trying to help my friend Bobbie's mother free herself of a demon. Cole and I had argued about his reluctance to venture outside the mansion where he "lived." I'd found out that ghosts who traveled outdoors could regenerate by channeling natural sunlight. He refused to listen to me and disappeared for several days. Then he came back and all was well. But now it had happened again. Were we destined to always be at odds because of the unique situation we found ourselves in? It seemed that every time we quarreled, he went into extreme brooding mode. Didn't he realize that we were going to have fights and that was just a fact of life?

But that was the issue. A fact of *life*.

Cole wasn't alive, and the rules were different. He could disappear for years if necessary and only reemerge when he felt like it.

I'd be dead and in the ground by then…Would I be able to find him in the afterworld? Just thinking about it made me feel a jolt of panic.

Was it my destiny to be alone forever?

I took a hot shower to relax before bed. Standing beneath the shower head, the water poured over me, soothing my frazzled nerves.

Steam filled the bathroom in a heavy fog of condensation and after about ten minutes of bliss, I turned off the water and stepped out of the shower.

Reaching for a towel, I pulled it on and wrapped my body tightly in its gentle folds and stood in front of the bathroom mirror, my hands gripping the sink. Even though the mirror was all steamed up, I could see my pale face staring back at me. My eyes were sunken in and looked dark and sad. My wet hair hung limply, the white streak barely visible in the haze.

And then I saw him.

A figure stood behind me. He was dark and his face was unrecognizable, but I knew one thing for sure. He was evil. Turning around quickly, my arm accidentally knocked over a set of perfume bottles and sent them crashing to the ground.

And then he vanished.

My bathroom now smelled like a flower garden gone amok. It took me about half an hour to clean up the mess, and luckily, I managed to pick up all the broken bits of colored glass without slicing my hands into ribbons.

Jane stood in the bathroom doorway and snorted at me in discontent. Her nostrils twitched at the strong smells, and she sneezed periodically, making me giggle at the insanity of the whole situation. Jane always had a way of making my mood lighter, even during bad times.

Especially during bad times.

I wasn't sure if my surprise visitor had been a Rasha or just a wayward spirit. My mental lever had dropped upon seeing Adahy, and I hadn't shut it off, so anything was possible. It was becoming harder and harder to block out the spirits, because lately, I'd begun to see some of them whether my lever was on or off. So, I wasn't sure what kind of ghost had chosen to appear behind me.

Jane sneezed again, reminding me to hurry up, so I quickly

dried the floor and threw out the glass shards. I tapped my dog on the nose, and she gave a soft bark, then turned and went to the front door, letting me know she wanted to go out for her bedtime pee.

Okay girl, I hear you.

If anyone ever tells you that dog owners are in control, don't believe it. Dogs tell us what they want us to do. But I wouldn't have it any other way.

Later on in bed, I stared up at the ceiling and pondered what I'd seen in the bathroom. I wasn't sure if it was a Rasha, or just my imagination, but whatever it was, my apartment now felt different—as though I wasn't quite safe in my own home.

Pulling the blankets up to my chin, I closed my eyes and tried to think of pleasant thoughts but all I could see was Cole's face filled with hurt as my insensitive words slashed him.

My eyelids grew heavy and the day's events finally took the wind completely out of my sails. The last thing I thought about before falling asleep was Katie lying in the hospital bed while her mother watched her in sad silence.

Chapter 8

Renda…Renda…

The whisperings were so low that they could have been easy to miss. But what wasn't as easy to ignore was the buzzing by my ear.

The sensation woke me up out of a deep sleep and I shrieked, jumping out of bed in one fluid motion as I spotted the big black beetle on my pillow. I hate insects, and nothing freaks me out more than having a creepy crawly critter anywhere near me.

The sudden movement also woke up Jane who snorted in irritation and stood up, instantly alert.

I went over to the window and opened it, hoping the bug would fly out. The Florida air was humid and still, but I could smell the earthy fragrance of the nearby palmetto trees and wet grass. The cicadas were singing at full volume and occasionally, I could hear a car pass by, its tires whooshing across the wet pavement.

Finally, the fat critter managed to find its way out, and I let out a sigh of relief.

That took care of the source of the buzzing. But I had no idea what or who was whispering my name.

I checked my watch and saw it was three in the morning.

The witching hour.

I read about that somewhere long ago, but couldn't recall the details. It didn't matter anyway. I was up and there was no getting back to sleep. I'd be dead at work later…

Maybe I should call in sick?

I decided it might be best to take Jane outside for a late-night pee, so I coaxed her out of the bedroom and outside. She didn't seem very excited about the idea of taking a walk at three o'clock in the morning. I didn't blame her.

As we stepped outside, I was amazed at how warm it was. I've lived in Florida my entire life, but the unbelievable humidity—even in the middle of the night—never failed to surprise me. Usually, after the sun goes down, the temperature should drop as well. But in Florida it's forever hot and humid.

Jane raced ahead and found her favorite spot, leaving me alone to muse and stare at the sky. It was a cloudless night and the smattering of stars in my vision shone brightly. It was actually quite beautiful, and I sighed into the stillness of the dark.

Jane finished her business, turned, and ran back toward the apartment. I turned to go in as well when a strange thing happened.

The most gentle of winds fluttered through the stagnant air, and with it, a small, sad voice spoke to me...

Renda. I need you. They're here and I can't get away...Help me.

I stood frozen in place for a moment. And then, every cell in my body vibrated to answer the call that had been sent out telepathically from the otherworldly realm.

Hang on Katie...I'm on my way...I'm on my way.

I said it in my mind, over and over again, like a mantra.

Rushing back inside, I yanked on some sweatpants, slipped my feet into a pair of flip-flops and ran out of the apartment, turning on my outdoor light, and locking the door behind me.

Inside, Jane whined unhappily, but I didn't have time to soothe her, as I headed straight for my car.

I sped through the streets of Cale in my anxiety to get to Katie.

When I pulled up to the hospital, it was noticeably quieter than during the day. The visitors' lot was nearly empty, and the majority of the remaining cars were parked in a staff area closer to the building.

I parked the car and got out, taking a quick look at the multi-level structure. Most of the windows were dark, but a few were still lit and glowed with a white-yellow haze.

I didn't know what I'd find inside. But I was prepared for the worst.

An empty chair faced a sparse desk and a blinking computer screen in the reception area.

Feeling a bit creeped out, I walked toward the children's ward. The hairs on the back of my neck stood up, and a tingling sensation moved through my body.

Where is everyone?

I ducked into a few rooms and was relieved to see a handful of patients sleeping, their snores amplified in the surrounding silence. But there were no nurses or doctors anywhere.

A beeping from down the hallway caught my attention. A room with a flashing light indicated a call for a nurse. I peeked in and glimpsed an elderly woman lying in bed, clearly irritated.

"Water," she rasped. "I need some water."

The poor thing looked absolutely parched, so I poured a cup of water for her and watched as her wrinkled lips wrapped around the edge of the glass as she slurped down the cool liquid.

When she was done, the woman smiled at me thankfully, displaying yellowed teeth. "Thanks, my dear. I've been trying to get the nurses to come see me for the past ten minutes, and no one seems to be responding to my call."

"You're welcome," I replied. "Have a good night." I'd turned to leave when I heard a deep cackle behind me.

I froze.

"You know where to go, don't you? She's waiting for you. We're all waiting for you."

I swung my head back to face her, but the woman's eyes were closed and she appeared to be asleep.

Fuck.

My flip-flops smacked against the tile floor as I went from fast walking to running. No one stopped me along the way, or scolded me for racing through a hospital in the middle of the night. The nurses' stations were deserted. The entire floor was empty.

Finally, I reached Katie's room. The door was closed and I couldn't hear anything.

I knocked, but no one answered.

Gently pushing the door open, I braced for a scolding from

Katie's mother but was surprised to find that Anne wasn't in the room.

Where the hell is everyone?

Katie was lying on her bed and appeared very still. As I walked over and stared at her gentle, sleeping countenance, I wondered if Katie had truly called out to me telepathically or if I was just imagining things. Then again, something weird was definitely going on at the hospital.

A thought suddenly occurred to me. My sight was "off." It was something that happened when I fell asleep. I needed to turn it back on or I wouldn't be able to figure out what was happening.

Taking a deep breath, I concentrated on the spot in my mind that allowed me to lift the lever to the next realm. As soon as I did, I felt the air change around me. It became cooler and was accompanied by an intense feeling of being watched.

I was afraid to open my eyes.

And then an icy hand curled around my wrist. When I opened my eyes, I was staring straight into the black eyes of something that had been dead a long time.

It was the same little man I'd seen in Katie's bedroom a few days ago, but now, he was larger and easier to see—though I wished he'd stayed away. The spirit was skinny to the point of being emaciated, and long white hair flowed from his pockmarked scalp. He was smartly dressed in a three-piece suit, but everything was wrinkled and fitted poorly, the folds of the fabric hanging on his sparse frame.

The man's face was skeletal and offset by a pointy noise and flinty eyes. He resembled a caricature from a horror movie, but the worst part of his appearance was the wide, rotten-toothed grin that he flashed at me. As he floated over Katie, he chortled and spittle ran down his mouth.

I yanked my arm and managed to pull away from his snake-like grip on my wrist. Terrified, I forced myself to speak, "Who... who are you?"

The specter chuckled. "I'm surprised you don't know. We've been watching you for a long time."

A chorus of cackling laughter resonated around the room, assaulting my ears.

"My name," he continued, "is Norman Ceaser, and I am one of Katie's...friends."

"You mean, you're a Rasha," I said, keeping my eyes firmly planted on his. I didn't want to convey any weakness or fear.

Norman's eyes narrowed and his grin turned into a scowl. "Well, if you know what I am, then you also know what I want."

Yes, I knew what he wanted. But there was no way I was going to let him take the sweet, beautiful girl lying on the bed.

"You can't have her. You and your...friends need to leave. There's nothing here for you. There never will be. Now, get out!"

The Rasha started snickering and the whole room shook as his eerie laughter turned into a deafening rumble.

I lost my balance as the furniture tilted at crazy angles. It was a mystery to me why no one had shown up yet, but I couldn't wait for a rescue. I was the only one who could protect Katie, so with all of my energy, I flung myself forward to cover her body and landed firmly on the hospital bed.

The shaking finally stopped but instead of Katie's slight form, all I felt was the crinkly cotton of the bedspread.

I was lying facedown on the bed.

Alone.

Anne's scream pierced the silence.

"Are you sure she was here when you came into the room?" the detective asked me for the fifth time.

"Yes, she was lying here. I don't know what happened. One minute she was here and the next minute, she was gone."

"What were you doing here? Why were you lying down on her bed? And can you repeat why you came to the hospital in the middle of the night?"

I sighed and tried not to lose my patience. The police had been questioning me for the past few hours, while investigators searched the hospital for Katie.

Anne sat opposite my chair with an accusatory look on her face as tears coursed down her cheeks. She hadn't said much to me since the incident, and I wondered where she'd come from as she wasn't in the room when I'd first arrived.

I was unable to talk to her however, because as soon as Katie had vanished into thin air, the world returned to its normal state, and the hospital room filled up fast with cops and medical personnel.

They eyed me suspiciously, and I was surprised that I hadn't yet been arrested. After all, I'd shown up out of the blue and was discovered lying in the little girl's bed. How much more guilty could a person look?

As I calmly answered all of the detective's questions, a little voice inside my mind silently considered calling a lawyer. Was it safe to be talking to the police? It had all happened so fast that I wasn't exactly thinking clearly, but now that the adrenaline was beginning to wear off, I wondered if perhaps I should stop talking.

There was no need to ponder that thought further however, because the detective finally finished grilling me and went to talk to the administrator who'd just walked in. In a hushed tone and with a grim look on her face, the administrator confirmed that no one had seen Katie. They'd checked the entire hospital. With a dark glance in my direction, the administrator told the detective that the security guards were checking the cameras that recorded movement from all building exits, but so far, the only strange occurrence had been a redheaded woman dressed in pajamas, entering the building in the middle of the night.

I rubbed my temples and looked down at my lap.

Great. That's all I need. More suspicion directed at me.

Tears of frustration threatened to spill when a moment of clarity struck. There was one place they hadn't looked. The place where I knew she would be.

The cemetery.

Just the thought of returning to where I'd been attacked the other night, made my stomach clench. There was such evil dwelling on the other side of the cemetery gates, and I didn't exactly have a team of experts who could help me fight the Rashas.

No Cole either.

A small ember of anger ignited deep within my heart. Yes, I loved him and missed him terribly, but this was ridiculous. Even though he was angry with me, he should have been helping me through this.

Wasn't that what love was all about?

If he ever returned to my world, I'd be sure to tell him a thing or two. Our relationship would need to change if we were ever to move forward.

"Ms. Bloodmane?"

The detective narrowed his eyes.

I knew he didn't have enough evidence to detain me, and that he'd possibly hit a dead end for the time being.

"Yes?"

"You're free to go. But don't plan on taking any trips out of Cale anytime soon. If we have more questions, I want to be sure you're around to answer them. Do you understand?"

I nodded and glanced over at Anne. She was talking to two nurses and had her back to me.

I left the room and slowly walked back down the hallway, looking around as I passed the nurses' stations and patient rooms.

The world had gone back to normal.

Nurses were bustling around as they checked on their patients. Despite the late hour, there was quite a bit of activity—a stark contrast to what I'd found upon my arrival.

I wasn't sure if the Rashas had hit a "pause" button within the hospital, but somehow they'd been able to abduct a child with no one but me to witness it.

Then I remembered someone else who'd been awake and alert as well.

I walked back to the room where I'd given water to the elderly woman. When I entered, I was surprised to see an orderly placing new sheets on the hospital bed.

"Can I help you?" he asked me.

"Um, I was looking for the patient who was in here earlier. She was an older woman?"

The heavyset orderly scratched his bald head.

"Ma'am, this room has been empty today. I'm just getting it ready for the next patient. Are you sure you have the right room?"

Not answering him, I backed up and ran out of the hospital.

Chapter 9

I was flying.

The sky was blue and it was a beautiful sunny day. Not a cloud to be had. Drifting along, I spotted someone up ahead. As I got closer, I could see a little girl with blonde hair. She was curled up in the fetal position in a little black box, just floating. I tried to fly faster but I couldn't get to her. I flapped my arms harder and harder but I couldn't reach her. I began to spiral down towards the ground. I shut my eyes, bracing for an impact that would surely kill me...

My eyes flew open.

I was in my bed, staring up at the ceiling.

But something was off. Someone or something was in bed with me.

My heart started pounding. Was it the Rashas again? They seemed to have a honing signal on me and could easily get to me as they did the day before when I was visited by one in my bathroom.

Still, it was better to face the fear head on, and I was learning that life would no longer allow me to simply hide under the covers. I turned my head and was shocked to see Cole lying beside me—his chin propped up on one hand.

His lean, sinewy form was stretched out on the bed, and he was wearing one of his more "up-to-date" outfits: a black shirt with faded jeans that fit his muscled thighs like a second skin. I had no idea where he got his clothes and how he managed to appear so alive in them. But I didn't care. Because he was beautiful. And he'd come back to me.

My immediate reaction was to smile. I was so happy to see

him that I didn't resist when he leaned down and kissed my mouth. I felt the initial tingle of his energy and then warmth as it radiated into my heart, and then flowed through my body like warm honey.

I was instantly aroused. Beyond aroused. I was desperate for him. I reached out and pulled him toward me.

Cole moaned in my ear, his erection straining against the denim of his jeans. He was so hard that I wondered if he'd split the seams.

He stretched out above me, grinding his cock against me. It didn't matter that Cole was a spirit—his passions were as strong as any living man's I'd ever met.

The sounds of our heavy breathing and moans filled the air while Jane—bless her heart—continued snoring in her doggie bed.

My body became liquid and I couldn't stop writhing underneath Cole. Somehow, we managed to get our clothes off without letting go of each other.

Cole never wore underwear, and his throbbing cock was red hot against my soft skin.

Without any hesitation, I stroked his shaft and began guiding him toward me, but then I heard a police car speed by, sirens blaring, and I suddenly stopped.

Everything came flooding back. Our argument. My fear. The Rashas. Adahy's visit. My birth parents. Katie vanishing. The fucking cops questioning me. Everyone at the hospital staring at me suspiciously. Anne's coldness. Everything.

Cole stared at me incredulously. "Can't you feel how much I want you?" he asked, his breath coming in short gasps.

Despite my incredible desire for the gorgeous man lying next to me, whom I loved more than anything in the world, I couldn't stop the roiling in my gut.

I was angry.

Groaning in lustful agony, Cole rolled over on his back and stared up at the ceiling.

"Where have you been?" Anger and hurt seeped into my words.

"I felt like it was best to give you your space." He blew out a breath and continued. "But, I forgive you now. Clearly, you didn't mean what you said."

He forgives me?

Red-hot anger flooded every cell in my body, but I warned myself to remain calm. The last time I'd allowed my temper to take over, Cole had disappeared and despite how disappointed I was in his behavior, I didn't want him to leave again. We had to work this out. So I decided to choose my words carefully.

"It's true, I didn't mean what I said, but you can't just run away every time I say something you don't like. There's been a lot going on here, and I could've used some help, some guidance, you know?"

Cole leapt from the bed, and I couldn't help but admire his lean, muscular body. *Damn.*

He grabbed his pants and yanked them on. Dragging his hands through his hair, he locked eyes with me. "You don't think I know that? You don't think I watch over you, even when I'm not here? I didn't abandon you. But maybe I should have."

"Yeah?" I asked, my voice now rising as well. "Then you obviously need glasses, because you clearly weren't 'watching over me' when a Rasha popped into the bathroom after my shower last night. And certainly not when Norman, the crazy Rasha, took Katie from me! Not to mention when that horde of Rashas was chasing me through the cemetery. Where were you then? Huh?"

I wanted to stop, knew that I was going down the same angry path that I'd traveled down before. But there was no way to keep my mouth shut. I loved Cole more than anything in the world, but I couldn't let him treat me like a part-time mistress, available whenever he got the urge to fuck. If we were going to be together, he would need to be there not just for lovemaking but for the tough stuff too.

I loved our sexual intimacy, but there was a time and a place for it. Right now, I needed Cole to help sort through this Rasha mess. If we had sex, he would expend too much energy and then vanish for hours in order to regenerate. And I couldn't let him do that.

There was too much at stake.

Cole's shoulders suddenly sagged and to my horror, his energy quickly evaporated in front of me.

"I'm sorry," he said. His eyes filled with remorse as he gazed at me. "You're right. But I was watching you sleep for several hours and combined with our near lovemaking session, I've expended too much energy. Forgive me, I can't stay and talk this out—I didn't do a great job recycling my essence. It's just because I was so excited to see you."

I got up and tried to touch him, but my hands passed through his arm into thin air.

"I'll be back," he said softly. "And we can finish this discussion. Just...be safe."

As the words tumbled from his lips, he closed his eyes and vanished.

Getting ready for work was difficult. I continued to run the morning's events through my mind but wasn't sure if Cole and I had made up, or if we were in worse shape than before.

Still, I was thoroughly relieved that he had returned to me. And even though things were uncertain, and I wasn't happy about his quick disappearance, I understood it. Sometimes, when Cole got mad or extremely aroused, he forgot to recycle energy through his spiritual body and ended up draining himself more quickly. Just as I needed to control my temper, he needed to control his emotions as well. Otherwise our time together would be very limited indeed. It was so damn frustrating. But we both needed to learn to keep calm when we argued. Otherwise, we'd never get anywhere.

In the early days, Cole had been unable to touch me because he'd immediately lose his energy. My body would absorb it like a salve. But Adahy had taught him how to control this phenomenon and instead, recycle the energy through his system. This "recycling" allowed him to remain with me for longer periods of time, but it wasn't a perfect science.

And now, I had a full eight hours of work ahead of me in the library, and I was a mess of thoughts, nerves, and expectations. I knew that Cole wouldn't be able to return to me for at least half the day, maybe longer. So for now, I was on my own and would have to continue on—in my own way.

The library wasn't very busy, which was a relief.

I pulled Larlene aside and talked to her about the morning's events as well as what had happened in Katie's room.

Her eyes grew wide as I told her about Norman showing up and snatching Katie.

"That's some serious shit. What are you going to do now?" she asked.

"Well, I'm going to try to figure out who this guy is. I have to do some research."

"Excuse me. Where can I find books about bees?" asked an elderly woman, interrupting our discussion.

Larlene gave my hand a squeeze and walked away to help her.

I was disappointed that we couldn't discuss the matter further, but now that I had a quick moment to myself, I headed over to my stash of books about demons that I kept handy just in case I needed some quick information. I perused the books but came up empty handed. Given my past experience with a demon and what I'd read about them—they liked to "strut their stuff" so to speak. Possessing a body and controlling it. But from what I'd seen with the Rashas—they were very secretive and tried to remain hidden. They'd literally made Katie vanish. Their goals and methods were different.

Sighing, I put the books away and tried to think. The best way to find information about Norman Ceaser would be to search online. Avoiding the computers in the staff office, I slipped into the empty conference room. I locked the door and took a seat at the computer terminal stationed there. Typing *Norman Ceaser* into a search engine, I blew out a breath and waited.

When the results popped up on screen, many different *Normans* appeared but as I scrolled down the list, I couldn't find anything that seemed like a good fit.

Then, I came upon a link to a newspaper site that archived Florida news articles. Norman's name appeared within the text of an article that talked about a child murderer, but once I clicked on the link, I was instantly asked to provide a username

and password. At that moment, my boss poked his head in and
asked how the budget was coming along.

I smiled and told him I was plowing through it.

He nodded, clicked the door shut, and walked up to chat
with Karen, a new librarian, who was going through a pile
of returns. Weird. My boss was usually hands-off. He rarely
ventured onto the library floor.

Damn. I'll have to get back to this later.

Clicking off the browser, I tried to focus on the library's
latest project, a major fundraiser with a local art gallery that
combined art and literature. But after an hour of working on the
budget and timetable for the week-long events set for late next
year, I found myself thinking more and more about Norman.

He wasn't a demon after all. He was just a restless human
spirit and possibly a child murderer.

I glanced out the wall of windows of the conference room.
My boss was nowhere to be seen, and Larlene was busy with a
group of school children. Taking a deep breath, I went online
again and ended up back at the newspaper archiving site.

The site requested that you pay for usage, so I quickly typed
in my credit card information, wincing at the forty dollars a
month price tag, and after answering a few questions was given
access.

I immediately clicked on the *Cale Tribune*, which was a small
newspaper outfit that had been around for decades but had
eventually folded in the early 2000s when the Internet exploded
in popularity. The traditional newspaper business had been
going downhill ever since. As a librarian, it saddened me, but at
least I could access the archives of old newspapers online.

The familiar insignia of the paper appeared alongside
numerous options. Instead of trying to mess with the different
tabs, I typed his name into the search box and waited. Within
a few moments, the article I'd been seeking revealed itself on
the screen. The article was from 1972 and was a retrospective
on various closed cases. The section that talked about Norman
was lengthy and contained a photo of the man. Despite the fact
that the picture had been taken of Norman in earlier years, well
before his death, I could see the resemblance between the figure

in the photo and the man I'd seen floating over Katie's hospital bed.

The write-up was long, so I focused on the important parts:

Authorities believe that Norman Ceaser, also known as the "Basement Killer," had been luring children back to his home for several months. Allegedly, once a child was in his custody, he would keep the youngsters captive in a hidden room in his basement, that he'd secretly built. In this prison, he forced them to listen to hours of scripture, while keeping them in a semi-starved state.

In a positive turn of events, police rescued one of the victims, a six-year-old girl, whose whereabouts were discovered when a neighbor heard her screams. After the neighbor called the authorities about the suspicious sounds, police entered Ceaser's residence and found the girl chained to a wall in the basement. She'd been starved and was dehydrated but after medical intervention, was able to describe her captor.

The girl told authorities that Ceaser was crazy and had forced her to read the Bible throughout the day while he yelled out different verses and screamed at the sky. Despite her young age, the child vividly described to them how the man had kept her chained to the wall for weeks, not even allowing her to use the toilet and forcing her to urinate and defecate on the floor.

Prepared to make an arrest, police waited for Ceaser to come home, but he never did. Instead, his body was found hanging from a tree at the Cale Cemetery, where he'd committed suicide.

Further investigation revealed that Ceaser had abducted and killed five other little girls from as far off as Miami. His suicide prevented the grieving parents from receiving the justice they so desperately wanted...

I skimmed through the rest of the article and found that Norman had been buried in Cale's cemetery, but his grave had been desecrated so many times by vandals, due to the atrocities of his crimes, that he was eventually moved to an unknown location within the cemetery—to an unmarked grave.

Chills racked my body as I thought about how evil the man had been. A true monster.

Even though he's dead, he's still a monster.

And he has Katie.

My car sat idling outside of the Marcks' home as I thought about how to best approach Katie's mother.

Despite it being the middle of the day, I'd raced out of the library with only one thought in my head.

I have to save Katie.

Every minute that she was lost to the world of the living, her soul would become weaker and more vulnerable to the evil energy that surrounded her. And sitting in a library doing research wouldn't help me any longer. I now knew what I was dealing with. I knew what Norman Ceaser had been in life and what he had become in the afterlife.

It was time to *act*.

To my surprise, the front door opened as soon as my car pulled up the Marcks' driveway. Both of Katie's parents stared at me solemnly. It was the first time I'd come face-to-face with Katie's father, my uncle, and I had a feeling that he'd been waiting for me.

I stepped out of the car and slowly made my way over to them. The heat of the day was incredible—the air around me so humid that it felt as if I was wading through soup. It was hard to breathe, but I forced my legs to propel me forward.

When I was close enough to the couple to speak, I found myself trembling. They were my family, and somehow, we'd been pulled together because of this tragedy. My uncle Brent was tall with reddish blonde hair and brown eyes. He looked very much like my father as he appeared to me before crossing over.

But my mind didn't have time to register any more questions, because before I knew it, my uncle reached his arms out to me and hugged me close to him.

I nearly collapsed against him, the feelings within me so powerful that they threatened to overtake all sanity. Tears poured down my cheeks as all of the emotions that had held me in their unforgiving grasp finally exploded.

My uncle was now the closest link I had to my parents.

After a few moments I pulled away and stepped back, a bit embarrassed. It wasn't every day that I bawled my eyes out in front of strangers, even though they were family. But things had changed forever and there was no going back.

"Renda. My sweet Renda." My uncle sighed. Sorrowful eyes gazed down at me. Glancing first toward Anne, who remained solemn, he turned back to me and motioned to the door. "Why don't you come in so that we can talk?"

As I entered the house, it was noticeably silent despite their little dog nipping at my heels. I figured she smelled Jane's scent on me, so I knelt down and petted the creature's soft head. In return, the little terrier tried to lick my face.

I smiled and then stood up and focused on the Marcks.

My uncle was already sitting down at the kitchen table with Anne, so I joined them. The chair was hard underneath me, and I suddenly became anxious. There were so many unanswered questions. Did Anne blame me for Katie's disappearance? She barely looked at me and when she did—her eyes were narrow slits of accusation.

"So, I'm sure you've got lots of things you want to ask me," Uncle Brent said. "But you've got to understand that we didn't tell you sooner because we wanted to protect you. You see, we think the creatures that took Katie are the same ones that killed my brother. Are you sure you're ready for this?"

I nodded and waited for him to continue.

My uncle took a sip of coffee and stood up. He walked over to the window and gazed out for what seemed like a long time, as though he were looking back into the past.

"When I finally met him, your father shared a secret with me...He always knew that he was different. He constantly had these weird dreams and imaginary friends who no one else could see. The crazy thing was that he could also predict the future. Not big stuff like who was going to win the World Series or anything, but he could tell you if you were going to hit a home run at your next game, or if that girl you liked was finally going to notice you. Just little things. And then, he met your mother."

At this point, my uncle paused and turned back to me. I wasn't sure what he was waiting for, so I just nodded again.

"You look a lot like her. She was such a beautiful woman, and she really swept your dad off his feet. When they met through a hiking group, he told me that it was love at first sight. And they were really happy for a while. But after they'd been married for about a year, your mother got pregnant and things started to change.

"Your father confided in me that he felt like he was being watched by an evil presence and that something was trying to possess him—take over his mind or something. He couldn't sleep, couldn't eat. It scared the hell out of him.

"The last time I saw him, he was on his way to talk to a priest. He felt like he was being attacked by a demon. He was in his car, when something went wrong and he veered out of control and slammed into a tree. He wasn't wearing a seatbelt and his face went into the windshield.

"There was no other car involved, Renda. It was so shocking. He just…lost control."

Tears were once again pouring down my face, but I somehow managed to find my voice. "What w-was his name?" I asked shakily.

"Your father's name was John, and your mother's name was… Evelyn."

Evelyn!

When I was in Macon helping Bobbie's mother through her possession, I'd had a dream about a woman who'd been talking with an elderly man. He'd called her Evelyn.

It was my mother. I saw her in my dream. And she must have been the woman who helped me in the woods after the demon Elial had overtaken my body. I hadn't made the connection when I'd seen my mother and father in Adahy's vision, because their images had been so blurry. But it was all so clear now.

Would I see her again? I hoped so. But first, there were other things I needed to know.

"Is my mother alive? I've seen her in my dreams, and she appeared to me in Macon."

My uncle and aunt exchanged glances and then, Aunt

Anne spoke. "We don't know, Renda. After you were born, she disappeared. We have a feeling that she was running from the same things that attacked your father, but we're not sure. And she's never contacted us."

There was a pause and then she continued, nodding toward her husband. "After I married Brent he told me the whole story— that he searched for you—"

"You tried to find me?" My eyes flew to my uncle's face. He nodded, tears in his eyes.

"I didn't know how or where to look for you. But I did some research and found out you'd been adopted by good people." He blew out a breath and raked his hands through his hair. "I thought it was best to let you grow up free from all this. As the years passed and everything seemed okay, I thought it best to just let it go and let you live your life.

"I understand," I said quietly, staring down at my clasped hands.

Aunt Anne quietly interjected. "But then Brent and I met, got married, and we had Katie and…and strange things started happening. That's when Brent told me the whole story."

I glanced at her, my eyes widening. So that's why my aunt had been so angry and accusatory. She'd had no idea what she'd married into, until after Katie was born.

"You have a gift," Uncle Brent said, drawing my attention back. "Most likely inherited from both your mother *and* father. We now know that Katie has a similar gift—"

"We need your help to find our daughter," Aunt Anne interrupted in a desperate tone. "We can't lose her to those monsters."

I wasn't sure what to say. The Rashas had probably killed my father and now they wanted Katie. With Elial, there had been some direction—Adahy had provided guidance. But now, I was up against a slew of evil spirits that made Elial look like a boy scout in comparison. How could I succeed?

As if reading my thoughts, Uncle Brent opened a kitchen drawer. He pulled out an envelope that looked worn and handed it to me. Three simple words were written on it.

For my daughter.

My heart nearly stopped in my chest as the impact of the words seeped in.

"We wanted to give you this letter sooner, but honestly Renda, we were very scared about the impact. Plus, your adoptive parents don't know about us, or any of this stuff. We were frightened, and just didn't want to create trouble for anyone. And I promised your father I would never read this letter, so I left it locked away for you. I thought that when the time was right I would give it to you. I think that time is now. We need your help to find Katie, and I think this might be the answer. I know it seems selfish to only share this with you now, but you have to believe me that we were trying to protect you."

I nodded again, feeling like I was standing in the middle of a tornado. The constant flow of new information was making my head spin, and there was simply too much being shared for me to process anything.

"We'll give you some privacy while you read it. Come on, honey."

And with that, my aunt and uncle left the kitchen and went into the living room.

With shaking fingers, I opened the envelope and began reading the handwritten letter.

Dear Daughter,

Right now, you are still protected deep within your mother's womb. But I'm worried for you, and this may be the best way to preserve my thoughts so that you make better decisions than I have.

Your mother and I love you very much. We wanted a child since we met on that special day, deep within the Georgia woods. I hope one day you get a chance to visit there and experience the same beauty that we did.

If you're reading this letter, it means that something has happened to me and your mother, and I'm not there to tell you this personally. Please don't take what I'm about to tell you, lightly. Your life may depend on it.

By now, you may have noticed that you have certain "abilities." You may be able to see spirits, or talk to creatures that no one else can see. You may be having strange dreams and feeling as if you are being watched. If these things have happened to you, don't be afraid.

If these things haven't happened to you yet, then you can put this letter away and read it at a later date. I don't want you to think that your father was crazy. I'm just trying to help you.

Your mother and I both have an ability that we like to call "the special sight". Some people call us "The Chosen," but no matter how you look at it, we're different than other people. We have the ability to see the dead, predict the future, and travel to places outside of our dimension.

These gifts can be wonderful and can lead to a richer, more exciting life, but they can also be dangerous.

There are creatures who have recognized this ability that we have. They are called "Rashas" and they are evil masses of dark spirits who seek to overtake us. For some reason, people like us contain strength in our souls that is like food for these horrible, restless spirits. The more of us they can possess, the stronger they become.

And there's more…

Your mother and I have sought counsel from some of the wisest members of The Chosen and it appears that there is a prophecy predicting that the Rashas will be able to transcend life and death if they become strong enough. They are strong now, but in order to fully transform, they need to possess a special soul.

The Rashas aren't sure whose soul they are seeking, because as the prophecy tells us, there is one of The Chosen who is stronger than the rest and who has inherited the gifts of the Elders. The primary gift that the Rashas seek to encompass is the gift of full immersion—that is, the gift to change form from death to life, and back again.

I know this is confusing Renda, but your mother and I have reason to believe that you might be that soul. We aren't sure, because you haven't entered our world yet, but the Rashas have begun their assault on us. Your mother and I are in grave danger and it's because of you.

Please don't think that either of us blames you for being special. We are here to protect you and ensure that you're safe, but I fear that if you're reading this, you're on your own already.

I have some advice as to how you can defeat the Rashas if they come after you or someone you love: The Rashas are a mass of evil energy, though they do contain some ringleaders within their core. Hopefully, you will never meet any of them, but if you do, we've been given guidance on how you can fight them.

First of all, you must find a religious leader. This can be a pastor or priest, whichever you choose. The importance here is that the person be of strong mind and spirit. It really isn't the sect of religion that's key, rather it is the condition of the person's soul.

Then, you must find a crucifix. This is crucial as it represents the most powerful symbol of religious piety to the Rashas, and given that they were all once human, they understand and fear it. I know that God is on our side in this fight.

When you are near the Rashas, you must have the religious person recite the following passage over and over again.

"Hear ye' Rashas of the blackest spirit. Be gone or face the purest and holiest of energies from God and his truest followers. Return from where you've come."

I know it seems silly, but trust me, it works. I've seen your mother protect herself many times and she's recited these words over and over. We actually have a family friend who's a pastor and he's helped us too. It seems to work better when he says the verse and your mother approaches these awful beings with a cross in her hand.

But then, once you've come close to them, you've got to be forceful and speak without fear. They feed on fear and seem to gain strength when they sense that you're afraid.

My darling daughter, I need you to be brave, but what I say next is crucial for your survival and the survival of your loved ones, and those who need your help.

If the Rashas have abducted a living soul, you must act quickly. There is only one thing you can do. You must enter their realm, reclaim that soul, or doom that soul for eternity.

I have to tell you, neither your mother nor I have ever entered their realm. We've been lucky enough to ward them off by reciting the verse and holding steadfast to our faith. But lately, the creatures have

been hounding me day and night. I can't seem to get away from them.
They're everywhere! I fear for my loved ones. I fear that through me the
Rashas can take hold of your mother and you. I need to act, and soon.
But before I do, I need to tell you something else.

If we are gone by the time you read this, and you are fighting the
Rashas on your own, please be careful. There is much that we don't
understand, so I'm hoping that you've received some counsel from the
spirit world. There is one spirit who may contact you. His name is
Adahy, and he is a wise Native American who was alive when the first
English settlers arrived on our soil. You can trust what he says and
should follow his advice. I hope he finds you before all of this starts to
unfold in your life.

Hopefully, I'll find you and tell you how much you mean to me.
I love you baby girl,
Daddy

A tear dripped down my cheek and splashed onto the letter. I'd seen my father in the library on two different occasions. The first time, he appeared as he'd died—with half of his face missing. At the time, I assumed that it was due to a gunshot wound and hadn't known who I was looking at.

But the second time, my father appeared as he had looked in life. In those few minutes together, I realized that despite feeling lonely most of the time, I was never really alone. There were people in the spirit world who had always watched over me and still do. Even though my father had finally moved on to the other side where he could be at peace, the brief exchange gave me comfort in knowing who my biological father was, and that he loved me always.

And now, after reading his letter, I was even more determined in my purpose. Strangely, it didn't frighten or overwhelm me. If I really was the strongest of my kind, then I was also the best equipped to handle the trials that came my way. The Rashas had killed my father, but I'd be damned before I'd let them take anyone else I loved. And now I had the guidance necessary to make my preparations for the battle to save Katie.

My second battle, but certainly not my last.

I slipped the letter in my pocket and made my way down the darkened hallway to join the Marcks. As my eyes adjusted, a strange thing happened.

My second sight turned on—on its own.

It was the first time my sight completely activated without any effort. Lately, it had been flickering periodically, allowing a few spirits to appear but usually I had to concentrate to lift the lever in my mind, and the special sight remained until I turned it off or fell asleep.

But in that moment, the sight had been turned on unexpectedly, and I was staring at my aunt and uncle who were deep in conversation as they sat on the couch together, and didn't realize that there were dark clouds swirling above their heads.

Without hesitation, I pulled the letter out of my pocket, burning my father's words into my memory. I then quickly walked up to my aunt and uncle and glared up at the dark clouds hovering over their heads. With as strong a voice as I could muster, I shouted, "Hear ye' Rashas of the blackest spirit. Be gone or face the purest and holiest of energies from God and his truest followers. Return from where you've come."

My aunt and uncle were stunned by my actions but miraculously, the dark clouds dissipated into the lukewarm air, leaving the room empty once more.

I didn't wait for either of them to say anything. There wasn't enough time.

"I've got to go. Thank you for sharing my father's letter with me. Please do me a favor and stay close to home. I'll be in touch within the next few days. Trust me, I will do everything in my power to save Katie."

My aunt pulled me into her arms. The accusatory look she'd had earlier was gone and I was glad she'd reached out. As we embraced, she whispered in my ear, "Thank you. Please save my baby."

When I returned to the library, it was late in the afternoon. My boss was standing near the door and gave me a disapproving look. I knew I was in trouble, so I made up a tiny lie about having to go home and search for Jane, who had somehow gotten out of the apartment. It was a fib, but it worked and I was able to get away with a stern reminder that I needed to let someone know if I was going to leave unexpectedly, as the library was short-staffed, and my absence had caused a strain on the remaining personnel.

I knew this was complete bullshit, because the library was practically devoid of patrons, but instead of arguing, I smiled demurely and apologized for the hundredth time.

As soon as my boss walked away, Larlene sidled up next to me with a grin on her face. "Well, looks like you got into a bit of trouble. Don't worry about it though. That asshole spent the entire afternoon on the phone in his office. Probably phone sex or something." She let out a giggle and pulled me aside to one of the nearby reading tables.

"So, tell me what's going on. Where were you?

I tried to give Larlene as much of the story as possible, including Cole's most recent re-appearing act. But, no matter how I described it, it didn't come across the right way, and I knew that Cole sounded like an unreliable jerk.

"I'm not sure about him," Larlene said. She pursed her lips and shook her head. "I mean—he needs to get a grip and stop disappearing on you all the time. I know you love him and things in the relationship aren't exactly normal. But, seriously."

Even though it felt good to confide in Larlene about the day's events, I didn't want to stand there talking to her about Cole. I actually had other things that I needed help with. Urgent things.

"Do you know anyone religious? I haven't gone to church in ages, and I don't know any…I don't know, what are they called? Men of the cloth?"

Larlene laughed again. "You are so funny, Renda. I don't think anyone actually calls a priest or pastor that. You're watching way too many classic movies on the BBC. But don't worry. I have a cousin who's a recently ordained minister and he should be able to help you out. He lives in Thomasville, but I'm sure he'd be willing to come down here. Why do you need him?"

I explained what my father's letter had outlined and the fact that I needed someone closely connected to God to accompany me as it helped to weaken the hold of the Rashas.

Larlene raised her eyebrows but then shrugged and called her cousin while I anxiously watched and waited.

Surprisingly, her normally chatty nature was on mute as she got right to the point and asked her cousin to come to Cale to meet a friend of hers who had recently found God and was looking for a church to affiliate with. She laid it on thick as she explained how keen her friend was to join his congregation.

I found the whole thing ridiculous, because why would I want to join a church in a town that was an hour away? But somehow, it worked. "Cousin Gary" was coming to visit.

"Really, Larlene," I said as she clicked off the cell. "You are super-sleuthy."

She winked at me, and we headed off to finish up our work for the day.

My second sight remained on for the rest of the day and no matter how hard I tried, I couldn't shut it off. Thankfully, the spirits in the library were mostly calm apparitions so they didn't bother me much. But I nearly lost it when an old ghost woman poked her head through the bathroom stall door as I was sitting on the toilet.

With the dead, there was rarely any privacy.

The only benefit of seeing spirits constantly was that it kept my mind sharp. I knew there was a fight coming with the Rashas, and I had to be on my game and aware of my surroundings.

Knowing that the rest of my life would be a constant battle with these evil forces made me yearn for my old existence. Yes, having clarity about my biological parents was a true gift, and Cole…well, Cole was a wonderful addition to my world. But all of that had come with complications.

For so long it had been just Jane and me. My weekends used to be ordinary. But there was a comfort in that routine: Grocery shopping on Saturdays, and a visit to my parents, or coffee with a friend. Saturday nights were movie nights, usually classic Hollywood romances, with Jane providing her own snoring soundtrack. Sundays were reserved for laundry and tucking into a Jane Austen or a Georgette Heyer novel. Sometimes there was a lame date with a local guy I had nothing in common with.

But mainly, I just stayed home.

And now? Oh, how I wished for that ordinary, boring routine.

I wished that my boyfriend was a living person and that dead people didn't constantly pester me with their life stories—or rather—death stories.

I wished that my biological parents had been regular people and not in possession of some strange, supernatural gift that made them targets for hordes of evil spirits.

And I wished that I could be normal. Like everyone else.

As I drove home to let Jane out before heading to Larlene's, it was impossible not to notice the numerous spirits walking the streets. It reminded me that some spirits, once they discover that the sun can help them regenerate, make it a point to wander around outside as much as possible.

At one point, I stopped at a red traffic light, and an emaciated, bald young woman stepped in front of my car. I gasped until I realized she was dead. Still, her eyes were calm. As she stood in the middle of the road, she waved at me hesitantly, the wind ruffling the light pink hospital gown that hung loosely over her frail body.

I waved back and smiled slightly.

When the light changed, I felt badly about hitting the accelerator, but I knew that my vehicle would simply pass through her. As I drove, I could actually smell the scent of baby powder float around me as her gentle, warm wind washed over my arms and face.

It was moments like these, when I appreciated my gift. These spirits remained stuck, unable to go back to their lives, but reluctant to move on. For the most part, they were alone. That's why the connection with a living person was so important to them.

It was a link to the past—a way to remember the life they used to have and an acknowledgment that someone could truly see them.

The idea made me think of Cole and the fact that somehow, he was more real and more dynamic than many of the people I interacted with on a daily basis. His entire being was condensed into a powerful, burning energy. It fed me like an addiction.

A shiver passed through my body, and I sincerely hoped that he would return soon so that we could finish our conversation. I knew that he was angry with me for taking such dangerous risks, but I had no choice. This was my purpose.

I was no longer the same person he'd met weeks ago at the Trillos'.

Trying to focus on the task at hand, I maneuvered my car onto the side road that led to my apartment complex. I parked the vehicle, but as soon as I stepped out, I felt a prickling sensation on my skin. It wasn't a spirit. It was a foreboding that something wasn't right.

My pulse accelerated as I walked to the front door. Hands trembling, I inserted the key and turned the lock.

Jane should have been barking in anticipation.

But all was eerily quiet.

The door slowly swung open, revealing the darkness inside.

Jane didn't run up to greet me.

"Jane?" I called out, fearful of what I might find. "Jane?"

A low growl raised the fine hairs on the back of my neck.

It came from my living room, but my eyes needed to adjust to the darkness. As everything came into view, I could see that my yellow Labrador was backed up against the wall.

She looked terrified but ready to fight, her large eyes staring straight ahead, her jaws set in a snarl, her paws planted firmly on the ground, spread out as if she was about to pounce.

At first, I couldn't tell what she was looking at, because there was nothing in front of her.

But then, I saw it.

A giant spider was hanging from the ceiling, but when its head turned to leer at me, my heart literally stopped in my chest.

It was Norman Ceaser. His body was contorted into a human-sized spider, his legs bent in an impossible manner and his head at a strange angle. His neck twisted like a pretzel as his crazed eyes peered at me.

"Hello, darling," he said in a voice that made my skin crawl. "How's about we give you a little spin?"

Before I could even scream, the monster swooped down on me. Jane raced forward, as she tried to protect me from the hellish creature. But it was faster than she was.

Icy-cold tentacles wrapped themselves around my chest and squeezed the air out of my lungs. Desperate to get away, I pushed and shoved against him, but he was too strong, and seemed to be growing legs in every direction, wrapping around me like a deadly twine.

As though from a great distance, I could hear Jane barking and growling. She must have tried to bite the creature, because in the next instant I heard her whimper.

Jane!

My chest ached to pull in oxygen, and as I clawed at nothingness, a mortal fear set in.

Oh my God. This is it. This fucking freakish spider is going to suffocate me—

Just as I felt a dark despair as the air was choked out of my body, a blast of heat swept through me. The monster's hold loosened and then vanished altogether.

Norman Ceaser was gone...

For now.

I fell back to the floor and coughed, gasping to suck in as much air as possible while I struggled to regain full consciousness. Jane barked and then started nuzzling my face. I laughed and sobbed at the same time, as I hugged her close. I managed to sit up and finally got a good look at who'd saved me.

Cole stood a few feet away. He was breathing heavily and bent over in exhaustion—odd for a ghost.

I started to say something, but he put up his hand to stop my words as he regained his composure.

We stared at each other for a few minutes. I still trembled, but Jane was determined to provide me with comfort in the only way she knew how—by licking my face and sitting on top of me.

I couldn't help myself. I burst into laughter again.

One minute a crazy ghost spider is strangling me and the next minute my dog is washing my face with her tongue.

I looked up at Cole with relief and gratitude shining in my eyes.

But Cole wasn't smiling. His eyes were dead serious.

"Are you okay?" he asked.

I nodded and waited for him to reprimand me again for putting myself in a risky situation. Instead, he surprised me by sitting cross-legged on the floor the way Adahy did, and stared back at me with a concerned expression on his face.

"Thank you for saving me," I said softly.

He nodded and reached for my hand, kissing my palm.

"Renda, this is very difficult for me to say, but it must be expressed." He closed his eyes and seemed to be grappling with himself. "I don't know if you realize it, but I keep trying to leave you."

My mouth dropped open, and it felt as if someone had just kicked me in the heart. Where was this coming from?

Cole's gaze softened. "Please understand that I don't want to leave you. It's just that I think you would be so much better off without a *romantic* distraction like me in your life. I will always watch over you and try to help you in any way I can, but as you've said a few times, I *am* dead. And you'll never have a normal relationship with me. So perhaps it's best if we go our separate ways."

I couldn't believe what I was hearing. I'd just survived the spider-of-death-squeeze by that cadaverous lunatic Norman Ceaser, and now my beloved was trying to break up with me?

Mustering all of my remaining strength, I pulled my hand away and stood up, motioning for Jane to go outside. I couldn't have this conversation now.

"So, you're just going to walk away from me?" Cole asked, surprise in his eyes.

"You saved my life," I choked out. "For that I am truly grateful. But I cannot have this conversation. Not now. I was just attacked by a Rasha, and Jane has to go out, and I have to meet with a minister who might help me save Katie. We need to talk. But not now. Please understand."

I turned around and watched as Jane ran out to the trees and began sniffing around the bushes. A warm wind tickled my arm and I didn't have to turn around to see that Cole had disappeared. It would have been impossible to see him anyway through the blur of tears filling my eyes.

Chapter 10

It was difficult for me to imagine that Larlene and her cousin Gary were both of the same genetic makeup. She was typically loud, full of energy, and the center of attention.

But her cousin was the complete opposite.

Despite being a minister and leading his own congregation, Gary didn't seem to be as socially comfortable in person as he might have been from behind the pulpit. As Larlene did the introductions, he gave me a gentle handshake and an awkward smile.

Gary was a short, round man, with a head that looked like an oversized egg. A couple of thin wisps of hair covered the top of his scalp.

Surprised by his shyness, I silently beseeched Larlene for some help.

"I haven't told Gary anything yet," she said apologetically, as she handed us each a glass of iced tea and motioned for us to take a seat on her white leather sofa. She sat across from us on a poppy-red accent chair. An identical one was strategically placed on the other side of the white ottoman coffee table. Darlene loved splashes of bright color. I was with her the day she'd discovered the chairs at a local thrift shop. She'd almost squealed in delight.

Oh, to go back to those carefree days.

"Gary arrived just before you got here, and we were talking about some family things. So, feel free to fill him in."

I was annoyed. Larlene was leaving the full responsibility on my shoulders, and given my recent exchange with Cole, I wasn't exactly in the best of moods. I tried to explain what was going on in the most matter-of-fact manner possible.

At first, the minister could barely look at me as I spoke, and instead kept his gaze fixed on his glass of iced tea. But as I continued telling him about Katie and the Rashas, he looked up at me, and his eyes grew hard and serious. I could tell that despite his quiet demeanor, Gary had an inner strength that wasn't immediately apparent.

Finally, I came to the crux of the conversation—the fact that I would need him to accompany me in the battle against the Rashas in order to save Katie. I managed to finish the entire request in one breath, took a gulp of tea, and waited for him to respond.

The minister carefully placed his glass on the coaster on the coffee table, then leaned back on the couch and closed his eyes.

After about a minute of waiting for him to speak, I glanced up at Larlene questioningly. It looked as if he was praying, but perhaps he was just contemplating what to do.

Larlene jumped in quickly. "Look, Gar," she said, "If you think Renda's crazy, she's not, I promise you. She's fighting against some pretty bad spirits and all we need is for you to stand there and just recite a passage over and over. It has to be a religious person."

In truth, I knew that if things went the way we expected, the small-town minister wouldn't just be standing in place. He would probably be praying for his own life, while I struggled to rescue Katie. But that wasn't something he had to know about right now.

Finally, he opened his eyes and spoke.

"I'll do it. But never ask this of me again. I counsel people through their marital, family, and health struggles. Life is hard enough without looking for trouble by battling the Devil himself. There are other spiritual leaders who do this work regularly, but it is not my calling. I will do this to help the little girl. She's a child of God and she's an innocent. She didn't seek this out." His eyes probed mine. "I am ready to begin, if you are."

I let out my breath, unaware that I'd been holding it while he was speaking. I was relieved that he would help me, but my inner voice was telling me it wasn't the right time of day. We would have to go at night. Not to mention, I was exhausted and I didn't feel strong enough to face what was ahead. I needed to regenerate my own energy and prepare myself for what could be the fight of my life. I had a feeling that the Rashas were using Katie to get to me. Norman Ceaser's appearance at my apartment was proof of that. They wouldn't harm her for now.

I also needed to study my father's letter again and be sure that I was completely prepared for what lay ahead. Once everything was set in motion, there would be no room for error. Ready or not, I had to do this. Katie's life depended on it.

The idea of going back to my apartment didn't thrill me either, given my earlier encounter with the Norman-Rasha-creature. It might still be there, lurking in the shadows and waiting for the perfect time to strike. Leaving Jane behind had been difficult.

Still, there was no choice. I had to go back.

We agreed to venture into the cemetery the next night. With the full moon making its appearance, we would have light to help us navigate through the darkness.

Larlene insisted on going with us, and even though I really didn't want to involve her in the paranormal mess we were in, I finally gave in and agreed. She'd helped me find the minister after all, and there was strength in numbers.

We said our good-byes and after giving my friend a hug, I drove home.

My arrival at the apartment was uneventful. I was relieved to see Jane run up to me, barking in exuberance.

She raced outside to find her spot and left me standing in the doorway. Thankfully my apartment was devoid of any spirits.

I was still seeing the dead everywhere I looked and couldn't believe that my inner sight was still stuck in the "on" position. But I was doing my best to block them out, and it was starting to become easier for me to navigate around them.

As nightfall was fast approaching, they were out in greater numbers, but none of them entered my apartment and mostly remained a few yards away as if they knew that my home was sacred ground and a private place where they couldn't venture.

When Jane and I went back inside, I turned on the lights and gasped when I saw who was sitting on the couch.

Cole was resting his head in his hands. He looked so forlorn, I just wanted to wrap my arms around him and hold him close.

I knew that he was having trouble coming to terms with what was happening. During a large portion of his spiritual life, he'd been roaming the halls of my friend Bobbie Trillo's grand mansion in Macon, awaiting revenge on someone who had cheated him in a duel. That revenge of course, would never come, because the spirit of the man who had killed him was no doubt in a different place. But the terrible fate of spirits like Cole was the never-ending obsession to take care of the "unfinished business" that plagued them.

This desire to correct the wrongdoing that had taken their lives was what kept many spirits like Cole out of the light and stuck in limbo between the world of the living and the darkness. Many haunting spirits were so gripped by their past, that they could not truly let go. In Cole's case, he had attained a spiritual awareness of his motivations. He understood that he could move on and cross over. But he opted to remain as he was, and stay frozen in the land of unrest.

All because of me.

Did he regret that decision?

I walked over and sat beside my lover. His dark hair had fallen over his hands, and I could see his firm muscles straining against the fabric of his shirt. His body was my temple, and I couldn't help but feel sexual energy course through me whenever I was near him. We hadn't made love in a while, and I ached for him, but I also wanted to comfort him and be comforted by him.

"Cole," I whispered. "It's okay. I don't want you to leave me. Please. We'll figure this out."

He looked up at me, and I could see his dark eyes shining in the light. His face, always so strong, reflected a softness and vulnerability that I hadn't seen before. My heart bled at the sight of his pain.

I instinctively knew that he needed me because I needed him too.

I reached out and touched his cheek gently with my finger. A slight jolt passed through me as his essence warmed my skin.

Cole opened his mouth and a barely audible moan escaped his lips. This was different than any other time we'd been together, because this time, I was in charge. I would pull him back to me and make us whole again.

Slowly, I knelt in front of him and pulled of his shirt.

Strong, muscles twitched gently as I ran my lips over his chest, using my tongue to taste his skin. I always marveled at that. He tasted earthy and musky and wonderful. As my tongue traveled down his stomach, I planted light kisses down his belly and over the scar that remained as a sign of where his mortal wound had been inflicted.

I could see Cole's erection begin to fill out against the jeans he wore, and ran my fingers lightly over him, feeling him harden further as his excitement grew. My own passions were burning and I grew wet in anticipation.

I took his pants off and pushed him back against the couch, my eyes capturing his. He moaned as I stroked his cock. Giving him a siren's smile, I shed my clothes and positioned my naked body over his.

In one quick movement, I enveloped his cock, his hardness filling my softness with an incredible, delicious heat.

We fit perfectly, and as our bodies rocked together, I kept my eyes open and watched his eyes grow wilder as his body stiffened before his climax.

When Cole was about to explode, he pulled my face close to his and whispered, "I love you."

His words made me soar over a precipice of light and love, as tears poured down my cheeks.

Lying in Cole's arms, it was much easier to tell him what was going on without the fear that he might chastise me for taking too many chances. To my relief, he didn't judge my plan but instead, listened attentively.

When I was done, he regarded me steadily, his chin propped up on one hand. "You know, I always want you to be safe," he said. "But I also know how relentless some of these spirits are.

And after what you've just told me, it's clear that you are now in more danger than ever before. As long as you understand that and know how to handle the risks, I'm not going to try to stop you. You need my support, and I'm here to help you in any way I can."

My mouth quirked as I tried to suppress my laughter. It wasn't that Cole had said anything funny, but I knew how hard it was for him to let go and allow me to handle things. I sometimes forgot that he was from another time, and even though he'd been "around" for the past few hundred years, his notions about women were certainly out of step with today's world.

I reached out and pulled his face to mine, giving him a gentle kiss. "Thanks for trusting me. I'm no longer that scared girl you met at Bobbie's house."

"I know. It's just so hard watching you walk right into the jaws of danger. Please understand that I may be a part of another realm, but because of that, I have a clear view of these entities. The Rashas are not to be trifled with. They're incredibly strong and evil."

If Norman Ceaser was any example of how horrible the dark spirits could be, there was no doubt I was swimming in the deep end. But there was nothing else I could do. Katie was family, and I needed to find a way to save her.

"How do you feel about discovering that you have biological relatives?"

Cole's question surprised me. We normally didn't discuss our families, and even though I'd met the ghost of his mother back in Georgia, I'd never told him. I was wary of bringing up pain from his past life. I would never really have a normal relationship with Cole—no kids, no carpooling, or family game night. Thinking about the past or the future made me too sad. I needed to focus on the present. On the beautiful moments we shared together.

"Well, I'm happy about it. I love my adopted parents, but it is nice to know I have blood relatives. Family connected to my parents. Unfortunately, I haven't really had time to enjoy it, given what's happened to Katie. We've all been kind of operating in crisis mode."

Cole was silent, so I decided to push in a direction that we normally avoided. "What about your family?" I asked tentatively. "Do you still miss them?"

He sighed, taking his time to answer.

"Sure, I miss my parents and sister. But I rarely think about them anymore. At first, I was just focused on revenge and felt like I couldn't rest until I found the man who'd betrayed me. But after I met you that anxiety went away, and I could focus on other things."

"What was his name?"

Cole paused and stared into space. "His name was Sebastian Carter. He was a family friend, or so I'd thought. But he never had our best interests at heart and he stole from my father. When I discovered what he'd done, I challenged him to a duel. But, despite a promise to fight fairly, he shot and killed me as we were preparing."

While he spoke, Cole ran his hand over the scar along his stomach. "He shot me right here."

"That must have been so painful," I said, my hand covering his over the scar.

"Yes, it was at first. When death set in, my entire body became numb and the world just seemed to float away. I could see a light in the distance and felt a warm presence guiding me toward it. But right before I closed my eyes, I caught sight of Sebastian standing in the shadows, watching—waiting for me to die. It disturbed my peaceful transition to the life beyond, and I swore at that moment that I would avenge my death and what he'd done to my family. Only then, would I allow myself to transition over."

"But you had another opportunity to pass on, didn't you?"

"Yes, after I helped you in your battle against Elial, a light once again appeared in the distance, and then grew closer. Adahy encouraged me to follow the path to peace, but I just couldn't imagine ever finding that comfort unless we were together. And I didn't want to wait for your death, before we could be in each other's arms again."

His words were like tiny arrows that pricked my heart. I didn't want Cole to remain in limbo because of me. It wasn't fair. I was being selfish. But I couldn't help it. I loved him and didn't want him to leave. Even if that meant that he would be caught up in my complicated and dangerous life for years to come.

Gathering up all my courage, I sat up to face the man who I couldn't live without.

He hoisted himself up next to me and took my hand.

His body flickered like the ending of an old movie running through a projector. His energy was dissipating fast. But, I didn't rush my next words.

"Cole. I've never told you this. But I want you to know. I love you."

Chapter 11

The sun made its appearance much too quickly, casting its unforgiving rays through the bedroom window. Warmth seeped through the sheets and flowed through the fabric until it touched my legs.

Jane continued to snore in her bed across the room and didn't seem ready to budge even though it was already seven o'clock. I was going to be late for work.

I stretched under the covers and smiled. Memories of making love to Cole flooded my mind, and my face flushed as I recalled how wanton I'd been when I'd discovered him in my living room.

The old Renda would never have acted that way, and privately I wondered if Cole had sparked my "sexual revolution" or if it was because I was changing, becoming more my own woman. My body seemed to have a mind of its own lately, and when I was around Cole, my desire for him was powerful.

But there were other things on my mind, too. Dark things. Things I hadn't stopped thinking about since Katie had disappeared.

Before the day was done, I'd be back at the Cale Cemetery.

It wouldn't be easy, and I hoped that the minister and I would be enough to set Katie free. It could be dangerous rushing into things, and even though I worried about Katie, it was imperative that I armed myself with knowledge and strength. Just as Cole had to rest to regenerate, I too had needed a good night's sleep to gather my own strength for the battle ahead.

I had a feeling the Rashas were waiting for me and wouldn't harm Katie in the meantime. Still, every minute that passed nearly drove me mad. All I wanted was to save my precious little cousin.

If my father had been right, there was a special strength that existed within me that would help me find Katie and save her. But what if he was wrong? What if this battle was too complex and I got lost within the Rashas' evil vortex?

There were so many questions I had about my parents' past. Aside from the few visions I'd seen, I knew virtually nothing about my mother. Where was she? Was she alive or dead?

It was too early to begin pondering everything that plagued me, so I pulled the comforter over my head and closed my eyes until Jane's snorts became loud and insistent.

Groaning, I untangled myself from the bedding and stumbled into the shower.

My eyes were alert as I made sure my apartment was safe to move around in. The hellish Norman-Rasha spider that had attacked me the previous day was nowhere to be seen, but that didn't mean I was still alone. From now on, I would have to be on my guard, even when I was home.

The drive to work was quiet and unassuming. Spirits ambled up and down the sidewalks, but given the early hour, the streets were peaceful.

Though worn out, I felt calm. The past few weeks had been nonstop turmoil, but the psychological revelations of the past few days had wreaked havoc on me. My myriad feelings were conflicting—I felt exhilaration at the knowledge that I had blood relatives, but despair at losing Katie, and fear of Norman Ceaser and his Rasha cohorts. Not to mention the ups and downs with Cole.

I took a deep breath and then blew it out as I arrived at work, trying to gauge the feel of the day.

"Hey, I was looking for you." Larlene's voice interrupted my musings as I was slipping my purse into my desk drawer. "Gary is hanging out at my place and 'spiritually preparing himself' for tonight," she said using air quotes. "Are you still up for it?"

Her words were like sharp electrical jolts punching through my veins.

No, I am not ready. Not yet.

"I'm okay. Just need to get through the day in one piece," I replied, trying for a smile.

Larlene squeezed my shoulder, giving me an encouraging smile, but her eyes held concern.

I became more restless as the day progressed. Perhaps it was the growing awareness that once again, I would have to step into the heat of another battle, but there was more to it.

I was getting tired of living with the mysteries in my life. I knew I would feel more empowered if I had all the facts about my mother, my family, and my supposed gifts. But how was I going to learn about all of those things if I was constantly in reactionary mode and trying to fight off evil?

It just didn't seem fair. And now, the life of a beautiful little girl hung in the balance.

Katie's disappearance had been broadcast non-stop on the news as an amber alert for the past twenty-four hours. The reporters showed pictures of her and her family and video clips from her last birthday, as well as interviews with the neighbors.

Luckily the police hadn't followed up with me yet but I was certain they were looking into my background and it was only a matter of time before I'd hear from them. It was crucial to take care of matters before I was possibly hauled in for more questioning. After all, I was the one they found on Katie's bed. I was the last person to see her before she vanished.

My mom called me to say hello and chat about what was going on in town. She had no idea what was really happening, and I wanted to keep it that way, so the conversation was short and strained. I felt badly about the fact that I wasn't forthcoming with the woman who had raised me—the only mother I'd ever really known. But there was no time to engage her in deep discussions about all of my recent discoveries, let alone the supernatural things that were happening to me. I figured she wouldn't understand any of it, anyway. And my father was so involved in his business and golfing buddies that he didn't notice anything odd about my recent distance from them.

It felt weird, because my adoptive parents had always been

my anchors. My childhood had been free from any pain or stress, and in a sense had acted like a protective cocoon for me.

And now, I realized just how sheltered I'd been. My world had become a strange place unfolding its secrets daily, like a rose slowly unfurling each petal to reveal its mysterious depths.

A rose with many thorns.

I was in the midst of a metamorphosis. The shy, meek librarian still lingered on the periphery of my being, but I was also becoming a woman with a purpose that no one could have ever predicted. Which made it difficult to stay connected to people I'd known all my life.

If I ran from everyone, what would I have left? Who would have I left?

Taking a deep breath, I tried to focus on the computer screen before me. I'd been given another business plan to create for the library, because we were petitioning for more money from the county and my boss wanted me to inventory key items that were needed.

The work was tedious at first, but then began to take my mind off everything else. I found myself in a rhythm that lasted well after lunch.

Outside, the sun began to make its transition as it peaked and then descended into the horizon. I barely noticed the shadows lengthening outside the windows, and I was still deep in concentration when Larlene burst into my workspace.

"Are you ready? It's almost quitting time. You might want to grab some dinner before we head out to the cemetery."

Tearing my gaze away from the screen, I looked up at Larlene. My brain was still fuzzy from all the numbers and forecasting I'd been immersed in. "Sorry I'm so out of it," I apologized. "I've been in here all day working on the fiscal addendum proposal."

"I know. It's probably a good thing. I didn't want to interrupt you, but the detective on Katie's case was in the library earlier."

"Really?"

"Yeah, he was asking some questions about the last time Katie visited here, because I guess they heard from someone that she liked to hang out in the children's section, reading and coloring, and he was doing his due diligence, or whatever it's called."

I swallowed hard. "Did he ask to speak to me?"

Larlene coughed and looked away. "He might have asked if you were working today, and I might have told him that you were out delivering books to the sick and elderly."

"Larlene!"

"What?" she asked, pasting an innocent look on her face. "I just didn't want him harassing you. You've got a lot to do today, and I didn't want you to get anxious before tonight."

It was impossible not to laugh. Larlene always had my back.

The sun beat down mercilessly on my shoulders as I headed out to my car for the short drive home. The air was thick and heavy and even the setting sun didn't provide a respite from the Florida heat.

As I sat behind the wheel, I gazed up at the library, a comforting place that had given me so much over the years. A heavy sense of foreboding had begun to swirl around my head, and I felt as if I was at a crossroads.

Shrugging off the feeling of dread, I pulled out of the parking lot and headed home. As I stopped my car at the intersection beside the cemetery, I scanned the area for any strange movements.

The trees leading to the entrance were motionless in the hot, humid air. A few cars were parked in the lot, but everything was quiet and calm. In the daytime, the cemetery looked entirely different than in the darkness of night.

"A nice final resting place," my adoptive mother always said.

A car honked behind me. The light had turned green, and I was still sitting in place.

I hit the gas pedal and continued home. When my apartment complex came into view, I was surprised to see Cole waiting for me.

He was sitting on the steps outside my door and smiled as my car pulled up.

"I thought it might be a nice surprise if I met you at your doorway, like a proper gentleman," he said, with a grin.

That was the thing about Cole. He embodied the old fashioned ways of the past, but had also quickly adapted to present-day customs. It was sweet. Most of the time. When he wasn't being bossy. Then I'd remind him what century he "lived" in. His language had also changed to a more modern way of speaking, which sounded super sexy with his English accent.

Smiling, I wrapped my arms around him and felt the telltale spark that always ignited whenever we were together. As his hardness rested against my sex, I whispered in his ear, "Don't you think we should take it easy? You'll need your energy for tonight."

Cole murmured in my ear, "I agree. Allow me to take control, my dear, and you'll have nothing to worry about."

He took my hand and led me into the apartment.

Jane quickly went outside and did her business and when she was done, Cole and I made our way to the bedroom. I got on the bed and lay back reaching my arms out to him.

He groaned and quickly shed his clothes, but instead of passionately grabbing me and devouring me with his mouth, he gently positioned his body over mine and we slowly made love.

It was sweetly satisfying, as we both knew it wasn't the time to expend heaps of energy. It might be our last time together before I faced the unknown and it was all I could do to keep from crying at the beauty of being with him.

Afterwards, we rested next to each other on the bed, both of us staring at the ceiling. We were careful not to touch so that Cole's energy could remain intact.

I glanced at my watch and felt my chest tighten with the realization that I was expected at Larlene's in less than one hour.

"I know," Cole said. "It's time, isn't it?"

"Yes."

We remained on the bed and quickly went over the plan for the evening:

We would drive to the cemetery with Larlene and her cousin, Minister Gary. Jane would remain at home where she'd be safe.

Once we arrived, we would walk into the cemetery together as a group and approach the mausoleum where I'd seen the Rashas the first time. The minister would begin to recite the passage that my father had shared with me, and then Larlene would join in and recite it as well to help strengthen the spiritual message.

I would approach the Rashas with Cole and together we would recite the chant and weaken the Rashas enough to somehow extract Katie from their clutches.

The idea of entering their realm scared me to death. Even with the minister by my side and the chant that my father wrote down, I wasn't sure if I could fight them.

But I felt better knowing Cole would be there. Between the two of us and with help from the minister, we would rescue Katie. It had to work.

I took a quick shower and changed into a T-shirt and shorts. It was hot and humid outside, and I didn't want anything to weigh me down. If my experience in Macon had been any indication, I would be heading into one grueling battle.

I might need to be light on my feet...I might need to run fast...

Pushing the disturbing thoughts out of my mind, I ran a brush through my wet hair and avoided makeup entirely.

"Are you ready to go?" Cole asked from the other room.

Staring at my face in the mirror, I could see the fear and uncertainty stamped on my features. I had to muster all my courage or I wouldn't be any good to Katie. I took a deep breath and let it out slowly.

"I'm ready."

Chapter 12

When we arrived at Larlene's townhouse, Cole shifted to the back seat. Typically, most people passed right through his body when he was moving about the living world, but each time that happened, it extracted some of his energy, and we wanted to avoid that at all cost. We needed Cole to be as strong and powerful as possible.

I left my car idling in the driveway and ran up to Larlene's front door. But I didn't need to knock, because she opened it as soon as I reached out to tap the wood.

"Finally!" she exclaimed. "We've been waiting for you. Are you ready?"

"As ready as I'll ever be. How about you guys?"

"We're good," Gary answered from behind her. As he approached, I was surprised to see him all dressed up as if he was preparing to give a sermon.

He gestured to his suit. "I figured it was probably a good idea to be as traditional as possible. So, I dressed for the occasion." He gave me a small smile, but his eyes were somber.

It was quite possible that he would experience things that he'd never seen before, so I was reassured by his serious demeanor. The last thing I needed was someone cracking jokes.

"The sun's going down," Larlene said, interrupting my thoughts. "We really need to get going, don't you think?"

I looked out at the darkening skies behind us. The sun was definitely making its descent, and I knew that Larlene was probably terrified of being in the graveyard in complete darkness so I nodded and we headed out to the car.

Larlene's breathing quickened with every step. I stopped

and turned around, looking into her eyes.

They held fear.

I hugged her fiercely, feeling her body tremble. "Don't worry," I whispered. "It's going to be fine."

"I know, I know," she whispered back. "I'm just kinda scared."

"Ladies, we need to proceed," Gary said calmly.

For some reason, hearing his commanding voice broke up the tension, causing the two of us to burst into nervous laughter.

We continued chuckling as we got into my car and to my relief, Cole shifted over just as Gary got into the back seat. Larlene sat in the passenger seat and stared out the window.

I took a deep breath and pulled onto the main road.

Gary carried all of the required materials: Crucifixes, a Bible, and he wore a vial of holy water around his neck that hung from a simple leather strap. It looked rather intimidating. I hoped it would have the desired effect on the Rashas.

Cole seemed unaffected by Gary's presence and kept his gaze on me as we drove through town. His strong energy enveloped me, like an embrace.

It took us about fifteen minutes to get to the cemetery. The sun had lost its battle and was now sinking dutifully below a darkening sky, while scattered clouds drifted aimlessly. In the west, it seemed like groups of larger, heavier clouds had gathered, signaling a brewing storm.

Standing in the rain, while battling the Rashas, wasn't my idea of fun, but there was really no choice. We were heading toward the darkest evil I'd ever encountered and bad weather or not, our objective was clear.

We arrived at the cemetery with its imposing gates standing sentinel. The parking lot was empty, save for a few rustling leaves.

Despite the air conditioning in my car, beads of sweat had already formed along my hairline, as my heart rate began to pick up speed. My stomach was twisted in knots, and nausea threatened to overtake me. As I stole a quick peek around the car, everyone else appeared as sick as I felt. Even Cole seemed to have become nervous and was anxiously shifting around in his seat.

I finally pulled the car into an empty parking space and turned off the engine.

No one spoke for a moment and we all sat in silence, staring at the pathway ahead that led through the tall trees and into the central part of the cemetery.

"Okay, guys," I said nervously. "It's time to do this. Are you ready?"

"I guess so," responded Larlene who looked as if she was going to throw up.

"Let's do it," said Gary who shifted over and to my horror, went straight through Cole to get out of the car. Passing through the ghost didn't seem to bother the minister one bit, but I could tell that it shocked Cole.

Once Gary was out of the car, I looked back at Cole who seemed dazed and confused. I knew that when a human passed through a ghost it could cause an immediate diffusion of energy because of the body's mass literally tearing through the spirit.

Thankfully, Cole hadn't completely dissipated, but he was definitely weaker.

Damn—I'm so stupid. Why didn't I tell him to meet us here?

While angry and frustrated thoughts flew through my brain, Larlene exited the car and left no time for me to sit and fume.

I got out and looked back again at Cole who was unsteadily making his way out of the vehicle. He took a few steps back, lest someone try to pass through him again.

In the meantime, Gary, who was none the wiser, continued speaking while he rubbed the crucifix that hung from his neck. "Okay, I think we really need to make this quick," he was saying, "It won't do us any good to hang around here. Any additional time we spend is time where they can suck the life out of us. I've been doing some reading on evil spirits and it's a battle of strength. If they can outlast you, then they've got you. These are strong fuckers."

Both Larlene and I gaped at him.

Gary laughed at our expressions. "It's okay, I do curse sometimes. And right now, there's no need to be politically correct. Let's just get it done."

Our footsteps echoed in the stillness of the surrounding forest like thrumming drumbeats, beating in unison. We forged along the path, not knowing what our fate would be. No one slowed down, no one stopped—we just kept our pace and moved forward.

When we were halfway to the mausoleum, I glanced back at Cole, and to my surprise, he wasn't there. I wondered if perhaps he'd decided to go on up ahead. Ghosts could move faster than us just by disappearing and reappearing at whatever place they chose.

I just hoped that he had enough energy to help me get through this.

As we continued to make our way down the path, the rich scents of damp grass, dark soil, Magnolia and Mimosa trees, all blended in a heady perfume that floated around us. Every once in a while, a warm wind would pass through and tickle the leaves on the trees, as crickets chimed in with their song of the night.

It would have been a pleasant interlude had we been out for a stroll, but our purpose was anything but casual. We were heading straight into Rasha territory.

The pathway came to an abrupt stop and was replaced by grass and the expansive spread of headstones. The mausoleum loomed in the distance, the night shadows making it look like a misshapen monster.

"I don't know if I can do this," Larlene whispered brokenly.

"It's okay," I said, trying to soothe her. "If you can't go any farther, head back and wait for us in the car."

Tears welled in her eyes, glinting in the moonlight as she shook her head. "So sorry, Renda. Please forgive me. I'm too chicken."

"It's okay. Just go back to the car. We'll be fine. Promise." With those words, I handed Larlene the keys to my car and gave her one final hug. She nodded and headed back to the parking lot.

I turned to face Gary. He was pale but calm. As if to answer my unspoken question, he put his hand on my shoulder and squeezed it.

"Don't worry, I'm staying," he said.

We looked at each other and a strange understanding passed

between us. We were going forward, together.

Slowly, we made our way, passing headstones on either side and trying to maneuver through the grass so that we avoided stepping directly onto the graves. It seemed to me that this visit was going a lot more slowly than my solo jaunt a few days prior—maybe it was the anxiety of knowing what lay ahead, or the stress of the past few days, or a combination of both.

We finally arrived at the entrance of the mausoleum and to my relief, Cole was there, standing off to the side.

He smiled as I approached, as if to give me a sense of comfort, but I was worried that he'd been weakened. It was hard to tell from where I was standing, but he appeared slightly translucent.

I wasn't sure how much help he was going to be.

Gary took out his Bible and flipped through it to find the passage he'd chosen to focus on before the Rashas arrived. He'd agreed to recite the phrase that my father had shared, but he also told us that he wanted to say a prayer for our strength and safety.

It didn't really matter to me. I just wanted him to follow directions when we engaged in the actual confrontation.

But the battle itself was a mystery to me. Now that we were in front of the mausoleum, I wasn't sure what we were supposed to do next. While Gary stood and prayed behind me, I pulled out my father's letter again and scoured the words, trying to figure out how to call on the evil spirits to bring them forward. In the past, they'd simply appeared, but now they were playing with us—keeping away while we anxiously awaited their presence.

I couldn't find anything. Frustrated, I decided to recite the passage from the letter, when suddenly a gentle wind rustled behind us.

I turned around and was shocked to see that Gary had turned as well. I came face-to-face with someone who I'd never expected to see...

Adahy.

Chapter 13

As the Native American sage walked toward me, I was alarmed at how frail he looked.

If it was possible, he had even more wrinkles than before and they were etched deep into his face. His eyes were barely open, and were moist to the point of looking watery. His gait was pained, and he walked slowly with a limp that I didn't recall from the past.

"Adahy," I whispered. "What are you doing here?"

To my shock, Gary's eyes followed Adahy's movements as well.

Could he see him?

"Gary, do you see someone?"

His eyes widened with fright. "I see a light, like a light bulb. It's coming toward you. What is it?"

"Don't be frightened," I assured him. "He's one of my spiritual advisors. His name is Adahy."

Adahy glanced over at Cole and nodded. Cole nodded in return. I wondered at the silent message that passed between them. Adahy's breathing was labored, and his eyes solemn.

I feared his time was short.

"Yes, my dear. You're right," he said, as if hearing my thoughts. "My time to depart this realm has come. In a way, I think it's because I've been able to serve you and the others. It saddens me that I must leave now when you are facing such great peril, but thus are the mysteries of life and death. "

Despite my need to remain calm, tears flooded my eyes and tumbled down my cheeks, obscuring my vision. I had grown to love the wise sage and wasn't ready to say goodbye.

There was too much that I still didn't understand.

"Please don't leave me," I whispered.

Adahy came even closer and was now standing directly in front of me.

Powerful energy emanated from his essence in slow, undulating waves. Even as he neared the end of his time, he radiated more brightly than most spirits who were still shackled to my realm.

He reached out and grasped my hand in one quick movement. It all happened so fast that I didn't have time to respond.

My dark surroundings suddenly burst into bright yellows and greens, and I was transported back to the woods where Adahy was standing with my parents. Except now, I was standing beside them as they listened intently to the sage's advice.

"You must go to the water. Go to the waves and you will find the answers you seek. It is there where the true protection of your inner strength lives."

As Adahy finished speaking, the colors around me began to fade and dissolve. Summoning as much strength as I could, I turned to face my mother and somehow found the ability to grasp her hands with my own. She felt warm and soft, and when I touched her, she actually turned to face me.

I saw her face clearly for the first time.

She can see me.

She gazed at me in awe, her eyes shimmering with tears... and then, everything receded and I was pulled back once more. The bright hues of the sky dimmed and I found myself once again standing in the cemetery, staring at my hands that had only moments ago, clasped the hands of my mother.

Though I could no longer see him, Adahy's voice whispered in my ear one final time.

Be strong. Look for the heat. And never give up the gift of the Chosen.

Farewell, my child.

The woodsy scent of smoke wafted in the air, dissipating, and taking Adahy with it.

He was gone.

I looked over to where Cole was standing, in the shadows. It was hard to see his face in the darkness but I could sense his sadness at Adahy's departure.

Suddenly, another type of wind blew through the cemetery. This one however, was not like the warm wind signaling the departure of my dear friend, but something sinister...wicked.

The wind tickled our skin at first and then picked up in intensity, howling as it flew over the headstones. Traveling around the mausoleum, the biting air emerged again to strike us directly in the face. This wind wasn't pure, and carried with it small stones and dirt that stung our eyes.

Cole shifted his stance, as if to brace himself for the coming battle.

As the frequency of the gusts began to increase, Gary shouted out to me, "I think something's happening, Renda. Are you ready?"

"I'm ready."

It was that simple.

Every action I took, every second that passed was another moment in time without my cousin Katie. She needed us and this was the only way to save her.

Taking a deep breath, I stole another quick glance at my father's letter and then placed it into my pocket. I stepped forward—my feet were heavy, and the ground almost seemed to be vibrating under my shoes—but I continued onward.

The wind formed a small swirling tornado right in front of the mausoleum's entrance. But instead of moving in a scattered fashion, it remained in place as it grew in size.

It reminded me of the tornado we'd encountered back at Bobbie's home in Georgia, when her mother had been shackled by a demon who'd tried to destroy her. I wondered if this was how evil spirits harnessed their power before an attack.

As if moving on its own, my body continued forward until I had to shield my eyes from all of the wind that continued to fly past me. Little pieces of gravel and dirt hit my face and began to cover me in a sheet of filth. A face formed in the center of the tornado.

It was Norman Ceaser, laughing from within the depths of the whirling mass. The wisps of hair atop his head flew back and forth in a wild frenzy and his eyes were crazed with pure evil.

Remembering my father's guidance, I called out to the Rashas that seemed to be gathering with Norman.

"Hear ye' Rashas of the blackest spirit. Be gone or face the purest and holiest of energies from God and his truest followers. Return from where you've come!"

I then stepped even closer and with all of my might, I screamed out, "Give Katie Marck back to me! She is not one of you and never will be. She belongs in the land of the living!"

The wind was blowing so hard now that it was difficult to hear anything, and it felt as if the sounds of my words had been snatched directly out of my throat. Cole moved closer to the centrifuge, chanting the same words as Gary.

"Hear ye' Rashas of the blackest spirit. Be gone or face the purest and holiest of energies from God and his truest followers. Return from where you've come!"

The sounds of Cole and Gary's voices started to merge into one, as they shouted as loud as possible to be heard over the screaming winds.

Suddenly, a thin cloud of black smoke emerged from the centrifuge and reached out toward me like a crooked finger. It extended until it nearly touched my face.

And then, I heard Norman's voice whisper in my ear, "You want her? Come and get her."

I hesitated. It could all be a trap, and once I was inside, I could be lost forever, falling into an infinite black hole of evil.

Closing my eyes, I decided it was time to ask for help.

I prayed.

Dear God, please help me. Please guide me and help me choose the right path. If I proceed and can't help Katie—then it's all over. I don't want to die. Even though death would bring me to my father and perhaps to my mother if she's in your embrace…and to Cole. But I'm not ready to go yet. I've just discovered my purpose. I need to help the living fight the dark forces in this world. I need to save Katie. She's young and good. She's perfect in every way, and she has the gift. She's Chosen. Please help me...

It was at that moment when the answer came to me. Katie and I were the Chosen Ones. We would live or we would die together. There was no other way. I couldn't go on, knowing that I'd turned my back on the only person in the world who knew what I knew. Who could see what I see.

Cole and Gary were shouting in the distance, but their words no longer mattered. I stepped forward into the blackness and smoke, almost choking from the putrid air.

The ground suddenly evaporated from beneath my feet, and I was swept away into a screaming mass of hell...

Chapter 14

Darkness surrounded me on all sides.

I was lying on something hard and cold and realized it was a dirty concrete floor. I took a deep breath as I struggled to sit and couldn't help but notice the wet, moldy smell in the air. I slowly moved my legs and arms to see if everything was working properly. It felt as though someone was turning on all of my nerve endings, one by one.

Where the hell am I?

As my eyes adjusted to the dark, it became apparent that I was in some sort of cellar or basement. A large worktable was pushed up against one wall and a bunch of corroding boxes sat in a pile against the opposite wall. But other than that, the room was bare.

Or at least I thought so, until I heard the sobbing.

Turning around, I was stunned to see Katie. She was pressed up against the wall, her knees pulled up to her chest. She was clearly terrified, and she stared at me with huge eyes. Even in the darkness I could see the tears glistening on her cheeks, like tiny little stars.

"Katie," I whispered as I crawled over to her. "I'm so glad I found you."

"I'm glad you found me too," she whispered, her voice sounding raw and pained.

I wrapped my arms around her and held on tight. "Do you know where we are?"

"It's the bad place, Renda. We're in the bad place with the bad man. He does a lot of bad things to kids. He said he was coming back to get me. He told me to be quiet as a mouse or he would hurt me."

My mind raced back to the day in the library when I was researching Norman's past. He was a child murderer who lured children down to his basement and then killed them. Was that why he'd brought us here?

Oh God. Was he going to try to kill Katie? I couldn't let that happen.

The little girl looked exhausted, and I wondered how she'd survived for so long without food or water.

"Are you okay, sweetie?" I asked. "You've been down here a couple of days."

Katie looked confused for a moment and then shook her head. "No I haven't. I just woke up here a little while ago. The man woke me up and said I'd better be quiet or I'd be punished. He wasn't very nice. He used to be nice to me. But now he's just mean. I want to go home."

She began crying again, and I rocked her as she sobbed into my shoulder. She was so small and fragile that an intense determination to protect her washed over me.

"We're going to get out of here," I whispered in her ear. "You and I together."

But Katie wouldn't move. She was frozen in place, fear clearly evident in her eyes. "No, we can't go. He'll find us, and then he'll hurt us.

He won't hurt you anymore. I promise. But we've got to get out of here. Don't you miss your mom and dad? We have lots of games to play and tea parties to have. But we can't have all that fun if we stay down here, now can we?"

The child seemed to be mulling over my offer, those little wheels turning in her mind as she weighed her options.

Time seemed suspended in this strange place, and it had a numbing effect. I felt *drowsy* somehow. As if there was a sedative in the air. Everything seemed to move slower in the dark captivity of the Rashas. I wondered if Cole was able to enter this place and what type of impact it would have on him.

He and Gary must be so worried. I wonder what's going on in the real world. Hope they're all right—

"Okay. Let's go." The sound of Katie's voice interrupted my thoughts, and I was pleased to see that the little girl was getting up off the ground.

For the first time, I noticed that she was still wearing her hospital gown. It was dirty and wrinkled, and hung loosely on her tiny frame. But despite her frailty and tender age, there was a conviction in her eyes that I hadn't seen before. Somehow, in the span of the past several weeks, she'd been forced to grow up.

It reminded me of my own life. How easy things had been for me in Cale before I'd discovered my birthright. Before Cole and the Trillos and Norman Ceaser.

I shuddered. Norman was hiding somewhere in this nightmare. We'd have to be careful as we navigated through the house and found our way out.

If we found our way out.

Grabbing Katie's hand, we made our way to a set of wooden stairs that led to what I hoped was the main floor of the house. For a moment, I considered trying to squeeze our way out of the little window, but it looked too small for either of us to fit through. And I was also worried about what might be on the other side. I wasn't sure if the house was real or some kind of twisted dream, fabricated from Norman's life.

A few years ago, I'd read a book about Hades, written by a paranormal psychic. The book chronicled the story of several lost souls a psychic had helped to cross over. Even before I knew who and what I was, I had always been fascinated by the occult. The psychic wrote about three different souls who had communicated with her and related what Hades felt like. It was a horrible mid-place between Heaven and Hell. A stopping point of sorts, where souls could get lost forever if they didn't have guides. The book was full of illustrations including a depiction of souls falling into a black hole, while a myriad of creatures watched them tumbling through what could only be described as an infinite nightmare.

For some reason, that image popped into my head. I certainly hoped we weren't in that stopping place.

An open door at the top of the stairs beckoned to us. Taking a deep breath, I squeezed Katie's hand and slowly, we ascended the stairwell.

Each step we took made a squeaky, creaking sound, echoing

through the silence like a demonic siren call. It certainly wasn't helping us achieve any aspect of surprise and could definitely be alerting the ghosts or creatures ahead that we were on the move.

Still, we had no choice. We had to continue upward, though I eased Katie along a bit faster than before.

As we reached the landing, we stepped into a hallway. To our right was the front door and to our left, the hallway led toward a kitchen. Straight ahead was another set of stairs. No doubt the second floor of the house where the bedrooms were.

Everything was sparsely furnished and impersonal, as if we were inside a model home that hadn't been fully decorated yet. Bland paintings adorned the walls with unimpressive nature scenes and a few contained biblical images of Jesus after he'd been crucified. His pained eyes stared at me in the darkness as if he too was sorrowful of our predicament and wanted to save us from our torment.

Katie and I were faced with a big decision.

Do we leave through the front door, or try to find another way out? Normally, the front door was the most logical way to leave a house. But I wasn't sure that in our present circumstance, it was the right option.

"Katie," I whispered. "Do you remember how you got here? Did you come in through the front door? Or did the bad man bring you into the house from another place?"

She bit her bottom lip and shook her head. "I don't remember, Renda. The only thing I remember is waking up in that dark place with that man. The one I met in the cemetery who used to play with me in my room. His name is Norman. He used to be nice, but now he lives in this house and keeps little kids in that dark place down there."

Swallowing hard, I nodded and closed my eyes.

Think! Think! What is the answer? When he was alive, Norman lured children here and killed them. What is the most logical way to get out? The basement? No, that's the way I got in. That won't work. What about the front door? Do we search the rest of the house? What do I do?

My mind worked furiously as I thought about everything Adahy had told me about spirits and the way to resolve conflict.

There was something I was missing. There was something that tied all of the positive spirits together. Something that would give me a way out.

I had to search for...

What was it?

What was the only thing that they all had in common? The one thing that evil could never possess and instead was constantly seeking out?

And then it hit me.

The one thing the Rashas could never truly have—the thing that was always absent from them and the one thing that always led me home—

Heat.

It was the source of all energy and the way that Cole always came back to me. It was the way I always knew that there was a wandering soul nearby who needed me. It was the embrace of the dead.

I had to find the warmth in the house. And it wouldn't be easy, because everything felt cold and drafty and *dead*.

"Katie, I know it's usually hot where we live, but where's the warmest place in your house?

She scrunched up her face in concentration and then widened her eyes. "The kitchen! The kitchen is where it's always the warmest. It's where Mommy cooks good things and where we have dinner. It's one of my favorite places because it's where we're a family."

Nodding, I grasped her hand and we crept along the hallway, toward the kitchen. Just before we reached the end of the hallway, I noticed a door to our left that opened into a large sitting room.

The house was very quiet, not a good sign.

We slowly entered the kitchen.

A small table and chairs were set in the center of the kitchen. A dated fridge and an old-fashioned oven with a stove-top lined one wall. To my distress, there was no sense of warmth here, just cold and darkness.

The fridge was plugged in and working but was dark, the only food—a jug of milk. Worried that it might contain some kind of drug or poison, I didn't touch it. I tried the oven, but it didn't work. It remained cold and dark like the rest of the house.

The countertops were bare, and a quick study of the pantry revealed the same.

Norman had certainly worked hard to make the house as unwelcome as he could.

A thump reverberated upstairs. It was muted, but echoed throughout the house.

"Should we look up there?" Katie asked, pointing overhead.

I wasn't sure. Instead, I walked over to a door that was located in the far corner of the kitchen and tried to open it. If we were to escape, we had to at least try the doors. Even if we weren't sure what lay beyond.

Putting my hand on the knob, I tried to turn it, but it wouldn't budge. There was no opening for a lock or anything to indicate how the door could be opened. It was solid wood, so I couldn't see outside.

Thump.

"Renda, what are we going to do?"

"Wait," I instructed as I tried to open a kitchen window.

The entire windowpane was sealed shut and when I peeked outside, all I could see was darkness. An attempt to turn the light switch on in the kitchen was also in vain. It seemed that, although the refrigerator was in fine working order, nothing else was functional.

Thump.

The recurring sound upstairs was undeniable now, and I wondered what or who was making the noise. The thought of trying the front door crossed my mind, but I quickly abandoned it. We were trapped in the middle of some strange dimension and the only way out was hidden somewhere within the house.

I searched for a source of heat but couldn't find any, all the while, hearing the strange thumping upstairs. It remained at the same pitch and volume, never getting any louder or quieter—just repeating every few moments as a reminder that there was something upstairs that wanted our attention.

"Well, there's nothing down here. It looks like we've got to check the rest of the house. Are you okay?" I asked Katie who was standing next to me, trembling in the darkness.

"Yes," she whispered.

We walked back into the hallway and I was about to step into the sitting room when we heard the thumping sound again. Only this time, it was followed by a child's cry.

"There's someone else here," Katie whispered. Her eyes were wide.

Anger flooded my veins. If Norman had brought another child to this wretched place, we had to find him.

"Come on, Katie. We've got to go upstairs."

She nodded and didn't speak. Together, we slowly made our way up the staircase. It was extremely dark and hard to see where we were going, so I held on to the banister tightly with one hand, and grasped Katie's hand with the other.

Finally, we reached the top of the stairwell and found ourselves in another small hallway.

There were three bedrooms on the second floor. Two of the rooms were open, but the door to the one at the end of the hallway was closed.

We peeked into the first bedroom and exhaled in relief. There was nothing there other than typical bedroom furniture. The room was dark and devoid of any moonlight through one single, dirty window. As we left the bedroom, we heard it again.

Thump.

The sound seemed to be coming from the last bedroom in the hallway—the one at the very end with the closed door.

My heart hammered in my chest, and every horror movie I'd ever seen flashed in my mind. I knew that whatever was on the other side of that door was something very bad. But despite our fears, Katie and I walked toward it. Looking down at the little girl, I was amazed at how brave she was. Her eyes were focused straight ahead, and she seemed to be barely blinking.

Maybe she's in shock. Whatever it is, I'm glad she's not hysterical. We'll need all the strength we can possibly pull together.

Seconds ticked by until we finally stood outside the closed door.

I hesitated for a moment, feeling my cousin's warm little fingers wrapped in mine. In that moment I knew we'd been brought to this horrible place to face whatever stood on the other side, and I couldn't help but wonder if there was any warmth or energy source in this cold, wretched place. Or were we going to be trapped forever in Norman's house of the damned?

I reached out and turned the knob.

Chapter 15

The door swung open slowly, revealing another bedroom. This one however, was fully lit. I blinked as my eyes readjusted to the brightness.

Without warning, something pushed me forward. It was like an invisible hand, shoving me from behind.

Katie must have felt it too, because she stumbled forward as well. Our hands disconnected and a surge of panic flooded my body. Gasping and without looking at anything else, I raced to her side and quickly gripped her soft palm in mine.

"Oh, so very concerned, are we?" asked a mocking voice.

I whirled to see Norman standing at the other end of the room. He was holding a ball in one hand and had a sinister grin on his face.

He appeared much younger than when I'd encountered him last. His hair was still wispy, but now it was a dark brown, giving it a creepy, comb-over look. His face was less lined and wrinkled, but his eyes were still beady. And evil. His clothes were reminiscent of the 1970s era—both his paisley shirt and brown, polyester pants. The ball he held in his hand was brightly painted in red, yellow, and blue; it was the only cheerful thing in the entire house.

My mind filled with fear, but I tried to hide it. Helping Katie up, and never taking my gaze off of the ghost, I forced my voice into an even tone.

"So, we're here. What do you want with us? Why have you brought us here?"

Norman chuckled and bounced the ball again.

Thump.

"Well, I'm always happy to bring new friends to my house. Especially you, little Katie," he said and winked at the terrified child. I pulled her closer as his gaze shifted to mine. "And you, Renda Bloodmane. Hmm. You're one of the few who can communicate with the dead. The Chosen as you're called. I think some have prophesized that you would be the one to bridge the gap between realms, for the greater good. Yes, some think that you might be able to defeat us. That you might save the world." He sighed as if the thought pained him.

"But you are only a mortal. You're a living person with the same weaknesses we all have. Or in my case, the weaknesses I *had*. You see, now I'm dead. And somehow that's made me stronger and more powerful than ever."

An ice-cold wind whipped through the room. I shivered, pulling Katie closer, and quickly looked around for the source, but the only window in the room was closed.

Norman continued, his voice getting louder now, "Yes, I'm more powerful than I was in life. Every time one of my young houseguests died, it filled me with such pity, because then I had to go to the trouble of seeking out a new guest. And I would have to start my lesson plan all over again. But I was still, after all, only mortal. My time was limited here amongst the living. And a mortal man has many flaws, after all. I knew they were after me. I had nowhere else to go. So I decided to go to the other side. And then an odd thing happened. Quite extraordinary, really. After I died, I began to understand my true calling. Oh, 'regular and boring' people follow that paltry light to 'everlasting peace.'" He paused to snicker contemptuously. "But that isn't where you will find the truth. And so, I've joined others who are just like me, and we are a force to be reckoned with. You see, the more humans who fear us, the stronger we become. You are Godless and we are strong. We are the Righteous Truth."

"You're not strong," I interrupted, raising my voice over the rising rush of the arctic wind. "You're just a pathetic little man who can't enter Heaven because of all the horrible things you've done, and you're too chicken to go to Hell. So, instead, you haunt the living. That doesn't sound powerful to me. It's just an excuse not to face what you really are and what you've done. God isn't with you. All you want to do is hurt people and cause fear and pain. But you're too afraid to face the one who really wants you. Lucifer."

Norman's face turned red with anger, his fists clenched at his sides. I was scared but I had to stand firm. He'd taken one of the most valuable things in my life, and I was willing to fight to the death to save her.

"You think I'm weak?" he shouted. "Let's see how weak you think this is!"

And with that, he flung the ball in our direction, but in mid-air it transformed into a huge ball of ice.

I screamed and ducked, pulling Katie as close to me as possible.

Behind us, the ball connected with the bedroom door and slammed into it at full speed, splintering the wood into small pieces.

Both Katie and I cried out as bits of wood flew at us. Trickles of blood appeared along my arms and legs as the sharp slivers pierced my flesh. Katie was also marked with blood and began crying in pain.

Without thinking, I pulled her out of the room.

Norman's cackling followed us as we ran down the hallway. Literally dragging the girl after me, I raced down the stairwell, nearly slipping on the last step. But just as my body was about to twist and tumble, I grabbed the banister and held on for dear life.

Thankfully, I didn't break my ankle or fall, but the action slowed me down—giving me a second to think.

Need to find the heat. It's the only way out. Where can I find a source of heat that will also serve as an escape route?

"Renda, we have to hurry!" shouted Katie. "We've got to get out of here. He's coming. The bad man is coming!"

A shadow loomed at the top of the stairs.

The fireplace! Go to the fireplace!

The voice that popped into my head was one that I knew and trusted.

Cole.

He'd somehow managed to connect with my mind and was

sending me the direction I so badly needed.

"Let's go!"

I urged Katie to the living room. It was dark and cold, with no available light. But as I ran over to the large wood-burning fireplace, I was thrilled to see that someone had left several logs and kindling inside. And to my amazement, there was a book of matches on the floor. Somehow, Cole had managed to send help our way, and I wasn't going to waste the opportunity.

Instructing Katie to stand back, I lit one of the matches and threw it against the logs. But the cold wind found us and blew against the flame, putting it out instantly. With shaking hands, I lit another match and this time, got closer to one of the pieces of kindling and it began to smolder as it slowly caught fire.

I reached for another match, when a voice stopped me in my tracks.

"You're really going to do that? Oh come on. Don't you like my house? It's rude to leave without saying goodbye."

Norman glared at me from the entrance. He looked ready to pounce, so I knew there wasn't much time left. I had to stall to give the logs more time to catch fire. But then what? Would the flames bring other spirits in to help us?

Without putting down the matches, I attempted to play upon his ego. "So, how did you create all of this? I can't imagine it was easy."

The spirit seemed caught off guard for just a split second and then quickly regained his composure. As he began speaking, he moved slowly into the room so it would be only a matter of time before he pounced on us. I wondered if it was possible for him to attack from where he stood, but when he'd taken Katie, he'd been hovering right above her. So, perhaps he needed to be physically close in order to get at us.

I put my hands close to the ground as if to simulate defeat, but could hear the crackling from behind me. The fire had begun to take shape and if I could just get one more match onto the logs, I would be able to get the fire roaring.

"This was my home at one time," Norman was saying. "It was my sanctuary against the evil world we live in. People never understood me. Never took the time to understand me.

But here..." he gestured around. "Here was a place where I could live out my life and take what I needed to survive."

Yeah, like poor innocent children, you bastard.

While Norman seemed engrossed in his story, I motioned for Katie to come closer.

"I didn't want to kill my little houseguests," he was saying. "But they wouldn't allow me to put the voice of God inside of them. The world is full of sinners. Full of horrible, Godless people. But not me. I needed those children to see what they were. They were born out of sin. They had to die. Don't you see? We are all born of sin..."

Norman continued gliding toward us, but Katie had also been on the move and was now standing next to me. For the first time since I'd arrived in Norman's nightmare, I could feel heat. The fire was radiating warmth off my back. And then in one terrifying realization, it hit me. What we needed to do defied all reality, but then, this world wasn't real either.

Find the heat, Adahy had told me just before disappearing. And it was this heat that would either save us or kill us.

"The world doesn't care about the suffering of its people," Norman was still speaking. "Just look at the cemetery. I gave up my life and hanged myself from one of those trees. I had to do it. But it only made me stronger. I can spend eternity purifying as many souls as I want. And now, it's your turn."

Norman stood very close to us now. Looking over at Katie, I slightly inclined my head to the flames and then back at her.

Her gaze widened when she figured it out. But amazingly, she didn't flinch. Instead, she came closer to me and stood facing the fireplace, her back to Norman.

"I wouldn't do that," he said quietly. "When you play with fire, you're sure to get burned."

I glared at Norman's evil face, which was now only a few feet away.

"Go to Hell. It's where you belong."

And then, I took Katie's hand, turned around and together, we stepped into the fireplace and walked right into the waiting flames.

Norman's shrieks filled the air, as the heat surrounded us.

The fire intensified, causing my skin to bubble and rupture. Strangely, I felt no pain. I glanced at Katie and could see she was calm as well. Together we remained in the fireplace, holding hands and burning.

In a flash of light, the flames grew higher and higher, until it seemed as if we were encircled by a wall of flames. But the fire had turned white and, the heat had receded to a gentle warmth.

Are we dead? Is this the entrance to Heaven?

In the overwhelming brightness, Katie stood beside me. She was all aglow and kept her face forward, eyes shut.

A whistling filled the air. It sounded like a jet plane racing down the runway and we were suddenly picked up by a wind that propelled us forward.

The force of the unnatural propulsion caused me to let go of Katie's hand as I went shooting forward like a human bullet. In the recesses of my panicked mind, I imagined that I'd become a rocket blasting up into a blindingly white sky.

The breath had been completely knocked out of my lungs and yet, I wasn't suffocating. In essence, I was simply *existing*. A soul traveling at an incredible speed toward some unknown destination.

But where am I going?

I tried to turn my head to find Katie, but I couldn't. The wind was too strong.

Then, I saw it. A black sphere up ahead. It was like a disc, hanging in mid-air and it cut through the brightness of the atmosphere like a puddle of ink. I hurtled toward it—faster and faster, until it had grown in size and was threatening to swallow me.

No! I don't want to go into that dark place! What if that's Hell? What if I have passed straight through purgatory into Hell? Oh dear God. Help us. Please help Katie and me make it out of this nightmare alive.

And at that moment, my body shot through the sphere and spit me out into a different kind of darkness...

Then everything went black.

Chapter 16

I opened my eyes.

Flames shot upward in the distance. It was hard to identify anything at first because I was now lying on my stomach in the grass, but as I lifted my head, I realized one of the large oak trees near the mausoleum had burst into flames.

I was back in the Cale Cemetery. But before I could even process this, a shrieking sound tore through the air. It sounded like a group of people being burned alive and it pounded through my skull like a hammer.

"Oww," I muttered, sitting up and placing my head between my knees.

"It hurts," a small voice moaned nearby.

Katie!

Tears sprang to my eyes as I saw her lying on the grass a few feet away, her little face scrunched up in pain.

With as much energy as I could muster, I shuffled over and put my arms around her as the shrieking faded away. Together we sat on the grass with our arms around each other and watched as Norman's tree burned to the ground.

All around us, the spirits haunting the cemetery watched in awe.

Cole was the first to find us. He appeared in the distance, standing by the burning tree, his body aglow in yellow-orange light. And then, in a flash, he was by our side, concern and relief warring in his eyes.

Katie saw him too, and now frightful of anything "unreal," buried her head against my shoulder.

"Renda, I'm so happy you're okay!" He knelt and gave me a huge hug. His embrace felt warm and wonderful.

My little cousin however, was terrified and she backed away, watching us warily from a distance.

"Cole," I managed to ask. "Was it you? Were you able to help us?"

"It was hard to find you. When you disappeared into the Rashas' vortex, I wasn't sure where you'd gone. For the first time ever, I couldn't see you. Everything was hazy and dark and even though I was trying to attach to your spirit, I kept hitting a wall. Then I saw something. It was like the tiniest blast of heat. I think you generated it when you were inside somehow."

I thought back to Norman's "dream house" and remembered my flash of anger. I wondered if perhaps anger could elicit the same amount of energy as love or excitement.

"When I saw the light, I followed it. It grew stronger and stronger until I was standing outside a house. But it was in the midst of darkness, and I couldn't get in. So, I conjured the logs, kindling, and matches and sent them down the only available open space."

"The fireplace!" I exclaimed.

Cole smiled, the fire from the blazing tree reflected in his eyes. "Yes, it was the only way in."

"And the only way out," I concluded and looked over at Katie. She was watching us, a curious expression now on her face.

I motioned for her to come closer and she slowly inched over, looking up at Cole with shyness. "Who're you? Are you Renda's boyfriend?" she asked.

"Yes, I guess you could say that," Cole replied softly, taking my hand in his. "But I'm your friend too. And I'll help you make new friends. Ghosts who are good to you. Okay?"

"You have a cool accent," Katie responded. "And I'm glad you're my friend."

A voice piped up from behind us. "You're glad who's your friend?"

I turned and saw Larlene and Gary rushing toward us. When I turned back, Cole was gone.

The cemetery was quiet.

The Rashas had disappeared, and I wondered if the destruction of Norman's tree and our escape had destroyed them, or if the mass of evil was merely weakened.

Either way, we weren't hanging around to find out.

Despite the fact that the fire was miraculously starting to die down, we knew that the flames had probably been detected by nearby locals and it was only a matter of time before the fire trucks arrived.

So we'd need to make a quick getaway.

As we walked toward the car, Gary and Larlene shared what they saw after I'd disappeared into the vortex.

Gary had continued shouting out the prayer I'd given him. According to what he'd experienced, I'd only been gone a minute or two, when the oak tree burst into flames. At the time, he'd raced back to the parking lot to find Larlene and figure out what they needed to do.

It reminded me that the dimension we'd visited moved at a different rate of speed than the world we lived in. So despite the fact that it felt like we'd been gone for hours, it had only been a matter of minutes in the living world.

Even though we'd only been gone a short while, Gary and Larlene had a billion questions for us.

"What happened to you?"

"Where'd you go?"

"Why'd that tree go up in flames?"

"Who were you talking to when we found you?"

The questions went on and on and eventually, Katie just leaned her head against me and fell asleep as Larlene drove us back to the little girl's house.

When we arrived at the Marcks' home, I was exhausted from answering questions and from evading Gary's perceptive stare. He'd seen something happen at the cemetery, and I could tell that he wasn't yet satisfied with my answers. In truth, I couldn't blame him for his new burning curiosity, because once you had undeniable proof that spirits existed, it changed everything. In essence, it changed the way you looked at the world, what you believed, and basically—it changed you. So, I didn't mind the intrusive way he probed me, but it was late and we'd been through a lot. All I really wanted to do was get Katie home and fall into my own bed after giving Jane a much-needed hug.

Katie awoke suddenly and looked around.

"I'm home!" she shrieked joyfully, and before I could say anything, she opened the car door and ran to the house.

I was still getting out of the car when Anne ran outside and swept her daughter into her arms. They hugged and twirled in a circle as Katie laughed and laughed.

The sound was music to my tired ears and gave me the strength to make it to the front door where Aunt Anne was waiting.

Tears coursed down her cheeks as she wrapped me in her arms and hugged me tightly.

"You did it. You saved my daughter. Thank you, thank you!"

Aunt Anne and Uncle Brent had many questions—all of which I tried to answer as honestly and clearly as possible. It was hard to explain how we'd jumped through fire and escaped back to the living world, so I condensed that part and simply said, we'd left the house together and made our way back to the cemetery.

Aunt Anne also wanted to know if Norman was gone forever. Was Katie now safe?

It was hard for me to answer that question. I needed to speak with Cole to better understand how the Rashas functioned and if escaping their clutches through the will and power of good energy was able to destroy them. So instead, I described how upon our return, we were no longer impeded by any dark force, and we'd been allowed to leave unharmed.

That seemed to be enough for Katie's parents who were just happy to have their daughter back safe and sound. There were many tears and hugs as I reveled in the presence of people who were now part of my family.

We decided to wait to tell Katie that she was my cousin, because the child had already been through so much and was falling asleep on her feet. I gave her a hug goodnight and a soft kiss on the cheek, before Aunt Anne ushered her out of the kitchen and into her bedroom.

Those of us who remained in the kitchen spoke of the future and of how thankful we were that everyone was safely back where they needed to be. I was relieved and happy but exhaustion was quickly overtaking me as well.

Uncle Brent offered to drive Larlene and Gary back to her place, allowing me to go straight home.

Before we parted ways, Larlene gave me a hug and whispered in my ear, "Woman, you are absolutely amazing. We have lots more to talk about, okay?"

I smiled and nodded at her and Gary. Then, I wished them both a good night and slowly walked to my car.

The drive home was a blur. I didn't even care if Cole was coming to visit, because my body was screaming out for sleep. It was difficult to keep my eyes open as my car navigated the quiet streets of Cale—the majority of people already fast asleep within their beds.

When my apartment complex appeared in the distance, relief flooded over me. All I wanted to do was get into my pajamas and curl up in bed with Jane.

As soon as I parked the car and opened my front door, Jane came bounding out and leapt up on me, covering my face with slobbery dog kisses. I felt badly about leaving her in the apartment by herself all night. But the situation hadn't been a safe one and even though I knew that Jane was a brave soul, she would have gotten herself hurt or likely killed protecting us against the evil of the Rashas.

After Jane finished her midnight business on the grass, we went back inside. I took off my grubby clothes and hopped into the shower. I wanted to wash off any lingering remnants of Norman Ceaser's house.

Slipping into a pair of comfortable sweatpants and a T-shirt, I climbed into bed and called out to Jane, allowing her to curl up beside me.

Mercifully, I fell into a deep sleep.

Chapter 17

The insistent buzzing of my alarm woke me out of a peaceful slumber. I sat up groggily, noticing that Jane was now lying at the edge of the bed, snoring loudly.

I decided there was no way I could go to work and quickly turned off the alarm and called the library, leaving a message for my boss that I was not coming in because I was sick with a cold. Then, I turned over and went back to sleep.

About three hours later I awoke again, this time because my bedroom was filled with sunlight and I was hot and sticky in my pajamas. Groaning, I rubbed my forehead and looked around the bedroom.

There was no sign of Cole, and now Jane was whining to be let out, so I slowly got up from the bed. I made a quick pit stop at the bathroom, and then led Jane to the front door. I hardly got it opened before she bounded out into the small front yard and headed straight for her favorite spot.

To my surprise, Cole was sitting underneath the tree in my front yard, deep in thought. Seeing him outside like this was strange because he normally came directly to me when he materialized. So I wasn't sure what was going on.

I walked over to the tree and sat down next to him. Most people living in my complex had already gone to work, so we were alone, and I was able to speak freely without appearing like a nutcase who was talking to herself.

"Hey, you," I said, plopping down next to him.

Cole glanced at me and smiled, but seemed pensive as we watched Jane run around and sniff at the grass.

"What're you doing out here?" I asked.

"Just thinking about things. I didn't want to disturb your sleep. I'm glad you were successful last night, Renda. You were able to seriously weaken that particular group of Rashas, so hopefully we won't be seeing them again."

I was confused. "What do you mean, *that* group of Rashas? There are others?"

Sometimes Cole had a way of making me feel like one of the dumbest people on the planet. This was one of those times. He regarded me closely and sighed.

"Yes. There are others. Evil exists everywhere and finds a way to gather in the most persistent and effective way possible. This particular clan was made up of certain unsavory types of criminals from the Cale Cemetery. But there are more—not only in Cale, but also around the world."

Cole seemed very concerned, and I wasn't exactly sure why.

"So, what does that mean for me?"

"Renda, please listen to me very carefully. Before Adahy allowed himself to pass over to the other side, he spoke with me. You see, it is possible for spirits to communicate with each other, even while we're regenerating."

I nodded, unsure as to where all this was going.

"Yesterday, while you were at work, I was in our protective spirit realm. And while I was there regenerating, Adahy came to me. His energy is so rich and alive that it's impossible not to notice. It's not going to be the same now that he's gone." Cole looked down at the ground, and I touched his knee, sympathetically.

"Adahy came to me and explained that he didn't want to pass on, but he needed to. He was tired of being trapped in limbo and yearned to return to his family members who were all waiting for him. But there was something he needed to do before he left—it was the same thing that had kept him here with us for so long."

"What was it?" I asked.

Cole turned to face me and took my hands in his. I felt a tingle as we connected, and realized that what I was about to hear was going to be difficult. So I took a deep breath and prepared myself for the worst.

"There is something looking for you," Cole said carefully, as if he was choosing each word. "It is the same force that killed your father. The group of Rashas that is searching for you is the most evil and powerful of all the darkest forces in the world. They are black to the core and not all of them were human. Some of them are demons. This group is so powerful that it caused some of the worst crimes in history. These Rashas are prophesized to become real—alive, unless you stop them. Renda, we believe you are the strongest of The Chosen, but you're also in grave danger. Adahy knew this and also knew that you would need training to survive what is yet to come."

I wasn't sure what to say. A fresh wave of terror washed over me. Was I doomed? Why should I even try to fight against something so powerful? My life was basically over. Once the Rashas found me, they'd destroy me.

Tears welled in my eyes, and I pulled my hands away from Cole's. This was all too much.

"Don't," he pleaded. "Please don't pull away. There's more."

"More?" I asked incredulously. "What else is there? I'm basically screwed. I have no future. Hell, I might as well just end everything now. It would be better to finally be with you all the time. Instead—"

"Stop!" Cole roared, interrupting me. His reaction was so out of character that I just sat back with a stunned expression on my face.

"I'm sorry," he apologized, "but you need to hear the rest. Before you were born, a wise Elder prophesized to your mother and father that you were going to be the one to bridge the gap between the dead and the living. It's something that's been repeated by the other spirits who I used to see in the halls of my former home. But I'm also beginning to hear it from spirits in other places too. Spirits you've seen or talked to. And last night, the Rashas were whispering the same thing in my ear. They know you well, and they were only too happy to try to destroy you. You see, all Rashas are connected, and they all know about you."

Cole's words cut through my heart like razor blades.

The sky was blue, the sun was shining brightly, but inside I felt as if the world had turned dark.

I was a fugitive. Someone who would be hunted all her days until it ended in a fiery mess. The knowledge left me exhausted and without any words to express my utter defeat.

Cole cupped my face in his hands.

As I gazed into his eyes, I could see that they were glistening, and I found it a wonder that even as a spirit, he could demonstrate such deep emotion.

"I'm not going to let you give up. I love you, Renda and there's so much for you to live for. Believe in yourself. Believe in us. Otherwise, I can't go on. I'll tumble into the darkness and never find my way out again."

He was trembling now. Every word he'd said pressed against the wall of defeat that I'd started to build. The bricks came crashing down, and all I wanted was to feel loved.

As if sensing my desperation, Cole lifted me up and carried me inside, Jane quietly following us.

The cool sheets caressed my back as Cole laid me down on the bed. He smiled and then stretched out on top of me, his muscles quivering against my skin.

At first his kisses were gentle—healing. He caressed my lips with his tongue, flicking it against my mouth and then slowly, pushed past my lips and explored my mouth. Our tongues played and danced in a sensual rhythm.

My worry and despair faded as I became more and more excited. I pulled Cole closer to me, wanting him to touch every inch of my body. Despite himself, Cole was allowing some energy to escape, and it was causing heat to glide over my body, permeating my skin.

It was driving me insane with passion.

Not wanting to wait, I pushed Cole onto his back and straddled him. I could feel him throbbing against my own wetness and the aching hunger of my femininity increased tenfold. I yanked my shirt off and then wiggled out of my pants.

Getting Cole naked wasn't hard to do. He was wearing his typical worn jeans and button down shirt. And as usual, he wasn't wearing any underwear.

Dear God. I might pass out from loving this man.

He looked at me with a vulnerability I'd never seen before. Usually he was brave and strong, but after what he'd just shared with me, I knew he was scared.

I leaned down and whispered in his ear, "Don't worry. It will all be okay."

Kissing Cole's mouth, I began to explore his body. My tongue tasted his chest, his nipples, and then moved down to his taut stomach, tracing the outline of his scar. I made my way down to his cock and licked him, tasting the salty wetness of his tip.

Cole moaned and quivered, but didn't stop me, and allowed me my moment of complete control—knowing full well that I wasn't really in control of what was happening in my life.

The frustration and desperation tearing through my mind was painful, and I knew that the only way to shut it out was to have Cole inside me. So without saying a word, I sat up and straddled him, positioning myself to take him in.

Cole helped by shifting his hips and with a small groan, lifted himself and fully penetrated me.

The sensation was amazing and for a moment, blotted out all of my pain and anguish. My emotions became a mixture of pleasure and need, tears rolling down my cheeks as I hung onto the only thing that mattered. The only thing that would keep me from losing myself to despair.

I'd come so far, only to learn that the road might end in turmoil. No matter what, I would always have to battle for survival.

But right now, I wasn't battling against anything other than sweet release. We began an age-old rhythm as our passions took us higher and higher.

And just when I thought I couldn't take anymore, I heard Cole moan loudly and the sound alone set off the fireworks in my body. Wanting to watch him in full orgasm, I leaned forward, hands capturing his beloved face as we both let the waves of our ecstasy wash over us.

Afterward, Cole wrapped me in his arms and rolled me onto my side.

Without even realizing it, I started crying into the crook of his neck. There were simply too many emotions rolling through my body...My love for the man who I adored, my joy at finding my new family, my fear of the future.

It was too much.

Sobs racked my body, and I let the feelings flow out like a river of pain. It felt like I cried for hours. Cole stayed with me as long as he could, but when he began to vanish, I felt him retreat like a warm kiss in the wind.

I slept for the rest of the day.

My cell phone rang several times, and in the deep recesses of my consciousness, I could hear the telltale ping of multiple messages. But I just didn't have the energy to listen or God forbid—answer anyone's inquiry. It was easier to remain under the covers and try to block out the horrible truths that Cole had shared.

Eventually though, Jane started getting antsy and began whining and pawing at my bed. When I managed to drag my body into an upright position, I noticed that the sun had already gone down and dusk was quickly turning into night.

Groaning, I swung my legs over the side of the bed and slowly walked out of my bedroom. The apartment was dark and empty, and I didn't sense any spirits lurking about.

I opened the front door and Jane raced ahead to her typical spot and began sniffing at the grass. She seemed very relaxed and happy, which calmed me a bit. But then I thought about what life would be like for my darling Labrador if something were to happen to me. I was her mother. She needed me.

My breath caught in my chest and for a minute, I thought that I might pass out. I grabbed my cell phone from the coffee table and sat on the steps outside my apartment. A calming breeze ruffled my hair and it felt better to be outside in the fresh air than in my stuffy apartment where I'd been sleeping all day.

I dialed into my phone. Four voice messages greeted me. The first was Larlene. But this time, she wasn't speaking in her normal, pushy tone. The events from the prior night had no doubt affected her.

"Hi, Renda. It's Larlene. So, I decided to stay home today too. I'm totally exhausted after last night. That was totally crazy! How're you

doing? You're probably sleeping all day. Or hanging out with your man-ghost. Okay, call me back when you can. Bye."

I smiled. Larlene was such a character.

I'll call her back in a little bit, I thought. Let's check the rest of these messages.

The next one was from my adoptive mother. She was chiding me for not calling my aunt on her birthday.

"Dear, you really must be more mindful of these things. Your dad and I want to see you for dinner this weekend. Please call me back so that we can plan, okay? Love you."

The third call was from Aunt Anne who sounded like she was in a great mood.

"Hey, Renda. Hope you're doing well. We just wanted to check in on you. It's been quite a day, trying to explain to the authorities how we found Katie. Brent made up some story about a relative who was trying to get back at us by snatching our daughter from the hospital. Not sure they bought it, but we didn't know what else to say. I mean, how do you explain that your daughter was kidnapped by a bunch of angry spirits?"

I shook my head. It couldn't have been easy. I knew that the detective from the hospital was pretty sharp. He was probably shaking his head over the whole situation. Given my own predicament, I was glad that I didn't have to deal with it.

"Anyway, Katie's doing great, and she's been asking about you. We'd love to have you over for supper or sometime over the weekend just to catch up. I'm sure you've still got lots of questions and stuff. Not sure how much more we can answer, but it might help being around family. Speaking of family, have you told your adoptive parents about us yet? Sorry for the rambling message. We'll talk to you soon."

It was a good question. When was I going to tell my mom and dad about discovering my relatives? And how would they take it? Might not be an easy pill to swallow—having to share me with people they didn't know.

There was so much to consider, and I wasn't sure how much I wanted to involve my parents. If Cole was right, things could get very dark for me, and I didn't want to drag anyone else into this brewing nightmare.

The last message popped on. It was a telemarketer, but something about the message caught my interest...

"Hi, this is Beach Vacations Plus calling. We're the leading provider of timeshares and rentals on the west coast of Florida. Our portfolio of vacation homes ranges from single family to mansion-sized properties, perfect for reunions or even weddings. Have you been wanting to get away? Now's your chance. You can visit us on the web, or call us toll free at 1-555-759-7767."

The message went into repeat and began to echo in my head like a mantra. I knew that the universe was sending me a sign. And I had to answer the call if I was to continue on this journey. I hung up and gazed at the darkening sky. Things were so scary and unpredictable that maybe I needed to get away for a while. Somehow, the idea of staying in Cale made me feel like I'd be bumping into Rashas when I least expected it.

Evil spirits existed everywhere, but I didn't want to be anywhere near the Cale cemetery. Shit, I didn't even want to *drive* by it. And then, I remembered what Adahy had said to me.

"You must go to the water. Go to the waves and you will find the answers you seek. It is there where the true protection of your inner strength lives."

I needed to go to the ocean. I didn't care if the library fired me for taking more vacation time so soon after my trip to Macon. I couldn't function or survive if I stayed.

It was that simple.

Chapter 18

"What do you mean, you're leaving?" shrieked Larlene.

She wasn't taking the news very well. After all, I'd just told my boss that I needed a break from work for a while, and he'd promptly agreed that it was best that I "not come back". He was keen on looking for ways to cut back on the budget, so I'd just given him an easy opportunity.

So much for that.

Normally, getting fired would've been devastating. But now, all I could think about was how I was going to survive the prophecy and the responsibilities that came with it.

Finding another job wouldn't be easy in small-town Cale, but having a nervous breakdown wasn't going to be any better. I had to leave and figure out what Adahy had been trying to tell me.

Taking a deep breath, I tried to explain to Larlene my reasoning for escaping the confines of Cale. "It's just something I have to do. Last night was incredibly traumatic and now, I'm afraid for my safety. There's darkness everywhere in this town, Larlene. I just need some time away to think about what my next move is going to be, and I can't do that working at the library. I can't define the rest of my life while I'm pushing books up and down aisles or finalizing budget spreadsheets or helping clueless patrons. Please try to understand and don't talk me out of this, okay?"

"You're making a mistake," she said quietly. "You can't escape your life, babe. It's better to face things head-on rather than stick your head in the sand. In this case, you're literally doing that," she chuckled—clearly trying to make me laugh. But it wasn't working.

"I promise to call every day," I assured her and realized at the same time that Cole had materialized and was standing behind me. "I've gotta go. I'll call you tomorrow."

When I hung up the call, I could feel Cole's heat gently radiating against my back. Since he'd mastered the ability to recycle his life source, he didn't feel as warm around me but I could still tell when he was close by.

Without turning around, I spoke. "I'm leaving, Cole. I've quit my job, and I'm going to rent a bungalow in a community called 'Whispering Pines'. It's a small seaside neighborhood where I can take the time to figure out what I'm doing and where I need to go. Please don't try to talk me out of this."

"Renda, you know I would never try to talk you out of anything. Why would I be upset that you're doing this?"

I turned to face him.

His black hair lay in mussed up waves over his forehead. His black T-shirt clung to his torso, outlining the muscles in his arms. His faded jeans stretched across his taut legs.

His beautiful eyes smiled into mine.

He was too damn appealing for his own good.

But I didn't feel any sense of arousal—only pain.

"You can't come with me. I've got to do this myself. As much as I love you, and as much as I don't think I can live without you, I've got to make this part of the journey on my own."

Cole's face furrowed in confusion. "What do you mean? Why can't I join you? Damn it, Renda! Why are you doing this?"

Tears flowed down my cheeks.

"If I'm going to survive the Rashas and live out the prophecy that Adahy kept telling you about, I've got to do this on my own. Basically, I've got to start over. I've been forced into this insane new life, and I can't continue to live in reactionary mode. I need to claim this prophecy as my own. And I can't do that if I'm leaning on you constantly and distracted by our love. With you in my life, it's impossible to think about anything else. All I want is you. And I can't do that anymore. There is so much at stake now. You said it yourself. They're hunting for me. Please, it won't be forever. Just until I can figure out what steps I'm supposed to take."

"And what about Jane?" Cole asked angrily, though I could see the pain in his eyes.

I looked down at my beautiful, furry daughter who was panting and drooling on the floor.

"She's coming with me. I think she's a part of this, too. Somehow, she's connected to this and is supposed to be with me. She'll help to protect me in the days ahead. I just know it."

My heart was erupting in pain, because the last thing I wanted to do was be away from the love of my life. He was everything to me. But at the same time, I knew that I was doing the right thing and eventually, Cole would realize it too. Because one day, we'd be together in a world where I could live without fear and the terror of what might be hiding around the corner.

I reached out, and as soon as my fingertips touched Cole's arm, he pulled me tightly into his arms.

As we embraced, I could smell his musky scent and feel his passion for me—it made leaving him all the harder.

"I love you so much," he whispered. "Being away from you is painful and makes me feel lost and restless. But, I'll honor your wishes and give you the space you need. I'll stay away until you call for me. But please don't forget me. I can't exist without you."

"How could I forget you?" I sobbed into his shoulder. "You're the best thing that's ever happened to me. And just when I've found you, I find out that my life has been predetermined to either continue in a place that's better than anything I could ever imagine, or end with me losing my soul to the darkest and blackest precipice of hell. I can't give up. I won't give up."

Cole's arms held me so tightly that I could feel the warmth of his strange spirit-like essence enter my skin. For one moment our love fused us together as one.

And then, he was gone.

He left so abruptly that I tumbled forward off-balance. I grabbed onto the nearby sofa as I slipped to the floor.

I cried until it felt as if I had no tears left.

The rest of the evening continued to be difficult.

When I called my parents to tell them I was leaving, my

mother was surprisingly calm despite the fact that I'm sure she was upset with my decision to quit my job and take off for the west coast of Florida. But then my father got on the phone and began lecturing me about "responsibilities" and "taking accountability for my actions".

"Dad, I'm only going away for a month or two. If you could just loan me a little bit of money, I promise to pay you back as soon as I find another job."

He eventually acquiesced and agreed to help me, but only after lecturing me some more and reminding me that I was no longer a child and that this was the "last time" he was going to loan me money.

When we hung up, I felt like another boulder had been lifted off my shoulders and there was only one more call to make.

When my biological aunt and uncle heard the news, they were silent for a moment. Then, my uncle cleared his throat and spoke quietly.

"You're just like your mother, Renda. Your biological mother. She made some very tough decisions, and didn't listen to anyone who told her otherwise. Don't know if she's still alive, but if she is, your best chance of finding her is by the ocean. She always loved being by the water. Godspeed, my beautiful niece, and I wish you the best of luck."

Then, Aunt Anne was kind enough to put Katie on the phone so that she could say goodbye.

"Hi," she said shyly.

"Hey there, Katie. Did your mommy tell you that I'll be going away for a little while?"

"Yeah, she did. Are you going with that nice ghost who likes you?"

I swallowed hard. "No, baby. I'm going by myself."

She was quiet for a minute. And then—

"Thank you for saving me. I'll miss you. Please don't go away for a long time."

"I won't. I promise."

"And Renda?"

"Yes, baby?"

"Stay away from the dark people. The people like Norman

who're bad. They don't play with me anymore, but I think they still want you."

Her words chilled me to the bone, but I swallowed hard and managed to answer her, "They may want me, but they aren't going to get me. Don't you worry. I'll see you soon, and I love you."

"I love you too."

My bags were packed.

Jane was up early and ready to go, as usual. But I wasn't going to be rushed. I sat on my sofa and sipped my coffee, trying to make sense of everything that had happened. I didn't know why I was the Chosen One. I didn't know what I was supposed to do to keep the world safe from the Rashas. But I did know one thing. I wasn't going to find my answers in Cale.

It took getting onto the highway and driving toward the coast, before I finally began to relax. The realization of what I was doing had set in.

There were no more tears left, and truthfully, I had no need for them. Jane and I were heading toward the unknown, yet I had no doubt that the decision I was making was the right one.

In the distance, a seagull flew overhead and led the way toward my future...

About the Author

Sara Brooke is an Amazon bestselling author of horror, paranormal romance, and suspense fiction.

A lifelong avid reader of all things scary, Sara's childhood dream was to write books that make readers sleep with their lights on. She hopes that isn't too troubling for the thousands of readers worldwide who have purchased her books.

Sara has been published alongside horror legends Clive Barker and John Carpenter. She has written nine novels, and numerous novellas and short stories.

Sara resides in beautiful South Florida. She can be reached via her website at www.sarabrooke.com. Sara welcomes feedback and questions from readers.

Curious about other Crossroad Press books?
Stop by our site:
http://store.crossroadpress.com
We offer quality writing
in digital, audio, and print formats.

www.ingramcontent.com/pod-product-compliance
Lightning Source LLC
Chambersburg PA
CBHW020335180626
46812CB00001B/212